the dog walker

LESLEY THOMSON grew up in west London. Her first novel, *A Kind of Vanishing*, won the People's Book Prize in 2010. Her second novel, *The Detective's Daughter*, was a no. 1 bestseller and sold over 500,000 copies. She lives in Lewes with her partner and her dog.

By Lesley Thomson

Seven Miles from Sydney

A Kind of Vanishing

The Detective's Daughter Series

The Detective's Daughter

Ghost Girl

The Detective's Secret

The House With No Rooms

The Dog walker

The Runaway (A Detective's Daughter Short Story)

Lesley
THOMSON

the dog walker

HEAD
of ZEUS

First published in the UK in 2017 by Head of Zeus, Ltd.

9 7 5 3 1 2 4 6 8

A catalogue record for this book is available from
the British Library.

ISBN (HB): 9781784972257
ISBN (XTPB): 9781784972264
ISBN (E): 9781784972240

Typeset by Adrian McLaughlin

Printed and bound in Great Britain by
CPI Group (UK) Ltd, Croydon CRO 4YY

Head of Zeus Ltd
First Floor East
5–8 Hardwick Street
London ECIR 4RG

WWW.HEADOFZEUS.COM

For Alfred, who gave me the idea

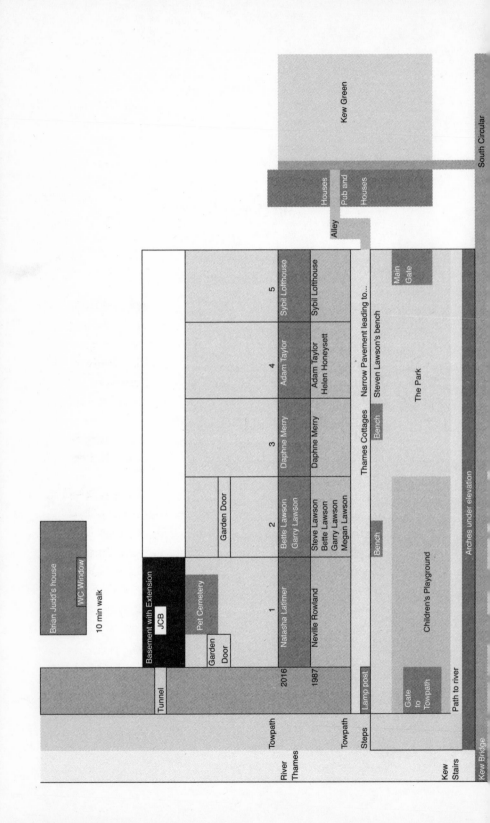

Prologue

On a hot summer's day the Thames towpath between Kew Bridge and Mortlake Crematorium is stippled with sunlight spilling through willow fronds and shading oaks. Birdsong twitters above the rumble of a District line train crossing Kew Railway Bridge. Although in London, the leafy towpath resembles a pastoral idyll. Cyclists weave around strolling couples and families straggling with scooters and pushchairs.

In deepest darkest winter, lamplight from the north bank is absorbed in the black waters and only joggers and dog walkers brave the towpath.

On this night, a figure walked briskly beside the Thames. The sweeping arc of a torch picked out puddles in the mud. A dog nosing along the bank cocked its ears. The person – a man or a woman in baggy waterproofs – paused. There was the thud of footsteps. Emerging out of the gloom came a jogger accompanied by a dog. The dog walker moved to the river's edge to make way.

'Good evening!' the dog walker hailed the receding figure. No reply. The jogger's dog was circling on the path; he pooed and, kicking his back legs in triumph or relief, raced away.

Clear of trees, the path was stained by the orange of the light-polluted sky. The dog walker strode on along the path, seemingly unfazed by the slap of the river against the bank and rustling in bushes that might suggest a creeping assailant.

The arch of Chiswick Bridge was a tomb in which ice cracking beneath the dog walker's step was amplified.

It's the dog walker with their inquisitive pet straying off the beaten track who's likely to come upon the body of a murder victim. Bent on their daily routine, rarely does it occur to them that they themselves could be a victim.

'Oh, it's you!' The words hung in the wintry air.

Chapter One

Stella Darnell headed smartly along Shepherd's Bush Green, trim in a green waxed jacket, wool-lined collar zipped to her chin against the searing wind, flat-soled black-leather ankle boots clipping on the frosty pavement, a styled pixie bob framing a lightly made-up complexion. A leather rucksack on one shoulder. A diminutive apricot poodle, shaggy and unstyled, 'Crufts-trotted' at her heel.

The morning had started badly because it had started late. For the first time in Stella's memory she had overslept. Embroiled in a dream in which she shot up with the alarm, dressed and searched without success for her boots, she had been stunned to wake at seven to find she was in bed. By half past the Great West Road was snarled up and what would have been a fifteen-minute journey at six took an hour. One reason was a collision between a Range Rover Evoque and a Fiat 500 on Hammersmith Broadway. The Evoque's registration was 'Pow3r 1'. Jack said a personalized plate was a sign of the owner's character. Stella's, a birthday present from her brother Dale, was 'CS1'; it stood for Clean Slate, although several clients had jokily suggested 'Crime Scene Investigation'. Jack suggested that Dale intended it to signify the two sides of her life. Stella, a cleaner for most of the day, was, with Jack Harmon, for the rest of the day and much of the night, a private detective. Her decision to open a detective agency, made a couple of years ago, wasn't yet official. She and Jack operated on an as-and-when basis.

As her van drifted past the accident, Stella took in the scene. The driver, a blonde woman in an embroidered coat, high heels and huge sunglasses despite there being no sun, was hectoring a bespectacled man with thinning hair who gazed forlornly, hands stuffed in the pockets of his cord jacket, at the crushed wing of his Fiat. The Evoque was undamaged. With the trained eye of a police officer's daughter, Stella saw, from the angle of the vehicles, that Pow3r 1 had swapped lanes and rammed the Fiat's offside. The Evoque was at fault, but as she drew level Stella heard the man apologize.

Stella shouldered the street door up to her office. It was locked. This was unheard of. She had lost count of her reminders to the insurance brokers on the top floor to keep the door locked against intruders. Emails, laminated notices and personal entreaties were ignored, resulting in delivery couriers – usually for the brokers – coming to Clean Slate on the first floor.

Stella was unused to needing her key and had to search for it. She was crouching down, digging in her rucksack, when the door opened. There was a shriek and Stanley let loose a barrage of shouty barks.

'Stella! I didn't see you sitting on the ground!' Beverly was Clean Slate's young office assistant. Permanently cheerful, she attacked her work with an unbounded enthusiasm that Stella could find overwhelming.

'I'm not sitting...' Stella found the key and stood up.

As ever Beverly looked immaculate. She wore knee-high boots, a short black dress, thick black tights and a skimpy green bolero jacket. She squatted down and vigorously petted Stanley, presenting her face to be licked. 'I'm popping next door for milk and Jackie says to get *biscuits*! We've got that woman coming in about the toilet cleaning job.' She flapped Stanley's ears merrily.

'Washrooms, not just toilets...' Stella exclaimed. 'She's coming to the office?'

'Yeah, bummer! We've been here since dawn deep cleaning. But you can't turn a sheep into a wolf or whatever. Do you fancy anything from the shop?'

'No, you're all right, Bev, thanks.' Stella spotted Dariusz Adomek, the owner of the mini-mart, frowning at an aubergine on the vegetable display outside his shop. She waved.

'Get chocolate bourbons. They're her favourite!' Dariusz winked at Stella. 'A gift from me.' Before Stella could object, he followed Beverly inside.

Pausing by the open door, Stella considered that she did like bourbons best. Like her, Adomek made it his business to know what his customers liked. She sniffed. The air in the passage was tainted with stale cooking although no one in the building cooked. The greasy smell somehow seeped in from a hamburger place two shops down. Jackie wanted Clean Slate to move to a larger and more attractive office. Stella was reluctant; she hated change. And she'd miss her chats with Dariusz Adomek. But when a major potential client insisted on coming to the office, as this Angela Morrish had, Stella saw Jackie's point.

Beverly called to her across the fruit and veg, 'Ooh, I forgot, there's two women waiting for you. One's in a bad mood, the other's well weird!' She did a 'bad mood' face and swooped into the shop.

'I haven't got anyone in my diary...' Stella always kept the first week after New Year free. Then again, she never overslept. Could she have forgotten the appointment?

Leading Stanley up the steep staircase, she considered how threadbare lino, peeling Anaglypta wallpaper and the cloying odour of meat would do nothing for the woman's mood.

On the landing, Stella smelled something else. Orange, rose and jasmine cut with patchouli. Her hypersensitive olfactory sense identified Chanel's Coco Mademoiselle. The visitor had expensive taste. Nerving herself, Stella went inside: 'Sorry I'm late.'

'Late for you who's always here before dawn! It's only nine, love.' Jackie Makepeace, Stella's PA, office manager and perhaps her closest friend, took Stanley's lead from her. Nodding at a door marked 'Stella Darnell, Chief Executive', she dropped her voice. 'You've got visitors. They came on spec, but insist on seeing you, or one of them does. I offered them drinks. One doesn't drink caffeine; the other said she's in a hurry.' Jackie's expression betrayed nothing.

A woman sat in Stella's swivel chair; she was tapping a Clean Slate branded pen on the desk, a slow beat that counted Stella in. 'I expected you'd be here.' She didn't look up.

Stella moved to the guest chair and, looking at the woman properly, had to contain astonishment. Blond hair, embroidered coat, sunglasses pushed up on to her head. Pow3r 1. Stella was less incredulous at the coincidence – Jack said there were no such things as coincidences (or accidents) – than that Pow3r 1 had got to the office before her. Up close she was younger than Stella had supposed, in her twenties, not thirties. Stella's assessment had been formed from a hazy assumption that a younger woman was less likely to own a car which left little change from thirty-five thousand quid. Stella's dad whispered in her head, as he often did since his death, *'Observe closely, never assume. Work with what you see, not what you think you see.'*

The woman shot a peremptory hand across the desk, clearly keen to dispose of pleasantries. 'Natasha Latimer.' Her grip was crushing.

Knuckles smarting, Stella enquired, 'How may I help you?'

'I want Blank Slate to do a job.'

'It's Clean Sl— I can come and do an estimate.'

'That won't work. You won't see a thing in a short visit.'

Stella nearly shouted with surprise. A woman with long hair braided at the ends with brightly coloured beads was brooding at the window. Wrapped in a custard-yellow cloak possibly adapted from a blanket, she wore flared maroon cords, blue shoes with crepe soles, a loose-knit cardigan – loose in that the

6

stitches were giving way – over a red cotton smock that reached to her knees. This had to be the visitor whom Beverly had dubbed weird. She wore a woollen hat with a bobble the size of Stanley that protruded behind her. It gave her the look of a chess piece – the bishop, Stella vaguely thought.

'She will see all she needs to see.' Natasha Latimer readjusted the sunglasses on her head. 'This is my sister.' She spoke as if referring to something unfortunate that couldn't be helped.

'Claudia. Greetings.' The woman floated over to the coat stand. For a ludicrous second, Stella caught a resemblance between her and the stand. 'You need to be there a good long time to appreciate it.'

'How is that?' Stella didn't say that three decades of short visits to do estimates had proved a success.

'You won't see her in broad daylight.' Claudia was kindly.

'She will see what's necessary.' Natasha Latimer beat a tattoo with the pen.

'Daytime's usually when—' Stella began.

'When's the last time you saw a ghost?' Claudia might have been asking Stella when she'd last caught a cold.

Stella had just redrafted the company's 'lone-working' policy so was up on the risks of being by herself with a client. Or two. Jackie was the other side of the wall. She didn't air her opinion that ghosts didn't exist – she wouldn't contradict a potential client even though she guessed Latimer would be right there with her. What she did know was that a job for two sisters who had already exhibited polar opposite opinions was bound to end in disaster. She was debating how to refuse the job without offending one or both of them. Clients who saw ghosts might also see non-existent stains and dust and quibble over invoices.

Stella's cleaning business was successful, bolstered with a mix of commercial contracts and domestic clients. She only took on clients who gave clear cleaning briefs and were respectful to the operatives. Natasha Latimer was brusque and ill-tempered.

Her sister would probably be fine, but whatever she asked the cleaner to do, Stella was pretty sure Latimer would object to. Her likely wealth – evidenced by the coat, the car and wafts of Chanel – was no guarantee of good manners or regular payment. Stella focused on how to get Jackie's help in ushering Pow3r 1 and her sister out. She took a subtle approach. 'I've actually never seen a ghost.'

'And you never will!' Latimer was snappish.

Jack could chat on happily about spectral sightings – he claimed to encounter ghosts all the time. Since her dad's death, Stella sometimes got the impression Terry Darnell had left a room as she entered it and, as just now, his voice broke into her thinking. But she didn't believe his pearls of wisdom came from beyond the grave. Latimer was talking.

'... so I moved in before Christmas. My new deep basement is double the square meterage of the house. I've gone right under the garden. Everything is "smart", no extraneous switches, and it's soundproofed. In and out. A humidifier keeps out the damp. You can't hear it... floor's water-resistant. The property is now worth millions. It's old and was crying out for a makeover. The location is totally perfect, what with the river and Kew Gardens, and there's only a few properties in the street.'

'It has a lovely community feel,' Claudia interposed, her fearsome bobble hat nodding. 'Tucked away by the river. You can get right in touch with your soul there. The river speaks—'

'Yah, community, *right*!' Latimer whipped off her sunglasses and spun them around by one of the arms. 'Bunch of robots.' She plucked at her coat with manicured fingers.

Claudia smiled to herself. 'When I step inside she's waiting for me.'

'Who is?' Stella hoped they hadn't already told her.

'That fucking woman!' Latimer spat out the words, her eyes blazing.

Stella wished she'd gone with Jackie's advice of a panic button under the desk. Claudia didn't appear dangerous, but with talk of spirits, she was only marginally more reassuring. Jack would be in his element. She mustered herself. 'Which fu— Which woman?' Did she mean her sister?

Latimer whacked the pen on the desk, sending a staple remover whizzing on to the carpet. Bangles clinking, Claudia waltzed over and picked it up. Stella reassured herself that her office wasn't soundproofed; she could shout for help. Except that would be rude. Not for the first time, she considered how being polite could be the death of her.

'Helen Honeysett has found peace there.' Claudia projected an air of patient explanation. 'I've told Nats to chill. The girl is harmless, a gentle soul.'

'Who is harmless?' Jack believed using a modulated voice calmed a person in a frenzy. To her own ear, Stella sounded as if she was addressing a halfwit. It would explain Claudia's peculiar lilting delivery; she'd be used to her sister.

'*Was*, not *is*! Helen Whatsit. That estate agent.' Latimer uttered the term like a swear word. 'Claudia says she's haunting the house.'

'Ah.' Stella understood. Natasha Latimer was blaming the estate agent for disappointment in her purchase. Sometimes clients blamed Clean Slate for their new home, despite a thorough clean, not being what they hoped for. 'Your estate agent should have returned the key when you complet—'

'Not that one! The girl that went missing in 1987. The year I was born.' Latimer huffed as if personally affronted by this fact. 'She lived in *my* street. She went out jogging in the dark on the towpath that runs right by my property and was never seen again. Claudia says she's haunting me!' She clicked the pen rapidly. 'Claudia, I said leave this to me.' Latimer flashed a warning look at her sister smiling beatifically by the coat stand.

That Estate Agent. Stella had been twenty when Helen Honeysett vanished in January 1987. Stella had remarked to her mum that it was a mistake for the woman to jog on a footpath at night and Suzie Darnell had told her off for 'blaming the victim', yet had forbidden her to jog anywhere. Not that Stella needed to jog; cleaning kept her fit. Terry Darnell wasn't involved in the investigation, but had told her that detectives believed Honeysett was murdered within hours of going missing.

Latimer was still talking. '... obviously it's tosh. Ghosts don't exist. But all you need is a rumour of haunting and the property value drops like a fucking stone.'

'You bought it without knowing so when you come to sell it...' Stella didn't want to discourage dishonesty, but surely phantoms wouldn't show up on a survey and you couldn't be blamed for not declaring the existence of something that didn't exist.

'The old man who lived there – the sitting tenant – told Claudia. It was to put me off buying. I got rid of him.'

'No one is "got rid of",' Claudia observed placidly. She was swaying as if in time to an inaudible tune.

Stella unzipped her jacket and shrugged it off. 'Would you like tea? There's chocolate bis—'

'... I hear her. Squeaking and shuffling. She's never been laid to rest, that's what it is, and Nats has dug down into deep time with that extraordinary basement – I keep telling her. It isn't only those left behind who agonize. Now the dead have no home.'

'Claudia, enough!' Latimer barked. 'The sooner I sell the better.'

Stella knew that old houses made odd noises; her own did. 'Have you actually seen her...?' She had forgotten the ghost's name. She was teetering on a tightrope of seeming to treat both Latimer and her sister seriously. She wouldn't make the mistake of assuming, for all her fancy gear, that Latimer held the purse strings.

'I hear her *breathing*!'

Natasha Latimer gave an exaggerated shudder. 'The way Claw talks, you'd think it was Mrs Goddam Grace Poole!'

The bobble hat dipped. 'Actually Mrs Rochester.'

'Do ghosts breathe?' Stella mused.

'Of course not.' Latimer examined her nails with a furious expression. 'It'll be one of that lot trying to get me out. They're all barking!'

'The basement was more change than the community could bear.' Claudia soothed her sister.

Belatedly Stella understood that Latimer had bought her house to make a profit, not to join a community. Stella had done jobs for several clients who made money from improving properties and selling them on. In a secluded neighbourhood, that wouldn't go down well, especially, Stella supposed, with the old man who'd rented the house before Latimer evicted him.

'If Clean Slate is going to take on the job, they must have the subtext.' Claudia glided around the desk and began massaging her sister's shoulders. Stella was surprised when Latimer slumped down in the chair and shut her eyes. 'What happened to that poor girl was terrible. I was three.' Claudia shook her head; the hat shook with her.

Surely Claudia had no recall of something that had happened when she was so young. Jack could remember the day his mother died – he'd been about four – but that was different.

'How can I help?' Stella meant to imply Clean Slate could *not* help.

'Get rid of her!' Latimer jumped up. Claudia stayed where she was, her hands in mid-air. 'I'm not idiotic enough to think there actually is a ghost. But people are incredibly thick. I need to quash the haunting rumours and get it on the market.' She was ferocious. 'Wipe out this Honeysett girl!'

'That's not a good way to frame it, Natty.' Claudia appeared to float back to her place by the coat stand.

That someone had very likely 'wiped out' Helen Honeysett appeared to be lost on Latimer. Stella resorted to her spiel. 'We do cleaning. Along with basic tasks of vacuuming and polishing, we clean carpets and upholstery, polish internal glazing and if necessary we can perform a scheduled deep clean which involves sanitiz—'

'I want all of that.' Latimer waved the ballpoint pen like a conductor's baton.

'It might be an intruder. Perhaps the police...' Stella was mildly cheered by the vision of Martin Cashman, Chief Super at Richmond Police Station and her dad's old colleague, negotiating Claudia in her blanket and bobble hat telling him about the ghost of an estate agent.

'No one can get in. The property is alarmed; there are cameras and most of it's underground, for Chrissakes.'

Stella tended to think that radiators, putting in draught excluders and filling cracks in floorboards did the trick. 'The Church does exorcisms,' she offered brightly as the thought occurred.

'Claudia had them round. A priest chucked water about and made a flood. My lovely hippy-dippy sister got one of her faith healer friends to sneak about burning weeds. He set off the sprinkler. I'm still getting rid of the stink.'

'It was sage. It's healing.' The 'hippy-dippy' sister puffed with contentment. 'We brought comfort to her.'

'How long did Helen Honeysett live there – I mean when she was alive?' Stella would balk at living where a person who was murdered had lived, however comforted they were. It was strange enough being in – she still had trouble calling it 'living in' rather than 'visiting' – her dad's place since his death five years ago.

'She was never there! She lived at number four. The husband's still there, swanning about with some new girl every week.' Latimer clicked the pen on and off.

'Wouldn't she be more likely to haunt her husband?' Stella tried to sound neutral.

'She's not haunting *anyone*.' Latimer flung her a look of exasperation. 'The point is that the neighbours *think* she is and neighbours talk! Claudia's not helping with incantations and nonsense.'

'I see.' Stella moved towards the door. 'Maybe you need a

PR agency?' Stella's commercial success was based on promising only what she could fulfil.

'I advised Nats to get a stringent clean – twenty-four/seven occupancy, no dust must settle, ghosts love dust. A clean home is like garlic to a vampire.' Claudia was opening and shutting the jaws of the staple remover in time to her speech. She appeared to have forgotten that Helen Honeysett was a 'gentle soul'. Although, as to method, Stella was with her every step of the way.

'Claudia's away with the fairies, but that did make sense,' Natasha conceded.

Stella felt ill equipped to comment on vampires or fairies, but did see the endless advantages in a clean house. 'We can do that. I can't guarantee it will get rid of—'

'I want a live-in housekeeper who can scotch any suggestion of some estate agent clanking her chains in my basement.' Natasha Latimer tossed the Clean Slate biro down; it lay between them like a gauntlet.

Stella picked up the pen. 'We have just the person.'

Chapter Two

'Champagne, darling?'

Megan mechanically put out a hand for the glass that the lady in the zebra dress with feathers sticking out of her hair was holding out to her.

'She's too young to drink, Mrs Honeysett.' Garry tugged at the sleeve of Megan's red cotton tunic dress. 'She has to have juice.'

'Oh, call me *Helen*, please! "Mrs H." is my august mother-in-law, the Horse on the Hill. Whoops, mustn't call her that!' The lady covered her mouth and winked at Megan. 'Gotta say, Megan, you look jolly grown up to me. And you, Garry Lawson! Haven't you got a *gor*-geous bro, Megan!'

'Garry keeps budgies.' Megan had waited for her chance to tell the new people at number 4 this information. They would see how lucky they were to have come to the street.

'Incredible!' Helen Honeysett marvelled. A response that satisfied the seven-year-old but annoyed her soon-to-be-teenaged brother.

He finished his orange juice in a long draught and admitted stiffly, 'I *breed* budgerigars.'

'Coo-elll! Can I have one?' Helen Honeysett drank from the glass she had offered Megan and exclaimed, 'Hot damn! Now I've got three on the go!'

'Garry sells them for a pound each and two pounds if they're albinos. That's white all over and it's a good thing so it costs double the blue and yellow ones. He hasn't made one yet, have you, Gal?' Megan looked up at her brother.

'Shut up, Megs.' Reddening, Garry pushed up the sleeves of his black nylon bomber jacket and shuffled his feet, clad in black Converse high-tops new on that morning.

'I want a blue and a yellow one. Two, so they don't get sad and lonely,' Helen Honeysett crooned absently, her eyes roving the crowded room.

Helen and Adam Honeysett had moved to Thames Cottages, one of a row of five terrace houses off the towpath near Kew Bridge, the week before. The next day they dropped cards through the neighbours' doors inviting them to a 'Real Honeysett Yuletide House-Warming'. The card was a Christmas tree. Balls hanging from the branches were inset with the faces of the occupants of the other four cottages. The words 'Adam Honeysett Design' were by the greeting. Megan pointed out happily that her dad was at the top of the tree by the star. Her mum, Bette, was less pleased to be on a lower branch. Next to Bette was Sybil Lofthouse from number 5. 'They must have hidden in the hedge to take me. Sneaky, I call it.'

'He's hoping we'll hire him to design stuff,' Steve Lawson had told Megan. 'Not a bad idea. Shall I stick a U-bend pipe through some letterboxes? Could bring in loads of work!'

'Everyone already knows you're a plumber,' Megan had said. 'You fixed Mrs Merry's leak.'

Megan had been astonished that the inside of the Honeysetts' cottage was bigger than the Lawsons' because from the pavement the houses looked the same size. The living room went right through to the back. It was topsy-turvy, with rugs on walls and bare floorboards. None of the chairs matched and there were bulges and dips in the velvet-covered sofa. There were toys everywhere. Megan particularly liked the mouse reading in a tiny rocking chair, glasses on the end of its whiskery nose. She had tried to get Garry interested in a carved tableau of a kitchen. The table and chairs were modelled to create perspective. It reminded her of her family's kitchen although they didn't have the dresser with plates propped on the shelves. Everywhere was something new and magical. Model cars and building bricks that were nicer than Garry's. The Honeysetts didn't have children so the toys must belong to them. Megan was envious that they didn't have to tidy them away, especially for a party. She had reached up to stroke a dog on the mantelpiece and Mr Honeysett had come up behind her and said that it was a nutcracker. He showed her how its mouth opened when she lifted up his tail. Her dad had whispered, 'Careful, Megsy, his jaws could crush your fingers!'

Before the party, Bette Lawson had instructed her children to be friendly. 'Don't stand in the corner like wet weekends.' Keen to keep Mrs... *Helen* talking to them, Megan asked, 'When did you take our faces for your card?'

Garry paled. 'Megan!'

'That was huge fun! I set up camp in our bedroom and waited for my moment! I take pictures at work. My job is to show people around houses and get them to buy them. I photograph boring empty rooms or houses that are horribly tidy. I saw you come from the towpath with your daddy and your dog and *snap*!' She mimed holding a camera, not noticing she had sloshed champagne out of the glass. 'Seems everyone takes their dogs down there.'

'Mum said it was sneak—'

Garry Lawson elbowed his sister and she staggered back into the Lawsons' Christmas tree, wincing as a branch scratched her arm. She breathed in the scent of pine.

'Now, kids, give me a rundown on everyone.' Helen Honeysett leant into the children conspiratorially. 'Dish the dirt!'

Brows furrowed, Megan cast about the cluttered room. 'That's Mr Rowlands by the door. With spectacles and strange eyes. He's at number one Thames Cottages. He's been there *all* his life and he's old. He lives with his mum. We call him the Lizard because he slides about. You don't know he's there and then he is.'

'I always know he's there,' Garry contradicted her fiercely. 'And so what? We live with our mum.'

'He does look pretty old and wrinkled. Is he scary?' Helen Honeysett widened her eyes.

'Yes.' Megan realized that he was.

'Is it a matter for the police? Have you told your parents?' Helen Honeysett looked serious and Megan felt a stirring of discomfort. She hadn't told her mum or dad. What would she tell them?

'She's making stuff up,' Garry said. 'She gets like this.'

'He looks a sweetie standing there, like a little boy lost.' Helen Honeysett squeezed Megan's arm. 'I'm afraid his mother wasn't on the card. I've never seen her out. Does she actually exist?' She did a face as if she'd been rude.

'Yes she does!' Megan exclaimed with delight that she knew something for sure. 'My mum says she's "failing" and will die. Mum's a nurse.' She sought to assuage any doubt about this extraordinary detail. 'Dad changed their boiler. He said she stays in her bed in the day. It's not Mr Rowlands' boiler because he's like us, he rents.'

'He's not like us.' Garry was gruff as he bounced on the balls of his high-tops, hands in the pockets of his brand-new Oxford bags.

'Is your jacket Levi, Garry?' Helen fingered the fur collar on the boy's denim jacket with manicured fingers. Her nails glinted dark red in the Christmas-tree lights.

'Yes! Mum told him it was ridiculously hot for indoors, but he won't take it off,' Megan piped. In case Helen had forgotten that she wanted to know about everyone: 'Miss Lofthouse is the one next to Mr Rowlands not talking. She never talks. She goes out early before anyone's up. I did once see her on the towpath. Her dog's called Timothy Trot. Daddy says it's cos he gets the trots!' She gave a squawking giggle.

'We named Baxter after the soup. I was drunk. It suits him though, don't you think?'

'Yes,' Megan said promptly and, not to be diverted, went on, 'Mum says Sybil Lofthouse doesn't like "idle chat" and prefers her own company. When she sees us she acts like we're invisible. Dad had to get our ball out of her garden once. She said no. He says she doesn't like children. Isn't that funny because she was once a little girl like us.' Megan was enjoying herself.

'I'm not a little girl,' Garry growled.

'Maybe she's always been a grown-up. Some people are.' Helen Honeysett sipped champagne. 'Or like Mr Rowlands, they never grow up. Look at him nibbling his finger. He's nervous, poor chap. I must rescue him from himself. And rescue Miss Lofthouse from the horror of company that isn't hers. I'm honoured she's deigned to come.' She put the champagne glass down on a shelf and adjusted the giant red clip holding up her hair. 'Miss Lofthouse gave Adam such a ticking off for taking her picture without permission. Hey, maybe she's a James Bond spy!'

'She's not,' Garry said reliably. 'She works at the Stock Exchange.'

'*Bor*-ing!' Helen flashed him a smile and, flustered, he downed his orange juice in one. 'Adam told her it was me who took the photo. Wasn't that mean! He grassed me up!' Her cockney accent was like the man in the Mary Poppins film; Megan would do it when she got home. *Grassed me up.*

'Yes it was.' Megan eyed her brother with puzzlement. He was gaping at Helen Honeysett as if she was from outer space. The last time he'd done that was when her mum accidentally shut his finger in the bathroom door. 'Mrs Merry is by your piano. She is very good at playing it.' Megan hugged herself. She was getting carried away. Mrs Merry did own a piano, but Megan had never heard her play.

'I recognize Daphne Merry.' Helen Honeysett nodded at a tall thin woman in a flowery dress talking with Adam Honeysett. 'She's holding her drink as if it's a Molotov cocktail!' Adam

Honeysett laughed loudly at something he'd said, prompting a thin smile. 'She brought us a cake the day we got here. I went and chucked out her old cake tin. That put the kibosh on good relations!'

Megan didn't know what this meant, so said, 'Mrs Merry cooks very nice cakes.' She decided to hold back the best bit about Mrs Merry.

'It was so battered and scratched, it never occurred to me she'd want it back. She asked for it and got quite shirty when I told her the dustmen had carted it off that morning. She wouldn't let us buy her another one.'

'Her little girl was killed.' Garry's voice was breaking; the last word came out as a squeak.

'*What?* Crap! When did that happen?' Helen Honeysett was aghast. Megan was dismayed that Garry had got in with the best bit of news first.

'Dunno. The kid was seven. Same as Megan, that's why she likes her. Megan is a substitute.' The boy flicked back his hair.

'Gosh, how awful. Did she drown in the river?'

'Substitutes are in football and it's not why she likes me. We're not meant to know about her child. It's secret.' Megan drew herself up. Mrs Merry had never told her, but still she saw herself as the Keeper of the Secret. Garry had completely spoilt it all.

'*Everyone* knows,' Garry scoffed. 'Her husband was driving back from France with her and her daughter. He'd got to England and fell asleep. The car smashed into a tree. He was killed. It was a silver Austin Allegro with a spoiler and power steering. Mrs Merry "got out of the car without a scratch on her".' Garry co-opted the phrase his father had used when he came back with the old newspaper he'd found lining a box in the shed.

'How absolutely bloody tragic! And now Adam's towing the poor woman through one of his interminable jokes. Megan, should I rescue her?'

Megan was astounded that Helen Honeysett was asking her opinion. Personally she didn't think that Mrs Merry ever needed rescuing and if she did, Megan would do it. She spotted a cue. 'Daphne's my best friend. I call her Daphne and I'm her De-Cluttering Assistant.' It wasn't as good as the dead daughter, but it was still amazing.

Helen Honeysett snatched up an Olympus Trip camera from a table laden with dishes – lentil bakes, sausage rolls, mince pies – brought by the neighbours. In a ringing voice that briefly muted the room, she called, 'Ste-eve, say *cheese*!'

Steve Lawson grinned at Helen Honeysett, eyes twinkling.

Helen lowered the camera. 'You're Paul Young's double!'

Steve toasted her with the Guinness that he'd brought himself and crooned the first few lines of 'Wherever I Lay My Hat'.

Bewitched, Megan watched Helen flit about the room, chatting to the neighbours. Flash light bleached faces as she weaved between her guests clicking the camera shutter, catching them unawares.

There was something on the floorboards by the piano. Megan squatted down and picked it up. It was one of the Christmas cards by Adam Honeysett. It looked different to their card, but she couldn't tell why. Tapping Garry's picture she told him, 'You're on the same branch as me. It's like a family tree!' Megan glanced at Garry, but he had gone. She peered through the press of bodies in time to see her brother slipping out of the front door. About to go after him, she saw what had caught her attention. One of the balls had been blackened out so that you couldn't see the face.

She counted the faces on the tree. Her dad was at the top above the Honeysetts. Daphne was opposite her and Garry, which was nice. Megan was unhappy that her mum was at the bottom near Mr Rowlands, even if he was a sweetie. She should be next to her dad. Who was missing?

She scanned the low-lit room and got her answer. Miss Lofthouse was going out of the door after Garry. She opened the card and read the writing inside: 'To Sybil, the lovely lady at number 5. Helen and Adam'.

A cold draught drifted in. The fire flickered. A candle on the window ledge went out. By the time Helen Honeysett glanced into the passage, the front door had closed behind 'the lovely lady at number 5'. Vaguely she registered that Sybil Lofthouse had left her party without saying goodbye.

Chapter Three

Monday, 4 January 2016

> '*One, two,*
> *Buckle my shoe;*
> *Three, four,*
> *Open the door…*'

The chanting was eerie at three in the morning.

Jack leant against the tunnel wall, oddly soothed by the cold from the tiles penetrating his coat. Above came the sporadic scrawl of a passing car or lorry. The Great West Road, a major route into London and to Heathrow Airport, was never quiet. But in the dead of night, he had the subway to himself. He shut his eyes and concentrated. He didn't have to wait long for the ghosts.

… here's your cocoa, drink that and you…

Mum, you are a…

… I'll put the dog out, you get that down you…

I love you, Mum…

In the 1950s, streets of houses had been demolished to extend the Great West Road. Jack was standing on the spot where the kitchen of 27 Black Lion Lane had been. At night, he caught snatches of chatter, the bang of pots and pans, cutlery clinking, a phantom domestic soundscape. He imagined himself in the warm kitchen, windows fugged with steam from washing on a drying rack while someone's mother made him cocoa.

I love you, Mum.

Get on with you. Drink that and get yourself upstairs!

Had he ever told his mother that? Had she ever made him cocoa? Oblivious to the tang of urine, Jack strained to hear what came next, but the voices were silent. He resumed his chant:

> *'Five, six,*
> *Pick up sticks;*
> *Seven, eight,*
> *Lay them straight...'*

Jack lifted the iron knocker on the front door. It was fashioned as a short-eared owl and he stroked its feathery chest with a finger. 'Hey, you,' he whispered as he lowered it. Swiftly he inserted his key in the lock and went inside. The piano lid was up. A music book was open at Beethoven's 'Pathétique', the second movement, his mother's favourite piece. Jack wandered into the dining room and dreamily traced the music notation. Modulated notes, poignant and haunting, filled the room. He flicked the page over, but was too late, the music stopped, the quiet like a rebuke. When his mother played, Jack had turned the pages for her; he'd never missed a beat. Now climbing the staircase, he remembered – or supposed he remembered – that he couldn't have done this. She had known the sonata off by heart. She hadn't needed him.

> *'Nine, ten,*
> *A big, fat hen;*
> *Eleven, twelve,*
> *Dig and delve...'*

At the turn in the stairs, he hunkered down and peeped through the banister spindles down to the hall.

Jack had left Bella, his erstwhile partner, an hour ago. (Erstwhile, because they had agreed they didn't want something serious.) She grumbled that he behaved as if he was having an affair with her, sneaking out of bed before morning to go home. At forty-nine, Bella Markham had declared herself in the 'monstrous grip of the menopause' and was suffering from what, post a trawl of the internet, she called 'mood disturbances'. Jack's sympathy cut no ice with Bella. '*Don't be some pony-tailed tosser in socks and sandals trying to be down with the girls!*' Jack, who would never dream of having a pony-tail, couldn't explain about needing to leave to hear the Great West Road ghosts. Or his other ghost...

His mother was craning over the table peering into the mirror. From this angle he couldn't see her face. He ran downstairs to her. There was an oval outline where the mirror had hung. It had broken years ago. His mother wasn't there.

The piano lid was shut and the music book closed. He hadn't touched the piano or closed her book. The room was icy. Not the grounding cold of the subway tiles, but profound, like bones in a winter grave.

> '*Thirteen, fourteen,*
> *Maids a-courting;*
> *Fifteen, sixteen,*
> *Maids in the kitchen...*'

His mobile phone was ringing. It was half past nine. He'd been sitting by the fire in his room – once his mother's den – for several hours. He was sure he hadn't been asleep, but time had slipped away. He looked around the room, vaguely taken aback that he was alone. Assuming it was Bella calling, upset that he'd left, he was surprised to see the name on the screen.

'Hey, Stell!' He was bluff and hearty. No point in telling Stella about his mother's ghost.

'Are you OK? You sound strange.' While tending to miss subtleties of expression or mood, Stella could surprise him with sparks of perception. Jack kept himself hidden, but Stella always found him.

'Yes. Is it another case?' He and Stella had solved several

high-profile murder cases. The last one was over a year ago. They rarely met socially and even less since he'd started seeing Bella. He missed her. He got up and going to the window, surveyed the square below.

'Not as such.' Stella sounded cagey.

Jack pressed his face to the glass. A woman and a little boy were pottering along the pavement towards the church. The boy had a toy steam engine. Jack blinked and looked properly. The pavement was empty.

'… sure you're all right?' Stella was concerned.

'Perfectly sure.' If he told Stella he had seen his mother's ghost – or worse, his own ghost as a boy – she wouldn't be reassured. When Stella worried about him, she offered him cleaning shifts, her cure-all. When he wasn't helping Stella solve murders, Jack took time from driving the Dead Late shift on the District line to work for Clean Slate.

'I have a job for you.'

'Murder or cleaning?'

'Neither.'

After he hung up, Jack sat in his mother's armchair watching the dying fire. He realized with a jolt that it wasn't his Great West Road ghosts, the real reason he'd left Bella's was that he didn't want Stella to call while he was in bed with someone else. Stupid. Why should she care? And Stella could call any time.

It was utterly unlike Stella to accept a job that entailed a ghost. In his head, clearer than his thoughts, more distinct than all his phantoms, Jack heard singing, light as spring air,

> 'Seventeen, eighteen,
> Maids a-waiting;
> Nineteen, twenty,
> My plate's empty.'

His plate wasn't empty, Stella had offered him the ideal job. He would leave his ghosts behind and live with someone else's.

Chapter Four

Christmas Day, 1986

The setting sun sent orange rays over the river, turning its surface to gold. Shards of light speared through leafless branches. It was freezing; the muddied towpath by the River Thames was as hard as concrete.

Two people made their way along the path towards Kew Railway Bridge. A tall thickset man in a donkey jacket, Dr Martens and jeans. A little girl, her cherry-red Puffa jacket slipping off one shoulder, skipped by his side, swinging her hand in his. Sometimes he raised his arm to give her hopping and jumping more scope. They walked in companionable silence. Behind them a brown Labrador sniffed among scrub at the edge of the bank.

Megan had been happy when Steve Lawson agreed she could walk Smudge with him. Mostly he liked to be on his own. Garry said she was too old to hold her dad's hand. She loved to be her dad's 'best girl'. Mostly he was a plumber, mending pipes and installing baths and toilets, but it was Christmas Day and he didn't have to work. She was happy Garry hadn't wanted to come because he would have gone on about football and other important boy's business.

Still Megan felt disappointment. The walk wasn't as she'd planned. She saved until they were under the bridge to tell her dad that Garry was giving her one of his baby budgies when

Topsy had her babies. But when they got to the bridge, a train had gone over and she'd had to shout. Her dad hadn't understood.

'Daddy, Garry's giving me one of Topsy's—'

'You be careful. Garry's put a lot of work into those budgies.'

Megan felt hot with dismay at his response and nearly told him that Garry said the word 'budgie' was babyish. 'I'll put a lot of work into it too!' She decided to give up her other great news of the day, hoarded up since the end of last term – the arrival of the new class hamster – there and then. Her dad had only said, 'That's nice, darlin'.' After she'd told him, Megan didn't think it quite so amazing either.

Her disappointment deepened when, long before they even reached Chiswick Bridge, Steven Lawson announced they must go back since it was getting dark. Blinded by the low afternoon sunlight, his daughter nearly asked where the dark was. She couldn't know it was inside him.

Absorbed in their thoughts, neither of them heard the footsteps. 'Hi, you two!' Helen Honeysett, kitted out in tracksuit and leg warmers, jogged up to them. Her wire-haired terrier darted about in front of the Lawsons' Labrador, who ignored it.

'Oh, hi, Helen. All right?' Her dad let go of Megan's hand. 'How far did you go today?'

'Just to Hammersmith. Need to step up for the marathon, I'm number one weed!' Helen Honeysett was running on the spot.

Steven pulled a face. 'Don't know how you do it.'

'In your business you work up a sweat!' Helen stopped jogging as if to visualize this image. 'I exhaust myself showing yuppies round over-priced houses!' She flashed him a smile. 'I bet you'd do the marathon in record time. Hey, you should join me!'

'I wish!' Steve gave a low laugh and pinched the collar of his donkey jacket together.

Megan was sure she could race to Hammersmith Bridge and back again and would say so if Helen wanted to know. She liked their beautiful neighbour, whose name, like the lady herself, belonged in a fairy tale. She scratched the lady's dog under his chin. 'Hello, Baxter,' she told him.

'You did brilliant work rescuing our ridiculously fangled sound system at the party last night. Adam bodges everything he touches. And as for your fancy footwork! God, if you hadn't fixed the amp, we'd have been stuck with dear Daphne Merry's litter-collecting lecture. Makes me long to come here and toss our rubbish on the towpath. Am I terribly bad?'

'You *are*.' Steven Lawson frowned, and then broke into laughter. Megan tried to make her face smile, although she didn't see why it was funny. If that happened there would be more litter to collect. She wished her dad had listened as hard about the budgie and the hamster.

'You take a nice photo. Remind me to show you the pics I took when they're back from the developers. Ignore the ones of me, I always look an absolute fright.' She began doing leg lunges.

Steven Lawson was quick to contradict her. 'You could be a glamour model.'

Megan remembered that at the party the evening before Mrs Honeysett had stuck a record on the turntable and pulled her dad off the settee next to her and made him dance. Her mum said they were 'half cut'. Garry said dancing was 'stupid' so it was just as well he'd already gone.

Her dad said Helen Honeysett was a welcome ray of sunshine to Thames Cottages. Megan considered Adam Honeysett very handsome and that if he was her husband, she would be called Megan Honeysett. Hoping Helen would hear, she repeated loudly, 'Hello, *Baxter.*'

'Me a model? Crap, Steve! Oops!' Grimacing at Megan, Helen Honeysett clamped a hand over her mouth. '*You* can talk. Like I said last night, you're a spit of Paul Young on a bad day!' She launched into 'Come Back and Stay'; crooning into a pretend mike, she leant across Megan to Steve.

'Get away with you!' Steven Lawson did a funny dance on the towpath.

Megan saw that his boots had got muddy. 'Dad...'

'I'd better be off.' Helen Honeysett darted forward and gave Steven Lawson a peck on the cheek. She jogged away, her dog bounding after her. It seemed to Megan she must have wings because in seconds she had completely gone.

Megan Lawson saw that her dad was right about the dark. The sun had dipped below a band of cloud. Kew Railway Bridge was lost in gloom. The river was grey. Thinking about him saying Helen Honeysett was a ray of sunshine, Megan imagined she had taken the sunlight with her.

'We need to get a move on.' Her dad gripped her hand; this time Megan didn't like it because he was hurrying and she couldn't keep up.

At the lamp-post for Thames Cottages, Megan heard distant barking. 'Daddy, it's Baxter!' She pointed into the gathering dusk and, tugging free of his hand, scampered along the towpath. She stopped at Kew Stairs, a set of steps that led to the river. The stone was worn and slippery with slime. With the river no longer a highway, few had reason to use the old access point. A wire-haired terrier, whitish in the dim light, ignoring the steps, was trying to go up the cobbled slope to the towpath. It kept slithering back down. As it did, it emitted a dreadful drawn-out bark, hollow and bleak.

'Watch it, Megs.' Steven Lawson grabbed his daughter.

'He's stuck, Daddy!'

'He's a dog, Megs. He got down there, he'll get up.'

'He doesn't understand about climbing stairs. We can't leave him. Helen Honeysett will be very, *very* upset,' Megan insisted. 'We must rescue him for her.'

'Don't move Megs!' Steven Lawson began to descend. Slipping and sliding, clutching at bushes, he kept his balance down the steps to a beach dotted with bricks and glass. Slathered in mud, the dog had stopped barking and was yelping piteously. Lawson swished Smudge's lead from around his neck and went towards it. Impassive, the Lawsons' Labrador sat beside Megan up on the towpath watching Baxter, frightened now, flounder at the edge of the incoming tide. Steve Lawson's feet sank into the claggy ground. Mud sucked at his boots. He staggered to firmer ground and heard a cry. Megan had fallen on to the first step. He yelled, 'Megsy, stay up there! Keep hold of Smudge.'

Megan got up and yanked her Brownies belt from her jeans. She looped it through the Labrador's collar. She heard her dad swear and was uneasy. 'What's the matter?' Darkness was all round. She couldn't see him. Peering back the way they had come she saw something on the towpath. She looked properly, but only saw shadows.

'He won't come, he's scared.' Her dad sounded far away. 'I'll go out further.'

Megan heard water trickling. 'What's happening?'

'The river's filling. *Fucking shit!*'

'Daddy!'

Smudge whimpered and tried to go down the steps. It took all her strength to hold him. She heard a whine and felt goose-bumps rise on her arms. Smudge jerked her and, flailing, she pitched forward. 'Help!' Megan cried at the top of her voice. A hand grabbed her.

'It's me.'

Megan smelled lavender.

'Megan love, it's Mrs Merry.'

'Megs!' There was more scraping and swearing. Steven Lawson clambered up the steps, Helen Honeysett's terrier lolling in his arms like an overgrown baby. 'Oh, it's you.' He fumed at Daphne Merry: 'You scared the living daylights out of her!'

'Megan is made of sterner stuff.' Daphne Merry let go of Megan and smacked mud off her long oilskin coat.

'Mrs Merry saved me from the river.' Megan's voice wobbled. 'I thought you'd died, Daddy.'

'I nearly did.' Lawson lowered the dog to the ground and held its collar.

'People should be careful, letting their dogs run wild.' Daphne

Merry tsked. 'It hasn't been trained, that's the problem.' Like Steven Lawson, she was in her thirties; her auburn hair, coiled into a bun, gave her an authoritative air confirmed by her decisive manner.

'They've got minds of their own.' Steven pushed back his hair. 'What did you do with Smudge's lead, Megsy?'

'You had it.' Megan said it quietly. 'I think you must have dropped it by the river when you rescued Baxter.'

'I wouldn't go looking for it, Mr Lawson. It'll be floating past Hammersmith Bridge by now,' Daphne Merry advised. 'Have this. I always carry a spare.' She handed Steven a lead and taking off her glasses began vigorously to wipe the lenses with a cloth.

'The river's flowing towards Kew because the tide's coming in.' Megan piped up proudly. She had just done about tides at school. 'His lead will be going towards Teddington Lock.'

'Thanks, Mrs Merry.' Grudgingly, Steven Lawson clipped the borrowed lead to the terrier's collar.

'Thank you for saving my life, Mrs Merry,' Megan announced.

'Megan don't be silly—' Steven began.

'I didn't save your life, but your father did save Mrs Honeysett's dog so I hope Mrs H is grateful. Careless to run off and leave it. In another few minutes it would have drowned.' With this, Daphne Merry went off along the towpath. Steven Lawson took Smudge's makeshift lead from Megan and led both dogs towards a pool of lamplight up ahead.

The lamp-post lit a flight of worn stone steps that led to a narrow pavement of flagstones in front of the five cottages. Opposite, a little park was enclosed by a high privet hedge. The first cottage, closest to the towpath, was in darkness. The windows in the second house, upstairs and down, were lit. This was home to Steven and Bette Lawson and their two children.

'You go in, I'll take her dog back.' Steven Lawson sounded weary.

'I'm coming too.' Megan let the Labrador into a small plot with a path lined with plastic pots in which weeds had died.

She shut the gate and caught up with Steven Lawson as he was ringing the doorbell of number 4 Thames Cottages where the Honeysetts lived.

Megan hoped that Helen Honeysett's handsome husband was in too. She planned to impress them both with her dad's bravery.

The front door opened and light flooded the path. The dog scampered into the house.

'Baxter old man, you're disgusting! Bath for you, methinks!' A man dressed in a baggy green shirt tucked into chinos and no socks continued munching a stick of KitKat.

'Baxter ran away. My daddy—'

'How often have I said to her, "Do *not* lose him." My wife's mind is a sieve!'

'It could happen to anyone, especially while jogging,' Steven Lawson said.

'Nice of you to defend her, er...' Honeysett nodded at Steven.

'Steve.' Steven Lawson didn't remind Honeysett that the night before at his house-warming party, he'd been his 'best buddy ever'.

'My daddy rescued Baxter from drown—'

'Thanks for scooting him round!' Adam Honeysett was closing the door when Helen Honeysett appeared. In a silk kimono decorated in swirling gold and red, her hair in a towel turban, she bent to pet Baxter, who was weaving around her legs, dirtying the silk. Megan caught a glimpse of her cleavage. She glanced at her dad, and saw he had seen it too.

'Steve, you saved Baxter!' Helen Honeysett came out on to the path and kissed Steven Lawson's cheek. Sashaying away down the hall, she began to sing, 'Every Time You Go Away'.

The door shut. Steven and Megan Lawson were plunged into darkness.

Chapter Five

Barking echoed around the auditorium. Stella shrank into her jacket; she would warm up if, like everyone else, she were chasing about the equine centre, but Suzie insisted on 'working' with Stanley. Stella didn't mind, except that it gave the impression she was prepared to let her elderly mother run around the jumps and tunnels while she lounged on a chair.

Stanley, Stella's poodle of indeterminate age, had been attending agility classes for about a year. Occasionally, when he wasn't driving a train or with Bella, Jack had come, but when her mum returned from staying with Stella's brother Dale in Sydney she had insisted on accompanying her. Although it complicated the expedition – Stella had to collect Suzie and return her to her flat in Barons Court – Stella liked these evenings. They started with a takeaway pizza which they ate in the van outside the equine centre. Stella had supposed her mum would enjoy seeing Stanley dash over the sand, leaping over jumps, trotting along a plank called 'the dog-walk' and shooting through a polythene tunnel, but on her second visit, Suzie had wanted to take Stanley around the course. With her, he did everything perfectly, prancing along the seesaw that up until then he had 'refused' and weaving through a series of poles without touching them. At the agility Christmas party Stanley had won first prize for the dog who had learnt the most. His yellow rosette was fixed to Suzie's computer monitor in the office.

Every week, driving to the centre near Wormwood Scrubs, where her dad had grown up, Suzie Darnell would grouse about the man she had left when Stella was seven. Terry Darnell was her 'wrong turning'. His death hadn't lessened this dissatisfaction, if anything it had become worse – Terry might have annoyed her mum only yesterday.

As Suzie whooshed around the expanse – which smelled of horse piss and damp sand – with the agility of a forty-year-old, Stella reran Suzie's old gripe.

'We met at the Hammersmith Palais. He was the best dancer – that man could twist for England. After we married, it was all work work work.'

Suzie was taking few turnings now. She was no longer running about; as if directing traffic, she stood in the middle of the arena signalling Stanley over jumps, through the tunnel and a suspended hoop. If there was a rosette for dog handlers, her mum would win it, Stella thought as she watched Stanley perfect a flawless English Finish (circling her mum's legs and finishing in a sitting pose facing her).

That evening, munching on a slice of Margarita, Suzie hadn't mentioned Terry. She had devoted herself to instructing Stella how it was about time she settled down. 'You set your sights too high.'

'You think I should make do?' Stella had been surprised: Suzie never compromised. Jack reckoned that Suzie's wrong turning was the day that she signed divorce papers and that Terry had been the love of her life. Stella conceded that there had been no one since and Suzie did talk about him a lot.

Whatever the truth, watching the Darnells' marriage fall apart had put their daughter off commitment; Stella was inclined to view any relationship as a wrong turning.

'Mr Right could be under your nose but, blinded by pre-conceptions of what he should be like, you can't see him.' Suzie extracted an olive from her pizza and snapped it between her teeth. 'Your biological clock is ticking.'

'The clock has stopped, Mum. I'm nearly fifty. Too old for children.'

'One is never too old. More women than ever are having kids in their fifties,' Suzie had told her.

Stella had begun to wish her mum would grouse about Terry and, to put her off, told her about the supposed ghost. It was a desperate move, but Suzie maintained the customer database so would find out soon enough. Suzie had embraced Stella's decision to open a detective agency, but 'ghostbusting' might test her tolerance.

'Those deep basements undermine the foundations,' Suzie had retorted. 'I've read about them: some go down more than one floor. Crazy.' Taking on what Stella had said, she asked, 'Why would this ghost be that estate agent? Why would she haunt Latimer's basement when she lived a couple of doors along?' She peeled the last slice of pizza out of the box and took a generous bite.

'Natasha Latimer doesn't believe it's Helen Honeysett's ghost. That's her sister Claudia. Latimer is worried it'll put off buyers. She bought to sell at a profit.'

'Sisters! I'd have advised you to steer clear. As for the ghost, I bet it makes it worth more. There'll be plenty of murder tourists who'll snatch at the chance to potter about the house with a murdered estate agent. Mind you, the police never found her body; she might not be dead.'

'Latimer wants a live-in housekeeper. Jack's agreed.' Any minute, her mum would grasp the significance of this. As Jackie had said, Jack could not be in two places at once.

'If there's a ghost, Jack will root it out,' Suzie reasoned complacently. 'Is there a deadline?' She flashed a smirk at the pun.

'I gave them a fortnight.'

'Is that a typical period for expelling ghosts?'

'It's all the leave Jack can take from the Underground.'

'Where is Helen Honeysett's ghost supposed to go after you cleanse the house of her?' Suzie appeared to have accepted the ghost's existence. 'Have you an exit strategy?' She scrubbed her hands with one of the damp flannels she always brought along.

'No.' A detailed planner, Stella was appalled by this realization. Latimer might well use that as an excuse not to pay. Ghost or not, she shouldn't have accepted the brief.

Her mulling was interrupted by hectic barking. Across the arena Stanley was leaping around someone sprawled by the seesaw.

'Mum!' Soft sand hampered her progress and by the time Stella reached her, Suzie had draped herself over the dog-walk. 'Are you OK?'

'We need to go to hospital.' Suzie was calm. 'I've broken my ankle.'

Chapter Six

'Those china bits should go. You'll have a clear surface and an uninterrupted view of your garden. Let's do the Three Reasons test.' Daphne Merry smiled at the elderly woman who was nervously fingering a porcelain rabbit, one of a crowd of rabbits dressed as bishops processing across the window sill.

'They were my mother's. She collected them right from when she was a girl.' The woman dotted her hand over the bishops, their long ears poking up each side of their mitres. Megan, perched on a leather pouffe out of the way, pondered how she would not be allowed to throw anything out that belonged to her mum. It would never be clutter. She had promised not to speak so she couldn't say she liked the rabbits – they had friendly faces.

Megan had come with Mrs Merry to De-Clutter. She was overjoyed when the lady – Megan had to call her Mrs Crockett – asked if she was 'Mrs Merry's daughter'. She'd been confounded when Mrs Merry had said 'certainly not'. Her spirits raised when Mrs Merry explained, 'Megan is my assistant.' Mrs Merry – Megan thought of her by her first name, 'Daphne' – was Megan's best friend. She had moved next door when Megan was six and made up for Megan's first best friend Keith, who'd lived there before, going to Australia. Her dad had put a gate in the fence so that Megan and Keith could call on each other without going out to the pavement. Now the gate was the way through to the magic world of De-Cluttering.

'This is about *your* life, Norma dear. Can you give them back to your mother?' Daphne Merry said you had to be friendly, but firm. Mrs Crockett was in her mid-eighties, the question had been rhetorical, but she answered in good faith, her hand hovering on a china dancing maiden picking up her voluminous skirts.

'Mother is no longer with us.' Mrs Crockett did a squawky laugh which Megan found dreadful. If her mum – or Daddy – were dead she would never laugh again.

'I do understand that it's dreadfully hard to part with knick-knacks, but this is about shedding other people's baggage – your mother's – which will fill you with light and air.' Mrs Merry's notebook was divided into two columns, 'In' and 'Out'. There was nothing in 'Out'. 'Are these ornaments useful?'

'Not really...' Mrs Crockett picked up a clay figure of a bearded man bending over one of the rabbits. A label on him read 'The Good Samaritan'. Megan's class had read the bible story last year. She had got into trouble for saying her dad was a Good Samaritan because he mended taps and things for people and he had saved Baxter the dog. The Good Samaritan couldn't be clutter.

'Are they beautiful?' Mrs Merry scowled at the Good Samaritan.

'Not exactly, although Mother loved—'

'They are not!' Mrs Merry shook her head. 'Do they make extra work for you, all that dusting?'

'Oh, yes they do.' Mrs Crocker seemed pleased to be able to agree wholeheartedly.

'Fail! We need three out of three or it's clutter. You think I'm brutal, but that's why you called me in. Sometimes we need others to make these tough decisions.' Mrs Merry gestured at one of the plastic removal crates she had brought. 'Megan, time to declutter!'

Megan snapped to, her sadness that the rabbits and all the other ornaments were clutter overtaken by delight in having a job. With tongue-biting care, she wrapped each piece in newspaper and placed them in a crate.

'This cupboard has a few lovely items lost in a mêlée of nonsense. If you had three things per shelf – say that shepherdess, or just the vase and the jug – they'd have pride of place.' Mrs Merry was scrutinizing a cluster of sundry ornaments through the glass-fronted door of a teak cabinet. 'Were these your mother's?'

'They were *her* mother's. My grandmother died before I was born, these help me to know her...' Norma Crockett shook her head.

'Out!' Daphne Merry scribbled 'Misc. figures, clerical and period' in the right-hand column of her notebook.

Mrs Crockett tipped her head to one side. 'Those sweet little koala bears are mine.'

Megan stifled the notion of taking the pottery pig and the fluffy bears on a trip around the cupboard. She was a De-Clutterer. She wasn't there to play.

'Remember, three good reasons why you should keep them.' Mrs Merry underlined the word 'Out' in her notebook and stabbed at the page.

'It's like throwing away my mother.' Mrs Crockett pulled a face at Megan. The girl couldn't hide her horror at this idea.

'Your mother has passed; she has no need of these.' Daphne Merry pursed her lips. 'When someone is dead they are beyond our protection.'

She must be thinking about her dead little girl and husband. Megan tried to think of something to deflect her. 'They are very sweet.'

'If our ancestors had kept everything that belonged to their forebears, we'd be hemmed in. I've had clients who cannot move for stuff.' Daphne Merry had told Megan the biggest stumbling block was persuading customers their treasured possessions were clutter.

'If you keep one item of your mother's on that shelf, once you've cleared all those books out, you will have light and air.' Smiling at Mrs Crockett, Daphne Merry waited for this to sink in.

Megan heard an Underground train pass underneath the house. The ornaments in the cabinet jiggled.

'Could I keep the koalas?' Mrs Crockett wheedled. Her voice was like a little girl's, Megan thought.

'It's up to you,' Daphne Merry replied pleasantly, then arched her eyebrows. 'Three reasons. One...?'

Megan imitated Mrs Merry cupping a hand under her chin, her other arm folded across her chest.

'It stupid, but they're sort of... well, they're my friends. I've had them since I was eight. Yes, you are right, they are sweet.' Mrs Crockett looked to Megan for support. But Megan, a would-be devout De-Clutterer, met her with a steely gaze.

'Once you make exceptions...' Daphne Merry warned.

'You're right!' Mrs Crockett rounded on Megan. 'Would *you* like my bears? I bet you'd give them a good home.'

'Yes, I—'

'We don't keep clutter disposed of by clients.' Mrs Merry was peremptory.

Megan looked wistfully at the koalas.

'I want light and air!' Mrs Crockett gasped.

Megan was saying goodbye to Mrs Merry at the garden gate when her mum called across from the kitchen doorstep, 'There you are! Daddy's been down the river looking for you.'

'Megan was with me, Mrs Lawson.' Mrs Merry stepped into the Lawsons' back garden and, frowning down at Megan, said, 'I assumed she told you.'

'I told Garry,' Megan muttered, scuffling her fringed suede boots on the grass.

'Telling your brother is like telling the wind, you know that, Megs,' Bette Lawson said.

Mrs Merry said, 'Megan's been a great help this afternoon.'

'Has she?' Bette Lawson sounded sceptical. 'Megsy love, go and wash your hands and next time, ask me before you wander off.'

'It wasn't Mrs Merry's fault,' Megan told Bette Lawson when they were in the kitchen.

'She should have checked with me. Of all people she should know we have to know what our kids are up to.'

'Why of all people?

'Cos her kid died in a car crash.' Garry wiped tomato sauce off his chin with his sleeve.

'Garry!' Bette Lawson made a shooing motion as she put a plate of beans on toast on the table for her daughter. 'Hands. Wash. Now!'

Drying her hands on a scratchy towel, Megan decided it didn't matter about the koalas. When you were a De-Cluttering Expert all that mattered was light and air.

Chapter Seven

Monday, 4 January 2016

Stella used Google Maps on her phone to find Thames Cottages. With the audio muted, Stanley snuffling at her side, the blue line on the map took her down an alley off Kew Green, left, then right. Thames Cottages was a terrace of five houses – she was outside number 5 – set back from narrow front gardens. The app showed the Thames at right angles to the steps at the end of the pavement as a cheery lighter blue ribbon as if it was the seaside. The towpath ran to the left and the right of the little street.

Late at night was hardly the best time to scout out Natasha Latimer's 'haunted house', but after a long wait in Accident and Emergency – Suzie's ankle was badly sprained – Stella needed to clear her head. She would scope the ghost-hunting escapade – her mum's term – from the outside.

St Anne's Church clock struck eleven forty-five. The chimes, floating on the cold air, seemed to come from all around. The cottages, essentially one building subdivided, were in darkness, chimneys black against the orange-mauve sky. Stella had relied on the occupants being asleep; she hoped to go unnoticed.

Keeping Stanley close, she trod softly to a lamp-post at the top of the steps. Natasha Latimer had said her 'property' was nearest to the river.

Latimer had decamped to a flat she owned in central London – Stella had gathered the impression that Latimer owned several properties – until 'you've done the business'. A gust of wind swished through a hedge on her left. The map showed a park. Stella felt a frisson of unease. At night with only Stanley for company, she couldn't so easily dismiss the possibility of ghosts.

From the outside Latimer's house looked like a typical country cottage; it even had roses growing around the door. However, the garden, flagstones set in gravel and three large black marble cubes, undercut this image. Stella, a fan of simplicity, found herself preferring number 2's scrubby patch in which plastic pots spilled over with dead weeds.

Stanley tugged on his lead. Feeling apologetic – he had missed most of his agility class – she let him pull her up the steps to the towpath.

Stella wasn't prepared for the lack of light and tripped, and just avoided falling on to the shingled path. She unclipped Stanley's lead. He chased off into the spangled darkness. Stella made out a pale shape before it vanished. This was out of character; she'd presumed that he'd potter about near her sniffing and then lift his leg. He must have smelled a fox or seen a cat. She fumbled in her pocket for her phone to turn on the torch app, but couldn't find it. She must have dropped it when she tripped. She scrabbled around on the shingle. Gradually her eyes became accustomed to the dark. In both directions, the towpath, a pallid strip, tapered into blackness. Stanley had gone off to the right. Stella nearly shouted with relief as her fingers touched the leather case of her phone. She switched on the torch.

Stanley wasn't on the path. She pointed the light over a low parapet to the river below. The wall was about thirty centimetres wide. With his agility skills, Stanley could walk along it. But he was clumsy and one false step would send him tumbling. The tide was in; she could hear water sloshing against the bank. She couldn't see Stanley, but if he had fallen, he would have been washed downstream. She went numb with dread.

Dry-mouthed, Stella ripped open her jacket and yanked out the whistle from around her neck. Aware she was near houses, she blew gently. The low hollow sound signalled terrible reality. *Stanley had drowned.* Reckless of tripping she ran along the path, swinging the torch into scrub either side. The light accentuated the darkness. It was so thick, she felt she would suffocate.

She stopped and this time blew hard on the whistle. In the ensuing quiet she heard the wash of the river and the hiss of wind in the trees. Suddenly she was in the open. Facing the river was a detached house, double-fronted with a gabled roof. It was dilapidated, guttering hung loose from the roof and when Stella crossed a grass verge and neared the house, she saw cobwebs slung across the window sashes.

Stanley trotted out of the porch. Stella rushed over to him. He was too quick and her fingers only brushed his collar. He ran down the side of the house. She plunged after him, calling his name in a fierce whisper for fear of waking anyone in the house. Abruptly, as if reminded of his obedience classes, Stanley sat down. She fixed on his lead. He wouldn't budge. Giving up on a tug of war that Stanley would win because she couldn't hurt his neck, Stella scooped him up and raced across the grass to the towpath. The back of her neck prickled with the sense of being watched from the dirty grey windows. With leaden legs – Stanley got heavier with each step – she stalked back along the towpath. Blood coursed through her veins like an electrical charge. At last she saw the lamp-post by the steps to Thames Cottages. She broke into a trot, veered off the path and down the steps. She hurried past the little terrace of cottages and into the alley.

She didn't stop until she reached her van on Kew Green. Suddenly aware she was panting, she secured Stanley into his jump seat and slid shut the door. The church clock on Kew Green chimed midnight. She had been by the river for fifteen minutes; it felt like forever.

She reached down to the ignition. There was a tap on the glass. Nerves frayed, Stella stifled a shout. A face was at the window. Pale and gaunt. *The ghost.* She opened the door, thinking too late that it was the very last thing she should have done.

'Stella Darnell?'

'Ye-es.' Fifties. Brown suede jacket. Brown polo-neck jumper. A two-day beard. He looked 'respectable'. And he looked real flesh and blood. She was a poor judge of character. She needed Jack. She needed Jack anyway.

'I saw the name on your van. Amazing coincidence! I was about to call Clean Slate.'

'You need a cleaner?' His hand was on the door. She couldn't close it.

'No! Cleaning's one thing that I'm good at. I want a detective.' He raked a hand through his mop of greying hair. 'I want you to find my wife.'

Chapter Eight

Wednesday, 7 January 1987

'I'm having one of Topsy's baby budgies.' Megan tipped the pudding bowl towards herself and scooped up the last of her banana custard.

'Megs. Manners!' Bette Lawson was spooning instant coffee into two mugs by the kettle. The family's nightly routine was in full swing. 'Tip the bowl away from you.'

'It makes it harder to eat,' Megan returned placidly. Surreptitiously she wiped her mouth on her sleeve.

'It's not definite.' Her brother Garry was toeing into his shoes by the back door.

Welling up, Megan dropped her spoon into the bowl. 'You said I could. *Ages* ago! Her family doesn't love her, you said. I *will* love her.'

'Chick, not "baby budgies" and *budgerigars* do not have families.' Garry gave a low whistle as, on one knee, he knotted his shoelace. 'The mother bird's hatched lots of chicks and she can't look after them all. I said perhaps you can look after one. And it's not about *love*.'

'You'll do a grand job rearing the chick, with Garry's help, Megsy. You'll make it feel well loved.' Steven Lawson winked at his daughter as he began clearing the table. 'Lucky me and your mum only have two chicks. Think of eight of you clamouring for bird seed!' Passing Megan on his way to the sink, he ruffled her hair. He stacked the dishes on the draining board. His back turned, his expression was careworn as if even two children were too much.

The Lawsons lived at number 2 Thames Cottages. Built in the 1850s, their house had escaped the gentrification of 1980s London. Then as now, it was a worker's cottage. The rust-stained geyser above the sink was testimony to Steve Lawson, a plumber, putting business before home improvement. One chair had a broken strut, the table was scored with dents and the wallpaper bulged with damp yet, as on this particularly dark and gusty night, the Lawsons' kitchen was cosy.

'I'm going to be a De-Cluttering Expert when I grow up,' Megan announced.

'What happened to breeding budgies and being a plumber?' Steven handed Garry the dishcloth. 'The birds can wait, lad.'

'I'll be those too,' Megan said. 'Mrs Merry told this lady called Mrs Crockett to throw out her mother.'

'I can imagine she did!' Steven Lawson nudged his son away from the sink and filled the kettle. 'Doesn't take prisoners, our Mrs M. What does she do with dads?'

'She didn't say that, lovey.' Bette Lawson scribbled on the calendar hanging on a cupboard door. 'That poor woman. She won't care for dads. I'd have killed you if you'd let anything happen to my two...' She caught herself and flapped at the January page as if to undo her words.

'I felt a bit sad for the lady. She said her bears and the rabbits were friends. Now she'll be able to see better. Mrs Merry gave her light and air.' Megan cheerfully echoed Daphne Merry's phrase.

'You're talking rubbish.' Garry turned on the hot tap. With loud pops, the geyser came to life. He sluiced dishes through the hot suds. Megan grabbed a drying-up cloth from a hinged plastic rail and, positioned importantly beside her big brother, stood ready for the first plate.

'That water's scalding, Gal. Use gloves.' Bette Lawson was still scrutinizing the calendar.

'Garry says gloves are for girls!' Megan announced.

'If she's blind, why does having clutter matter?' Garry's hands were already pink.

'She's not blind. With no clutter, Daphne says she'll have straight lines.'

'I hate this fad for having nothing on show. Customers want everything boxed in. All very nice until there's a leak and you can't trace it.' Steven Lawson blew on his coffee.

'It was nice of Mrs Merry to take you to her work with her. Although, like I said, you should have told us.' Bette finished with the calendar and left the pen swinging.

'She told me,' Garry remarked. His support of his sister, once solid, now swung between clumsy care and being crippled with embarrassment.

'You didn't think to pass it on?' Bette Lawson drank her coffee. 'I'm on lates tomorrow, Steve, you haven't forgotten?' Bette Lawson was a Sister at Charing Cross Hospital's A and E.

'I told you Betsy, I'll be here anyway.' The phone rang in the hall. Rattling aside the bead curtain Steven Lawson went to answer it.

Later Megan would fix on that moment as when everything went wrong.

'Who was it?' Bette Lawson asked. Steven Lawson dragged bead strings from around his shoulders as he pushed through the curtain. He snatched up the mug and gulped his coffee.

'Who was on the phone?' Bette Lawson's children continued washing and drying. Megan dried an already dry dish.

'That bloke in Chiswick, the one with the two MGs? He's had a flood from the washing machine. Says I installed it wrong.'

'Did you?' Bette spoke under her breath.

'Course not. It was second-hand junk. I warned him.'

'Was that the job where the wife called you in saying she was fed up with waiting for him to plumb it in?' Bette Lawson involuntarily glanced at the geyser. Now was not the time to mention living with a time bomb.

'Yep.'

'You going down there now?'

'No! He was calling to kindly inform me he don't ever want to set eyes on me and won't be paying the bill!' Steven Lawson crashed his mug down on the table, splashing coffee. 'He's charging me for reinstating his neighbour's ceiling. A full redeck, replastering, painting the lot!'

'He can claim on insurance.' Bette was unflustered. She dealt with real life-and-death dramas.

'He's not insured and nor is his downstairs neighbour.' Steven Lawson knuckled a closed fist against his teeth.

'Kids. Upstairs.' Bette Lawson waved at her children as if scaring them into flight.

'I haven't finished drying,' Megan protested. Her brother abandoned the sink and, with his hand on her shoulder, shepherded her out of the kitchen.

Megan heard her dad say: 'It's over, Bette, I'm washed up.' Which was odd because there were the pudding bowls to do.

Without discussion the children went into their parents' bedroom at the front of the cottage. Neither of them turned on the light. Megan mooched to the window. The park opposite was too dark to see the swings and the slide. 'Is Daddy all right?' Her breath steamed the glass.

'Course.' Garry sat on their mum and dad's bed, smoothing and resmoothing the yellow and brown flowered duvet, a leftover from the seventies. 'He hates cheapskates. So do I.'

'He gets quite cross these days,' Megan observed as the idea occurred. 'He was cross with Mrs Merry when we rescued Helen Honeysett's dog Baxter.'

'No he doesn't,' Garry said crossly.

Megan plumped for safer ground. 'When can I start rearing my chick?'

'It's not *your* chick. You're going to be looking after it and not on your own, I'll be watching,' Garry retorted. He hadn't changed out of his uniform; his shirt collar was unbuttoned. He sat forward, elbows on knees, tie dangling.

'Yes, but when can I start?' Her brother's moods didn't faze Megan.

'This weekend. Maybe.' He wandered over to the window and looking up at the sky said inconsequentially, 'That's the Plough.'

'It's Helen Honeysett!' Megan's excitement about the chick and her usual interest in stars was subverted by astonishment that it was the very person she had mentioned. 'She's running with a torch and Baxter's there. She'd better not lose him because me and Dad aren't there to rescue him.' She added quietly, 'I'd be scared to go to the river by myself.'

'That's stupid,' Garry said without conviction.

The children heard the front door shut; Steven Lawson was running up the towpath steps. A moment later a slant of light fell across the path and their mum was at the gate.

Megan made to bang on the glass.

'Don't!' Garry pulled her away.

'Steve!' Bette Lawson called into the darkness.

Garry went to his bedroom. Megan watched her mum come into the house. Then she crept downstairs.

Chapter Nine

Tuesday, 5 January 2016

A sharp wind whipped up from the river carrying with it the smell of mud.

Midnight. Jack looked along the towpath, beyond the light cast from a lamp-post on the steps to Thames Cottages. He had come to see where he would be living for the next two weeks. Number 1 Thames Cottages was empty. Stella had said Natasha Latimer wanted the ghost got rid of. He didn't say that ghosts were not 'got rid of', they were accommodated. That would sound too much like the sister. He rather liked the sound of Claudia. As for Latimer, scratch the surface and most people harbour a suspicion that the dead walk. She had listened to her sister and come to Clean Slate.

Latimer's high garden wall was parallel to the towpath. It was topped with glass, no deterrent for spirits, but it put him off climbing over. He would have to wait until later that day – twenty hours away – when he and Stella were meeting Latimer in the cottage to see the garden.

Or perhaps not. There was a door in the wall. Natasha Latimer sounded like someone who would cover all points of entry, particularly a door in the seclusion of the towpath. The solid oak door fitted snugly into the wall, leaving no gaps for a foothold. There was no handle. It opened only from within the garden. Jack checked he was alone and switched on the tiny

Maglite he kept on his key ring. He shone it on the lock. Jack knew there were few locks that couldn't be picked. The digital lock – responding to a key pad and recently fingerprints – was his enemy. But luckily there still weren't many of them around. Despite the apparently state-of-the-art basement, Latimer had fitted a deadbolt lock on her garden door. Or someone had; neither the door nor the lock looked new. A deadbolt could be picked if you had the right tools. He had the right tools.

Jack switched off the Maglite and waited for the darkness to dissolve so he could make out the outline of the towpath. Experience had taught him there were always others creeping along the alleys and byways of London for whom night was a friend. Few murderers were afraid of murderers. Jack never assumed he was alone. He began to count... *eight, nine, ten.*

The breeze had died. Far off he could hear traffic on the Great West Road, but, like the sea in a shell, it might be his blood circulating. He slipped his hand inside his overcoat and was rewarded by a clink. Grimacing at the sound – careless – he extracted his steel lock picks, 'borrowed' from someone with no more right to them than he had. He had to work with no light and rely on touch. He must be at one with the lock. He could pick a lock and enter a property without damage. Not even a scratch. If he were a burglar, with no evidence of forced entry, no insurance company would pay up.

The door opened on greased hinges. Not good: someone used the door regularly. He pushed it to, but didn't lock it. Never cut off a point of egress. Long grass reached to his knees; buddleia crowded in. Latimer had skimped on the garden; perhaps funds had run out.

His shoe caught something. He cleared away weeds and grass. A headstone. Jack tore at matted roots around the marble.

HERCULES 1981–1987
A FAITHFUL COMPANION
STILL MISSED

Confident that the next-door cottage had no view of the end of the garden, Jack swung the light around and saw another headstone. And another. There were five. He had stumbled upon a pet cemetery.

He cleared moss and soil from the other monuments. All of them only about thirty centimetres high. 'Max 2000–2012 Lost to us'; 'Rex 1921–1930 Forever a friend'. Basil had lived from 1966 to 1976 and Bunter ('Dear one') from 1930 to 1941. There was no pattern to the arrangement of the graves: two were side by side, Max and Hercules, the most recent. Latimer must have been loath to dig up the graves of pets belonging to previous occupants of the cottage, but she hadn't kept them tidy. Given her attitude to rumours of a ghost, he doubted she had much time for death. Still, that she had kept them pointed to a degree, however meagre, of sensitivity. Although thinking about it, the sister – Claudia – was probably responsible for saving them. Were they to meet, Jack fully expected to like Claudia. He supposed Latimer would tell them about the graves later, because surely this, if anywhere, was where a ghost would haunt. Jack had no doubt about the existence of phantoms, but in Latimer's case, he tended towards the malicious rumour option. Or it could be that, like Rillington Place and Cromwell Street, the backwater of cottages would be tainted beyond living memory by murder.

He protected his face with his coat collar and edged around a holly bush. Ahead was a sweep of gravel, another enemy. The point of gravel was that it was impossible to tread quietly on it. A rectangular pond was divided by a little bridge to French doors. He progressed over the gravel gingerly, as if avoiding land mines. The room beyond the doors was in darkness, pin-pricks light of what he guessed were standby lights for electrical equipment (TV, hifi etc.) glowed through the glass. The pond was two squares of green glass: skylights. The basement beneath must stretch beyond the extension under the garden. It was a wonder indeed that Latimer had stopped at the pet cemetery. Good old Claudia. Jack hoped she'd be there later. He had no idea if someone was watching him through the French doors. Never assume that no light means no one's at home. He wouldn't push his luck. Swiftly he made his way over the gravel, around the holly bush and across the pet cemetery. He closed the garden door firmly, the lock clicked.

Someone was coming along the towpath. A bright light moved steadily closer. Jack daren't conceal himself in bushes on the bank: the slope was steep. Besides, a True Host would know he was there. A True Host, Jack's term for someone who had killed or was going to kill, would find him. Jack's self-imposed mission was to hunt out creatures of the subterranean night and learn their habits and routines. He tracked men – and women – with minds like his own. The risk was that a True Host got inside his own mind. After his and Stella's first case, Jack had tried to halt his quest. Stella, strict about means to ends, didn't approve that, in a bid to prevent murder, he was an uninvited guest in anyone's home. Yet his mission was the point of living. Long ago he had failed to stop a True Host from shattering lives. He had to atone.

'Good evening.' The man wore a head torch. Jack was blinded. He caught the glint of a dog lead dangling from the dog walker's hand.

'Evening,' Jack replied. A dot of light floated on his retina after the man had gone. Jack let himself breathe. It wasn't only True Hosts who were out on lonely paths late at night. Dog walkers were not afraid of the dark. He moved on along the footpath towards the Kew Railway Bridge.

Chapter Ten

Sunday, 11 January 1987

'I know her!' Megan couldn't hide her pride.

'How can you know her? My dad was talking about her at breakfast. He says there's a monster on the loose. She's on the telly – you can't know her.'

'I do. She's probably just lost.' Megan was annoyed that Angela Parker didn't believe her. Angela had broken friends with Becky Fox and had asked to go around with Megan. Although Megan liked Becky better, she had cautiously agreed. 'She lives there, by our house.' Megan waved a hand over the hedge and added for good measure, 'Her husband is very handsome. He took a picture of me in secret.'

'You're a liar,' Angela pronounced.

'It's true, in fact.' Used to Garry contradicting her, Megan was equable. She murmured, 'She takes pictures of people's rooms and sells them.'

The children were scrutinizing an A4-size poster tied with loops of string to railings in the park. Rain had soaked the string and loosened it, so that the poster, encased in plastic, hung askew. The face of Helen Honeysett looked through the clouded plastic at them, as if through dirty water. The word *Missing* was printed in bright red. Like blood, Angela had said.

Missing. Missing who? Megan had missed her family when she went on Brownie camp. She had never thought of a person *being* missing, let along Mrs Honeysett, who was as beautiful as a queen and was going to have two of Garry's budgies.

'She looks scary,' Angela pronounced. 'The way she's smiling like it's fun to be missing. I think she's hiding.'

'She didn't know she was missing when that was taken. My dad took it at their Ewell-Tide Party when they got here. She's very nice. My dad likes her. He saved her dog from drowning.' Megan remembered how happy her dad had been at the party, dancing and singing. Since the man's washing machine had gone everywhere, he was always cross. He had said 1987 was cursed. 'Helen Honeysett says he's the best plumber in London.' Megan sniffed to cover her confusion because she wasn't sure Mrs Honeysett had said that.

'I 'spect she's drowned in the river. That's what happens. Your dad should have saved *her* not her dog.' Then in a burst of munificence Angela conceded, 'Amazing you know a famous person. Have you got her autograph? I've got that man from *Dad's Army* and Basil Brush.'

'She wasn't famous until she became missing.' This fact struck Megan as peculiar. Surely a person had to be there to be famous?

'I wish Becky was missing,' Angela said as they wandered across the playground to the gate that opened on to the towpath. A blue-and-white plastic tape marked 'Police Line Do Not Cross' was tied from two tree trunks beyond. A metal sign propped on the path told them 'Road Closed'.

The girls craned over the tape. Uniformed officers were moving along the riverbank, poking sticks and shining torches into tangled scrub.

'My dad says her husband killed her to get her money,' Angela said.

'You said a monster took her,' Megan reminded her.

'He is a monster. He murdered her.' Angela giggled at the word 'murdered'.

'She's missing. She's not murdered,' Megan insisted.

'How do you know?'

'Her husband is handsome. He's called Adam and he's not a monster.'

'Dad says the police are questioning him. They won't care he's handsome.' Angela wavered. 'I shouldn't think so, anyway.'

'I'm rearing a baby budgie.' Megan had been saving up this nugget for her new friend. 'My brother breeds them and I help him. I give her bits of grated carrot and apple. She's beginning to *feather up*.' She pronounced the 'technical term' with aplomb. 'You can visit her, if you'd like.'

Impressed, despite herself, by a missing famous person and a baby budgie, Angela agreed.

Another poster was wrapped around the lamp-post by the towpath steps. With no protection, the photograph had bleached. It had a dated quality. Only missing a few days, Helen Honeysett already belonged to a distant past.

Chapter Eleven

Tuesday, 5 January 2016

A fire burned in the grate. Stella's deep-cleaning eye roved over opened post on a table, letters and circulars stuffed back into envelopes, CDs out of their cases splayed around a tower of audio equipment; a ripped packet spilling Digestive biscuits lay on top of copies of the *Metro* and the *Evening Standard* piled on a chair. Stella had seen truly untidy rooms, with every available surface buried under mounds of clutter and nowhere to sit, but this was different. She might not be a great judge of character, but Stella could assess the habits of a client from just one room. This man was restless, flitting from one unfinished task to another like a butterfly.

Stella reminded herself she wasn't here to do a cleaning estimate. Only then did it strike her that she'd allowed a stranger to lure her into his home in the middle of the night. When she was little, her parents had forbidden her to answer the door or the telephone even if they were upstairs. Tired after hours in the hospital and preoccupied with Natasha Latimer's commission, too late she heard her dad's advice: *'Always say where you are going. Don't trust anyone, especially not the respectable ones: appearances deceive.'*

Stanley barked, sharp and shrill, his warning tone.

'I have to go,' Stella said.

'You can't!' The man – he had told her his name, but she'd

forgotten it and this somehow made her predicament worse –
shovelled papers off an armchair and motioned to her to sit.
He pulled the curtains. Despite the warmth of the fire, Stella
was chill.

As if watching a film, she saw herself shutting the van door
and driving back to Hammersmith. Instead she had gone down
an alley and now she was trapped. In electric light the man
didn't look respectable. Crumpled shirt. Trousers blotted with
muddy paw marks. Scuffed shoes. His wired manner, bright eyes
and twitchy movements didn't reassure. Was he on something?
Her mum would presume Stella had gone home after she left her.
Jackie supposed she'd been to agility and was at home. Jack too.
No one was wondering where she was.

Natasha Latimer had said there was no 'community'. No
one had welcomed her. Stella could understand that digging
out a basement might alienate the neighbours. But what if
they weren't friendly anyway? Helen Honeysett – ghost or not
– had disappeared from this street. In such cases, it was often
the husbands. If she shouted for help, who would come? After
midnight there would be few passers-by. She should have waited
and come with Jack. He would be with Bella asleep or... Stella
closed down the thought.

Stella could have no idea that Jack wasn't with Bella but, at
the moment she was taking in the enormity of her mistake, he
was outside. Had she called for help Jack would have heard.

Stella sat down in the armchair. The man – his name was
Adam Honeysett – was pacing up and down the long room.
This wasn't easy as there was so much stuff: toys and books, a
baby grand piano. When he had his back to the door, she could
make a run for it. Yet her curiosity took over. She said, 'You
wanted to talk about your wife?'

'Have you heard of Helen Honeysett?' Adam Honeysett
stopped and, interlocking his fingers, cracked his knuckles.
An old trick designed to unsettle.

'The missing estate agent?' Guessing he expected her to know,

Stella was fleetingly grateful to Natasha Latimer for refreshing her memory that morning. To hear about the woman twice in one day was extraordinary.

'She was my wife.' He puffed out his cheeks as if this was an inconvenience. 'Early on the morning of the eighth of January 1987 Helen went jogging with the dog along the towpath by the river at the end of these houses. She never returned.' Looking at Stella with strange intensity, he said again, 'She's dead. I want you to prove it.'

'Why now, twenty-nine years later? Why not years ago?' This might antagonize Honeysett. Her dad had asked awkward questions, but he could radio for help. She never antagonized cleaning clients.

'With no new leads, there's no active investigation. The police review it annually, but Helen is a "cold case". There was nothing cold about my wife. I want you to find out what happened to her.'

Stella had been about to protest that since the Met police hadn't solved the case she doubted she and Jack could, but then she remembered how her mum grumbled that Stella and her father's first response was always 'no' and also that she and Jack had solved four cold cases. She should at least listen. Not that she had a choice. Stanley stood by her chair, tail down. A bad sign. In the grate, a lump of wood had burned to grey ash; the flames died. She said nothing and huddled in her jacket.

Adam Honeysett grabbed a silver frame placed next to the model of a dog with a long tail on the mantelpiece and gave it to Stella. 'That's my Helen. Please find her.'

Stella knew the image. In 1987 it had been all over the press and TV and on missing posters stuck around West London. Stella had been starting out on her cleaning business then and – no van in those days – had seen 'Missing' posters on trees, fences and lamp-posts as she walked between jobs. A blonde woman, with hair piled on her head, strands curling around her face, laughing into the camera. Stella considered how a murdered person became known for one expression. Usually a smile that grew as familiar as the Mona Lisa's. Stella stared at Helen Honeysett and Honeysett stared back. Stella blinked; she could imagine Honeysett coming out of the photograph and asking why Stella was in her house so late. Stella laid the frame on her lap. It seemed rude to give it back to Adam Honeysett or to return it to the mantelpiece.

Honeysett took up a poker from beside the grate and pushed the log about on the embers. A lick of flame engulfed it. Still grasping the poker, he leant on the piano. 'She never learnt to play this.' He smacked the poker in his palm. Stella wished he would put it down. 'In a few days it'll be the anniversary of when Helen vanished. I read in the local paper that you found some killer from the seventies and that you solved your father's case. You see clues that the police miss. I want a fresh, objective eye.'

Lucie May had written an article after what Lucie called 'The Kew Gardens Murders'. It had netted a couple of cleaning jobs, but no detection cases. Stella had been vaguely grateful; although she had decided to open a detective arm to her cleaning business, she remained ambivalent. A detective burrowed into people's personal lives, something that as a cleaner, despite entering clients' homes, Stella made a point of not doing. However, Helen Honeysett was the focus of two jobs within twenty-four hours. If not one of Jack's signs, it was something that might be worth pursuing. She got out her Filofax. 'So you think your wife is dead?'

'Some days I feel it here.' He thumped his chest. 'In what's left of my heart. Natasha in the end house accused me of starting an absurd story that Helen's haunting the street. I told her, that's not my wife's style. If anyone, she'll haunt me for putting her favourite silk shirt on spin.' He spoke on a sigh: 'If she was alive, I'd know. I want to move on.'

Natasha Latimer had said something about Honeysett having a 'new girl every week'. A missing wife must cramp things a bit. Stella wouldn't probe that for now.

Honeysett laid the poker on the hearth. He grabbed a lever-arch file from under a heap of magazines. 'I've got together newspaper cuttings, stuff off the internet, photos and police letters. You probably do things your way, but...'

'I'd like to hear it from you first.' Terry used to say that how someone told a story provided clues. Stella noted that he'd only recently assembled the material; the file wasn't the result of decades of obsessive research.

A cloud passed over the man's face. Perhaps he was used to doing things his way. Hugging the file he began to talk, without emotion, as if he'd said it many times before. In her head Terry's 'ghost' voice advised, *'Even a well-rehearsed lie reveals a grain of truth.'*

'I left Helen that morning. She was asleep. I had a pitch in Northampton. I kissed her on the cheek, careful not to wake her. Had I known it would be the last time, I'd have shaken her, told her I loved her, told her I'd never...' He wiped a hand over his mouth and brooded at the dying fire.

'Hold the silence. Into the void, a clue will fall.'

After some moments Honeysett continued, 'Helen started work at ten in Hammersmith. At eight, she went for a jog with the dog. Every day, same time, same route. If someone were stalking her, he would have got her routine in no time. It never varied. These days we'd call her OCD; then she was disciplined. It makes it so hard.'

'Makes what hard?' Stella hadn't meant to speak and not to ask an absurd question. His wife being missing and presumed murdered was hard.

Honeysett said, 'Hard to remember that morning. It was the same as any other. I said to the police, days merged. They still do, but then it was because I was blissfully happy, now I don't care what happens.' He fell silent and scratched his stubbly chin.

Stella brought him back. 'Was it usual for you to go to Northampton?'

'No. I was presenting worked-up concepts for an annual report to a firm that made plastic cogs. After Helen, that job – any job – seemed banal. I'm a graphic designer. Was. Not much going now. Few want to hire a murder suspect. Recently it's picked up, younger guys think it's edgy. And as long as the price is right.' He pushed out his lower lip and gave a shrug in mock powerlessness.

Stella had scribbled Honeysett's initial words in her Filofax. 'I want you to find my wife.' She could be alone with a killer. She tried to hear Terry, but his voice was silent.

Honeysett was still talking. '... nevertheless, I live under a cloud of suspicion. If you'd set up a pitch for graphic design companies, would you invite the one that killed his wife?' he asked bitterly.

'I choose the work I like best.' Stella had sat through design pitches when Clean Slate rebranded. 'If I liked your ideas, I'd choose you.' Honeysett had said 'killed his wife', not 'might have killed'. Was that a slip?

'God! If I hadn't gone to Northampton, Helen would be talking to you now.' He went to the window and tweaked the curtain aside, as if looking to see if his wife was outside. He returned to his chair.

Stella didn't say that she wouldn't be there if Helen Honeysett were alive. She asked, 'Were you the last person to see your wife alive?' A family member or someone close to the victim was statistically likely to be the killer. More than once Stella had seen a weeping partner on *Crimewatch* pleading for his loved one to return, only to hear later he'd been charged with murder. That Honeysett had brought her the case didn't rule him out as a suspect.

'I got back at eight that evening. Helen wasn't there. I didn't worry as I guessed she'd gone with the dog for her run. She went twice a day. Eight in the morning and eight at night.'

'Where did she used to go?' Stella posed questions that prompted clear-cut replies. If Jack were here, he'd encourage Honeysett to ramble on. He said people gave themselves away when they went off the subject. She wanted a foundation of facts.

'Along the towpath, to Chiswick Bridge and back.'

'When did you realize Mrs Honeysett was missing?' She wasn't on first-name terms with the potential victim.

'About ten that night. Helen was always out for an hour.'

That meant that Helen Honeysett should have got back by nine. Despite her strict routine, her husband only started worrying an hour after that. Had the police decided he was innocent or did they lack the evidence to prove him guilty?

'Sometimes she'd go as far as Hammersmith Bridge. She was a friendly person. I guessed she'd met a neighbour on the towpath and gone in for a drink.'

'Did she do that a lot?' A spontaneous visit to neighbours didn't fit the OCD profile. Nor did it fit the kind of neighbours that Natasha Latimer had described. But it was about thirty years ago; perhaps there were nice ones then.

'Never. She borrowed two baking potatoes off Daphne Merry. She liked the family at number 2. She flirted with Steve Lawson, the husband.' He shrugged as if it was unimportant. Stella wrote, 'Check Steve Lawson/Helen Honeysett.'

'When you got worried, what did you do?'

'I tried every house. Bette Lawson said Helen wasn't there. I didn't call on Sybil Whatsit next door at number 5; she did early shifts at the Stock Exchange so I knew she'd be asleep. Besides, she keeps herself to herself. She walked out of our party without saying goodbye. No way would Helen have gone there.' He put a finger to his lip. It made him look like a small boy. Stella wondered if it was meant to. 'That Merry woman didn't answer. It turned out she'd been walking her dog and had found our dog down by the river. She'd tried me, but of course I was on the towpath looking for Helen. Old Neville Rowlands lived at number 1, the cottage closest to the river. Tash kicked him out when she bought the house, turned out he hadn't told the people he rented from that his mother had died! The cottage was part of a portfolio of properties, the consortium who owned it hadn't kept tabs on the tenants or they'd have realized she had to be about a hundred and thirty! Rowlands was lucky not to be done for fraud. Anyway, that night he behaved as if I'd accused him of kidnapping Helen. After that I told the police to try there first. Helen used to call him an "old grouch" but she was sweet with him. She was nice to everyone. He wasn't old, he was only in his mid-thirties then. He was that classic type that looks middle-aged even as a kid, lives with his mother and does some boring old job. It's the quiet ones who turn out to be murderers.'

'Do you think he's a murderer?' It surely wouldn't be this easy. Stella put down about Rowlands' dead mother paying rent. It might have no relevance to the case, but it was the sort of fact that Jack appreciated.

'Rowlands has an alibi.'

'What was it?'

'He was in the house nursing his mother. He went out for five minutes with the dog, but went the other way along the towpath to Helen. He saw Daphne Merry, but she didn't see him. He saw her with the two dogs, he corroborated her story and his own.'

Corroboration could also be collusion. 'Are Neville Rowlands and Daphne Merry friends?'

'No one in this street are friends!' He gave her wry look.

Terry had said that relatives provided the best and worst alibis. 'Was his mother still alive then?'

'Yeah, just. She died not long after. I'll save you time, Rowlands is in the clear.'

'Are these people still living in the street?' Stella knew that no one was in the clear. Least of all a man whose alibi was his mother. She wrote 'Old Grouch' and added 'SUSPECT' in capitals. She scrawled a diagram of the five cottages and filled in the names she had so far. She'd need Sybil Whatsit's surname, but wouldn't interrupt Honeysett's flow.

'Tash caused a stink by digging a hole deep enough for a double-decker bus under her house!' Honeysett grinned. If he had been inconvenienced by the basement, he gave no sign. So, Natasha Latimer ('Tash') had 'kicked' Neville Rowlands out. What could that mean? Had Latimer been scathing about Honeysett because he'd dumped her for another woman? One of his 'new girls every week'?

'Like I said, I went to the towpath. I forgot to take a torch and nearly fell into the river. I was scared Helen had done that. She couldn't swim and even if she'd been able to, it was January, the water's freezing. Like tonight. You'd be paralysed and sink in seconds into the steely depths!'

'Perhaps that's what happened.' Stella didn't stint on bald possibility. The simplest explanations were generally the right ones.

'If so, her body would have resurfaced downstream. The river doesn't keep its victims.'

Stella shot him a glance. Honeysett had what Beverly, Clean Slate's office assistant, would call 'a right way with words'. He might be telling a ghost story by the fire. She knew that he was wrong. In winter, with fewer people on the towpath or sitting outside pubs and restaurants, a body could be trapped under a bridge or among weeds unseen and, as it decomposed, not smelled for months. Or it could be washed downstream to the sea and never found. During summer months a corpse's gases were released faster so the body would rise to the surface quicker. Stella didn't say this.

'I had to identify the clothes of two female bodies pulled from the Thames that year. Someone's found drowned in the river once a week. I wasn't allowed to see either woman as they'd been submerged for weeks. Their faces were disfigured, pecked by seagulls and battered by bridges and boats. Helen wouldn't have been seen dead in the clothes they showed me.' Honeysett was able to face grisly detail; Jack might say he relished it. Stella noted this down.

'What about your dog?'

'I whistled and when he didn't come, I knew he'd gone into the river and she'd gone in after him. Idiotic thing to do.' Honeysett looked cross. 'Dogs always survive and their owners drown trying to save them.'

'You said Daphne Merry found your dog.' She wound up the pressure. Stella made a show of consulting her notes.

'I meant that, at the time, I thought that's what had happened.' Honeysett snatched up the poker again. Stella decided her tactic was misguided. Terry wouldn't have upset a suspect holding a potential weapon. 'I *hoped* she'd gone home and was there, worrying about me. I had a car phone; she could be ringing it. She should have had one. With her job she went into empty properties with strangers, but in those days the phones were as heavy as car batteries. When I got back, I thought I saw her, but it was Daphne Merry with the dog. She'd found him on the towpath. She made me call the police; I didn't want to bother them. Not yet. "That's what they're there for," she said. When I told them Helen was nearly twenty-seven, they asked if we'd quarrelled. I said no.' He frowned. Stella wondered if they had argued and thought again about the hour between nine and ten when he'd done nothing. 'Once they knew her age, they weren't interested.'

'An adult can go somewhere of their own volition; a child's more likely to have been abducted,' Stella explained.

'They as good as suggested she'd dumped me.' Honeysett was scratching at a stain on the arm of his chair.

Stella reminded herself that she was being a detective, not a cleaner.

'We'd only been married two years, couldn't keep our hands off each other. Helen had a career, she was in love and we had this house, why leave?' Another shadow darkened his face. 'When I told them Helen wouldn't abandon the dog and that she did the same thing every night they started taking it seriously.'

Stella knew that most kidnap victims are killed within twenty-four hours of abduction. The police would have had to move fast once they had decided it was abduction.

'What was Helen like?' Wishing he was there, Stella asked a 'Jack' question. She used the first name to put Honeysett at ease.

Honeysett sighed. 'Perfect.'

No one was perfect. Stella bit her lip.

'Kind, funny, beautiful, cared about people and animals, not a bad bone in her body. Every day I pinch myself that she loved me – she could have had anyone. She'd have been a brilliant mum.' He raked his fingers through his greying hair. Stella couldn't shake the impression that Honeysett was conscious that the gesture drew attention to his good looks. She wrote 'Vain' under 'Relishes grisly facts' and then added 'SUSPECT'.

'You said Helen was *addicted* to running.' Stella stuck a poker into the missing woman's flawless image.

'She was on an endless diet. Ridiculous – she was a string bean. Her wrist fitted in here.' He made a circle of his forefinger and thumb. Stella envisaged a stick insect. 'She was even talking about getting a boob job. She hated how she looked. She said she had flat feet!' He laughed uproariously.

Stella tapped her pen on her chin. Honeysett was increasingly coming across as a plausible suspect. 'Could she have gone into the river deliberately?'

'So *not*! She was full of life. Plus she wouldn't have taken the dog with her.'

'What was its name?'

'Who?'

'The dog.'

'I, er, I don't remember. Why?' Honeysett looked at her as if reassessing whether she was up to the job.

'I want salient detail.' Stella supposed in twenty-nine years' time she would remember Stanley's name, especially if he'd been involved in a tragedy. She wrote down 'Lack of recall'.

'They took this house apart while they grilled me in a room without windows for hours. I'm claustrophobic, I need light and air. I was desperate to get out of there and look for her. They made me dredge up the minutiae of our last days. And of course I couldn't distinguish between them. Why hadn't I gone looking sooner? Why hadn't I gone with her? Did I think it was OK to go jogging in the dark by the river? Had we fought? They kept asking that. They checked my hands and fingernails for signs of violence and trapped skin.'

Stella had been about to ask Honeysett these questions herself.

'... they were wasting precious time. The abductor was out there. He is *still* out there.' Again Stella wished Jack was with her. There was something Honeysett wasn't telling her. Jack would have wormed it out of him.

She heard a shifting; the lump of wood tumbled on to the hearthstone. Adam Honeysett grabbed tongs from a silver companion set beside the fireplace, snapped the wood between its teeth and threw it back on to the embers. He smacked his hands on his trousers, smudging the wool. Stella was put in mind of an ageing Heathcliff – *Wuthering Heights* was the only novel she'd read from start to finish – as he slumped brooding back in the armchair. 'Helen was the love of my life.' He nodded at Stella's chair. 'We'd sit like this, telling each other's fortunes in the flames. I said Helen had a bright future. How crap was I!' His forefinger went back to his lower lip.

It wasn't the first time a client had told Stella she was sitting in the chair of a dead wife. At least Helen Honeysett hadn't died there. *Or had she?* Keeping her voice calm Stella asked, 'Did the police connect the case – Helen – with Suzy Lamplugh's disappearance? They were both estate agents, similar age and they worked in West London.'

Suzy Lamplugh had gone missing the previous July, in 1986. Terry had cancelled an early birthday celebration with Stella in a Chinese restaurant (she was twenty a week later) to join the search, so putting off her first go with chopsticks. Her dad often cancelled their outings for his work. Stella had grown adept at containing her disappointment, but her mum had fumed that Terry was as unreliable a father as he had been a husband. Stella knew about murders and abductions, but – perhaps *because* her dad was in the police – until Suzy Lamplugh had gone missing, a woman close to her own age, she had never considered the possibility of danger to herself.

'Yes, the police explored that line of inquiry. How could they not? Neither woman has ever been found. It could suggest a man skilled at disposal, but besides thin circumstantial coincidence, no link to the cases has been found.'

Honeysett spoke like a detective. Perhaps nearly thirty years of liaising with the police had familiarized him with their terminology. She brought him back to the personal. 'Did your wife have family?'

'Her parents were divorced. The first thing her dad asked me was had she made a will? He gave us money for this place; the bastard wanted it back. But the cottage is in both our names. So he could whistle! She wasn't declared officially dead until 2007. I had to wait twenty years before I could access her funds.' Honeysett rummaged in the log basket and tossed more wood into the grate. It killed the tiny flame. A chill closed in. 'Her mother died in 1988. Cancer. The father died of a heart attack months after. My poor Helen is an orphan.'

Stella noted the present tense. She didn't think it was an error. She felt that Adam Honeysett chose his words carefully. Did he think she was still alive? That might be a problem. Stella, remembering what Terry had said, was certain Helen Honeysett was dead.

'Did she have brothers or sisters?'

'She was an only child. So were her parents, no cousins and what not. No one but me.' Honeysett got down on his knees and tried to encourage a flame from the embers.

Convenient, Stella noted.

Honeysett was revving up. 'The press camped out there. They shouted abuse through my letterbox. "Wife-Killer." "Where did you bury her?" "Living off her money, Adam?" They talked like we were mates. The police did nothing.' He scratched his stubble, making a rasping sound.

'Did they rule out a connection to Suzy Lamplugh?' Stella mused out loud. From his own testimony, Adam Honeysett could have killed his wife. He had been in Northampton, but it was only his say-so that she was alive when he left that morning. Why hadn't the police charged him? A second later she got an answer.

'The police arrested someone for Helen's murder with an alibi for the Lamplugh disappearance.'

The air was icy. Stella pulled up the collar of her jacket and hurried down the alley to Kew Green. Her footsteps rang on the frosted pavement. Stanley trotted alongside her. This time she checked for anyone lurking in the shadows. Her van was ethereal white. Adam Honeysett said he had recognized it because he saw the livery on the panels. Stella preferred anonymity. Hers was the only plain vehicle in the fleet. How could he have known it belonged to Clean Slate?

Chapter Twelve

'Stand out of the way,' Garry instructed his sister.

'Can I hold it?' Megan pleaded.

They were in the aviary in the back garden. Steven Lawson had constructed a wooden cage attached to what had been the outside lavatory when the family moved in three years ago. Steven's first, and only, plumbing job in the cottage had been to instal an indoor toilet. He stowed his tools in the lean-to.

A bicycle lamp fixed to a bracket cast a light into Garry's budgerigar aviary. One side of the aviary was given over to perches on which were huddled two blue-feathered budgerigars. There were ladders and a swing held by wires threaded with painted wooden balls on which a yellow bird oscillated dramatically. Cylindrical bird feeders were suspended from the mesh roof. At the one end, under tarpaulin, was a cupboard with shoebox-size drawers cut with circular holes. From these came a constant cheeping.

'You can fill the bird feeders,' Garry informed Megan. 'Unhook them and take off the cap at the bottom. Do *not* spill any seeds. They're expensive.'

'There's some there already.' Megan pointed at a scattering of seeds on the impacted earth at their feet. She wanted this established should Garry accuse her of dropping them.

Garry didn't look. 'They're husks.'

'I want to hold my chick. Please!' Megan shivered. She had come outside for the express purpose of seeing her Abandoned Baby Budgie. She didn't want to fill dirty old feeders, and suspecting Garry of fobbing her off with the boring chore.

Garry softened. 'After. Fill that jug with seed and pour it in. I've got to clean out the roosting boxes.'

'I'll help you, Megsy.' Their dad was outside the aviary, fingers hooked into the mesh. 'Mum wants you in for tea.' He unlatched the door and, careful not to let the birds escape, edged inside. 'Gal, give Megan her bird. Let me do the feeders.'

Garry extracted a tiny budgerigar with blue feathers from one of the roosting drawers and, holding it in cupped hands, passed it to his sister. 'She'll never learn to look after them if all she does is cuddle them. They're not toys,' he grumbled.

'The police have taken Mr Honeysett in for questioning. About Helen.' Steven spoke in a low voice because Bette didn't want him talking about it to the kids.

'Why?' Megan kissed the chick's head. 'She kissed me back!' she crowed.

'No, she didn't,' Garry said.

'Mr Honeysett was the last person to see Helen.'

'He's murdered her.' Garry swept out the last drawer and tipped dirty straw, moulted feathers and seed husks into a bin bag.

'No he hasn't!' Megan raised her clasped hands in horror, swooping the small bird upwards.

'Careful! Give her to me.' Garry took the bird and returned it to the freshly strawed box.

Seeing the effect on his daughter, Steven Lawson back-pedalled. 'We don't know what's happened. She might have fallen and be in hospital with no memory.'

'She's not in Charing Cross. I heard Mum telling you,' Megan told him.

'She's dead.' Garry was phlegmatic.

'Don't start coming out with that nonsense, Garry, you'll give Megan nightmares.'

'I don't want her to be dead. She's nice.' Megan bit back tears, as much for the tiny bird now in a dark box as for the missing woman. 'Mr Honeysett is so handsome. Angie says there's a monster on the loose.'

'What does she know?' Garry scoffed. 'He's not handsome and if he was, it doesn't mean he didn't strangle her and throw her in the river to be eaten by eels!'

'Garry!' Steven was properly cross. 'Give over now.' He took Megan's hand and led her out on to the concrete path.

Garry made a show of inspecting the filled feeders; then he gathered up the bag and eased out of the cage. He took his time latching the aviary door. Megan watched him so that if she was allowed to look after the birds, she would do it right.

'Chop chop, Megsy!' Steven Lawson grabbed Megan and lifted her off the ground. 'Gotcha!' he shouted.

'No you have *not*.' Megan struggled, but he had got her and was holding her tight.

'Love you, Megs,' Steve Lawson whispered into her hair.

'I love you back, Daddy,' she confided. When he let her go, she pushed past her brother and skipped up to the house, bursting into the kitchen, happiness restored.

Garry waited for his father by the back door and, sniffing, asked in a 'man-to-man' voice, 'Do you reckon they'll send Mr Honeysett to prison, Dad?'

Steve Lawson scraped his shoes on the step. 'I bloody hope so.'

Chapter Thirteen

Tuesday, 5 January 2016

'Excuse me. What are you doing?'

Jack whipped around. In the darkness he couldn't see anyone. 'Show yourself.' Clipped speech sliced the night air.

As if reeled in on the end of a line, Jack moved away from what looked like a dilapidated house. He'd hoped to have a look inside. Torchlight dazzled him, then the beam dropped to his feet. As the bright dots diminished, he saw an elderly woman, upright and dignified, white hair translucent in the moonlight. Faced with a tall pale man in black on a deserted towpath, she was unafraid.

'You don't live here,' she informed him.

'No... I...' Jack advised Stella that, if in a jam, say whatever occurs. 'I was clearing up.' He scooped out his coat pockets and displayed his treasures: sticks, dried leaves and special shaped stones. There were biscuits for Stanley and a Cadbury's wrapper for chocolate he'd shared with Bella on one of their night walks.

'Clearing up?' The woman peered down quizzically. She had guessed the motley collection belonged to him. She wasn't wearing a coat although it was freezing. A dog lead and what looked like a police whistle were slung around her neck. She must have a dog. Jack had to hope it wasn't as fierce as her.

'Litter had been tossed over the gate. Horrible for the owner to clear up. I was asked...' He wouldn't push it; too much detail got you in trouble. 'Ooh, is it *your* home?' He gave his best smile.

'No it is *not*! I couldn't live there.' Then she said in a softer tone, 'Good of you to tidy up after people. I can't bear clutter.'

'Me neither.' Jack was fervent although he collected clutter.

'Why are you here?' She wasn't pacified. 'Do you have a dog?'

'No, the thing is...' Jack wouldn't start explaining about how much he loved Stanley. He rammed his hands into his coat pocket and felt his phone. 'I'm at number one Thames Cottages' – an address might reassure – 'and it has no signal. I walked along a bit, but there's no reception here either.' He laughed as if this was of no consequence.

'All that disruption to a house that's more than adequate for a decent-sized family.' Lifting her whistle the woman blew a piercing blast like the hoot Jack used to summon station staff trackside in an emergency on the District line. Imagining a slathering mastiff, he nearly cried out in relief when a fluffy dog no bigger than Stanley pattered out of the gloom. He wasn't good on breeds of dog, but hazarded it was a Yorkshire terrier. The animal was wheezing. 'Come here, Woof! I'm sorry, but I think it's dreadful what you've both done. It is a form of vandalism and all in the cause of the dollar.' The woman set off in the direction of the cottages.

Guessing she was one of Natasha Latimer's neighbours, Jack fell into step. 'I'm only the live-in housekeeper.' He liked his new title, he could be in *Jane Eyre*.

'I see.' The woman was like Miss Marple, kindly yet, Jack knew, as sharp as a pin. 'Nothing "only" about that role. No wonder you were picking up litter. We do that.'

'Are you a housekeeper too?'

'I'm a *declutterer*.' This was clearly a superior role. The woman stopped at the steps down to Thames Cottages and proffered a hand. 'Daphne Merry.'

Expecting a strong grip to go with her indomitable manner, Jack just avoided breaking her fingers when she lightly rested them in his. Her skin was papery and warm. 'Jack Harmon. I'm here for a fortnight. I have to shoo off a gh— dust.' Daphne

Merry, like Stella, would have no truck with spirits. He warmed towards anyone who called a dog 'Woof'.

In the pool of lamplight Jack abandoned his detection technique of laying groundwork and gaining trust. If, despite Latimer's denials, Honeysett was haunting Natasha Latimer's house, he must learn about her. He must find out *why*. Daphne Merry was a woman who brooked no nonsense and he only had two weeks. 'I hear a woman went missing here years ago.'

'The towpath isn't a place to go after dark. You meet all sorts,' Daphne Merry said. 'She went jogging by herself. She had a dog – he was nothing but a nuisance. No training, you see. She never cleared up his mess. She cut corners. Careless. Sadly, we pay for our actions.' She did look sad.

No doubt Daphne Merry meant he was 'all sorts' and she'd be right. 'Do you think she's dead?'

'I don't *think* about her. What do you think?'

Jack was startled at having the tables turned. 'These days it's hard to disappear so comprehensively. But then…' Despite Daphne Merry's less than flattering comments about her, Merry mightn't welcome him saying that he doubted Honeysett was alive.

'Latimer bought that house to sell at a profit. She denies it, but it's obvious. I say, if you're going to do a thing, just do it. At least whoever moves in next can't do more to the building. Perhaps they'll leave us in peace.'

'You seem to have an affinity with this place born of longevity.' Jack was glad Stella wasn't there to hear him. She'd definitely lump him in with Claudia.

'I've lived here for over thirty years.' In the poor lamplight the cottages looked what they once were: squat workers' dwellings, prey to damp and draughts. 'In 1987 we had journalists nosing about, dropping food cartons, hiding in hedges, banging on doors. You have no idea of the disruption such an event causes to law-abiding citizens.'

Since he was being a housekeeper, not a detective, Jack didn't say that actually he did have some idea.

'What do you think happened to her?' He needed Stella's blunt insistence on keeping to the subject – he was no contest for Daphne Merry.

'She may have fallen in the river. Carelessness is costly. But if you want my advice, Mr Harmon, you'll stick to your cleaning, a most worthwhile occupation.' She turned into the gate of number 3, Woof at her heels with obedience worthy of Stanley. Merry lived next door to where he'd heard a dog bark. Perhaps it had been Woof barking, Jack thought.

'Goodnight, Mrs Merry.' Jack wouldn't call her Daphne. Yet.

'Sleep well, Mr Harmon.' She was brittle, as if doubting he would sleep at all.

Lingering outside Latimer's gate as if he could go in, Jack heard a key scratch in a lock and Merry's door close. It seemed that Natasha Latimer was wrong about at least one neighbour spreading rumours about her house being haunted. Daphne Merry saw Latimer for what she was, a rich, ruthless young woman intent on getting richer. So if it wasn't Merry, then who was it? Alone in the little street, Jack reflected again that he needed Stella.

As he came down the steps from the towpath, Jack heard barking. Probably the dog he had just seen. It sounded like Stanley, reminding him that he hadn't seen Stanley, or Stella, for a long time. Jack tended to see Stella if they were doing a cleaning job together, which was rare, or working on a detective case, which was rarer still. He'd enjoyed the agility classes with Stanley, but since he'd begun seeing more of Bella, couldn't fit them in. He would see Stella soon.

The barking had come from number 4 Thames Cottages. Through lace curtains he saw the blurred outline of two figures in the sitting room. Despite there being a 'guard dog', he opened the gate to get a closer look. Someone shut the curtains. He believed that the action was unconnected to him, but it was a sign to go. He'd taken enough risks tonight.

As he passed number 5, the last cottage in the terrace, an upstairs light went out. It could be yet more synchronicity, but this time Jack felt sure that someone had extinguished the light to see without being seen. He would find out who lived there. To have any success with ridding the street of any haunting rumours – or real ghosts – he'd get to know the other residents. He'd enjoy getting acquainted with Daphne Merry.

His phone buzzed. At the same moment St Anne's Church on Kew Green struck half past midnight. Bella. She'd ask where he was. Bella was a botanical illustrator and, if they weren't seeing each other, she was often at her drawing board until dawn. He couldn't say he'd been looking around the house he was going to live in for the next fortnight. He had yet to tell her about his assignment. His finger hovered over the answer button. Bella would want him to come over. Or – and this was more likely – she would want to join him. Over the last year, he had grown to like Bella being with him on his nocturnal journeys across London. Although recently she'd felt too tired to join him. Anyway, tonight after his visit to Latimer's garden, he wanted to be by himself.

Footsteps. They came down the alley that led to Kew Green. Jack ran back up the steps to the towpath and, dipping into shadows, kept perfectly still. To become invisible, he cleared his mind and kept his gaze unfocused, his breath even. If you held your breath you had eventually to breathe deeply and give yourself away.

A man lingered on the pavement outside Daphne Merry's house. Something dangled from his hand. A dog lead. *He had a dog.* No amount of invisibility fooled a dog.

The man unlatched Daphne Merry's gate and walked slowly up to her door. Mr Merry? Jack rejigged the Miss Marple image. But then the man returned to the pavement and, with deliberate care, latched the gate. He vanished down the alley to Kew Green. Jack ran on tiptoe along the narrow walkway, noticing as he passed her house that Daphne Merry's curtains were moving as if she had just closed them.

Had he not been preoccupied with the pet cemetery and guilt about Bella, Jack might have noticed, as was his habit, that the number plate of the van parked on Kew Green was CS1. Seeing it, he would have grasped that the dog he had heard barking sounded like Stanley because he was Stanley and that it was Stella whom he had seen through the lace curtains. Regardless of having to explain what he was doing there, Jack would have gone back to find her. Instead he passed her plain white van without even seeing it.

Dressed in black, his dark hair brushed back from strong aquiline features, on soundless rubber-soled shoes, Jack Harmon disappeared into the labyrinth of London streets, as insubstantial as a ghost.

Chapter Fourteen

Monday, 12 January 1987

'Answer the policeman's questions truthfully.' Bette Lawson hovered behind her children, a hand on each of their shoulders. Megan and Garry Lawson sat like shop dummies at the kitchen table, staring at their empty tea plates.

A smell of cigarette smoke and damp wool pervaded the kitchen. A plain-clothes detective sat opposite the children; a WPC stood by the bead curtain, perhaps unaware of the bead string draped over one shoulder.

'When did you last see Helen?' The police inspector, a thin-faced man with blotches on his cheeks and a military haircut, smiled reassuringly.

'We're supposed to call her Mrs Honeysett,' Megan replied promptly.

'Sssh!' Garry jabbed her with his elbow. 'That's not important.'

'It *is* important to be polite,' Megan hissed. 'Daphne says to take care with everything we do.'

'Mrs Merry, you mean!' Garry hissed.

'What did I say just now?' Bette Lawson squeezed their shoulders. 'Just answer the policeman.' She shot a look of apology to the officer, but he was smiling at Megan.

'You are quite right, Megan.' He nodded encouragingly. 'Always take care.' His mouth gave a twitch as if he had his own opinion. 'Now, Garry, tell me when you last spoke to Mrs Honeysett?'

'I saw her running along one morning on my way back from my paper round. She said, "Hello, Garry, you're an early bird!"' Garry mussed up his mullet hairstyle self-consciously.

'What morning would that have been, Garry?' The inspector readied his pad.

'Last Tuesday.'

'Do you deliver the papers every day, Garry?'

'Yes. Then I clean out the budgerigars and feed them. Then I get ready for school and then I have breakfast and then—'

'I've been helping with the budgies. Haven't I, Gal?' Megan interjected. Annoyance passed over her brother's face, but he gave a grudging nod.

'Good lad.' The detective leant forward. 'I bet you can tell one morning from another. What makes you say you saw Mrs Honeysett on Tuesday morning and not, say, Wednesday?'

'On Wednesday I have football and have to pack my kit.' Garry looked faintly impatient as if this was obvious.

'Could you have seen Mrs Honeysett on Wednesday and then packed your kit?' Honeysett's husband had seen her on the morning of Thursday 8th, so the boy's sighting on the Tuesday had no relevance, but it tested his credibility as a witness.

'No.' Garry pulled at his upper lip. 'I didn't see her on Wednesday.' He didn't say he knew this because, returning from his round, he had looked out for Helen Honeysett, hoping she would speak to him again, and had been disappointed not to see her.

'I saw Mrs Honeysett last Monday – exactly a week ago – when I was walking Smudge with my dad. She was galloping along the towpath with Baxter at top speed. She stopped when she saw us. And...' Megan clasped her hands at the memory. '... on Christmas Day Daddy rescued Baxter from drowning and he nearly drowned too! Mrs Honeysett was really pleased with him. Mr Honeysett told her off for forgetting him. Daddy makes her laugh.'

'Told her off? What did he say, Megan?' The officer put down his pad as if the answer would be of no consequence. He knew when to apply pressure.

'She doesn't eavesdrop, Chief Inspector Harper.' Bette clutched at Megan with both hands.

'Ouch.' Megan winced. 'I couldn't help hearing because I was there. It's only eavesdropping if you're hiding.'

'Still an inspector for my sins, Mrs Lawson!' the officer said. 'I'm sure Megan doesn't listen to other people's conversations, but she was present during the exchange between the Honeysetts so anything she heard could be very helpful.' Bugger manners, he liked eavesdroppers. 'Megan, take your time. Your dad hasn't told us he rescued the Honeysetts' dog. One to hide his light under the proverbial is he?' He bared his teeth at Bette Lawson.

Bette was tight-lipped; her husband hadn't told her. Recently there were many things Steve hadn't said. She snatched up the plates and, resisting washing them, laid them on the side and resumed her post behind her children.

'Megan, why did Mr Honeysett *tell his wife off*?' The officer emphasized Megan's words. 'Was she careless?'

'I think he was cross she left Baxter by the river to drown and forgot all about him.' Her palms clasping her face, Megan appeared to give the matter great thought. 'My dad told Mr Honeysett that it could happen to anyone and then Mr Honeysett agreed, but I think he was still cross. He called her "a sieve". My dad was happy afterwards.' Megan beamed at the detective.

'Why was he happy?' In a 'by-the-way' tone.

'Because of saving Baxter for Mrs Honeysett,' Megan rattled on. 'I like her. She always says nice things, doesn't she, Gal?' Garry didn't respond. 'She liked my new haircut and said our Labrador who's called Smudge is a "sweetie". She told my brother he was "one cool dude" which made him go bright red!' She nudged Garry; he grimaced fiercely and tweaked at an imaginary moustache. 'She's going to buy two of his budgerigars.'

'Have you seen Mr Honeysett get cross with Mrs Honeysett before, Megan?'

'No. When I see her he's usually not there. She said he goes away a lot for work. I think it makes her sad.' Megan was winsome. 'I had to go to school camp and I missed my dolls. Didn't I, Gal?'

Her brother, bright red, said nothing.

'You can't know she was sad, Megs.' Bette shook her head at the inspector. 'She's got an imagination!'

'Megan has been helpful. You both have. If you think of anything else, get your mum to call us.' He nodded at Garry.

'You was talking shit, Megs.' Garry rounded on Megan in the aviary. He was feeding the budgerigars. Megan sat on a stool feeding her chick. She was pleased to see she had got plumper. Holding her to her face she felt tiny wings whirr against her cheek.

'Shit?' She looked at her brother but, cleaning out the roosting boxes, he had his back to her.

'I don't care about Mrs Honeysett.'

'You do.' Megan popped a drop of milk from a pipette into the bird's open beak. 'You like her. So does Daddy. And so do I. Mrs Merry says she's a "man's woman". What does she mean?'

Garry didn't know and as his sister expected him to know everything, ignored her question. 'Dad likes Mum better.'

'Of course he does,' Megan said peaceably. 'We all do.'

Chapter Fifteen

A week after the disappearance of 26-year-old Helen Honeysett on a foggy morning beside the Thames, police have no clue to what happened to her. Last week, just after 8 a.m., the time Helen left for a jog, police reconstructed her usual movements. Accompanied by Helen's beloved spaniel, Baxter, a WPC dressed as the striking blonde in Nike running pants, yellow sweatshirt and white Adidas 'Three Stripes' gym shoes retraced Helen's final journey along the Thames towpath, a little-used secluded track. Apart from dog walkers and joggers, tragic Helen would have been alone. The WPC – who resembled the missing girl – was trailed by press and TV snapping and filming as she ran to Chiswick Bridge and back. She paused by Mortlake Crematorium to do stretches as the promising estate agent used to do. The run took a little over forty minutes. But Helen Honeysett, a girl with a brilliant career beckoning, never made it home. Her dog was found by a neighbour on the towpath yards from the dream cottage – roses around the door – that newly-weds Honeysett and Honeysett had for only three weeks called home.

'Helen's super-fit; if she was attacked, she'd have defended herself,' a distraught Adam Honeysett told us in an exclusive interview (page 4). The last person to see her alive when he left for work that morning, he said, 'My wife should be celebrating her 27th birthday on 31 January. She was born on the 29th February and on non-leap years we choose her birthday.' A large gift tied with pink ribbon waits for stunning Helen. Honeysett was questioned at Richmond Police Station for three days before being released.

The disappearance of estate agent Suzy Lamplugh last summer alerted detectives to a possible serial killer. But despite grilling every client whom Helen has shown around properties since starting work at Harrold and Sons in Hammersmith last September, they have drawn a blank.

Detective Inspector Ian Harper appealed for witnesses. 'Helen was an eye-catching girl. If you saw her in the vicinity of the towpath on the morning of Thursday 8 January, please come forward…'

Stella noted with only mild surprise that although the cutting was from the *Richmond and Twickenham Times* it was by Lucie May, now the Hammersmith-and-Fulham-based *Chronicle*'s chief reporter. May got everywhere. It was dated 22 January, a week after the reconstruction on the 15th and a fortnight after Helen Honeysett's disappearance on Thursday the 8th. Lucie May had been on friendly terms with Terry – Stella didn't dwell on how 'friendly' – and had helped her and Jack with previous cases. Stella was wary of her, but didn't forget that Lucie had once saved her life; she was good in a crisis. She and Jack were good friends. Like Terry, Lucie was never off the clock. Stella guessed this story (May viewed everything as a story) with no conclusion must have frustrated the reporter.

Stella sat in what had been her bedroom before her mum left Terry and took her to the flat in Barons Court when she was seven. When she was too grown up for access weekends, her dad had converted the room to his office. Terry Darnell had died in 2011 and left Stella his house. She had taken over the room (she didn't think of it as reclaiming) and Terry's new computer. At 3.30 a.m., with an early start, there was no point going to bed so, armed with an instant coffee, she opened Honeysett's lever-arch file. Stella had stressed that she wouldn't accept the case before discussing it with her partner, Jack. Honeysett had appeared hacked off, but hadn't argued.

Honeysett had only printed archive material from the internet in the last days and it didn't date back years. St Peter's Church chimed four and then five; Stella read on, stopping to jot notes in her Filofax. In his tartan-covered bed by the radiator, Stanley slept, four legs stuck straight up, his head twisted at an impossible angle.

There were several articles by Lucie May along with many from the nationals. Again and again, Stella came across the photograph of Helen Honeysett that was framed in the Honeysetts' living room; it was repeated in newspapers and news bulletins on several anniversaries of her disappearance. Sipping cold coffee, Stella read a piece from the *Sun* from 1997. Headlined *Fairy Tale Couple*, describing Honeysett and Honeysett as an eighties power couple, glamorous and gorgeous in Galliano and Westwood, cruising London in a red VW cabriolet with the top down. They had frequented New Romantic clubs and the coolest restaurants. Honeysett topped sales targets at Harrold and Sons and her husband *made loadsamoney* designing packaging for *fast-moving consumables* like confectionery and shampoo. Until the morning of Thursday 8 January, they'd had it all. Until, as Lucie May said in one of her luridly couched articles, *a monster stalking the banks of the Thames ripped their lives apart.*

Stella had worked for couples like the Honeysetts. People her own age, with nannies for their children and cleaners and gardeners for their homes. She never judged clients, any observation was to ensure that Clean Slate did the best possible job. She wondered now who had cleaned for them. Perhaps no one. Adam Honeysett had said he was good at cleaning.

In an article written in 2007, twenty years after the disappearance, was a picture of Adam on the footpath where a neighbour called Daphne Merry had found their dog. *Husband still yearns for Helen's return.* He was gazing out at the Thames as if the river was where Helen Honeysett would 'return' from. He was quoted: 'I know she's alive.' When had he stopped thinking this? Stella pondered. Or had he said it to keep the press interested?

She needed Jack. Jackie said Stella was logical and methodical while Jack was intuitive. She amassed and ordered facts; he saw signs everywhere: in telephone numbers, digital clocks, in shadows and the shape of chewing gum on pavements. He said he heard voices from the past in subways and old houses. She had chosen him for the Latimer job because he believed in ghosts and, especially, because he could clean. Stella didn't hold with making decisions based on squashed Doublemint gum but did admit that somehow Jack arrived at the truth. As detectives, they were least efficient when they worked alone. She reached for her phone and stopped, hand in mid-air. Again she decided that Jack would be with Bella Markham. He had met her when Stella and he were on the Kew Gardens murder case. Jackie said Bella was Jack's girlfriend, although, secretive about his private life, he hadn't told Stella this. Bella was teaching Jack to draw dried plants. He said it made him see life differently. He talked about patterns on leaf surfaces, in the patina of tree bark and hairs on a stem. It helped him 'deconstruct reality'. Stella had no wish to do anything to reality except face it head on. When she looked at a surface she wanted to see a polished sheen.

Jack would be pleased they had another case. They were a team. What if Jack brought Bella with him? No, he wouldn't. When they had a case they told no one except Jackie – and Lucie May if they needed her help.

For no good reason, Stella felt that Adam Honeysett had kept something back. She couldn't explain this suspicion. Jack was good at nuance. It wouldn't be the first time a client had lied, but why would he lie? She let it go and before she could change her mind, she dialled Jack.

'This is Jack, who are *you*? Tell me after the beep.'

Puffing out her cheeks, Stella cut the line. She reviewed the columns in her Filofax. Adam Honeysett said the police hadn't linked Honeysett to the Lamplugh case because they'd arrested a man with an alibi for when Suzy Lamplugh went missing. The man was called Steven Lawson. She went back through the file, but found nothing about Lawson being a suspect. She rolled back on her chair, thinking to get another coffee and heard crackling. The wheels were on a newspaper cutting that had fallen from the file. She got up and pushed the chair off it.

Lucie May had been busy on this case. As she read, Stella was increasingly bemused: the article was biased even for Lucie. She generally managed a nod to balanced reporting. Steven Lawson had been thirty-five in 1987, a plumber married with two children, Garry twelve and Megan aged seven. Stella had put on her map that the Lawsons lived at number 2 Thames Cottages. The Honeysetts were at number 4. Lucie described how, on Christmas Day 1986, Lawson had saved Honeysett's dog from the river. Lucie angled the story to suggest that Lawson deliberately put the dog in danger before he rescued it. Megan Lawson had seen her father following Honeysett to the towpath on Wednesday night, 7 January. May urged readers not to be fooled by Lawson's *baby-faced Paul Young looks. Forget that his kids claimed to love him. Monsters come in all shapes and sizes.* There was a picture of Lawson being led away by officers. Stella made out two faces, presumably Megan and Garry, at an upstairs window. In another photo – of Lawson with his wife Bette on their wedding day – she saw the resemblance to Paul Young. Bette Lawson reminded her of someone too, but Stella cleaned for many people; one client was likely to look like another.

She was puzzled by the police focus on Lawson because Adam Honeysett had left her sleeping the following morning, the 8th. Why did Megan Lawson's sighting the previous evening matter? Lawson was a neighbour, he had a dog and went to the towpath, but so did Daphne Merry and the man dubbed 'Old Grouch' by Helen Honeysett. Neville Rowlands lived with his elderly mother in the house that was now Natasha Latimer's.

Stella supposed that the police had allowed for the possibility Honeysett had broken her routine and, instead of jogging, abandoned her dog and gone away. It might be out of character, but Stella knew not to depend on people doing what was expected of them. Honeysett could have been abducted from her house and the dog let out.

'Presume nothing. Start as if with a clean slate.' Stella dimly recalled it was Terry's advice that had given her the name of her company. Suzie maintained it was her idea.

A brief report from the Guardian stated that after two weeks of questioning the plumber was released without charge due to lack of evidence. Lucie wouldn't have eaten her words, she 'didn't do mistakes'.

The church clock struck six. Caffeine zinged through her blood and, despite no sleep, Stella was ready for the day. She went for a shower.

Hot water pounded on her scalp and streamed down her face. Lack of evidence didn't absolve someone from murder. Absently soaping herself, Stella decided to interview the plumber, Steven Lawson.

It was only as she and Stanley were crossing the dark street to her van that, with a guilty jolt, Stella recognized that without consulting Jack, she had decided they'd take the case.

Chapter Sixteen

Saturday, 17 January 1987

'What are you doing here on your own?'

Megan jumped. She hadn't heard Mrs Merry come along the towpath. 'I'm taking Smudge out for a walk,' she announced decisively. Hands on hips, she pointed at the Labrador rootling about by the slope to the river.

'It's dangerous. Anything could happen to you and no one would know.' Mrs Merry was fierce. 'Remember Mrs Honeysett.'

Megan felt herself grow hot. She mumbled, 'Sorry.'

'Don't apologize to me: it's yourself you should be thinking about – and your poor parents. What if I hadn't come along? People don't think of the consequences of actions. Those left behind.' Mrs Merry frowned at where the dog was now circling. 'Is Smudge doing his business?'

'Yes. I'm to bring him back after.' Megan hoped Mrs Merry would see that she was doing what she'd been told.

'You must go and clear it up. A declutterer is always working.'

Miserably regarding the heap of brown mess, Megan proceeded towards it. She had never thought of poo as clutter and didn't know what to do with it. Did Mrs Merry mean use her hands?

'I'll do it.' Daphne Merry went down the bank, clutching branches and not once slipping. As if she had performed magic, she climbed up again in record time with the poo in a Marks

& Spencer's plastic bag. 'Would you let your dog mess in your home? No, you would not!' She secured the bag with a knot.

Megan nearly said that her dad didn't clear up Smudge's poo but didn't want him to be in trouble with Mrs Merry. In the gathering gloom, balancing on one leg, her other foot against the back of her calf, Megan was puzzled: since Mrs Merry was always right, her parents must be wrong. They didn't know about clutter. Eyeing the bag swinging from Mrs Merry's hand, Megan felt a surge of excitement. She blurted out, 'I saw Helen Honeysett this week!'

'What?' Daphne Merry dropped the bag of poo and didn't seem to notice. 'She's dead, how can you have done?' She gripped Megan's shoulder.

'On the towpath before school. She was running exactly where Smudge just did his...' The word 'poo' was probably rude. '... made clutter.'

'That was a police reconstruction! Didn't you realize?' Mrs Merry took her hand off Megan and clumsily stroked at her hair. 'It was a policewoman dressed up to make us remember. I prefer to forget very bad things. It was a waste of time and money. Still, they must think it works.'

'Um. Yes, I didn't remember anything.' Megan felt hot with stupidity. 'It did look like her.'

'It was meant to.' Mrs Merry stalked on back towards Thames Cottages. She had forgotten the poo. Megan hesitated, and then bent and grabbed it. There was a 'Missing' poster flapping on a tree trunk by the side of the path. She glanced up at it and then ran after Mrs Merry. What with the Poo and the Reconstruct-shon she didn't dare think of her as Daphne.

Wherever she went Helen Honeysett watched her. Crumpled on pavements, soaking in a puddle, on the lamp-post near her school, on *every* lamp-post around where she lived. The poster on the noticeboard in the park was upside down making Helen look scary so until she'd seen her jogging Megan hadn't been sure – a secret she'd saved for Mrs Merry – that she wanted

Helen Honeysett to come back. Although she knew a photograph wasn't real, Angie's comment about it being wrong for Helen Honeysett to smile considering she was missing still haunted Megan. In bed, unable to sleep, the little girl was positive that were she missing in the cold and dark she wouldn't smile at all.

'... we must clear up as we go along. Never let clutter collect,' Mrs Merry was saying.

'Then you wouldn't have anything to do,' Megan stated brightly, swinging the bag of poo as she trotted to keep up. 'My daddy says people who mend their own pipes put him out of a job.'

'It's not about me, it's about clutter. It's about *taking care*.'

Megan nodded fervently; then, thinking of her dad and keen to offer up a subject that set him firmly in Mrs Merry's camp, she announced, 'Daddy comes to the towpath all by himself. I bet he shouldn't do because it's dangerous, but he does brave things. He took care of Helen Honeysett the night before she was *Missing*.'

Mrs Merry stopped by the Kew river stairs. For a terrible moment, Megan feared she'd made her cross again. Then Mrs Merry asked kindly, 'What did you say, Megan?'

'Only that Daddy comes here on his own at night which is dangerous. Like you said. Except that time he wasn't really by himself because Mrs Honeysett was there. Garry and me saw her with our own eyes.' With Mrs Merry it was important to be accurate. 'He was after her.'

'Did you tell the police?' Mrs Merry was looking at her intently.

'No. Daddy was safe with Mrs Honeysett.' The notion that her father would be in danger was astonishing.

'That means your father was the last person to see Mrs Honeysett alive.' Daphne Merry regarded the bag of poo in Megan's hand. 'Here, give me that.'

'No. That was Mr Honeysett.' Megan and her friends were authorities on the facts of the Missing Neighbour. 'He's handsome, I think. Do you think so too?'

'Come with me.' Mrs Merry snatched the poo off Megan. She took her hand and frogmarched her past her house and up the path to her own cottage.

'We saw her on Wednesday night,' Megan declared.

'Are you sure?' Detective Inspector Harper was back at the kitchen table. Megan felt he wasn't as friendly as the last time.

'Yes, I *am* sure. I told Daphne. We had to go upstairs so that Mummy and Daddy could have one of their private chats. Me and Garry were watching out of the window. We saw Mrs Honeysett go racing past our house to the river. I was worried about her being on her own in the dark because Daphne says it's dangerous.' Megan paused because this wasn't strictly true, Mrs Merry had told her not to walk there alone *after* Helen Honeysett went missing. But she would have thought it at the time if Mrs Merry had said it, she decided. She resumed her account, speaking slowly and clearly to the policeman so he understood. 'Daddy banged the front door and went after her. That was good because he would have rescued her dog if he fell in the river.' Megan took in a gulp of air and added grandly. 'He's called Baxter.'

'So you both witnessed Helen going to the towpath from the window. What room would that be?'

'I think they were in our bedroom.' Bette Lawson's voice was barely audible. She sat squeezed between her children, hugging herself as if cold. She had told the police that Steven Lawson was still at work although she didn't know where he was.

'I see. Why did you go there as opposed to – instead of – your own bedrooms?'

'I like it there,' Megan said simply. She couldn't articulate that when her parents disagreed being in their bedroom made her feel better.

'How soon after Mrs Honeysett went to the towpath did you see your daddy follow her?' The officer smiled at Garry. The boy stared down at his hands, clamped between his thighs, his face chalk white.

'I didn't see anything,' he muttered.

'Yes you did, Gal, you were by the window too.' Megan leant across her mother, perplexed. 'You pointed out the Plough up in the sky.'

'I was looking at the sky, not at the ground.' Garry was firm.

'It's good if you can be accurate, Garry. It's best for everyone.' The officer was stern.

'I was looking at the sky,' Garry said again. 'I didn't see Dad. Or, or anyone.' His sister seemed about to speak but, wriggling on her seat, said nothing.

'Did your husband leave the house that evening?' DI Harper addressed Bette Lawson.

'He needed to clear his head. His business is having a few problems. Nothing he won't sort out.' She bit her lower lip.

'What time was this?'

'After we'd had tea.'

'At what time?'

'About eight.

'That's quite late for tea,' Harper commented. 'For the kiddies, I mean.'

'We wait for Steve, we like to eat as a family. I don't see what this is about? And it's upsetting my kids. Helen Honeysett was seen on the Thursday morning by her husband,' Bette protested. 'How can it matter what happened the previous evening?'

'We're looking at every angle, Mrs Lawson. Anything that will help to cast light on the disappearance of this young woman. Please try to think what you can tell us. Megan has been very obliging.' He raised his eyebrows at Megan and she patted at her hair with ill-disguised pleasure, picturing recounting the scene to Angie tomorrow at school. Then recalling her chat with Mrs Merry, she enunciated proudly, 'Dad is brave about the tow-path, he often goes by himself, usually with Smudge.'

The detective dashed something down on his pad, flipped it

shut and tucked it in his pocket. He got up and slid his chair under the table, leaning on it. 'I'll need to see Mr Lawson, to clear up a few loose ends. When is he back?'

Bette Lawson remained sitting. In a monotone she said, 'He goes to the towpath with the dog.'

'In the dark?'

'He has a torch.' Bette tried to pull herself together. 'He takes him out last thing.'

'Megan, you said "usually". Did your daddy not have Smudge that night?' DI Harper gathered aside the bead curtain; he eyed it as if he fancied one himself.

'No he didn't! That's what I must have meant,' Megan exclaimed. 'He *forgot* Smudge. That's funny, isn't it, Mum?' She was beside herself; it was always Garry who knew things.

'It does seem as if Mr Lawson might be able to answer a few queries.' The officer nodded at Bette. 'What time is your husband due to return, Mrs Lawson?'

'I don't know,' Bette mumbled.

'I'll call back. Please, don't come to the door, I'll see myself out.'

All three huddled in silence watching the bead curtain strings fall still. Suddenly Garry, eyes blazing, spat, 'Megan, see what you've done!'

Megan felt a wave of hot shame. *But what had she done?*

Chapter Seventeen

Tuesday, 5 January 2016

'Have you said yes?' In the evening gloom of the towpath, Jack couldn't make out Stella's expression.

'Not without talking to you.' A fractional pause. He guessed Stella had decided to investigate the Honeysett case, even if she hadn't told the client.

'You didn't call me.' He cursed himself. He was often out of touch and Stella never complained. All that mattered was that they had a new case.

'It was late, I thought you'd be with... busy.' Stella's voice in the darkness was disembodied.

They were on the Thames towpath. The river, hidden by dense scrub on the bank, was visible only where a light from the north side glimmered on the water. There was no wind; bare branches were black lines against the sky. The air was cold.

Jack drifted closer to Stella. He had been nerving himself up to telling her about Bella. He guessed that Jackie had told her. Being discretion itself, Stella wouldn't say Bella's name. He couldn't say that he hadn't been with Bella, but on the towpath. Or that the figures he'd seen through the lace curtains of number 4 must have been Stella with Adam Honeysett. Above all he couldn't tell her about Natasha Latimer's pet cemetery.

The appointment with Latimer was at eight. Stella had asked to see him at seven, 'to fill you in on developments'. Both punctual, they arrived at the Greyhound pub on Kew Green as St Anne's Church clock was chiming seven. Over ginger beers – neither drank alcohol before seeing a client – Stella told him about her encounter with the missing woman's husband. She had brought him a copy of Honeysett's file.

Watching Stella as she reeled off her list of facts, Jack had observed how having a case energized her. Always alert despite working longer hours than humanly possible, Stella was never languid, but tonight she was animated. Her energy was infectious. He felt excitement stir and when they left the pub, Stella in her smart waxed jacket, sharply cut hair mussed and tousled (Jackie said it was a modish 'wash-and-go' cut), had seen, with puff-pigeoned pride, that Stella attracted the attention of some men clustered around a table crowded with pints. Jack had drawn himself up to his full six feet – Stella's height – to indicate they were 'together', and then felt vaguely ashamed of the action.

Stella had brought them to the towpath ostensibly for Stanley to poo, but he soon realized the true reason.

'According to something I read, this was where Daphne Merry found Helen Honeysett's dog.' Stella was looking down at the river.

Jack had come with Bella to Kew Stairs on one of their nocturnal wanderings. He had first kissed her here. He'd thought the impulse a categorical mistake, that Bella would be furious. But she'd clasped him closer and relief had flooded through him. After that she often came with him on his night walks. Happiest drawing dead plants in intricate monochrome, she said she felt at home in the deserted dark of London. As did he. Not keen to tell Stella this, Jack blurted, 'Isn't this where you and whatsisname found Stanley?'

'Closer to Kew Bridge,' Stella faltered.

She must have forgotten that episode. Jack couldn't see her expression, but was cross with himself for his indirect reference to a relationship that had gone wrong. He'd made Stella feel awkward. Stanley had nothing to do with a woman missing, presumed murdered. 'It's strange how Adam Honeysett recognized your van. It doesn't say Clean Slate.' In the pub, he'd resisted saying this; he'd wanted to hear Stella's account of the case. He said it now to change the subject.

'I thought so.'

'I wonder if he was lying.'

'He could've recognized the number plate. You would have.'

'He'd have had to have seen you in the van,' Jack reminded her.

'He said he'd read about the Kew Gardens murder and other cases. He talked about wanting a fresh eye. He must have seen a picture of me.'

'He'd only have seen a head-shot,' Jack said. 'If he knew about Clean Slate, why didn't he ring the office like other clients, or come to the office, like I did?'

'Adam's not like other clients. He doesn't want us to clean or even to get rid of a ghost. We're not officially a detective agency; maybe he didn't know how to approach me.' Stella didn't sound convinced.

'Sounds like he had no trouble "approaching" you. The guy must have followed you.' Jack felt a coil of fury. He was inclined to say they shouldn't take the man's case. He barked, 'Do you check behind you when you're out and vary your routine?'

'No! Do you?'

'Yes.'

'Anyway, it's not the point.' Stella was watching Stanley pad about on the shingled path; she held an empty poo-bag at the ready.

'It *is* the point if Honeysett killed his wife. He could have followed her to the towpath. You didn't hear him until he was upon you.' Stella could spot a stain from twenty paces and identify the most obscure smell, but she tended to trust a person until they gave her a glaring reason not to. Jack felt a lurch of nausea that Stella might one day vanish without trace.

'Adam'd hardly ask us to investigate her disappearance if he killed her,' Stella said. Again she didn't sound certain.

'Not if he knows we won't find her, but wants to shore up his supposed innocence.' Already Jack disliked Honeysett, not least because Stella referred to him as 'Adam'. At best the man was insensitive – he should know better than to sneak up on a lone woman – anyone – in the dark. At worst he was a killer. 'Like you said in the pub, we should interview the plumber.' Once Jack was living in the street, he'd judge Honeysett for himself.

'Adam's file's not comprehensive,' Stella remarked. 'I think he cobbled it together for our meeting. That's what I really think is odd. Why didn't he keep track along the way?' Stanley stopped circling and, pulling on his lead, snouted along the towpath. 'Lucie May covered it – maybe we should contact her. There won't be gaps in her file.'

Stella only found out after Terry Darnell's death that Lucie May had had an affair with him. Lucie made no secret of resenting 'Darnell's daughter' for his putting her first. Stella never expressed a view on Lucie, but had been irritated when Jack had consulted her about one of their investigations without discussing it with her. Since then Stella had done the same. Not from revenge: she didn't work that way. However, proposing that they involve May so early in a case was new.

'Shall we hold off? Lucie has a habit of taking over,' Jack cautioned. 'Let's get familiar with the people involved first.' He went down the steps to the river, careful not to slip on mud. The tide was coming in; water slopped over the lowest step. He called back, 'Could Helen Honeysett have committed suicide?'

'Adam said she was happy.' Stella was lost in shadows on the bank.

'He would say that, wouldn't he?'

'Easy for the killer to push her into the river.' Ordinarily, Stella disliked discussing death, but she had been brought up on tales of cadaver dogs and the life stages of larvae in a decomposing body. She wasn't squeamish.

Jack came back up the steps and, Stanley having not pooed,

they continued along the towpath. Away from the lamplight, darkness thickened around them. 'It was a risk; her body could have resurfaced. Let's assume that the killer ensured that there was nothing to incriminate him. In which case, that makes it more likely the killer was strong enough to remove the corpse. It restricts suspects.'

'Unless she knew her killer and went with him or her to where she was murdered.' Stanley tugged on the lead and Stella stumbled forward.

They were by the dilapidated house that Jack had been about to investigate when he was accosted by Daphne Merry. Again there were no lights on in the windows. This time there was no sign of Daphne Merry to give him away, yet Jack felt an anxious twinge that Stella would know he'd been there.

'That's possible,' Jack agreed. 'If indeed she is dead. Maybe she left him.'

'She owned half the house. It's not likely she'd leave him all her stuff if she wanted to split up with him. Her account hasn't been touched or her Amex card used.' Stella flapped the unused poo-bag at Stanley. 'He ran here last night. Must be animal smells. Let's find out who lives there. Being out of the way, it's a good place to lure a victim. Talk about a haunted house.' She urged Stanley away and set off back along the towpath.

'I bet the police checked. Did your dad mention the Honeysett case?' Jack caught up with her.

'Not to me. Maybe Mum remembers. Except, thinking about it, they'd split up by then and were hardly talking.' Stella stopped. 'What was that?'

'What was what?' Jack held his breath.

'Nothing. Thought I heard something. Probably just the wind.' Stella looked behind her.

They walked on in a silence that from Jack's viewpoint wasn't companionable. He kept a lookout for Daphne Merry as he tried to concoct what to say if she mentioned meeting in the early hours of this morning. *Not if. When.* After what seemed an age, light from the lamp-post by Thames Cottages was visible on the path ahead.

Stella paused outside Latimer's house. 'This is a crazy job. Feel free to turn it down.'

'Best I accept since you've accepted the Honeysett case.' Jack regretted sounding resentful. He was intent on behaving as if the cottage was new to him. He hated lying to Stella – even by omission; too often he had a secret he had to keep from her. Stella would be alarmed that he had broken into a client's property, even if he was going to be staying there soon. He looked at the cottage. Two panels in the front door were glazed with a pattern of fleur-de-lis. Tonight the garden – if that described an area in which nothing grew – was bathed in lurid green light from lamps that rendered the stone shapes sinister. The green morphed to lurid blue and back again.

'They weren't on last night,' Stella remarked and Jack nearly agreed.

Next door's garden had organic matter. Weeds sprouted from plastic plant pots on a scrap of unkempt grass and had lifted tiles on the path. Given its state of neglect, he'd expect a ghost to be haunting no 2. The neglect suggested care that had long lapsed, perhaps due to illness or tragedy. Helen Honeysett had lived at no 4. Jack doubted ghosts got addresses wrong: why haunt number 1? He would speculate with Claudia.

As they reached Latimer's door light flooded the porch and a voice, tinny and monotone, demanded, 'State your name and reason for visiting.'

Jack and Stella remained stock still.

'State your name and reason for visiting.' The voice came from a silver panel in the wall. Jack's instinct was to run, but Stella stepped forward and in a matching monotone said, 'Names: Stella Darnell and Jack Harmon from Clean Slate. Reason for visiting: to discuss getting rid… cleaning.'

The front door swung open into an empty hallway.

★

'I fly all over the world, haggling with charlatans trying to fleece me. This was meant to be my haven; the estate agents described it as an area of peace and tranquillity. Instead, what do I find?' Natasha Latimer glowered at Stella and Jack as if they were to blame for her disappointment.

'A ghost?' Beside him on a plush silk-covered sofa, Jack felt Stella stiffen.

'No! It's malicious *shit*!' They were in Natasha Latimer's sitting room on the ground floor. She stood over them, a glass of wine in one hand, a remote control in the other. There was no television so Jack supposed it had operated the door. She hadn't offered them a drink. Chilled from the towpath, Jack contemplated requesting hot milk with honey, but Stella would do more than stiffen if he did. There was no sign of Claudia.

Latimer was familiar. Not because he had met her before – he was good with faces and knew he had not – but because she was a type. She was like the sisters of boys at his boarding school: confident, her hair snatched back in a velvet scrunchy, dressed conservatively in Russell and Bromley loafers, tapered slacks, pale blue cotton shirt, cardigan sleeves pushed above her wrists revealing a huge silver bangle like handcuffs. Not remotely like Stella, yet Latimer too was a woman of action. Like Stella she wouldn't ponder on a decision, but get on with it. There the similarity ended. They were divided by class. Latimer had a demeanour of entitlement and certainty that things would go the way she wanted. Rather like he'd thought Bella until he'd got to know her better, Latimer was obdurate and undoubting. Stella had no sense of privilege, she deferred and offered respect where it was due – and where it wasn't – to avoid conflict. Only a fool would mistake this as weakness. She was a match for Latimer who, as the Pow3r 1 number-plated Evoque on Kew Green signified, possessed merciless ambition. Latimer's voice penetrated Jack's thoughts.

'... you'd expect they'd be grateful. I've increased property values – I put it on the bloody map! There was a piece about my basement in the *Observer Mag* and *Tatler*. Last week Radio London interviewed me.' She contemplated her wine glass. 'But no! Mrs Prim-as-you-like-Merry at number three complained about noise and dust. Adam fucking Honeysett at number four started out charming, but he's a *snake*!' Eyes blazing, nostrils flaring. 'He took me to dinner. It was going nicely until he said that the vibrations from my digger could have damaged the street. He's a tin-pot artist not a fucking engineer!' She banged down her glass on a coffee table, spilling wine. Jack saw Stella twitch; wine was acid and could damage the wood.

'What about Neville Rowlands?' Stella asked.

'What about him?' Latimer whipped off her scrunchy and grabbed her hank of hair, rolling the scrunchy back over it, tugging it so tight Jack felt the sting on his own scalp.

'He could be harbouring resentment.'

'He's dead. Hey, maybe it's him haunting.' Latimer gave a ghastly smile.

'Where's Claudia?' Jack asked suddenly. Stella was staring at him.

'Who?'

'Your sister,' Jack told her.

'Oh, Claudia! She's at her drumming group.' Latimer appeared to bat a fly off her hair. 'I expected trouble from that nurse next door or the son with a hundred budgies. My surveyor had to have a word about damp on their party wall. And if this place wasn't soundproofed, those birds would drive me nuts!' She tossed the remote control on to a chair and leant on the mantelpiece.

'What is the son's name?' Stella enquired irrelevantly. Jack guessed it was a detective gambit.

'No idea!' Latimer was disdainful. 'Geoff, Gordon? He's at least forty. One of these weirdos married to his mama. Claudia is nice to him.'

'Garry?' Stella suggested innocently.

Go, Wonderhorse. Jack settled happily in his chair.

'No idea. Yes.' Natasha Latimer pushed off the mantelpiece

and retrieved her wine. 'The only one with her head screwed on is old Sybil Lofthouse at the other end of terrace.'

'Number five,' Stella murmured.

'... she was at the Stock Exchange, not married, could be gay, who cares? Has an ancient mutt. Says she's learnt to keep herself to herself. Sybil has been nothing but civil, she wouldn't blab about ghosts.'

Jack imagined that Latimer approved of anyone who worked with money. While she was talking, Stella had been writing. Glancing across at her Filofax, Jack read 'Budgerigars'. Stella wasn't listing cleaning requirements, she was capturing details of the neighbours. She was being a detective. Stella's moral code prevented her going undercover as a cleaner. Latimer had unwittingly handed them perfect cover. While being a detective for Adam Honeysett, Jack would be a cleaner in the same street. His heart soared.

'... it would be funny were it not tragic. The old chap Judd ambushed me on the towpath and ranted on like a madman. Said I'd ripped out its soul. None of his business, I said. "Go and tell the cops I said that!"' She guffawed a laugh and, grabbing a wine bottle from the coffee table, topped up her glass.

'Who is Judd?' Stella asked. Jack knew she would have taken notice of anyone described as a 'madman'.

'No one!' Latimer flapped an impatient hand. Her inference being that he really was 'no one'.

'Your sister told Stella you have a close community here.' Jack wasn't over his disappointment that Claudia was out drumming. 'Is Judd a friend?'

'This lot have mouldered here for centuries. They *need* me!' It came out as a strangled wail. 'No, he's not a friend.' Latimer might be strident and imperious, but she was also scared. Why was she scared?

'Who do you think is responsible for this rumour?' The likely suspect was Neville Rowlands, a candidate for the murder of Helen Honeysett, but he was dead. If they did find her killer then he'd wanted him or her to be alive. He wouldn't give up. 'Who is Judd?'

'Brian Judd is a slimy toad. I wouldn't put the ghost rumours past him. Shit-bag!' Hugging the wine bottle, Latimer was spiteful. 'I've got the place alarmed to the police. I caught Barry the Birdman skulking in the back garden; he pretended he was looking for one of his budgies. No manners. It could be him.'

Jack regarded his fingers assiduously. That he might have set off an alarm made him go cold. Absently, he corrected Latimer, 'Garry'.

'Only a ghost *could* get in.' Latimer quaffed her wine in one go.

'Please could we see the rest of the house?' Stella retracted her pen with a click and stood up.

Although Jack knew that Latimer had converted her basement, he wasn't prepared for the contrast between the traditionally furnished sitting room, complete with beams and polished oak floorboards, and what he saw at the turn of the passage. He teetered at the top of a glass staircase. As they descended, each tread was outlined with minute blue lights. Jack had the sensation of floating. He gripped a steel rail for balance. Stanley flattened on the first tread, ears back and claws skittering. Stella picked him up and carried him down.

When they reached the bottom row upon row of ceiling lights lit up, reflecting a floor sheened bluey silver like a sheet of ice. Latimer went ahead, drifting like a ghost. A glass panel slid aside, then another. The basement was cavernous. Jack knew that it went a long way under the garden.

'The playroom.' She paused by a large stainless-steel-lined area filled with sand. Against the wall was a tall steel rack on which sat a pristine teddy bear.

Stella was expressionless. She never asked clients personal questions or commented on what they told her about themselves beyond what was polite. Clients could round on her for giving them bad advice or for knowing something they regretted telling her.

Jack sighed. 'Fancy having your own sandpit.'

'It's not mine! It's to show how to use the space. Claudia wanted a meditation space.' Latimer flapped her hand at a glass wall and it swished aside. 'One has to lead buyers by the hand, give them ideas.' In the second 'room' was a bright red sofa – a Salvador Dalí copy, it resembled a lipsticked mouth. To the left of this stood a large galvanized steel box the size of a small car.

'Ta-dah!' Showing them her 'project' was cheering Latimer up. She pulled a handle and one side of the box swung away. Inside was a home office with a laptop computer, printer, drawers and one of those chairs without a back that forced you to sit upright. She shut the box again.

Black water, thick and sluggish as oil, flowed towards them. Flickers of light caught the surface. Jack stepped back and there was a shriek. He'd trodden on Stanley. The poodle held up a paw and fixed him with a baleful stare.

Stella picked Stanley up again. 'Did you film this?'

Jack saw that the water was a projected image on the wall.

'It's not a film.' Latimer went to the wall. She merged with the image as if she might float away. 'It's real time. There's a camera on the roof.'

'Wonderful.' Jack touched the wall, half expecting it to be cold and wet, to feel the current pulling him under. In the sparse subterranean space, it was like a window.

'I think so.' Latimer looked pleased and beneath the profit-margin mentality Jack glimpsed pride in her project. She added grudgingly, 'It was Claudia's idea.'

'Does it show the garden?' Jack was nervous.

'No, there's nothing to see.' She led them into the last room. This was bare with a white-painted brick wall at the end.

'Is this the meditation space?'

'No,' Latimer responded bluntly.

Jack looked up. Where were the rectangles of green glass that he'd mistaken for a pond? 'What's behind this wall?'

'Nothing.' Latimer was getting irritable.

'I wonder, could we see the garden?' Jack asked.

Latimer glared at Jack. 'It's dark. Besides, the squeaking comes from inside.'

'You didn't mention squeaking.' Stella kept her voice level.

'It's nothing. Just when I'm in bed. Claudia has heard it, but she imagines things.'

'The supernatural knows no boundaries.' Jack saw Stella quail.

'If you've got intruders, it's a matter for the police,' Stella said.

'They did one of their security checks. Gave me advice about window locks and setting my alarm. Patronizing plods!' She addressed Jack. 'No visitors. If you're tied up with a girl and think you can party-party, think again.' She stalked through the basement, heels clicking on the faux ice, the hiss of sliding panels insidious in the sealed silence. 'Stay close at all times.'

'I understand.' Jack resisted saying that he was always pining for someone and it didn't interfere with his cleaning. And he hated parties.

When they were on the doorstep Jack remembered Bella. *No visitors.* He had to keep close to the house. No night journeys either.

'When can you start?' Natasha Latimer demanded.

'We will draw up a contra—'

Jack interrupted Stella: 'Tomorrow.'

Jack and Stella walked up the path to the pavement.

'That one with the plastic flower pots is the Lawson house,' Stella whispered. She indicated the neglected garden next door to Latimer's. 'Natasha Latimer didn't mention Steven Lawson.'

'If he's in prison that would explain why the son feels protective towards his mother.' Jack had never had the chance to protect his mother. Or rather, given the chance, he had failed to protect her.

'If Steven Lawson is in prison for murder wouldn't Adam

have said?' Stella said. 'You'll be well placed for door-to-door interviews. I'll introduce you to Adam: we need your take on him. There's something he hasn't said.'

Jack had the conviction they were being overheard. To their right a tall hedge ran beside the park. He stood on tiptoe and looked over. Across the grass stood some swings and a slide. One swing seemed to be moving but, looking again, he decided it was the shadow of branches. Before Stella asked what he was doing, he said, 'It could have been a random attack on Honeysett by a stranger.' In case she was watching, he shielded his face with his collar as they passed Daphne Merry's house.

'It's likely the kind of person who did that would have killed again in the last twenty-nine years. The police would've checked for matches.' Stella stopped outside number 4. The curtains were drawn, the lights out. 'Looks like Adam's not in.'

'Perhaps the killer doesn't have an MO. Or they're dead.' Jack wasn't in a hurry to meet 'Adam'. 'Or the killer's in prison for another crime.'

'We have to assume the police considered that. Let's limit the scope or this will be too big to handle. Honeysett had a predictable routine so let's start with those who knew it.' Stella paused outside the last cottage. 'Sybil Lofthouse will be hard to crack if she keeps herself to herself.'

'I'll find a way,' Jack said.

'Two of them had dogs. Steven Lawson and Daphne Merry. It gave them a reason to go to the towpath.' Stella was already well versed with the facts.

'Natasha Latimer said Sybil Lofthouse had an "ancient mutt",' Jack reminded her.

'That's now. In 1987 she did early shifts at the Stock Exchange. She may not have had a dog.' Stella had missed nothing.

'We only have Adam Honeysett's word for it that his wife took their dog. He might have killed her and abandoned the dog on the towpath.'

'True. And there's Bette Lawson. If her husband was having

an affair with – or even fancied – Helen Honeysett, that's a motive for murder.'

'With those graves in the garden, Neville Rowlands must have had a dog.'

'He did. Adam told me he took a dog to the towpath for five minutes and went in the opposite direction to Helen Honeysett.' Stella stopped. 'What graves?'

'Latimer said there were pet graves in her back garden.' *Natasha Latimer hadn't mentioned the graves.*

'Did you see that?' Stella was looking back at Daphne Merry's cottage.

'What?' Dizzied by his mistake, Jack was barely capable of seeing anything. In case Daphne Merry saw him, he shrugged into his coat.

'Something moved by that water butt.'

Jack tried to sound dismissive and made the same suggestion as he had on the towpath: 'Probably a fox or a cat.'

'That was probably the sound Natasha Latimer heard.' Stella continued to the alley. 'Given Latimer intends to sell I've asked Jackie to price up the job based on our "Prepare for Sale" package. Are you sure about starting tomorrow? What about Bel—'

'Perfectly sure.' Jack felt weighed down with his secret. If Latimer had showed them the graves, he could talk about them as if that was when he'd first seen them.

'It seems Latimer's the only newcomer since 1987. The neighbours might have resented her regardless of her basement. People can be funny about change,' Stella said as if she herself was relaxed about change.

While they waited for Stanley to lift his leg against a tree on Kew Green Jack remarked, 'Going by Natasha Latimer's description of the residents of Thames Cottages, I'd say any of one of them could have murdered Helen Honeysett.'

Chapter Eighteen

Friday, 27 February 1987

Megan got the swing going, kicking at the tarmac when she swooped down to make it go higher. If her dad was here, he'd push her, but by herself it wasn't as good. He hadn't come back with Mum after work. She'd said he was on a job. When Garry asked, 'What job? I thought Dad wasn't getting—' her mum had shouted at him to go and feed his birds. Even though he was in his school uniform. She didn't see Megan sneak out to the playground. She would wait for her dad. The park was closed so she'd climbed over the gate. All the top windows in the houses were dark; from the swings, no one could see her.

Megan was also hoping to see Daphne Merry. She mustn't speak to her, but it couldn't be against the rules to *see* her. Since the police, her mum wouldn't let Megan be a De-Cluttering Assistant. She needed to tell Mrs Merry this (Megan didn't dare say Daphne, didn't dare say her name at all), but since she wasn't allowed to speak to her, she didn't how to let her know. She didn't want to stop assisting.

Megan had overheard her mum saying to her dad '... that Merry woman wants to make us feel as shit as her! I won't put up with...' She'd stopped when she saw Megan by the bead curtain. Megan had been as shocked by her mum swearing as she was puzzled by what she'd said because Mrs Merry only wanted people to have light and air.

Garry wasn't speaking to Megan. Nor was her dad, but he wasn't speaking at all. Before he went to work with her mum, he'd kissed her goodbye. She wasn't supposed to speak to Mrs Merry or Aunty El as they called her mum's older sister. Megan scuffed at the ground and walking the swing, she hurled herself towards the sky, straight legs thrusting her upwards. The hedge reeled away beneath her; to her right she glimpsed the river. She wanted to keep going up and never come down.

Mrs Merry was on the towpath. Megan blinked and looked properly. It really was her. Fleetingly it passed through her mind that her dad wasn't safely in the bright kitchen where her mum could see him.

Do as you would be done by.

Megan must warn Mrs Merry about being out by herself. She leapt off the swing and fell forwards. Palms stinging, she tore past the slide and the gate by the towpath. Behind her the swing oscillated wildly as if she was urging it on, the squeaking chains an echo of the long-lost soundscape of Thames barges creaking on their moorings.

She clambered over the gate. 'Mrs Merry—' Cold fingers clamped her mouth. She was dragged backwards. The park railings pressed into her like a rack.

'Megan. Come back indoors!' She smelled the aftershave Garry had started spilling on to himself. It was called Polo like the sweets she didn't like. She liked the smell, but her arm was really hurting.

'Actually you should both be indoors.' Mrs Merry was in front of them.

'So should you.' Megan hadn't meant it to come out cross.

'It's far too late to be out and where's Smudge?' She stepped closer. Garry jerked Megan away.

'At home. My daddy – ouch!' Megan squealed as her brother jerked her again.

'Megan, I was hoping to see you. We've got a decluttering job in Chiswick. An elderly couple are moving into a home. It's an important job. You'll be a tremendous help. I wonder if you'd be free to come with me. You can have tea with me as usual.' Mrs Merry added, 'We must of course ask your parents.'

'You do your own work. If you come near her, I'll, I'll *show* you!' Garry's speech was blurred. He circled his arm around Megan and, stumbling, steered her on along the path towards the lamp-post light.

At the steps, Megan twisted back. Mrs Merry was where they'd left her. She was standing still as if she had forgotten where she was meant to be going. Woof sat in front of her. For a tiny moment Megan felt a sadness so intense it might be for all the things that had ever made her sad.

Then she was on the pavement outside Thames Cottages. Then she saw the police.

'*Daddy!*'

Except he wasn't there.

Chapter Nineteen

Wednesday, 6 January 2016

Jack climbed over the park gate from the towpath. Keen to move into his new, if temporary, home, he had come at eight in the morning, twelve hours before Latimer had said he could go into the cottage.

He skirted a climbing frame shaped like a boat, a set of two swings, and a seesaw. One of the swings was moving as if a child had just got down from it. But the playground was empty.

He made for a high hedge that separated the park from Thames Cottages where there were two benches. He wiped droplets of dew from the nearer one and sat down. He remembered his impression the night before that someone had been listening to his conversation with Stella. From the bench, it would be easy to hear anything on the pavement half a metre away.

He hadn't told Bella about his new job. He was putting it off. She wouldn't see why, if she couldn't visit, he couldn't come to her. The prospect of holing up in this backwater for two weeks, away from his own ghosts and associations and, he had to be honest, avoiding any emotional complications, was attractive. Latimer thought that Helen Honeysett was haunting her basement. Jack, however, wasn't so sure. Despite saying to Stella that the killer could be a random stranger, he suspected that the answer to the young woman's disappearance was to be found close to where he now sat. Someone in one of the five cottages

– with the exception of Latimer, obviously – was keeping a secret about the vanished woman. Jack didn't like secrets. Unless they were his own.

There was an inscription carved into the bench. He cupped his hand over his Maglite and switched it on.

'Mabel Darby, who loved to sit here.'

The wood had bleached. It would be a long time since Mabel Darby had loved sitting here. Inquisitive, Jack made his way to the other bench to see if it commemorated someone. His light caught something in the hedge. He shone it on the leaves. The branches were snapped. It wasn't 'something' but nothing. A hole had been cut in the foliage. He leant over the bench and peered through. He could see the sitting room of one of the cottages. He jumped nimbly on to the bench and popped his head over the hedge. He was directly in front of number 3. Someone had sat on the bench – they'd have had to twist round – and watched Daphne Merry's house through a peephole. The hole was freshly cut. That someone would be back.

A brass plaque was affixed to the bench. Jack read it twice before he grasped the significance. With clumsy fingers, he took a photograph of the words with his phone and sent it to Stella. It was self-explanatory, no text required.

The message failed. When he'd met Daphne Merry on the towpath the night before last, Jack had unknowingly told the truth. There was no signal. He was in a dead zone.

Chapter Twenty

Wednesday, 6 January 2016

By ten to eight on the morning after meeting Latimer with Jack, Stella had been at her desk at Clean Slate for an hour and a half. She had assembled a spreadsheet from the notes she'd taken at Natasha Latimer's. Aside from cleaning, Stella relished spreadsheets. She was adept at constructing formulas that manipulated totals, attributed discounts and turned cells and fonts specific colours.

For the Honeysett case, Stella had taken Excel to new heights and created a map of the area around Thames Cottages. She divided the rectangles representing the five cottages into two levels. The top was crimson for 1987, the year of Honeysett's disappearance. She coloured the lower strip – 2016 – sickly peach. The colours clashed but Stella, whose appreciation of art was limited to a couple of Marianne North prints inherited from a friend, was concerned with layout and content. Other colours were broadly faithful: the pavement outside the cottages and the children's playground was grey. The front gardens were green, as was the grass behind the hedge in the park. Running vertically on the left-hand side of the frame, at right angles to the row of cottages, she made the Thames a turquoise column – in reality at best gunmetal grey – and inserted a grey strip for the towpath alongside.

She typed in the names of the neighbours and, where she knew them, their occupations. What people did might have a bearing on the case. Whatever Sybil Lofthouse had done at the Stock Exchange – perhaps a broker – would involve confidentiality. Adam had said Lofthouse kept herself to herself. As Stella had said to Jack, Lofthouse might be a challenge because she wouldn't be a gossip. Nor was Stella, but she heard Terry's advice, *'Gossip is the detective's friend.'*

Latimer had said Garry Lawson was married to his mother. That suggested that Steven Lawson wasn't around. For all her vague sense that he was holding something back, surely Adam Honeysett would have said that Lawson had been jailed for his wife's murder. She put a question mark next to Steven's name in the 2016 cell and considered again that contacting him was a priority. She added in Megan Lawson. What had happened to her? She was a child at the time, but in Stella's experience, even if they didn't understand what they had seen, children made good witnesses. She typed 'Budgerigars' in the peach cell for number 2 Thames Cottages. Terry said even a trivial detail could be a clue.

She flicked back to her list made after reading Adam Honeysett's file and confirmed her prediction about Lofthouse. 'Sybil Lofthouse refused to comment' was next to a reference for one of Lucie May's articles. Stella felt sympathy: she avoided being grilled by Lucie May herself.

A dog was a reason for being on the towpath at odd times. Stella wrote 'Smudge' in the 1987 section of the Lawsons' house and 'Baxter' at number 4. She didn't know the name of Daphne Merry's dog then or if Sybil Lofthouse had had a dog. Apart from living with a mother who'd alibied him and owning a dog, she had scant information on Neville Rowlands. She'd reminded Jack that they must keep an open mind about the suspects, but – disregarding the alibi – Rowlands was high on her own list. If, as Natasha Latimer had said, the old man was dead, it was possible that the truth of what happened to Helen Honeysett had died with him.

Stella sipped her already cold tea and reviewed the spreadsheet so far.

River	Towpath	1	2	3	4	5
		1987 Neville Rowlands (?)	1987 Steven (Plumber) & Bette (Nurse) Garry (12) & Megan (7) Lawson Budgerigars	1987 Daphne Merry (Declutterer)	1987 Helen Honeysett (Estate Agent) & Adam Honeysett (Graphic Designer)	1987 Sybil Lofthouse (Stock Exchange – doing what?)
		Dog (Name?)	Dog (Smudge)	Dog (Name?)	Dog (Baxter)	Dog?
		2016 Natasha Latimer (Property Developer) Is Neville Rowlands dead?	2016 Bette (Nurse) & Steven Lawson (?) Budgerigars (Garry & Megan?)	2016 Daphne Merry (Declutterer still?)	2016 Adam Honeysett (Graphic Designer)	2016 Sybil Lofthouse (Retired?)
		No dog	Dog?	Dog?	Dog (Name?)	Dog?
		Front Garden/ Basement	Front Garden	Front Garden	Front Garden	Front Garden
		Pavement				
		Park				

Latimer had been unpleasant about Daphne Merry. Stella didn't need to consult her notes to recall that in 1987 Merry was a professional declutterer. Stella seldom pre-judged; she classified customers according to their cleaning needs. Battling with her open mind, she was conscious of bias in favour of Daphne Merry. Clutter hampered cleaning. Stella would welcome a declutterer working in advance of her arrival.

The door to the outer office opened. Stella tensed. Someone from the insurance office could have left the downstairs door on the latch. It could be a stranger who had wandered in off the street.

Mewing piteously, Stanley tore out to the main office. Stella relaxed; Stanley knew the 'stranger'.

'You there, Stell?' Jackie called. Stella saved her spreadsheet and went out to greet her.

Jackie laid a bundle of post in Beverly's in-tray and unwound a blue woolly scarf from around her neck. She wore a dark green wool coat and her cheeks were pink from the cold. A handsome woman in her late fifties, shortish hair tucked behind her ears, she carried a capacious leather bag that Beverly called her 'Mary Poppins' bag because it held anything from painkillers and plasters to biscuits, tea bags and cleaning materials. Jackie Makepeace took crisis in her stride. She was happily married to Graham, a surveyor with Hammersmith and Fulham Council, and they had two grown-up sons, Nick and Mark. Jack and Stella each gravitated to their Chiswick home for warm, domestic stability. Jack did so consciously, Stella, unaware of such needs, was lured by Jackie under pretexts that typically involved cleaning and fresh vegetables.

Lauded in the local and specialist cleaning-sector media for single-handedly building a cleaning empire, Stella was under no illusion that this was true. Suzie Darnell had pitched in when Stella's office was her bedroom in her mother's Barons Court flat. It was Jackie who'd persuaded Stella to lease the two rooms in Shepherd's Bush and as office manager she had steered the company's growth with quiet efficiency.

'Suzie needs a new cleaner.' Jackie hung her coat on a set of hooks by the 'tea station' and flicked on the kettle. She took a litre of milk from her handbag and slotted it into a mini-fridge on top of which, besides the kettle, were tea and coffee things. She emptied the rest of a milk carton into two mugs. Stella's mug displayed a map of Kew Gardens, a key client. Jackie's, a gift from her son Nick who was a dancer in a West End musical, was decorated with 'Perfect Mum' within a red heart.

'Why? Has Mum complained about Jack?' Stella wandered to the pile of post and picked up the topmost envelope. Catching

Jackie's eye, she put it back. Opening post was Beverly's job; it upset the process when Stella interfered. Jack loved her mum; it would be Suzie who had found fault.

'Would Suzie complain about Jack?' Jackie rolled her eyes. 'No, but if he's going to be staying at the haunted house he can't do her cleaning.' She poured boiling water into a pristine white teapot and, giving the tea bags a swish with a spoon, replaced the lid.

'True.' Planning the cleaning schedule was one of Stella's favoured tasks and she was looking forward to doing it that afternoon. No amount of rejigging cleaning operatives would provide a solution to this problem. Her mum was hyper-fussy and at first had insisted on having only Stella 'ferreting in my home'. But with Stella's brother Dale living in Sydney, Suzie had determined that Jack fill the 'son' vacancy. She cooked for him and, according to Suzie, solved his problems. Stella didn't know Jack had problems although Jackie said losing your mother when you were four was problem enough. Stella remained dubious that anything her mum said to Jack could help. Suzie went on about her 'wrong turning' often enough. 'I'll have to allocate another operative to the Latimer job.' Stella rubbed at her temples; with little sleep over the last two nights, a headache was brewing.

'Jack's the only one who can confront a ghost.' Straight-faced, Jackie handed Stella her tea. 'We need someone else for Suzie and no, not you!' She wagged a finger. Given the chance, Stella would clean full-time; for the good of the business, Jackie prevented her.

'It'll have to be me. Since Mum sprained her ankle, I have to go after work to sort out her meals anyway.' For once Stella wasn't keen to take on a cleaning job. She relished challenging clients, but her mum considered her a poor second to Jack; she would be a challenge too far.

Jackie sat at her desk and switched on her computer. 'Jack said you have a new case. That missing estate agent. I can't think of her name – not Suzy Lamplugh.'

'Helen Honeysett went missing in 1987, the year after

Lamplugh. I haven't told Mum.' Stella always put off telling
Suzie about a case because her response could be anything from
proud that Stella was being a detective to complaining that Terry
Darnell's cases had taken him away from his family and that
Stella would be the same.

'All in good time,' Jackie replied evenly. 'Mind you, Suzie
might know your dad's take on the case.'

Stella sighed. 'She wasn't married to him in 1987.'

'She kept tabs on his work though.'

Stella had to agree that this was true. Regardless of Suzie's
negative opinion of her ex-husband, she seemed to store the
details of his major investigations in what amounted to a mental
database.

'I remember her disappearing.' Jackie sat back and Stanley
leapt on to her lap. He settled with his chin on her desk. 'I'd just
met Graham; we went for a meal in Kew. There were coppers
swarming about at the station, everywhere. It was like up north
before they caught Peter Sutcliffe, the Yorkshire Ripper. Women
didn't go out at night on their own. Graham didn't let me out
of his sight. Not that I'd have gone to that towpath in the dark.
It can feel creepy in the day.'

'She lived in the same street as the haunted house. Latimer
said there's a rumour she's the ghost.'

'For goodness' sake!' Jackie tucked a wrist-rest under Stanley's
chin for comfort. 'I'd guess from seeing her that Natasha Latimer
is used to getting what she wants. She'll have been enraged that
someone's saying her house is haunted – there's not much that's
more nebulous than a phantom!' She tapped on her keyboard
and set about her emails. 'How are you going to approach it?
It's like weapons of mass destruction: hard to get rid of a ghost
that's not there.'

'Jack will keep the house clean and keep a lookout for
intruders and talk to the neighbours. She mentioned hearing a
noise. I suggested the police, but she said they'd been. She didn't
have much time for them.'

'It's lose-lose, Stell. The best thing is that Jack's on the spot for the Honeysett case.' Jackie hit print and, tucking Stanley on her shoulder, got up and snatched a document as it spewed from a workhorse Hewlett-Packard printer on one of the filing cabinets by the door. She returned to her chair.

'I reckon Adam Honeysett wants to clear his name, although he didn't say that.' Stella rarely talked to Jackie about detective cases. In the early days this was because she had been an unwilling detective encumbered with an unsolved case of her dad's. Later she had worried that since Jackie discouraged her from cleaning in favour of pitching for business she'd draw the line at investigating a murder. When Jackie brought her a murder case, Stella had seen that, as ever, Jackie was right with her.

Stella's phone buzzed with a text. Jack Mob. An image filled the screen. Black writing on a blotchy background.

STEVEN LAWSON, A SPECIAL HUSBAND AND DAD
1952–1987

'... it's left a cloud over a few people. It was dreadful about that bloke,' Jackie was saying. 'At least the husband had an alibi so he was in the clear. What was that other bloke's name? I want to say Paul Young because he was a spit image. I'll look him up.'

'Steven Lawson.' It was too late to interview the plumber, nearly thirty years too late. Stella stared at the words on the phone screen.

Jackie leant into her monitor. 'Here we go: *Bankrupt Beast Murders Beauty.*' She snorted. 'What if Helen Honeysett hadn't been attractive?'

'What was the evidence against Steven Lawson?' Stella thought of the son still living with Bette Lawson. Was it because her husband had died or because Bette and Garry Lawson knew he was a killer and were harbouring the secret?

'Says here, Lawson was seen following Helen Honeysett to the towpath at night. The police arrested him, but quote "after extensive questioning, had to let him go" unquote. Makes it sound as if they thought he was guilty, but had no choice. The tabloids found him guilty anyway. They hounded him. The poor guy was already in financial straits; after that his business collapsed. I remember marvelling at how easy it is to be in the wrong place at the wrong time and for your life to fall apart. He went from "decent family man" to Evil Plumber.'

'He died the same year as Honeysett.' Stella continued looking at her phone. Had Jack found Lawson's grave? The lettering looked too small for a gravestone.

'He committed suicide. He drowned in the Thames. I can't remember the details. Sounds awful, but I was so mad about Graham at the time, nothing else mattered. Those were the days.' Jackie fiddled with Stanley's ears ruminatively. 'What with the Paul Young thing, Steven Lawson didn't look like a murderer!'

'That's how they get away with it.' None of those who had committed the crimes Stella had solved looked like killers. Not until she knew that they were.

'He had kiddies. A boy and a girl. Dreadful to lose your dad like that.' Jackie sat up; the sudden movement made Stanley sit up too, ears pricked, angled out from his head like wings. 'Changing the subject. As we know, Jack doesn't believe in coincidences.' Lowering her voice, Jackie did an imitation of Jack: 'Every confluence is a sign.'

Stella gripped her mug. One person being Jack was enough; she relied on Jackie for hard-and-fast reality.

'I allocated one of the recent newbies to those flats being prepared for sale on the North End Road. The young woman did a brilliant job, over and above the brief, and on time. What is it with me? I can't think of her name either. Beverly will know.'

'How is that a coincidence?'

'She's just joined us and she'd be perfect for Suzie.'

'No one will be perfect.' Her mum thought Jack was perfect and Stella tended to agree.

'We can at least aim for the stars.' Jackie grabbed an A4 diary. 'While I've got you, Stell, can we book a time to discuss the office move? What with your fledgling detective agency and these recent larger contracts, we're already bursting at the seams in here. Also, I had this idea. Why not try out Beverly on this case? Get her doing legwork?' Jackie, and Stanley, looked beadily at Stella.

Apparently not having heard, Stella muttered, 'I must speak to Jack,' and went into her room. Back at her desk, she pressed quick dial.

'This is Jack, who are *you*? Tell me after the beep.'

Chapter Twenty-One

Wednesday, 1 April 1987

'Whose dad's a murderer? Whose dad's a murderer?'

'Watch out, she'll kill you, like her dad did! April Foo-ool. April Foo-ool.'

'Kill. Kill. Kill!'

Megan ducked and twisted between trees on Kew Green and veered towards the main road. She didn't go down the alley to her street because she didn't want the children to follow her to her door. As she ran, Megan dimly knew this ploy was pointless because they already knew where she lived. Everyone knew where she lived.

She swerved down a lane beside the arches under Kew Bridge and arrived at the towpath. Vaguely, she was aware of railings... bushes... the park. She belted through the gate and dodged across the playground, past the rocking boat and the swings to the grass. A sign said 'No dogs allowed'. After her dad went, her mum gave Smudge away because there wasn't anyone to walk him.

Megan collapsed on to the new bench and leant on the arm getting her breath.

'Your dad's a murderer!'

'Kill. Kill. *Kill!*'

She could hear the chants, but couldn't see Angela or the other girls. She heard them all the time, shouted in the playground, whispered in the dinner queue and behind the coats in the cloak-room. Wherever it came from it was true.

The light was failing. The man from the council would come to lock the gates. Megan clutched the bench and rocked to stop herself crying. She turned around and buffed at the brass plate with the sleeve of her coat

STEVEN LAWSON, A SPECIAL HUSBAND AND DAD
1952–1987

Someone had gouged 'Killer' into the wood underneath. Megan's mum had come out with sandpaper and rubbed at it. But Megan could see it. Her mum said people were cruel and told lies. Megan knew, though her mum hadn't said it, that she meant her. One night Garry had screamed, 'It's your fault Dad's gone!' Her mum sent him to the garden, but never made him say sorry. He wouldn't let her care for the baby budgie any more and threatened to kill her if she went into his aviary. Otherwise he acted as though she wasn't there.

It was her fault. Mrs Merry had called the police and Megan had told the officer she'd seen her daddy and Helen Honeysett going to the towpath. Megan wasn't sorry he was arrested because she *had* seen him. She was sorry that her mum was upset. She was sorry about the budgie. The police had let her dad go. But one day when no one was looking, he'd gone into the river. She mouthed the shiny new word. *Suicide.*

Although Megan had seen her father's coffin, she couldn't grasp the full meaning of his absence. If she went to the towpath she might find him. He must be somewhere. She had come to his bench, but now realized that was silly because her dad didn't know about it. She had hidden Smudge's lead when he went away and fingering it now – she kept it in her school bag – she made believe that he was with her. Mrs Merry said the towpath was dangerous, but she had her daddy's wrench for plumbing tucked in her satchel. Her mum had given away all his tools to the man who took Smudge. Her daddy would be pleased she had saved his wrench. Were people pleased about things when they were dead?

Megan wasn't alone in her search for Steven Lawson. Unknown to her children, Bette Lawson walked the footpath while they were at school; she came to the bench to find him. Garry sat on a stool in the aviary that his dad had let him help build. The Lawsons were lost to themselves and each other.

'*Your Dad's a murderer!*'

Megan stuffed her fingers in her ears, but couldn't stop the voices. Angie said she couldn't be her friend because her mum wouldn't let her play with Megan. Angela was back to being best friends with Becky Fox. No one must play with a murderer's daughter.

'*Love you Megs.*'

'*I love you back, Daddy.*'

'*Kill. Kill. Kill!*'

Chapter Twenty-Two

A shadow flitted across the staircase wall. Then was gone. *She was gone.* Jack was four when his mother died. His memories of her were a procession of shadows and murmuring embraces as fragile as gossamer. He had looked at photographs, all taken in the later years of her short life. He feared that it was from these his recall derived. He took comfort from the soft lullabies that drifted around him as he walked through the London night. The caress of a breeze against his cheek.

He shut the front door and waited for her shadow to return, but apart from the damp stains – since his father's death years ago, he had never decorated – the wall remained blank. Whenever he saw his mother's shadow – ghost – she was running up the stairs. However long he waited, his hand on the marble-topped table, standing where he had last seen her in this house, she never came downstairs. The silence in the five-storey house wasn't of emptiness, but of her presence. *Come and find me!* She would never come looking. Once it had been consoling to feel her close, but recently it had begun to feel like purgatory. He needed to be free.

When Stella had asked him to live at Thames Cottages, Jack had been excited and impatient to get there. His discovery that Steven Lawson was dead had dampened his spirits. It was an absurd notion, since everyone dies, but in the photographs Lawson had looked too alive to die.

He carried his suitcase on to the porch, suddenly reluctant to leave. It was betrayal. He switched off the hall light and didn't linger to see if the dark would lure his mother down.

He cradled the short-eared owl door knocker, feeling the weight of his feathered friend. He stroked the bird's puffed chest with the side of his thumb. The body was light and warm, the feathers soft.

Fly away, Jack.

His slow progress down the steps triggered a far-off memory of stumping down these same steps when he was a small boy. In bright sunlight he saw the blue wellington boots he had insisted on wearing even in the house. Clutched in chubby hands was a red steam engine. Jack had a vision of red sinking into mud and being washed away on the turning tide.

It wasn't sunny now. It was dark and, at half seven in the evening, people were eating supper or had yet to come home. He glanced at the next-door house. His elderly neighbour Mrs Ramsay had died some years ago and he was only on 'hello' terms with the man and woman who lived there now. Resting his gaze on the top window he fancied he saw Mrs Ramsay's stern, angular face. He tipped a hand to her, but she too was a ghost.

The brown leather case had been his mother's. Her initials – K.V. for Katherine Venus – were embossed by the lock; the silver lettering had rubbed away.

'Off on holiday, are we?' Swathed in a mohair shawl, Bella Markham was ethereal in the lamplight. When he first met her Jack had been struck by her warm mellifluent tones; she had a beautiful singing voice. There was nothing warm about her now. She was smouldering with fury. He understood why. 'When were you going to tell me, Jack?'

'Bella. I've been...' He couldn't say that he had been pre-occupied by a new murder case. He couldn't say he had been so concerned with the dead he had forgotten to tell her he was going away and couldn't see her.

'I said at the get-go I don't do "serious". You claimed to be up for that. Now you're doing that classic shit of acting like I'm being the clingy nag. Putting pressure on you. Don't make me the enemy so you can feel justified in getting out. Okay so I've been a misery lately, but you're not exactly a laugh a minute. I haven't changed, I *still* don't do serious, I'm the girl who just wants to have fun. I thought we were having fun.' Her voice thickened. 'Where are you going?' She batted a hand in front of her face. 'Don't answer. It's not my business where you go any more than it's yours what I do and *who with.*'

'It's not what you think.' Jack was horrified to find himself resorting to the clichés used in such exchanges. Bella had been low recently, but he had no problem with that. She'd also been lethargic, too tired to come on night walks, which was disappointing, but he was used to going on his own.

'What do I think?' Bella asked sweetly.

'I'm doing a job for Stella.'

'Lucky Stella! I bet you're good!'

'I have to live in. I'm not allowed guests…' He was no good at this.

'How convenient.' Bella's shawl slipped, releasing a mass of curly dark hair. He moved to touch her, but checked himself. Bella didn't 'do' placation.

'We *were* having fun.' He saw from Bella's expression she had noted the past tense. It was a slip of the tongue. Or was it? When Bella wasn't there, he couldn't conjure her up any more than he could his mother. He had told her about his mission to find True Hosts – those who had murdered or will murder – and stop them. Instead of trying to keep him indoors, she had wanted to join him. He had stopped her. Now he was in a boat drifting away from Bella. Soon she would be out of reach.

'You know your problem, Jack?' Bella tossed her mane of hair. 'It's you who should lighten up. You think you've got a calling to rid the world of True Murderers or whatever you call them. Well, get this Batman, you're dirt human like the rest of us.' She hugged the shawl around herself.

'I don't think I'm Batman.' He rather liked the notion.

'I won't keep you from your mission. I will *not* chase you, Jack. I loathe this grasping person you're trying to turn me into.' Bella moved out of the circle of light. 'Tell you what. Call me when you're up for having fun. When you've got that woman out of your head.'

Jack protested weakly, 'Stella and me, we're just friends.'

Bella gave a mirthless laugh. From a dim shape in the darkness, her voice rang out strong and clear: 'Who said Stella Darnell? I meant your mother!'

Chapter Twenty-Three

Wednesday, 6 January 2016

Her mum's injury had altered Stella's routine. She arrived at Suzie's flat at 6.30 p.m. to make supper so that her mum could eat it with *The Archers*. Suzie could hobble, and insisted she was quite able to provide for herself, but Stella feared this would lead to a more serious accident than a sprained ankle. She would do the cooking.

That night Stella had heeded Jackie's advice about fresh food and planned to make them both an omelette. It would save her microwaving a shepherd's pie when she got back to her house. She had remembered that her brother Dale's omelettes – he ran a posh restaurant in Sydney – contained cheese and a garnish of parsley. She didn't see the point of parsley, but was going to serve it with a bag of salad from the mini-mart. She was not a cook; this was a leap into the unknown.

The omelette wasn't entirely down to healthy eating. Stella wanted to offer a something to soften the blow for Suzie that Jack wouldn't be coming for a fortnight. Besides supper ingredients, Stella lugged in a bundle of Clean Slate client files for Suzie to add to the client database until she could return to work.

Pulling closed the concertina gate of the lift, Stella pressed the top-floor button. The panel of buttons was grey with dust. Despite her mum's urgings, she refused to pitch for the building's cleaning contract. Suzie would be even tougher on her than with the present substandard cleaners. However, Stella was becoming progressively frustrated by the smeared brassware and stained carpet.

She was preoccupied by the image Jack had texted her that morning. He hadn't rung her back. Tonight he was moving in to Natasha Latimer's. She'd go round there after she'd finished at Suzie's. Adam Honeysett hadn't told her that Lawson was dead. There was nothing in the file. Beverly had combed the internet and printed up information for Stella. One piece was from a *Murderers Who Got Away* website that Stella thought must be libellous. The plumber was seen going to the river on the Wednesday night before Helen Honeysett went missing. Why was Lawson a suspect? Adam told her that he'd left his wife asleep on the Thursday morning. Stanley was staring up at her. The lift was at her mum's landing.

Outside Suzie's flat, Stella was again troubled by Adam Honeysett. Why hire a private detective and keep back key information? Perhaps she should bid for the contract in her mum's mansion block. It was simpler being a cleaner than a detective.

'I felt sorry for that poor fellow.' Suzie was sitting by the gas fire already reading the client files Stella had brought. 'The press killed him. Particularly that friend of yours.' She pursed her lips and enunciated, 'She *ripped him to shreds.*'

'What poor fellow and what friend?' Stella peered through the kitchen hatch. She was puzzling over when to add cheese to the omelette and had begun to regret passing up the frozen lasagne on special offer at the mini-mart. She had expected that her mum would become immersed in her database and let her concentrate on cooking. Instead Suzie was going to give a running commentary on the clients.

'Lucie May, the *Chronicle*'s old retainer.' Suzie picked up the file and hobbled across the room. Stella didn't see why her mum minded about Lucie May, since she was the one who'd left Terry. The animosity was mutual; neither woman missed an opportunity to snipe at the other.

'She's not my friend.' Stella cracked four eggs into a bowl. Two yolks broke and ran into the white. Sweat prickled on her forehead; it was ruined at the start. She reread Dale's email and saw that she would be whipping the eggs with a fork so it didn't matter if the yolk was broken.

'What a dish,' her mum murmured from the living room.

'What dish?' Dale's instructions were to serve directly on to one plate, slice in half and slide one half on to another plate. This struck Stella as tricky enough, but she had a greater problem. She was perplexing over a 'knob of butter'. The knobs on her mum's cupboards were a third of the size of the door knobs. Stella sliced a corner off the new pat of butter that was a compromise between the two sizes and dropped it into the frying pan. Instantly it sizzled and scooted across the hot surface. She raised her hands at this minor success and set about whisking the eggs, the fork blurring as she picked up speed. Belatedly she took in what her mum had said: 'What's Lucie May got to do with it?'

'Lucie May, *Raving Reporter*, good as murdered that man. I told Terry Lawson wasn't the only person to take his dog to the towpath. What was his motive? The chap had a family and his business was on the rocks: he had more to lose than to gain by murdering that woman. Terry had the grace to agree.'

Stella reread Dale's recipe. Grated cheese went in after the egg. She tipped in the mixture. Suzie wasn't talking about a client. Lucie May would never have Clean Slate in to do her house. She craned through the hatch. 'Did you did speak to Dad about the Honeysett case?' Suzie had spread the customer files over the table, covering the mats and the cutlery. One paper was propped against the salad bowl, another against the bottle of dressing.

'Terry depended on my theories.' Suzie rattled a paper in her hand. 'We were a team.'

The eggs were browning at the edges. Stella grabbed the cheese and teased it off the plate into the frying pan. She saw a similarity between cleaning and cooking. Both were time-sensitive. For cleaning a bath, her cleaning manual advised, *Squirt the liquid on the surface and work briskly to lift grime then sluice with hot water.* She slid the non-stick fish slice beneath the omelette, easing it upwards.

'Who did Dad think did it?' Jack didn't believe in coincidences, but it was astonishing that her mum was talking about Helen Honeysett's disappearance two days after Stella had accepted the cold case.

Her mum harrumphed. 'Terry never told me anything.'

The egg was brown in patches like countries on a map. Just like Dale's photograph of one of his omelettes. Stella cut it in half and transferred one half to the other plate. She carried the plates through to the living room and waited for Suzie to move the client papers. Suzie seemed unaware of her. Stella glanced at the papers and met the smiling face of Steven Lawson. She tipped the plate and the omelette shot towards the rim. 'Mum! What are you reading?'

Absently Suzie took the plate from Stella. She delved beneath the papers for her knife and fork and, still reading, mechanically began to eat. 'You were twenty-one that year. I wanted a party, but – *naturellement* – Terry was for a boring old scoff in a steak-house. Neither happened in the end.' Suzie pushed aside the folder and Stella saw her own writing on the card cover: 'Helen Honeysett 1987'.

'Mum, how come you have that?' She had left the Honeysett file in the van.

'Mmm, delicious, nearly as good as Dale's.' Suzie scrutinized another document. This was high praise, but, her appetite gone, Stella was impervious to compliments. She had given Suzie the Honeysett folder instead of the client file. She groaned, 'Mum, that's confidential.'

'How is anything in the *Chronicle* confidential?' Suzie Darnell munched serenely on her omelette as she read one of Lucie May's articles. 'Whatever Loopy May says, Lawson was innocent.' Far from open, Suzie Darnell's mind was a sealed vault. A trait Lucie and her mum shared. Pragmatic, Stella opted to make the most of her mum's knowing.

'Who did you suspect?'

'The husband. Look at Terry!' Suzie Darnell popped the last forkful of omelette into her mouth and clattered her cutlery down on the plate. She waved at the salad bowl. 'It's too cold for that, but nice thought.'

'Dad wasn't a murderer!' Suzie's disparagements of Terry hadn't lessened with his death, but she'd never gone this far. 'He was a detective.'

'Murderers and detectives are two sides of a coin,' Suzie said sagely.

Stella felt, as she often did around her mum, overwhelmed by a rolling fog. She tried to track back to the point. 'Why did you suspect Adam Honeysett?'

'The killer is usually someone close to or known to the victim. There was something else, but it's escaped me.' Suzie snatched up another article by Lucie May. 'Ooh, I'd forgotten this!'

'What?' Stella chopped off a square of omelette. It was cold and the cheese had solidified. Assiduously chewing it, she carved out another square. She didn't want salad either.

'Lucille mentions a Daphne Merry who called the police and made the girl confess she'd seen her dad stalking Helen Honeysett.' She frowned. 'Poor thing, that would have taken some doing. I'd like to hope you'd have been as honest about your dad's misdemeanours.'

'Do you suspect Daphne Merry?' Stella swallowed the last of the omelette and resolved to microwave lasagne the following evening.

'I told you it's the husband. Says here she was a declutterer.' Suzie waved at the papers strewn over the table. 'I want one of those.'

'Mum, you have a cleaner.' Not true. Stella had yet to break this to her.

'This woman isn't a cleaner. She strips out the inessential so it's easier to clean. Do you offer that?'

'You know we don't.' Stella leant through the hatchway and put their plates on the counter. 'She's probably retired.' She must find out.

'Declutterers, like cleaners, never retire.' Bundling up a sheaf of papers, Suzie lurched back to her armchair. 'You should have her in to declutter and pick up some tricks.'

'That's not honest.' Although she hadn't cleaned that day, Stella felt exhausted. In the kitchen, she snapped on marigolds and filled the washing-up bowl.

'Since when was a detective honest?' Suzie was arch. 'Take Terry.'

Stella was driving over Hammersmith Flyover when her phone rang, the sound resounding through the speakers. The dashboard screen read Jackie Home.

'Hi, hun, did you tell Suzie about Jack not cleaning?'

'Yes.' Preoccupied with Helen Honeysett, her mum had taken the news in her stride. Stella whizzed past the statue of the Leaning Lady and Rose Gardens North, the cul-de-sac where she lived. Bollards prevented access from the Great West Road, but tonight she was going to see Jack in Kew.

'Bev told me the name of that cleaner who I think would be great for Suzie. Stephanie Benson. She's patient and, like I said, super-efficient. Clients are giving her glowing feedback.'

'OK,' Stella said. After all, there was nothing to lose.

Chapter Twenty-Four

Wednesday, 1 April 1987

'Do *not* touch my birds!' Garry prised open Megan's curled fingers. He bent her forefinger back, the stretched skin like a burn, and wrested the now fully grown budgerigar from her and tipped it into the nest box. 'Get out!' he stormed.

'I was feeding her.' Megan's voice wobbled, but she wouldn't cry because Garry had hated it even before their dad...

Megan Lawson couldn't remember how it had been before Helen Honeysett went missing and her dad became the Monster. Angie and Becky and everyone said he'd killed her and drowned her body in the Thames.

'Go to the river and jump *in*!' Garry's voice, on the verge of breaking, cracked. He sounded funny and before Megan would have teased him. Even if he had been cross, she wouldn't have been scared because whatever he said wouldn't have been true.

'What's going on?' Bette Lawson was at the kitchen door. Behind, Megan saw Aunty El. Garry had seen her too because he whispered: 'Take *her* with you!'

Like her, Garry had loved Aunty El. When she turned up in her red sports car, smelling of perfume, they were guaranteed fun – scary fun, but fun all the same. But since Helen Honeysett went missing, her aunty was the Bad Fairy and she and her mum had hissing conversations and banged doors. Aunty El was the only one who was nice to Megan, but her visits weren't worth it for that because after she left, her mum would cry and Garry was horrible. Her eyes pricking with tears, Megan hazarded, 'Maybe if we could find Helen Honeysett it could be a bit normal.'

'You're an idiot!' Garry shoved her out of the aviary. 'Dad's dead. It will never be normal. You killed him.'

'Garry!' Bette Lawson's call was the scream of a rook. 'Stop!' She didn't say it wasn't true.

'Megan didn't kill your dad, Gaz.' Aunty El rattled the mesh on the aviary. No one did that, not even her dad. Aunty El was brave. 'I'm afraid your dad managed that all by himself.'

'Most people can't face the truth. You stand firm, lovey. Good will out.' Daphne Merry ruffled Megan's hair and gave her a glass of chocolate Nesquik. 'I won't criticize your mother, but she really shouldn't let your brother speak to you like that. Still, it's nice she let you come and see me. She did let you, didn't she?'

'Yes.' Megan dipped her face over the Nesquik. No one knew where she was. She would never ever go home again. Megan hadn't properly thought this. The brown liquid floated before her, a spot of powder eddying on the surface. 'Mum agrees with Garry.'

'I'm sure she doesn't. What your father did, he did on his own, as your aunt said.' As Megan had hoped, Mrs Merry took her up to her De-Cluttering Office. In Megan's cottage the equivalent room was her mum and dad's bedroom. It was still her mum's, although she slept in the spare room with the ironing board. Several nights, Megan had crept downstairs, squinted through the hinge crack in the door and seen her mum with a mug of tea staring at the kitchen stove.

After she had done a De-Clutter, Mrs Merry brought back a haul of clutter from a person's home. Balanced on a stool, Megan contemplated a stack of photographs. The top one of a man with his arms around two girls and a lady who might be his wife made her queasy. There were packets of letters and exercise books with sums all over the covers and a shoebox of pebbles.

'What are those for?' She was intrigued.

'Neither useful nor beautiful: what are they?'

'Clutter!' Megan called with triumph.

'Quite. My client's daughter collected them when she was a girl. She's a grown-up, but her mother has kept them. We will dump them on the riverbank where they belong.'

'Do they have pebbles there?' Megan was doubtful.

'These come from Brighton; the girl took them in 1966. If we all did that, there'd be no beach.' Mrs Merry nudged the box with the toe of her sturdy De-Clutter lace-up shoe.

The pebbles were round and shiny and Megan wondered about asking to take them home. But they were clutter so she couldn't. De-Clutterers didn't keep what they took; Mrs Merry said that would be wrong.

'Did you tell the police that your brother lied about seeing your father going to the river?'

'Yes.' Megan gazed out of the window. The view mixed with the reflection of the clutter was ghostly. It was the same view as on the night when she had stood with Garry looking at the stars and they had seen their dad going to the towpath after Helen Honeysett. 'Garry said he wasn't watching. The police believed him.'

'The two of you as witnesses would have weighed against the circumstantial evidence and reduced cause for doubt. Especially when you and your brother had every reason to lie to protect your father. You are braver than your brother. Your aunt told me she had never approved of Steven Lawson marrying her sister.' Daphne Merry appeared to have forgotten she was talking to Steven Lawson's daughter. The girl gripped her drink with whitened knuckles and watched Mrs Merry empty a box of detached dolls' limbs into a black sack. A decapitated head rolled on to the floor and came to a stop by Megan's foot.

'What does circumstantial mean?' Megan decided to ask.

'That the police have a confluence of events that could tie the plumber to Honeysett's disappearance, but no motive or concrete proof. That's why they couldn't charge him. Time will reveal the truth. Mark my words, you will be exonerated, Megan.'

'What if Daddy didn't kill her and now he's dead?' Megan didn't know the word 'confluence' and felt a stab of fear at the prospect of something called 'exonerated' happening.

'Oh, Megan! Is the moon made of cheese?' Daphne Merry gathered up the photographs and letters and tossed them into the sack. 'We'll never know the workings of your father's mind – he's taken that with him. I will never know how my husband could allow himself to fall asleep... Well, anyway.' She indicated a myriad of ornaments and trinkets on her work table. 'Stow those in this cardboard box and write "Hospice" in your lovely neat hand on the side. Hopefully they'll find good homes and raise money for what is a worthy charity.'

'Won't they be clutter there too?' Elated to have a task, Megan was still baffled.

'Doubtless.' Clasping the bin bag Mrs Merry glided from the room.

The felt pen squeaked as Megan wrote on the cardboard. She counted thirty-two pieces of clutter: photograph frames, a glass fruit bowl, a lump of glass with a shape of a swan entombed within, a bobbly-fringed lampshade, a matchbox of odd earrings and some old coins. She paused over a Donald Duck clock with a bell on top. If it belonged to her it would be such a treasure, not clutter. She remembered one of Mrs Merry's mottos: 'A clear home is a clear mind.' Megan's mind didn't feel one bit clear.

Chapter Twenty-Five

Jack dug a channel in the sand and drove his truck along it. The sand was dry and as he manoeuvred the truck along the trench, the sides gave way. He should sprinkle some water, damp sand was firmer, but not committed to the activity he remained on his haunches in the sandbox.

The truck had a flatbed behind the cab and was the one thing he'd brought with him. Jack loaded sand on to the back. When it was full he drove the truck from one end of his channel to the other. Weighed down, it was soon mired in the dry sand.

'I will make a mountain with the sand,' he announced.

'You want to make a mountain with the sand.'

'I will be king of my mountain.'

'You want to be king.'

'My mummy will be queen.'

'You want your mummy to be with you on your mountain.'

'Daddy can't climb mountains.' Fact.

'Your daddy can't climb up your mountain.'

'Mummy can climb anything, and I can too.'

'You and your mummy will be on your mountain.'

The back flap of the truck gave way and sand poured out. He looked up. There were boys all around him. With scruffled hair, in crumpled jumpers, they crouched in the sand. The boys were his reflection repeated in the glass panels. Jack was alone in Natasha Latimer's show playroom.

The voice wasn't his ghost mother. It was the therapist he'd seen after his mother died. Or the one he'd wished he'd seen. He made so many people up.

He should have told Bella what Natasha Latimer wanted; Bella would have understood. When she was immersed in a drawing, she liked to be by herself. Jack ran the truck back up the channel and shovelled on another load of sand. He tried to picture Bella, but she had gone. He only saw his own reflection in the glass.

He tipped the truck up and shook out the last grains of sand.

'I will make a mountain of sand to cover my daddy.'

'You want your daddy to be covered by sand.'

'If he's under the mountain he will be dead and gone instead of my mummy.'

'You want your mummy to be alive.'

Jack jumped up, scrubbing at his hair to shut out the voices. He pulled out his phone. He would call Bella and say he was sorry. He could go and see her. He pressed the phone to his ear. Nothing. He was in the dead zone.

He went back to the room with the River Wall. The glass swished aside. Luminous footprints appeared on the floor when he stepped on it. Ghost steps. Latimer would like to see proof of her impact as she moved about. Jack found the feature unsettling; he tried to move though life leaving no trace of his journey. It hadn't been there the night before so he hoped it was possible to switch it off.

The black water darkened the space. The reflection of a light on the north bank flickered on the surface. The darting dot of yellow was extinguished; perhaps a branch had blown in front of it. It reappeared. Jack touched the speck of light, thinking of it as a friend. He felt cold plaster, the light vanished and he was engulfed by desolation. He wished he could have brought the short-eared owl, but things and creatures had their rightful place. And besides, the sadness did not feel as though it belonged to him.

The ceiling lights flashed. The projection of the river disappeared. The outline of a figure filled the space. *Stella.* Jack ran up the glass staircase as if he was soaring in the air.

Chapter Twenty-Six

'I made you a cake.' The woman brandished a cake tin. Her look was timeless, flat brogues with tasselled laces, tweed skirt, shirt buttoned to the neck and a jacket with a fearsome brooch that resembled a medal pinned to the lapel. Her dark hair was cut into a bob. She made Jack think of Miss Marple and that made him realize he'd thought this before. It was the strict woman who'd accosted him outside the dilapidated house. Daphne Merry. Number 3. Jack was suffused with horror that she might so easily have visited him the night before when Natasha Latimer and Stella were there and given away that she'd met him.

'Ah, how lovely, thank you.' He took the tin. The base was faintly warm. The cake must be freshly baked. 'Come in.' Too late he remembered Natasha Latimer's rule about visitors.

'I see you've now moved in.' The lamp in the hall revealed deep lines on Daphne Merry's face, less, Jack thought, due to age than life; on the towpath he'd put her in her late sixties, but she was possibly nearer late fifties. He took in her comment. She had known he wasn't living at number 1 when she met him on the towpath. She truly was Miss Marple. With a burst of glee, Jack dismissed his qualms about having visitors.

'I hope you like Jamaican ginger?' Daphne Merry's tone implied that if he didn't, he should. 'It was my little girl's... It's my favourite.'

'I love it.' Jack nearly said it had been his mother's favourite, but was suddenly unsure that was true. 'Would you like a cup of tea? Oh! I can't offer you tea or indeed anything!' He smacked his forehead. 'I moved in today and I need to go shopping.' *Damn.* If Daphne Merry hadn't known he had lied, she did now. He was making a mess of both ghostbusting and detection. With reckless bravado, he said, 'We can eat cake!'

'I imagined you wouldn't have anything. I've brought tea bags and a carton of milk. That's what you do with new neighbours.' Smiling, she passed him a carrier bag. Jack reminded himself that not everyone suspected others of lying.

'Follow me.' A door at the top of the staircase to the basement led to what had once been a mean scullery, but was now a large steel-clad kitchen – resembling a morgue – with a glass door to the garden. The only items on the stainless-steel worktop were a set of silver Sabatier knives and a chrome kettle. The colour came from six bubble-gum-pink plastic chairs around a glass table. Jack drew one of these out for Merry, quelling an apology because the garish design must be ill suited to her taste.

'I haven't been in here before,' Daphne Merry commented.

Had Merry brought similar provisions when Natasha Latimer had moved in? He speculated whether Latimer had refused the Jamaican ginger cake; her svelte curveless figure suggested a regime of diet and exercise. He remembered that Merry was one of the neighbours who had complained about the disruption caused by the conversion. Perhaps she hadn't felt like bearing gifts. 'It's much bigger than it looks from the outside.' Jack scrabbled to wind back the absurdity of his remark: 'Have you lived in Thames Cottages long?'

'Yes.' Daphne Merry got up and said apropos of nothing, 'I expect you're hungry.'

Jack wasn't hungry. He made the tea while Daphne Merry opened and shut cupboards until she found mugs and plates. They came from Asda; Latimer had bought cheap for what was essentially a show home. 'She doesn't have a cake slice.' She sounded mildly censorious.

'It seems a friendly street.' Jack sat down at the table.

'It isn't, but that suits me. I didn't come here to make friends.' Merry wasn't drinking her tea. For a moment Jack thought she looked immensely sad, but then she smiled and the impression passed. Merry passed him a plate with a wedge of cake and a piece of kitchen towel folded into a triangle. Jack was reminded of Jackie who could make the least domestic space feel like home. Mrs Merry was the motherly sort. Nothing he'd read on the Honeysett case suggested that Daphne Merry had children, but they could be grown up and have moved away. Not that Garry Lawson had moved away.

'You've come to get rid of the ghost.'

Jack swallowed a lump of cake. He had been ready with Latimer's story that he was keeping the house clean and occupied while she was away on business. 'Well, er...'

'It's her, you know,' Daphne Merry remarked archly. She wiped her fingers on the kitchen towel although she hadn't touched her cake.

'Helen Honeysett? You think she's haunting this house?' Perhaps Merry wasn't being malicious and genuinely believed it.

'What? No I do not! Poor dear Natasha is, I suspect, rather neurotic. These money types are. She hadn't heard about Honeysett until she moved in and she whipped up quite a fuss about how it affected house prices. I pointed out that she'd bought her house, but to no avail. I should have told her that we carry our dead with us.'

Jack was interested. Had Latimer herself started the rumour? He agreed about the carrying the dead. He'd only been in the cottage an hour, but could feel his mother's presence. Not as a loving companion, but as a reminder of what he had lost. Bella was right, he was shackled to a woman he'd only known for four years of his life but loved more than anyone. He was filled with the urge to tell Daphne Merry his life story, to confess everything.

'At least it's free of clutter.' Merry regarded the kitchen with approval.

Jack had forgotten Daphne Merry was a declutterer. Despite her objections to the basement conversion, she must like the vast uncluttered space. Stella would get on with Daphne Merry.

'Besides, we don't even know if the girl is dead. One minute she was there; then she was gone. The path was empty.'

'Did you like her?' Jack remembered Daphne had said Helen Honeysett was careless.

'I didn't know her enough to like her or to dislike her.'

'Do you think Steven Lawson was guilty?' He knew he was pushing it.

'I am not a detective, Mr…' She appeared to have forgotten about her cake and her tea. Jack was loath to remind her in case she had changed her mind.

'Call me Jack.' He finished his cake. So much for not being hungry. He was ready to start on Daphne's slice.

'Mr Lawson had no alibi. With no body, the police had little to go on. He was guilty of selfish cowardliness; he ruined his little girl's life. The only saving grace is he didn't take his children with him.' Daphne folded the kitchen towel into a smaller triangle and laid it back on the table. Jack had gathered that she prized taking care. 'Megan had to find out far too young that her father was a flawed being. Some children pay dearly for those flaws.' She got up. 'I'll leave you to your ghosts, Jack. It's been a pleasure to meet you.' She took his hands in hers and looked into his eyes as if she really meant what she said. Jack blinked to stop the tears that stung his eyes. 'Please return the cake tin when you have finished with it. They are few and far between.'

'Of course.' In a flash, Jack supposed that Latimer had accepted the cake and she had never returned the tin. Careless of her.

After he had shown Daphne Merry out, Jack was in the basement sitting on the Dalí-esque sofabed – Latimer had designated it his sleeping place – when again the ceiling lights dimmed and a figure filled the River Wall. Daphne Merry had realized that she hadn't eaten her cake. Jack felt a flush of pleasure at the prospect of seeing her again.

'I've brought milk, tea and coffee.' Stella unclipped Stanley's lead to let him into the hall. Stanley bolted back down the path. Stella and Jack watched in dismay as he slithered under the gate and galloped up the steps to the towpath.

'Is he chipped?' Jack panted as they plunged after him, the torch on Stella's phone barely breaking the darkness.

'Yes and my mobile number's on his collar, but it won't help if he falls in the river.' For all his night walking, Jack wasn't a sprinter; Stella soon left him behind.

'Are we sure he came this way?' he called after her.

'He did last time,' Stella replied from far off.

Bushes gave way to grass. It was the dilapidated house. Stella was shining light over the crumbling wall. This time Jack saw that the wrought-iron gate hung off its hinges and that a window pane on the upper floor was broken and blocked with cardboard. He heard a noise.

'Someone's in there.' Jack lifted the latch. Stella put her hand on his arm.

'Wait!' She crept past, Stanley's lead dangling from her hand. 'Stan-ley,' she whispered. 'Stan-ley.'

Stanley was on his hind legs scratching at the front door. A sound like fingernails on a blackboard. Jack sucked his teeth. Stanley began to mew; the call, plaintive and dismal, might express every sorrow in the world. For no reason, he thought of Daphne Merry.

So intent was the little poodle on getting into the house that he didn't notice Stella until she clipped on his lead. In protest, he sat down heavily when she tried to lead him away.

'He did this last time too.' Stella lifted Stanley up.

'What last time?' Jack caught the significance of Stella's earlier comment. Why had she been to this house before?

'He came here the night I met Adam Honeysett. He must catch a scent of a creature or something.'

Stella told him easily; she had no secrets to keep. Envious, Jack fitted the gate on to the latch. He paused and swept his Maglite's piercing beam across the house. The night before – or early morning – Daphne Merry had interrupted him before he could examine it. Now he saw that the inside of the windows were draped with cobwebs like tattered lace and the sashes were rotten. It looked abandoned, but often houses that he found on nocturnal outings, crumbling and desolate, were someone's home. Others were empty – perhaps the owner had died and probate had stalled or a developer was letting the property deteriorate to justify demolition. One day the double-fronted house (it looked Georgian) would fall victim to a Natasha Latimer-type makeover. He saw a face peeping from behind the cardboard in one of the upper windows.

'Jack!' Stella hissed from the towpath. 'Come on!'

'I think someone lives there,' he said when he joined her.

'Very likely.' Stella was tight-lipped. 'It needs a good clean.'

As he had when they were outside Thames Cottages, Jack suddenly had the distinct impression that, somewhere in the shadows of the towpath, someone was there. He walked faster.

Stella stopped abruptly. 'If we were to carry on the way Stanley was going we'd get to Mortlake Crematorium.'

'Let's not.' Jack kept his tone neutral; no point them both being scared. In fact Stella wasn't easily rattled. The first time he'd met her had been late at night by the river at Hammersmith. She was poking about on the site of their first murder. As he pictured this, Jack anticipated what Stella would say next.

'Helen Honeysett went jogging at eight in the evening, two hours earlier than now. But, like tonight, it would have been dark and it was January.' Before he could protest, Stella had turned round and was walking back towards Mortlake, her footsteps diminishing.

Jack thrilled with the horrible possibility that from somewhere in the darkness either side of the towpath they were being watched. He caught up with her. It was scant comfort that Stanley was pattering along beside Stella, tail up, seemingly unbothered. Yet dogs picked up the slightest thing. They must be alone.

They were passing the dilapidated house. This time there was no one at the top window.

They stepped into the foot tunnel under the Kew Railway Bridge; it was chill and dank. Jack switched on his Maglite. A notice offered a number to call in case of a 'strike' and gave the bridge identification (SAR 2/29). He couldn't find significance in the letters and numbers. Stella didn't hold with his finding meaning in signs and if she was prepared to consider it, now wasn't the time to ask.

'That was Helen Honeysett's birthday,' Stella said.

'What was?'

'The twenty-ninth of February. She was born in 1960, which was a leap year. She only had a birthday every four years and was due to have one in 1988 and would have had one this year. She'd have been fifty-six this year. She chose her birthday on years where there wasn't a twenty-nine. The year she died it was going to be the thirty-first of January. Bit random.'

'No such thing as random.' Jack was elated. Stella had found a sign. Just when he thought he knew her, she confounded him with something supposedly untypical. She was *unknowable*.

'Or maybe the journalist – Lucie May as it happens – twisted facts to fit the story. It wouldn't be the first time,' she said.

Stella was negative about few people but Lucie May was one. Recently they'd had a rapprochement and acerbic comments like this were even rarer.

They passed iron railings on their right. These were dwarfed by swaying ornamental grasses beyond. In the light of Jack's torch the grasses looked bright red. Sinister. A pebbled path led off between the grasses as if through a maze. Beyond was a dull wash of light. 'That's a gated estate,' Stella said. 'We clean a couple of the houses. In 1987, according to an old *A–Z* of Dad's, this whole area was a sprawl of warehouses and scrub.'

'Easy to hide and ambush Helen Honeysett.' Jack shone the torch. The grasses were tinted red. Irrationally this intensified his disquiet. 'It's still easy.'

'OK, this is what we'll do. You stay here; I'll go on. After twenty seconds I'll call out to you. Shout if you can hear me. I'll walk for another twenty seconds and call again and so on.'

Jack stopped dead. 'You are *kidding*!'

'You can be the one walking if you like,' Stella said peaceably.

'No! Stella, we shouldn't separate at all,' Jack sputtered. 'Helen Honeysett was murdered on this towpath. At night in the dark. As you said, it was January and after dark. Like *now*!'

'She was out on her own. We're together. If you don't hear me on the count of twenty seconds, come as fast as you can. Plus I've got Stanley. Or would you like to keep him? He'll hear me even if you don't which is fine because most people down here would have had dogs.'

'I *will* hear you!' Jack shouldn't mind, not least because he might have dreamt up the idea himself. Before he could protest Stella was off down the towpath.

'Jack?' Already she sounded some distance away.

'Yes,' he bellowed. He forced himself to stand still and wait. After what seemed longer than twenty seconds, he heard her call his name again. Fainter this time. He shouted back, 'Yes I can hear you.'

'Jack?' Much fainter. He returned her call.

Jack counted to twenty, trying not to go too fast. Nothing. Another five seconds. Still nothing. 'Stella!' His throat hurt. Nothing.

How could he have been so stupid? He rushed forward, feet pounding on the shingled path.

She was there. Jack slowed to a walk. It wasn't Stella. It was the dog walker with the head torch.

'Are you all right?' The man sounded unflurried. The man

switched his torch to a dull red glow. It put his face in shadow. Jack could see the outline of a dog lead slung across his chest, it had the look of a military accessory. He held a bag of poo. Jack was always drawn to footwear; the man's shoes were black and scuffed. Jack kept his own shoes polished.

'Fine.' Jack swallowed hard. Something was wrong. He tried to keep the edge from his tone: 'Did you see my friend up along there?'

'I didn't I'm afraid.' Too pleasant.

Too ordinary for the middle of the night. Jack felt a rush of panic and resisted grabbing the man and shaking him. There was a rustling. Stanley struggled out of thick brush on the bank and began snuffling around the man's legs.

The man proffered the back of his hand – a man who knew about dogs – and Stanley gave an exploratory sniff. He murmured, 'Hello, dog. Is he obedient?'

'Mostly.' Stella climbed up from the riverbank. Jack wanted to clasp her close. His relief was immense.

'I must get on.' The man swished his lead from around his neck and with a brief 'Goodnight' continued along the towpath towards the dilapidated house.

'What the hell were you doing down there?' Jack stormed at Stella.

'I wanted to see if it was possible for a person to conceal themselves.'

'You can tell that without looking.'

'Only if a person goes by and doesn't see you.' Stella was reasonable. 'That man didn't see me. Nor did you.'

The lights of Chiswick Bridge twinkled. Across the Memorial Gardens, the grass frosted white, was the bulky shape of the Mortlake Crematorium.

'I called after twenty seconds. You didn't answer.'

'That tells us that if Honeysett had shouted then anyone more than twenty seconds away wouldn't have heard either.' Apparently content, Stella continued on to Chiswick Bridge.

'That dog walker should have come to help.' Scouring the obscure gloom of the towpath, Jack couldn't see the man or his dog.

'I didn't shout "help", I was calling you. Dad said if you're in trouble in a street shout "fire"; people are less nervous about responding to that than "help". They don't want to get attacked.' Stella stopped under Chiswick Bridge. Her voice resonated around the cavernous arch as if in a cathedral. She stalked between the towering supports. 'Odd that man was out now, don't you think?'

'Dog walkers come out at all hours. Look at us. Strange question about Stanley being obedient?' he said.

'Not really. It's a key quality in a dog.' Stella was looking up at the high swooping ceiling. 'I said he was, but that's not strictly true.' Stella would hate to mislead.

The path gave way to an apron of gravel, bollards blocked it from the road beyond. Jack welcomed lights in houses a hundred metres away.

'We're trying to solve a murder. I didn't like the look of him.'

'He seemed OK.' Stella's voice echoed around the curving stone ceiling.

'So would a murderer. He was too polite.'

'You can't be too polite. And he was nearly seventy.' Stella was looking up at the bridge.

'In 1987, he'd have been about forty,' Jack said. 'Anyway, how could you tell with his torch on, we couldn't see his face.'

'I thought he sounded seventy,' Stella said obscurely.

'Helen Honeysett's killer could have attacked here, bundled her into a car parked up on the bridge. It's double yellows, but it would only have taken a moment.'

'I read that Megan Lawson, the plumber's daughter at number two, heard her say "Oh, it's you!" close to Thames Cottages,' Stella said. 'Let's go.' She set off back the way they had come.

Jack had walked without fear on the towpath alone several times, recently with Bella. Tonight the ancient path had an eerie, desolate aspect. Honeysett's murder – assuming she was dead – was nearly three decades ago, but she could have vanished moments before. Their steps rang in the Kew Railway Bridge tunnel. *SAR 29/2*. The missing estate agent had chosen her birthday, but she had not chosen the date on which she would die.

'It's nice cake.' Stella swallowed a bite of Daphne Merry's cake. 'Strange to knock on your door like that.' She was looking at the upturned truck in the sandbox. She'd guess he had been playing there. One thing Jack loved about Stella was that she never judged him.

'She was being neighbourly.' Jack was about to tell Stella that Daphne Merry reminded him of his mother, but he hadn't considered this until now and couldn't explain it. At fifty-nine, if she had lived, his mother would be younger than Daphne Merry. Not that he knew how old Daphne Merry was.

They moved back to the red-lips sofa, the glass panels swishing open, and sat down. Stella balanced a plate on her lap, and rested her mug of tea on the 'ice' floor. Stanley settled, head on his paws, a steady gaze trained on the cake tin by Jack's feet. Natasha Latimer's commitment to minimalism meant there was no table and, as Daphne had observed, no clutter.

'Merry might have wanted to check out the basement. When Latimer said no visitors, she probably meant Daphne Merry.' Stella wasn't reproving.

'True. What with the cake, I felt I had to ask her in.' Jack opened the lid of the tin and took another slice. 'I suspect she'd have asked. She's a "no-messing" sort of woman. Literally.'

'You said everyone in this street was capable of murder. It doesn't sound as if Daphne Merry cared much for Helen Honeysett.' Stella finished her cake. 'Does she rate as a suspect?'

'Not liking Honeysett is a giant leap to murder.' Jack sipped his hot milk. It was claggy. He wished he'd had tea. Thanks to Stella and Daphne Merry he was supplied with a lot of milk. 'I suppose we should have her on the list. But I can't see her lugging a body away from the towpath or overcoming Honeysett and pushing her in the Thames. I still don't get it. Adam Honeysett saw her in bed that morning so why was Steven Lawson a suspect?' He wished he'd asked Daphne Merry, but she would have balked at his curiosity. She was canny.

'We'll keep an open mind,' Stella agreed. 'I shouldn't have let Mum see the file.' She laid her empty plate on the floor. Stanley yawned, got up and, stretching, meandered over. Not fooled by the apparent disinterest, Stella retrieved the plate and put it back on her lap.

'We reveal what we most want to hide.' Jack hoped as he said it that it wasn't true. 'At least you got a clue to what Terry thought about the case.'

'He didn't think it was Lawson. Adam Honeysett is the obvious suspect and I'm sure there was something he didn't tell me.'

'Let's do some research.' Jack was pleased that Stella's open mind extended to 'Adam'. Carrying his plate and mug, he went to the home-office box beside the sofa. Any movement intimating possible food, Stanley shadowed him. Patches of light pooled around their feet as they stepped on the floor. Putting the hot milk and plate on top of the box, Jack pulled on the handle and swung back the doors as Latimer had done.

'There's no phone, but there is internet connection.' Happiest in London Underground tunnels and night-time subways, Jack had found himself daunted at being sequestered in a deep basement with no contact with the outside world.

'I'm not sure we should use her computer,' Stella cautioned.

'Latimer didn't say we couldn't.' Latimer's task sheet stipulated he clean the 'Home-Office Pod' inside and out. The box resembled those used by magicians for sawing people in half.

Pulling his glasses out of his shirt pocket, Jack crammed them on and, sitting on the upright stool, typed 'Helen Honeysett' on the keyboard. Google returned pages of articles, blogs and websites devoted to her disappearance. Wikipedia gave the subject four headings. The first was *Missing*; Adam Honeysett and Steven Lawson were listed under *Suspects*. 'Adam Honeysett *was* a suspect in his wife's disappearance.'

Stella leant in. 'He said he stopped being a suspect when they arrested Steven Lawson. I'm surprised the fact that he ever was a suspect is allowed to be included. Isn't that defamation of character?'

'It was a fact so it's OK. Still, I'd bet Honeysett would like this to be expunged from the internet.'

'He spoke as if he still is a suspect. He wasn't charged and he's still free,' Stella remarked.

'So are many murderers.' Jack scrolled down to *Similar cases*. There were two, Suzy Lamplugh and the kidnapping of another estate agent called Stephanie Slater, but police had found no connection between the crimes. A man was jailed for the Slater abduction.

'*An estate agent has to be alone with strangers. Since the Honeysett and Lamplugh murders companies are wiser to the dangers*,' Jack read from the page.

'It's like cleaning. We have a rigorous drill for our staff.' Stella sat on the pink chair that Jack had brought down from the kitchen. Stanley shot on to her lap and peered at the screen as if he could read.

'Where in your drill does it say staff can go into the house of a potential murderer in the dead of night without telling anyone?' Jack was acerbic.

Stella didn't answer his question. 'Helen Honeysett was jogging so what she did for a living may not be relevant.'

Jack clicked on *Other missing persons*; the list dated back to Spartacus in 71 BC. He returned to *Suspects*. 'No mention of Neville Rowlands who rented this house.'

'What's this?' Stella clicked on a link on the *Chronicle* website entitled *The Secret Lover!*

Adam Honeysett has a cast-iron alibi for the hours when Helen Honeysett disappeared from the lonely towpath at Kew, Detective Inspector Ian Harper told a packed press conference at Richmond Police Station today. Adam Honeysett confessed to police that he was with another woman! Jane Drake, 19, is retaking A levels at South Thames College in Wandsworth. She occupies a luxury pied-à-terre paid for by her doting dad. The penthouse is a few steps from her lover Honeysett's Thames-side home. To protect his mistress, Honeysett lied. He couldn't have seen his wife in bed on the Thursday morning. He wasn't there!

Police ask anyone on or near the Thames towpath on the night of Wednesday 7 January to call with information...

Jack gave a whistle. 'By the time Adam Honeysett realized Helen was gone, she'd been missing twenty-four hours. This is what he failed to tell you!' He banged the desk, making the steel box ring. 'He was having an affair. Forget defamation of character, Honeysett did a good job of that himself!' He clicked back to Wikipedia.

'It gives him a motive for killing her,' Stella breathed. 'It says Honeysett avoided a charge of wasting police time because he had been punished enough. I was obviously going to find this out, so why not tell me?' She was stroking Stanley as if his life depended on it. 'He called Helen Honeysett the love of his life.'

'You can be in love with one person and in a relationship with another.' Jack rolled up a flapping shirt cuff. Not that he was in a relationship with Bella. Stanley, overburdened by Stella's attentions, made his way over to Jack.

Probably unwilling to discuss the ramifications and repercussions of love, a mystery she had yet to solve, Stella said, 'Honeysett's alibi put Lawson in the frame as the last person to see Helen Honeysett alive on the Wednesday night. It transferred the timing from the morning of Thursday the eighth of January to the evening of the seventh. The night Megan Lawson saw her father following Honeysett to the towpath. She implicated her own father.'

Jack read out another paragraph. '*Presumption of Lawson's guilt was cemented by his subsequent suicide. The father of two drowned himself in the Thames. His body was recovered downstream by Chelsea Bridge three days later.*'

Stella dabbed at the screen, and swooshed the page down and read out '*Helen Honeysett was declared dead in 2007.* Why is Honeysett bringing it up now? There was no evidence to charge him and it looks as if Lawson was, and still is, the prime suspect. He said he wanted to move on. Move on where?'

'Looks like he moved on even before Helen disappeared. If he's the killer, he's committed the perfect murder.'

Stanley tensed. He stared up at Jack, his pupils enlarged, eyes dark and unreadable; he was on alert. Jack looked behind him. On the River Wall, the fathomless water was motionless and dark. He shivered; the basement was a soulless place. He had once lived in a water tower, down by the river at Chiswick; he was disturbed to realize that he'd rather be high up than underground. Tunnels were his home.

It wasn't often that Stella read his mind. 'Will you be all right here? You know, on your own in this basement?'

'Oh yes!' Jack assured her.

'Would you like Stanley? For company? His barking is a deterrent and dogs pick up sounds we don't hear. He might flush out the squeaking Latimer mentioned.'

He was touched that, twice that night, Stella had offered him her pet. 'No, you're all right.' Jack thumped his chest like Tarzan, and then felt faintly silly. 'Ghosts don't float about in sheets and clanking chains. They are subtle. My boarding school had once been owned by a man who died in the Tay Bridge disaster in the nineteenth century. Boys claimed to smell his cigar smoke in the library. The true signs were the tomes on engineering that he left on tables opened at specific pages.'

'It could be an intruder.' Stella dropped her voice as if they could be overheard. She would have noticed Stanley. 'Regardless of the Honeysett case, I could pull you off this job.'

'This place is like Fort Knox!' *Not quite.* 'You both get off.'

After Stella had gone, Jack went to the sandbox and righted the truck. The sand was dotted with paw marks; grains of sand trailed to the sofa. We all leave traces of ourselves, he thought. Helen Honeysett had not vanished without trace. Somewhere a grain of sand would lead to the truth.

There were rib patterns on the river. Flashes of grey on black, skeins of scum swirled. Something had passed along and left a wash, a late police patrol perhaps. He checked his watch. Midnight. He should have seen Stella to her van to be sure she was safe. Bad, thoughtless of him. She would have objected, but he could have insisted. Too late to go after her; she would be long gone.

Soulless the basement might be, but Jack couldn't slough off a sense he wasn't alone. Natasha Latimer was as far from being spiritually in touch as it was possible to be, but that didn't preclude her house from being haunted.

Since meeting Stella, his first line of defence had become cleaning. Jack went to the trolley she'd left for him and found a duster and a canister of beeswax polish. In the magician's box, he lifted the mouse to polish Latimer's desk. The monitor came to life. He dropped the canister. It rolled across the floor, a scrawling that faded to nothing as momentum died. Words floated across the screen, ghostly grey like the veil of scum on the Thames.

Who am I and what have I done?

Chapter Twenty-Seven

Thursday, 7 January 2016

Jack would have been concerned for Stella's safety had he known that instead of returning to her van on Kew Green, she was on the towpath with Stanley. On the narrow pavement outside the cottages the little dog had drawn her to the right towards the steps, wheezing and coughing as his collar constrained his windpipe. Jackie said he was always at others' beck and call, it was fair to give him his way sometimes. Jack was close by if she got into trouble. Stella told herself that, at night, only dog walkers went to the river. She put from her mind that Helen Honeysett had gone to the towpath and never come back.

Stella was concerned by Adam Honeysett's economy with the truth. He couldn't claim to have forgotten he'd been with Jane Drake and not with his wife. Until his alibi Honeysett was the prime suspect. That his alibi was with another woman hardly discounted him from motive – indeed it gave him one. Except that it had discounted him.

She wouldn't let Stanley off the lead in case he went to the ramshackle house by the river. He led her into deeper gloom at the edge of the bank. She glimpsed treacherous water below, the surface rippled with currents and counter-currents. She was a step away from death by drowning. Stella, calm in a crisis, rarely felt fear; she had the ideal temperament for someone at the helm of a growing business who had to make decisions. The downside was, as Jackie had warned, that Stella sometimes took decisions without weighing up dangers.

Coolly she considered that Helen had jogged along this path. The mindset of a runner dwelt on speed and distance and not detail, smells and shadows. What had Helen Honeysett missed? Whom had she met? It wasn't evident when Helen Honeysett went missing: it could have been any time after eight p.m. on the Wednesday till around eight on the next evening when Adam Honeysett said he came back. Had the estate agent died on the Wednesday or had she spent time with someone before she was murdered? She hadn't gone to work that day. Stella had read that she'd never had a day off sick so it was likely that by then she was dead. Still, it left twenty-four hours unaccounted for. Adam had said he'd gone to Northampton that day. Presumably he had or the police would have arrested him. She checked the time. It was after one in the morning. Too late to call on Adam Honeysett. Besides, she wanted Jack with her.

Insipid light cut through the canopy of branches. Although London was never dark, Stella needed her torch app to see. Stanley tugged again. She hissed, 'Sit!' He ignored her command. Helen Honeysett wouldn't have had this issue; she had let her dog – Baxter was an odd name – run free.

A light in a house on Strand on the Green on the north bank cast spattering light on the swirling water. The pattern formed and re-formed. It was the image on the wall in Natasha Latimer's basement. Stella realized that she was by Latimer's garden. She squinted up at the cottage's roof and made out a shape on the chimney. The camera. She was pretty sure that the lens was trained on the river, so it couldn't see her and Stanley. *Jack couldn't see her.* Stella became aware of dull slaps of water against the bank. Of a silence beyond. The silence of presence.

On the cold static air, she smelled washing powder. Jack smelled of fresh clean clothes. Stanley gave a succession of sharp barks. He never barked at Jack.

'It's late to be out.'

'Who's there?' Stella demanded.

The figure was spectral. 'Stella, it's Adam.'

Adam Honeysett. She had just been thinking about him. Jack said there was no such thing as a coincidence. *A coinciding of events is a sign.*

'What are you doing here?' Alarmed by her tone, Stanley escalated to shrill cries and, teeth bare, he dived at Honeysett's ankles.

'Never admit to the culprit that you are frightened. Your fear is their objective. Don't let them know they have succeeded.'

Her dad's advice, given to the little daughter determined to be a detective, came to her unbidden. Stella had no need to pretend, she wasn't frightened.

'I'm walking my dog.' He moved closer to her. 'As are you. Another late-night dog walker, I see.' As if to prove this, a brown and white spaniel meandered into the hazy light of Stella's torch. When she visited him, she hadn't seen a dog. Thinking of her spreadsheet, she asked, 'What's your dog's name?'

'Tiffany. Not my choice, she's a rescue. Best not to change their names: they're already disturbed. I feel an idiot calling her!'

Remembering what she had been thinking, Stella blurted, 'How come you didn't tell me you were having an affair when your wife went missing?'

The river slopped against the bank. The sound was irregular and eerie.

At last Adam Honeysett spoke. 'It was irrelevant. It didn't change how I felt – how I *feel* – about Helen.' In the dark Stella couldn't see his expression.

'How isn't it relevant? It makes you a key suspect!' She shone her torch on him. He blinked in the light.

'Safety first: avoid being trapped with a person you suspect of murder, and if you are, don't say anything likely to inflame.'

Too late for that.

'For exactly that reason. I don't want you to treat me as a suspect. You'd have concentrated your investigation on me. I *know* I'm not guilty.'

'I don't know that. My partner and I need all the facts to make informed decisions and identify credible leads.' Stella put on her talking-to-difficult-clients voice. 'We keep an open mind and we don't rule out anyone without a concrete reason. You withheld a vital fact. If anything it puts you further up our list.' Stella was distantly aware that, aside from inflaming a possible murderer, she wouldn't tick off a cleaning client. It was their privilege to limit where a cleaner could go. She had often cleaned in houses with locked rooms.

'You think I did it?' Honeysett said quietly.

The sensible answer on a dark isolated path by the Thames long before dawn, was 'No, *never*!' Stella glanced up at Latimer's roof camera. She wondered if the live feed had sound. In any case, if she shouted would Jack hear? Was he still there? He was probably with Bella. She retreated and stepped on Stanley sitting – unbidden – at her feet. He gave a terrible squeal. The sound unnerved her.

'Watch your step, Stella.' A warning. Did it have wider meaning?

'I don't know what I think.' As Stella massaged Stanley's paw she recalled that Jack said honesty was over-rated.

'I can't have you working for me if you think I'm guilty. My private detective must have faith in me.'

Stella had one rule with all clients, whether cleaning or crime-solving: she didn't accept rudeness or unreasonable contractual conditions. Even if her life depended on it, she wouldn't be compromised.

'We will have to turn down the job. Thank you for giving Clean Slate the chance to consider it.' Stella pattered out her script for passing up a client. 'Just one thing.' She should leave it there, but as it had in Honeysett's lounge, curiosity won out. 'You said you recognized my van on Kew Green. I drive a plain white van; nothing links it to Clean Slate. You lied. Why should I have faith in you?' She spoke loudly in case Jack could hear. 'You referred to "the true killer". What makes you sure your wife was killed? If she knew about Jane Drake she might have left you.'

Although it was dark, it seemed to Stella that it got darker. Stanley gave a low growl.

'She wouldn't have left me.' Stella saw movement as Honeysett thumped his heart with a fist. The passionate gesture didn't convince.

'Everything all right?' A light bobbed along the towpath from the direction of Kew Stairs. A woman in her late fifties, in wellingtons and a donkey jacket several sizes too large, swept her torch across them. 'Oh, it's you.' She played the light over Adam Honeysett's chest.

'Bette, nice to see you too,' Honeysett said smoothly. 'Bette Lawson, Stella Darnell.'

'Is he giving you gyp?' Stella couldn't tell if the woman was joking.

'Of course.' Adam Honeysett wasn't joking. 'It's what I do, you know that. Late for you to be out, Bette.'

'I've come off a late shift. This is my evening. What's your excuse?'

'Couldn't sleep.' Adam Honeysett spoke heavily as if this was usual.

'You won't sleep wandering about out here.' Bette Lawson bid them goodnight.

Mentally Stella summoned facts from her spreadsheet. *A and E Nurse. Lives with grown-up son, Garry. Budgerigars. Latimer says weirdo. Daughter, Megan.* Bette was Steven Lawson's widow. Good with names, Stella was sure Bette Lawson had never been a Clean Slate client, but even in dim torchlight, she was familiar. Stella had seen her in photographs, but it wasn't just her features, it was her facial movements that struck a chord. Maybe it was that there were limited faces and voices in the world: sooner or later you found duplicates.

'If anyone has reason not to trust me, it's her.' Honeysett had waited until Lawson was out of earshot. 'My alibi put her husband in the frame. She could hate me, yet she doesn't. She believes Steven was innocent and is fanatical about proving it. If anyone could think I'm guilty it's Bette, but she has faith in me.'

'Mrs Lawson has known you for thirty years. I don't put faith in anyone after a few days. We trust no one. That includes Bette Lawson.' Stella started towards the light of the Thames Cottage lamp-post, Stanley beside her. The back of her head prickled with the likelihood Honeysett would attack her.

There was no light on at Natasha Latimer's. Jack would be in bed. Or he might be at Bella Markham's. But surely Jack wouldn't desert his 'post'. Since Bella had come on the scene, Stella had even less idea what Jack would do.

'Listen, Stella, I want a detective who chases the truth wherever it takes them. Someone who faces reality head on. Someone swayed by the head, not by the heart. I read about you and I came to your office to speak to you. I saw you driving off and took down the number plate. When I saw it on Kew Green on Monday night, I reckoned it had to be a sign. I still do. Shall we start again?'

Swayed by the heart rather than the head, Jack would approve that Honeysett had interpreted seeing her van as a sign. He made decisions based on cracks in pavements, cloud formations and dreams. She was reluctant to introduce him to Adam. Reality she could face, but the prospect of witnessing an enthusiastic exchange on the meaning of signs didn't enthral.

Honeysett was opening his front door. Moments later he reappeared clasping a cardboard box. 'If you'll keep on this case, here's the rest of the stuff. I've collected it since 1987.'

In the van, with the box on the passenger seat, Stella pondered on what she'd said. Should she believe in a client's innocence to accept their brief? She would never clean for someone she didn't trust. Her mum said Terry hadn't trusted anyone, not even his family.

A woman was coming along the pavement beside the green. Mostly if strangers' eyes meet, their gaze flits away, but the woman looked straight at her. Stella was glad she'd locked the van. The woman, dressed against the cold in a bulky duffel coat, had long wavy hair that vaguely reminded Stella of Bella who, although only a few months younger than her, could seem as if in her early forties. Diverted by thoughts of Jack's girlfriend, Stella became aware that the woman had disappeared. No ghost; the only way she could have gone was down the alley to Thames Cottages.

Stella unclipped Stanley – she wouldn't leave him in the van – and ran across the road with him under her arm, and along the alley. The woman was outside the cottages. Did she live in one of them? She was too young to be Sybil Lofthouse or Daphne Merry and Stella knew she wasn't Bette Lawson. Was she Megan Lawson? Or one of the 'new girls every week' Latimer had referred to? She inched closer, keeping in the shadow of the hedge. The woman was gazing at Adam Honeysett's house. Stella felt uncomfortable. She was essentially spying on a stranger; she should go back to the van. Yet a strong detective instinct urged her to stay. Adam had come to her years after his wife disappeared. Helen Honeysett had been declared officially dead in 2007. Why hire a private detective now? Jack would say spying was necessary.

The woman unlatched Adam Honeysett's gate. On the path, she caught her shoe on a stone and kicked it. Stanley tensed and took a breath, a prelude to barking. Stella clamped her hand over his jaws. He squealed and struggled.

'Who's there?' The woman sounded scared. Stella felt terrible. Nevertheless, if she answered, how could she explain hiding? She pushed closer into the hedge. It was no hiding place; if the woman had a torch Stella would be discovered.

Apparently satisfied that she'd been mistaken, the woman went to the door. Stanley mewed. Stella flushed with panic. How could she shut him up? No longer a faithful companion, he threatened to betray her. She could knock him out. He growled and on a reflex, she pressed him to her chest, thinking – or not thinking – to smother him inside her jacket, but it was zipped up.

He wriggled and she gripped him hard, blindly aware that she might crack his delicate rib cage. Fear of discovery had made her ruthless. He jerked free and let out a volley of outraged barks.

'Come out of there!' Now obviously frightened, the woman was back at the gate.

'I'm taking my dog for a walk.' Stepping away from the hedge, Stella did Jack's thing of opening your mouth and seeing what came out. What had come out was feeble.

'He's not doing much walking.' The woman nodded at the dog in her arms.

Stella gaped at Stanley as if she hadn't realized she held him. Free-falling, she opted for ground zero. 'Did you want to see Adam? Are you a... a friend?'

'*Adam*, is it?' The woman put up the hood of her duffel coat. Like a cowl, it gave her a sinister aspect.

'I just wondered.' She was making a mess of this. Jack was only metres away, but in the soundproofed basement, he wouldn't hear Stella shout for him.

'It's none of your business. More to the point, who are *you*? Why were you watching me?'

'Bella Markham.' What the *hell* had possessed her to say that?

'OK, Bella Markham, I wish you luck, he's all yours.' The woman rammed her hands in the pockets of her duffel coat and stalked down the pavement and up the steps to the towpath. The darkness swallowed her.

Stella was rooted to the spot. If there was a spy test, she'd totally failed it. She looked at Adam's house, hoping he'd not heard her. His windows were dark. She could rouse him and ask who the woman was. She obviously knew him. Stella felt reluctant to pursue it now: she needed time to think. Adam had given her the rest of his case file, yet she had a hunch – based on nothing she could put her finger on – that there was still something he wasn't telling her. No, she determined, client or not, she didn't trust Adam Honeysett. Stella shifted Stanley on to her shoulder and carried him back to the van.

★

If Stella had waited a moment more, she would have seen that someone else was out on that freezing night. A shadow passed through the lamplight at the top of the towpath steps going in the same direction along the river as the woman in the duffel coat.

Chapter Twenty-Eight

Thursday, 8 April 1987

> 'Ring a ring o' roses,
> a pocketful of murderers,
> kill one, kill two
> and they all *die!*'

The children jigged and clapped around Megan in a merry dance. She sat on her dad's bench barely aware of the blur of legs. Voices raucous, the song was punctuated by gales of laughter. Angela sang louder than the rest. Someone had scratched 'Killer' on the bench again and tried to lever off the plaque, bending the metal.

In the *Chronicle*, reporter Lucie May wrote that:

> ... schoolkids near where blonde beauty Helen Honeysett went missing acted out her murder in the playground. A boy, hands tied with a skipping rope, was taunted by his playmates. A psychological expert told us that it was 'healthy for children to express fears and anxieties through play, if monitored'. Do we want our kids playing 'murder' instead of hopscotch or marbles?

No one was monitoring these children in the park as, in failing light, they closed in on Megan Lawson, their taunts shrill.

Through her bewilderment Megan heard her mum. Springing to life, she pushed her way through the gang and ran out the gate.

'You've never been happy to let things be. Had to ruin it, didn't you? If you couldn't have it, you made sure I didn't. Satisfied now?'

Her mum was on the pavement. She was shouting at someone. Megan didn't need to go closer to recognize Aunty El. Her aunty's voice was low and because she wasn't shouting, Megan couldn't hear her reply. Her mum was waving a carving knife. *She was going to kill Aunty El.* Her mum hurled the knife on to the paving. It flapped like a bird at her aunty's feet. 'Don't come round ever again. Take that poison and leave us alone!'

The door slammed. Megan's Aunty El stayed outside. Since Helen Honeysett had gone, everything was horrible. Megan was about to call to her when she saw Mr Rowlands on the towpath steps. All the children hated him, but now they hated her more. Megan was too scared to move, no longer sure her Aunty El would protect her.

'Excuse me.' Megan thought her aunty was talking to her, but she was walking towards Mr Rowlands. They went inside his house. Megan knew he liked Daphne Merry, he was always hanging about her. When she'd told Daphne that she thought Mr Rowlands wanted to marry her, Daphne had been very cross. 'I'm not marrying anyone again, Megan. Trust no one!'

Don't come here again. Take this poison and leave us alone!

If Megan took her aunty's side she wouldn't be allowed home. Megan ran back to the park. The children had gone. She stayed on her dad's bench until it was dark and then crept home. Newspaper lay on the grass that her dad used to keep tidy. A De-Clutterer, Megan gathered up the pages. *Helen Suicide Suspect in Debt.* Steven Lawson's face was smiling at her. Megan lifted the paper and kissed him. 'Love you best, Daddy,' she whispered.

Chapter Twenty-Nine

Thursday, 7 January 2016

Natasha Latimer had asked Jack to check the area around the cottage for the ghost. At the precise time Stella was driving away from Kew Green Jack left the house and went up the steps to the towpath.

Who am I and what have I done?

The words on Latimer's computer floated across his thoughts. In her circumstances, he would ask himself that question too. Latimer didn't strike him as reflective. Had someone else put the question on her screensaver? It was too tangible an action for a phantom.

Every so often there was a gap in the clouds and a crescent moon sent light scattering on the water. Jack had begun to see Latimer's River Wall as reality so found it strange to see the scene 'live'. He couldn't know that, at the same spot on the towpath a few minutes earlier, Stella had thought something similar.

He walked until he reached the dilapidated house. He wanted to establish what had attracted Stanley there. He was alone. No sign of Daphne Merry. He lifted the gate off its latch and, avoiding the gravel, approached the porch.

There was a loud clink. Jack shone his Maglite down. He had kicked over a milk bottle. It hadn't been there earlier. Someone did live here. He righted the bottle and quickly slipped to the side out of sight of the front windows. The house was isolated, but close to Kew Green: he couldn't claim to be lost.

Searching for True Hosts, Jack made himself invisible so that he never had to justify his presence. If those he 'visited' sensed they weren't alone – many did – they couldn't substantiate their suspicions.

As True Hosts did, Jack Harmon kept watch for those who left their doors on the latch while they put recycling in the bin, or took their dog for a last walk. As well as hunting for a True Host, Bella had once said he was searching for his mother. He should ring Bella.

Through a partially glazed door, Jack tried to see beyond a corded lattice of cobwebs, but made out nothing. He felt a buzz in his pocket. He had a signal!

He had heard nothing from Bella since their – *her* – acrimonious parting outside his house. She had summoned the courage to come to him, so when they made up, he must make the first move. Perhaps she had been trying to contact him and he'd missed her messages. Bella would be drawing in her studio; he should go and see her.

Jack waited, but nothing downloaded. He keyed in *Bella Mob*. He couldn't invite her to the cottage and he was reluctant to leave the area. If you were to understand the signs that were all around, you had to immerse yourself. If he could articulate his feelings about Bella, it would take longer than a text and should be said face to face. He pressed 'Discard'. The signal had gone. He turned back to the window.

The pattern of fanning leaves on the frosted pane suggested a downstairs lavatory. There was little putty left and the wood was spongy with rot. Perfect, Jack concluded. Careful to avoid a splinter, he eased up the lower sash. Foul air drifted out.

If the face he'd seen behind the pane had heard, Jack would be entering a trap. He counted to ten. After a further ten seconds for luck he peered through the opening. A tang of urine stung his nostrils. A lavatory faced the window and beneath the sill was a sink with clunky brass taps. The wooden seat was up, a sign that the occupant was a man, unless there were two people. Jack suspected not. The house had an air of solitude.

He gathered his coat around him and climbed in. His soles scrunched on the floor. He risked the Maglite. Ceramic tiles were strewn with dried leaves. Oak and sycamore, the trees on the towpath. They must have blown in through the window when it was open. Why hadn't they been cleared up? He was thinking like Stella.

He shone his phone into the lavatory pan and recoiled. The water was black. He forced himself to look closer. The porcelain was encrusted and stained, but the water itself was clean. Stella would take a filthy lavatory in her stride. Armed with cleaning astringents, she cut a swathe through noxious odours. Daphne Merry gave her clients light and air and wherever Stella went she left the air fragrant and fresh. He liked to clean, but balked at toilets. Jack wished he'd called Stella. Ridiculous. She would only enter a house uninvited with very good reason. She wouldn't think Stanley's interest in the old house or Jack's curiosity justification. Jack entered many homes uninvited; never had he wished Stella were there, so why this time?

Jack crept to the door and, with practised dexterity, twisted the handle. The latch shifted, but the door stayed shut. *Someone was holding it from the other side.* He snatched away his hand. *Ten, nine, eight…* No held breath, no body warmth. He saw why the door wouldn't budge. It was locked from the inside.

Whoever had been in the lavatory must have left by the window. Jack whirled around. The dead leaves at his feet stirred. The open window hadn't dispelled the stench and he was relieved to stick his head out. The side path was criss-crossed with shadows. If someone was watching, they had taken care to be invisible. *Like a True Host.*

Straightening up, Jack lowered the window – against his better judgement, closing off his exit. He unlocked the door.

The faintest trickle of light allowed him to get his bearings.

There was no post by the front door. Someone had picked it up. He was puzzled to find the hall scattered with more leaves and twigs. A True Host was tidy. He turned right and moved soundlessly along the passage. As he'd anticipated, it was the kitchen. His light picked out a jar of instant coffee, a packet of Tate & Lyle granulated sugar, a kettle and a toaster clustered on a wooden work surface. Chunky beige mugs hung from a mug-tree. Jack unscrewed the lid from the coffee and tipped the jar. The granules avalanched forward. They were not stale.

A driver through centuries-old tunnels on the District line, Jack was expert on dust. From the whirls and drifts on counters – IKEA, early nineties – he guessed there'd been a cursory wipe about a month ago. It wasn't that someone lived here, only that they *existed*.

He smelled an olfactory palimpsest of roasted meats cooked there over years, he estimated. Stella would know. Something caught his eye on the floor. Set precisely at the intersection of four ceramic tiles was a tin bowl. Whoever 'existed' here had a sense of symmetry. True Hosts had an eye for balance and detail. Jack nearly dropped his Maglite. It was a dog bowl. Jack made it a policy never to be a secret guest in a house with a dog, or a cat. An animal would give him away. He should leave, but his mission pulled him on. He examined the bowl; the water was clean, which suggested that a dog hadn't recently drunk from it. Stanley left a silt of grit and specks of soil from his muzzle when he slurped. Jack sensed something dreadful in the house, the walls glistening with animal fat and window sashes strung with cobwebs weighted by dust. There had been no happiness here for a long time.

In the sitting room at the front, a standby light glowed on a television. Jack's impression of evil was strong. The steady light indicated someone living in the house.

He risked his torch. Daphne Merry would approve of the sparse furnishings: no clutter. Two armchairs and a table. An open bureau was piled with papers with compartments filled with stationery, unused envelopes, reels of sellotape, a ball of string, rulers plastic and wooden. A tin labelled 'Crème de Marrons' crammed with strips of unused staples and paper clips. The topmost paper was a British Gas bill addressed to Mr Brian Judd. Jack let out a breath; he had a name for his Host. Beneath this a water bill told 'B. Judd' he was due a rebate. Brian Judd might be defeated by cleaning, but he paid his bills by direct debit. A chill ran through him. Naturally not everyone on direct debit was a True Host. But, organized and precise, True Hosts never let anything slide. The still house held itself. A True Host lived here and, Jack realized, Stanley had sensed it.

It took too long for Jack to absorb the sound. The lavatory window had opened. Brian Judd. He would discover the door unbolted and know he had an intruder. *A True Host knew anyway.* Or did Judd have another guest? Surely he had a key to his own front door. Unless he'd forgotten it.

Jack knew that he wouldn't get to the door in time; whoever it was would be in the bathroom by now. He fiddled frantically with the window catch. It was the worst exit: he could be seen from the towpath. The catch was fused by layers of paint. Too much pressure and he could break the glass. He raced out of the room and, avoiding the dead leaves, ran nimbly to the front door.

He knew without trying it that the door was locked with a Chubb key. He had seen plenty of examples of people assiduously locking their front doors and leaving a back window open. He had never known someone to lock a room from the inside and leave by the window. The dread increased.

Stay close to the occupant. *The closer you are, the less chance they have of finding you. Empty your mind, be at one with your prey.* Jack's nerves were as poised as a mountaineer climbing a sheer face while, his back to the wall, he slid along to the lavatory. The door shielded him as it opened, slowly. Whoever it was knew they had company. A bluff of cold air from the open window blew into the hall, rustling the leaves and ushering in the stench from the lavatory. Whoever had come in had kept the window open. Why would Judd do that?

The intruder – was it Judd? – moved with the halting steps of the watchful down the passage to the kitchen. The room closest to the bathroom, it was logical to check there first. A burglar would move fast to the sitting room where there could be valuable electrical equipment.

Jack took his chance. He ducked into the closet and flung himself through the gap in the sashes. He darted down the side of the house to the towpath. Only when he was sure that he had left the dilapidated house behind did he look back. The towpath tapered into blackness. Not reassuring: a True Host would blend with the night. As Jack did.

There was a person outside Adam Honeysett's house. A woman in a duffel coat, the hood down. It was a coat that tended to make adults look like children, Jack thought. The woman had a lost look about her. She had seen him. She hurried down the alley. He gave chase. When he reached Kew Green, he couldn't see her. He meandered on to the grass: if she was behind a tree, she'd have to break cover or be discovered. He circled the trunks of the nearest trees, but she wasn't there. She must have made it to the South Circular. After that she could backtrack and be anywhere. He returned down the alley to Thames Cottages. If the duffel-coated woman was Helen Honeysett – ghost or not – she had vanished again.

Chapter Thirty

Monday, 29 February 1988

Megan had made up her mind to see Mrs Merry. She would be grown up and approach the front door. After she'd told Mrs Merry it was a special day, she could be a De-Clutterer again. When she was being a De-Clutterer, Megan forgot her dad was a murderer.

A hand yanked Megan backwards, nearly tipping her over. 'What do you want?' It was Mr Rowlands from number 1.

'I've come to see Daphne.' His fingers were like twigs.

Neville Rowlands was thirty-six, but early on had embraced middle age as a place of safety where less was expected of him. He shied away from the big-shouldered, big-haired, brash eighties.

'You mustn't call her Daphne! It's rude,' he told Megan.

Megan fixed on his salt-and-pepper brush moustache. 'I'm Daph— Mrs Merry's Assistant De-Clutterer. I've come to assist.' Megan was convinced her title would impress.

'Listen.' Neville Rowlands smelled of school soap. 'Mrs Merry has been nothing but kind to you, and what thanks has she got? Abuse from your brother, from your mother. It's your fault.' He nibbled at a finger. Helen Honeysett had called him a sweetie. Megan tried to think so too. 'When I was your age I was out from under my mother's feet. Mrs Merry has me if she needs help. Get along with you, hop it!' He squeezed his twig fingers into her shoulder.

'What is going on?' Mrs Merry was on her doorstep.

'I've come to help declutter. And the thing is today is the twenty-ninth of February. It's Helen Honeysett's real birthday, she'd be seven because it's a leap year, but really she'd be twenty-eight except she's de—'

'I've told the girl till I'm blue in the face that you're busy, Mrs Merry.' Neville Rowlands spoke over Megan. He smoothed the strands of hair trained over the beginnings of a balding pate.

'I don't need anyone's help.' Daphne Merry didn't appear to recognize Megan or Mr Rowlands. The eight-year-old had grown in the past year and her short hair (practical for De-Cluttering) was now shoulder-length. Her father's suicide and his presumed guilt for Helen Honeysett's murder had lent her a careworn aspect beyond her years. She was no longer the little girl who had touched Daphne Merry's heart. She struck her as gawky and unattractive. 'You shouldn't be here – your mother will blame me. Go and play.' She closed the door.

'I did warn you.' Neville Rowlands gave Megan a tepid smile. 'Like I said, best you run along.' He stayed on the doorstep.

Megan's legs were heavy. She blundered out of the gate, along the pavement and up the towpath steps. She stumbled beyond the watery light of the lamp-post along the path to Kew Stairs. In the sodium-stained twilight, trees were as insubstantial as wraiths. She plunged down the granite steps, slipping on mud to the river below.

'I don't need anyone's help.'

Thinking she would be decluttering, Megan had left the house without a coat. Her teeth began to chatter. Before her the black water, swaying and swirling like treacle, washed around the toes of her De-Cluttering monkey boots.

'Go and play.'

She saw herself walking through the water until it went lapping over her head, like Angie and Becky said her daddy had done. It wouldn't be freezing and full of eels like they'd said. It would be like Richmond swimming baths with her daddy holding on to her rubber ring while she swished her legs like a mermaid's tail.

'Daddy, it's me.' She gave an experimental whisper. 'Megsy.' In case, like Mrs Merry, he'd forgotten about her. A year was a lifetime to her.

Megan was struggling with an obscure sense of betrayal. Her father had drowned himself in the Thames. Mrs Merry wasn't her friend any more. With the clarity of a child forced to grow up fast, she understood that she would always be alone.

Chapter Thirty-One

Saturday, 9 January 2016

At half four in the afternoon, Stella was on her way to see Jack to discuss their next move. Embroiled with staff interviews and two estimate visits and a pile of paperwork, she hadn't seen him since Wednesday night. Stella hoisted her rucksack on to her shoulder; with the Honeysett papers under one arm and clutching her keys, she let go of Stanley's lead. As he shot away, she stamped hopelessly at the flailing leash. He skittered down the alley to Thames Cottages. Hampered, Stella couldn't run fast. Even empty-handed she couldn't catch Stanley; at full gallop he went like the wind.

She reached the narrow pavement outside the cottages. No Stanley. Dismayed, she knew he'd gone to the ramshackle house on the towpath. She allowed herself some relief; it was better than tumbling into the river or tangling with traffic on Kew Bridge.

'Excuse me?' a voice called. 'Hello there?'

An elderly woman was waving to Stella from the cottage at the other end of the terrace to Latimer's. Stella quelled a burst of impatience; with Stanley every second counted. He could after all be distracted by a squirrel or a bird by the river. She pictured him as she had first seen him, balanced on a branch above the Thames.

'I've got Whisky.' The woman was elegantly dressed in a fine wool cardigan, wool skirt and a necklace that might be pearls. Her grey hair was swept up into a coiled bun.

'I don't...' Stanley was sitting at the woman's feet, a paw raised; he was expecting a treat from her.

'Oh, there he is!' Stella flushed with relief. 'Would you mind grabbing his lead, please?' Although, pertly expectant, it looked like Stanley had no intention of going anywhere.

'Did he run off again? No titbits for you, my man!' The woman pronounced it 'orf'. She collected up the lead. 'Naughty Whisky!'

'He's not called Whisky.' Stella took the lead, and then, hearing how ungracious she sounded, said, 'Thanks for catching him.'

'I could have sworn it was...' The woman retreated into her cottage. 'I must go.'

'Thank you for catching him,' Stella said again. She heard another snippet of Terry's advice. *'Maximize the briefest exchange, that's how you get information.'*

On his access weekends and when she was a teenager, Terry had struck up conversations with strangers in cafés and pubs. Stella had been crippled with embarrassment at his probing curiosity. After his death, she realized the people he talked to weren't random strangers. Terry was never off the job. What better way to gain a suspect's trust or to worm information out of a witness than in the guise of a caring dad treating his daughter to a chocolate sundae?

'He's called Stanley. I'm Stella Darnell. My friend Jack and I are working at number 1 for Natasha Latimer. I expect you know her.' Stella was aghast at her temerity. She avoided specifics. Some of her clients considered conversing with a cleaner beneath them.

'I *do* know Natasha. A charming young lady. Her father was a broker.' Her hand on her door, the woman didn't offer her name. Stella pictured her spreadsheet. *Sybil Lofthouse. Stock Exchange – doing what? Dog?* Latimer had said she was unmarried.

'What did you do at the Stock Exchange?' She shouldn't know this. However, Sybil Lofthouse answered readily enough.

'I was an editor. We collected profit information from companies and passed it to the media for when the markets opened at eight. Or lack of profit, as the case might be.' Her eyes glittered with undisguised pleasure at the memory.

'Fascinating.' Stella had a ghastly vision of herself flattering an elderly woman to get her on side, just as Natasha Latimer had. She preferred the transparency of cleaning to the subterfuge of detection. However Sybil Lofthouse – more than one person had said Lofthouse kept herself to herself – seemed fired up by recalling her career. She took a punt. 'The early starts must be difficult with a dog.'

'I got a taxi at five a.m. sharp – no trains at that time – and got home around eight and took Dartie out. There was no one on the towpath then except joggers and dog walkers.' Sybil Lofthouse frowned and added in a confidential tone, 'If you reported an incorrect share price they flayed you alive.' With surprising suppleness – she must be late seventies – she stooped and tore out a weed from a crack in the path. 'He was creeping past the crematorium, like he does, stalking that poor Mrs Merry. I was the best editor at the exchange. I never made an error in thirty years.'

'It must have made for strong team spirit, everyone looking out for each other,' Stella hazarded.

'I kept my head down. See nothing, hear nothing. Those who got in trouble were tainted.'

'I see.' Stella agreed with Jackie that people learnt best from their mistakes.

'Sybil Lofthouse. Next time I see you I might find a little something to offer Whisky, if he's a good boy.' She wagged a finger at Stanley.

Stella didn't correct her again. She was perturbed at how smoothly Terry's tactic had worked. *Open Sesame.* Bringing up the Stock Exchange, as Latimer had known, had oiled the wheels, and Stella capitalized on it: 'Were you living here when Helen Honeysett went missing?'

Sybil Lofthouse's lips tightened a fraction. Had Stella not been forensically aware, she would've missed it. 'I was.'

'It must have been a shock.' A dead-end statement. Jack would ask an open question.

'I went the other way, I didn't see her. I didn't look down at Kew Stairs; my dog stayed on his lead. Then back, cocoa and bed.' Sybil Lofthouse retreated into her house. 'Goodbye, Whisky.' Tipping a hand at Stanley, she shut the door. Stella had been ticked off about dropping Stanley's lead. She had pushed it too far.

She trotted Stanley into the little park beyond the hedge and felt Steven Lawson's bench for damp before sitting down on it. Before going to see Jack, while it was fresh, she would record her meeting with Lofthouse in her Filofax.

'I never made an error in thirty years.'

Sybil Lofthouse had meant her work at the Stock Exchange, but was it true of everything she did? So far Honeysett's killer had committed the perfect murder. It was a stretch to number the thin, reclusive woman as a suspect. Still, Stella was keeping an open mind.

Chapter Thirty-Two

Monday, 29 February 1988

> '*Happy birthday to you,*
> *Happy birthday to you,*
> *Happy birthday, dear Mrs Hon— Helen,*
> *Happy birth-day to you!*

'It's me, Megan, by the way...' the little girl sang under her breath.

Megan let Smudge's lead dangle, and imagined the dog bounding off, paws splashing on the muddy track. Smudge darted back to her – her dad said he did it to report 'on progress' – and then with a toss of the head was off delving into bushes on the riverbank.

At four in the afternoon, the grey of the sky met the grey of the river and the houses on Strand on the Green on the far bank dissolved into an indistinct mass.

The bitter cold forced reality upon her. Mrs Honeysett wasn't having a real birthday – today was the day she'd been born – because she was dead. Daddy had been dead for over a year. He'd missed his birthday last year. Smudge had gone to live in a proper home with a mummy, a daddy and two girls who, her mum said, would 'love him as much as we do'. No one else could love Smudge like she did. She hoped he was somewhere nice.

Megan wrestled with the dilemma that had weighed on her

since Steven Lawson's death the year before. Traipsing along the empty towpath, she feared that, because her father had murdered Helen Honeysett, he was in Hell. She didn't want him to be alone, so she put Smudge in there with him. Except Smudge was innocent and she knew from school that the innocent went up to Heaven in white dresses. And Smudge wasn't dead, but living in a proper home.

Outside Mortlake Crematorium was a long black car. It was like the car they had used for her dad. *'Say goodbye to Daddy.'* Garry hadn't watched the huge box go behind a curtain, but Megan had promised her dad that when she was frightened she would never blink and look away so she hadn't missed a thing. *'Murderer. Kill. Kill. Kill!'*

Megan heard footsteps. *Smudge.* She whisked around. There was a person coming along the towpath. As they got closer, she realized it was Mr Rowlands again. She hesitated, hopeful that Mrs Merry was with him because he had said they were friends now. He was on his own. Something dangled from his hand. It was a dog lead. Megan looked for his dog but couldn't see it. He was watching her, his eyes boring into her. Megan was engulfed in prickling fear.

Quickly, she ran to the gate into the crematorium grounds and slipped through. She passed the sign that dogs weren't allowed, but luckily Smudge was invisible. She ran for her life, full pelt across the damp grass.

She heard music, sonorous and haunting, and she imagined she was running towards her dad.

'Love you, Megsy.'

She ran faster. As she reached the gravel drive in front of the building, the chapel doors were closed and the music – Samuel Barber's *Adagio for Strings* – faded.

Behind her damp fog drifted up from the river. She stared unbelieving. The long black car was rolling towards her. Silent and smooth, the fender gleaming. Megan shouted, but her throat felt squeezed tight and nothing came out.

Chapter Thirty-Three

Saturday, 9 January 2016

Grey clouds over the Thames hastened the impending night. A murky flat light cast no shadow, all was one-dimensional and monochrome. Dank air would penetrate the warmest clothing. The water had receded exposing the Kew Stairs and the foreshore littered with plastic bottles, rags, fragments of broken metal, iron and glass. Oozing mud, like quicksand, would suck the unwitting into its depths, a fathomless grave of bones and lost treasures.

Jack and Stella paused at the top of the granite steps. Stanley lifted a leg against a rotting post. This being the reason they were out, they could now go back to Natasha Latimer's cottage and debrief on the Honeysett case.

'You were going to ask me to come with you to talk to Adam Honeysett.' Jack was aggrieved that Stella had again seen the man he had dubbed the Grieving Widower without him. He went down the steps and stopped. In the mephitic gloom, a bouquet of chrysanthemums had been tied to the trunk of an oak sapling. The stems, wrapped in cellophane, were soaked by many tides, the heads bleached whitish-brown.

'I bumped into him here.' Stella had already told him this.

'In the dark? By yourself?' Jack was ashamed for being peevish.

'Stanley was here. I thought you were with Bella.'

'I wasn't... Stella, he's a suspect, the *main* suspect. You shouldn't be alone with him.' He hadn't meant to sound reproving.

'I asked him why he didn't mention he was having an affair. He said he didn't want to prejudice us against him. He threatened to sack us if we didn't trust him.'

'I *am* prejudiced now! Fishy, don't you think?' There was a card on the bouquet.

'For S. Loving you. Bx'.

'Everyone's fishy. Daphne Merry made no secret to you of disliking Helen Honeysett. Sybil Lofthouse shut the door when I brought up the subject. However, in 1987 she did have a dog – called Dartie – and did go to the towpath. If Helen Honeysett was pushed into the river, either of them could have done it. Or both. There's Neville Rowlands who, if Natasha Latimer's to be believed, may be dead. But even so he could have done it.'

'Montague Dartie married Winifred Forsyte.' Jack reread the dedication card; evening dew had blurred the biro ink. Had someone died here? How? Murder? Heart attack?

'Is she a client?' Stella asked.

'Winifred Forsyte? No, she's in *The Forsyte Saga*.'

'Is that related to this case?

'No! It's cos you mentioned the dog called Dartie... Oh, never mind. It's amazing you got Sybil Lofthouse to talk.' Jack was seriously impressed.

'Stanley helped. People talk to you if you have a dog.'

Having a dog had got Stella talking to people too.

A lavender bush, leaves muted grey in the dusk, flourished on the bank. Jack pinched a sprig between his fingers. The fragrance propelled him back to his mother's garden – his garden. Sometimes he fancied he saw her ghost wandering between the beds, trailing fingers caressing a swathe of Michaelmas daisies. His reverie was broken by a shout from the beach below.

'Having a good gawp, are you?' A woman came up the steps. 'You lot don't give up, do you! No respect for folk trying to live their lives. We're a story to sell your dirty rags!' Her voice carried across the water.

She clasped a fresh bunch of chrysanthemums. Jack saw a flash of silver and instinctively flinched. But it wasn't a knife; the woman snipped the twine around the bouquet with a pair of scissors. 'Bx'. Jack knew who she was and why she was there. Bette Lawson had come to the steps down which, in 1987, her husband Steven had walked to the river and drowned.

'I'm sorry. We were waiting for Stanley to...' Jack shut himself up and climbed back to the bank.

'Don't fob me off with your shit!'

Stella was waiting in the pool of light by the steps to Thames Cottages.

Looking back down the Kew Stairs, Jack saw Bette Lawson tying a fresh bunch of flowers to the oak sapling. Oak, the harbinger of wisdom. Jack carried an acorn as a talisman against mortality and illness. It was too late for Steven Lawson.

'I met her last night when I was with Adam. She was reasonably friendly; I want to keep it that way.' Stella opened the microwave and placed two shepherd's pies inside the oven. Hoping for a nice bone, Stanley was regarding Stella with a baleful glare.

She gave a slight nod; he knew she'd seen how sparkling clean he'd made it. Jack felt faint pleasure. Although she'd never told him, Jack knew from Jackie that Stella considered him her best cleaner.

He had spent the day cleaning the cottage. He was methodical, doing one type of task at a time. He washed skirting boards, walls, wainscots and window sills from the attic to the ground floor. He vacuumed and dusted and polished. He left the basement until last.

Like Claudia, Jack had expected to encounter phantoms in Latimer's newly dug basement. As in the home of a True Host, he was alive to the faintest presence.

He dismissed typical symptoms reported in haunted houses. Apparitions flitting out of the corner of an eye; mist in the room not explained by a shaft of sunlight or a boiling kettle. Strands of floating gossamer; ornaments that vanished and reappeared elsewhere or were found smashed to bits. Ghosts were outsiders; they eschewed stereotypical means of making their presence – or absence – felt. A fused light bulb, a drop in temperature or the creaking reported by Latimer were expressions of people's fears and terrors rather than proof of phantoms. A thorough cleanse wouldn't relieve Latimer of her demons, but would give him an intimate connection to the building. If Helen Honeysett had chosen to haunt the cavernous basement, he would find her.

Jack had relocated a glass figurine from the coffee table in the sitting room to the mantelpiece, rearranged cubes of coloured plastic and adjusted a battalion of toy grenadiers in the play-room. He took photographs that captured the position of each soldier. He moved the coffee table centimetres to the right. Inspecting at the end of the day, he was satisfied that nothing had moved. He was alone.

At intervals as he cleaned, although there was no signal, he had checked for a text from Bella. Pointless: she'd told him once that if she thought someone wanted to leave her, she wiped them from her life as she erased a pencil sketch of a plant if it was inaccurate or she wanted to move it to another part of her drawing. Bella would rub him out and start again. Like one of her specimens, he was extinct.

After he had finished cleaning Jack had flopped on the lips sofa and mulled disconsolately on what to have for supper. He had forgotten to shop and only had the milk Daphne Merry and Stella had brought him. He'd gone off milk. It was for babies. He reflected again on how soulless was the space Latimer had carved out from deep in the foundations. The sparse industrial aspect suggested that the objective of achieving a yawning sub-terranean extension took precedence over creating a cosy room.

He had been happy when the lights dimmed and Stella's face

appeared on the River Wall. She was holding the shepherd's pies and a tin of 'fresh' petits pois. He had taken them off her and gone with her to the towpath to get Stanley to pee.

'Show me that thing on the computer,' Stella said. Supper finished, they were side by side on the sofa.

Who am I and what have I done? Jack had forgotten he'd told Stella about Latimer's question. He got off the sofa and went to the steel Magic Box. He pulled open the steel office and jiggled the mouse. Nothing happened. He banged the mouse on the desk.

'Careful, you'll break it.' Stella stayed his hand. He hadn't noticed her get up. Her skin felt warm and soft. 'You've turned off the machine.'

'I didn't!' he snapped. Stanley was watching him, tail down. Jack spoke in an unnaturally bright voice to reassure him. 'I cleaned around it today. It was off then too.' He didn't know why he was tense.

'Has there been a power cut?' Stella was reasonable.

'I don't think so.'

'The microwave clock was showing the correct time, but it's probably some smart sort that knows the time whatever.' Stella wandered back to the sofa. 'The question is probably to do with this basement. After all the fuss from neighbours, maybe Latimer regrets what she did.'

'She didn't sound regretful the other night,' Jack said. 'This sounds like a threat.' He shivered. 'Natasha Latimer mightn't have written it.'

'Who else could have? Surely not Claudia, she's all about peace and love.' Stella was losing interest. The Honeysett case had taken over.

Jack pulled a face. 'The ghost?' He looked for his coat to put on, but it wasn't on the back of the sofa where he was sure he'd left it.

'Do ghosts use computers?' Jack silently applauded Stella for trying. 'Latimer only said about squeaking and creaking in the house. It could be an intruder. It's a matter for the police.'

Jack felt his skin crawl. It wouldn't be the first time a True Host had turned the tables on him. 'Did you see my coat when we came in?'

'It's over there, by that sandpit.' She waved an arm and the glass panel slid back.

Jack went through to the fake playroom. His coat was slung over the back of a chair he'd put by the sandpit. He remembered placing it there now. He put it on.

'Going by this evening, it's going to be hard to get Bette Lawson to talk to us.' Stella had opened her bag and was sorting through the bundle of Honeysett papers the Grieving Widower had given her. 'She wants to be left alone.'

'Especially if she thinks we suspect her husband.'

'It's telling his own daughter told the police she'd seen him with Honeysett.'

'Daughters can be wrong about their dads.'

'Yes, they can.' Stella went quiet.

Jack hadn't meant to remind Stella of her own unsatisfactory relationship with her father. She had really only got to know him after his death. He pulled his cigarette case from his coat, assembled tobacco and papers on his lap and began to roll a cigarette.

There was a noise. Jack jumped up, knocking over Stella's mug and spilling dregs of tea on to the liquid-resistant flooring. In the distance, through the glass panels, Jack saw Stanley. He was scrabbling at the white brick wall. He must have gone there when Jack fetched his coat.

'Enough!' Stella commanded. Stanley ignored her. Sighing, she got up and went to him, the glass panels swishing open for her.

Jack slipped the completed cigarette into his case and closed it. He followed Stella to the end of the basement.

'He might have found something,' he said.

'Maybe he wants another pee.'

'The garden's up there.' Jack pointed up at the green skylights. He put his hand to his mouth, he wasn't meant to know about the garden. No, it was okay, he could have been there. Besides it was obvious that the garden was above them.

'He forgets about stairs.' Then Stella exclaimed: 'There's a door!' Her surprise made Stanley stop scrabbling. He watched her eagerly. She pushed on the wall. 'It's moving!' she gasped. A slab of brick of about a metre square opened inwards and a stale smell drifted in from the darkness. Jack didn't need Stella or Stanley's preternatural olfactory sense to identify the stink of river mud. The temperature dropped.

Before Jack could stop her, Stella ducked through the opening. He went in after her. In light from the basement he made out a crude concrete ceiling.

The light went out. A negative impression of the ceiling flashed across Jack's retina and then dissolved to black.

'What happened?' He tottered and fell against cold brick.

'The basement lights respond to heat and movement. We're not there so they've gone off,' Stella reminded him. 'This must be the emergency exit.'

'Hardly a quick getaway.'

'Odd Latimer didn't show this to us.' Stanley started growling. 'Hang on, I've found a switch.'

A dirty bulb illuminated the ceiling. Instinctively Jack and Stella gravitated to each other. On a platform, gleaming bright yellow, was a mechanical digger.

Chapter Thirty-Four

Megan felt warmth between her legs and then cold, a sensation from early childhood. She had wet herself. If she was dead, she didn't care.

'Megsy!'

'What?' *Daddy!*

'Get up. It's filthy. Get *up*!' Hands grabbed her, snatching ineffectually at her school blouse. She sat up. The long black car had gone. A flock of geese flew overhead honking and dipped behind the roof of the crematorium. If she could hear, she couldn't be dead.

She clambered up. Her skirt was streaked with mud and had a damp patch. She bashed at it, but made it worse. Her knickers hung loose and sopping and her socks were round her ankles. Helen Honeysett had run along the towpath, she was running away from Daddy. When he caught up with her, he would have been kind.

'You shouldn't be here by yourself. Not at all! What if you'd been murdered like the lady? It's dangerous!' Garry stormed at her. 'The murderer is out here somewhere.' To Megan's astonishment her brother looked afraid. She tried to reassure him.

'He's not, Garry. The danger is gone.' *The murderer went into the river and drowned.*

Garry Lawson knew what his sister was thinking. 'You've got

to stop this. What would Mum do if you was murdered?' His voice was hollow over the darkening crematorium lawns.

'I was taking Smu—' The newspaper her mum had thrown at Aunty El said her dad liked Helen Honeysett more than his family. With no money of his own, he wanted to have hers. Megan faltered. Last night in bed, she'd tried to think what her dad looked like and only knew in the end because she found his picture in the paper.

'Come home. Ugh, you stink!' He took her hand like her dad used to. Like Garry used to. 'Mum will run a bath and stick your clothes in the wash.'

Megan Lawson wrestled with a double bind that would haunt her for years. She had loved her dad, but he was bad because, like her Aunty El and Angela and everyone said, he was a murderer. Her mum and Garry said he wasn't a murderer and he was good. If she thought that a murderer was good, then she must be bad. If she was bad she would go to Hell. If her dad and Smudge were there that would be all right.

Megan glanced over her shoulder. Mr Rowlands was there. Except Mr Rowlands didn't have a walking stick. 'Gal.' She tried to free her hand.

Garry hurried her along. When they reached Thames Cottages, she started to tell him that Smudge was with their dad, but suddenly she doubted it was true.

Chapter Thirty-Five

Sunday, 10 January 2016

'Call me when you get this message, please.' Keys in hand, Stella was outside her mum's front door. Since the night before when she and Jack had found a small JCB digger in Natasha Latimer's basement, Stella had been trying to reach her to ask why it was there. Latimer hadn't rung back.

'It's me-ee,' Stella called as she stepped into the hall.

Who is me? She waited to hear the ritual response. Nothing. The doors – her old bedroom, her mum's room, bathroom and toilet – were closed. Suzie kept them open to light the passage. This had been a point of contention for the teenaged Stella who, as she still did, prized privacy. Stella switched on the light and saw that the carpet and skirting boards remained spotless. Jackie said that incredibly Suzie approved of Stephanie Benson, the new cleaner.

She and her mum were going to take Stanley to Richmond Park: a regular outing dating from when Suzie had been depressed and had refused to go out at all. Since Stella had given her a job at Clean Slate, Suzie's spirits had lifted and she thought nothing of flying to see her son in Australia. Maybe Richmond Park was now run of the mill and the plan had slipped her mum's mind. From feeling mildly frustrated at losing an afternoon on the Honeysett case, Stella was also disappointed Suzie had gone out. When her mum wasn't complaining about Terry, she was good company.

Her mum had probably popped downstairs for a paper or milk. As she thought this, Stella was struck by the seemingly most unlikely notion that Suzie had gone to see her brother Dale in Sydney. She had long ago stopped being certain of her mother's movements, her likes and dislikes. It was quite possible that having conquered some kind of agoraphobia, her mum had gone off to Australia on a whim with a bandaged ankle.

'It's me,' she repeated as she opened the living-room door. Stanley bolted past her and came to a standstill on the carpet.

At first Stella thought the living room was empty – of her mum – but alarmingly of everything. Stanley shouldn't be able to sit where he was sitting. Her mum's armchair should be there.

Suzie's collection of playing cards – going back fifty years – was gone from the shelf above the TV. The dancing porcelain man and women in eighteenth-century costume were no longer on the mantelpiece. Her mum's armchair was actually still there, it had moved to where the little table should be. Where was the ashtray from Kent's Cavern, bought in Devon on one of the last family holidays they'd taken before they moved to Barons Court? Of the four dining chairs her mum had bought 'for a snip' after the divorce, there were two left. The sofa had been shifted from the wall by the window to opposite the television. Not a fan of art or objects that gathered dust and got in the way of a swift polish, Stella was nevertheless relieved that the print of Constable's *Hay Wain*, her dad's favourite painting that her mum had laid claim to, remained above the fire. Through the hatch to the kitchen she saw that her wish that her mum would keep less stuff on the counters had come true. But for the kettle and toaster, the worktops were clear, and gleaming. Stephanie Benson was indeed good. Dread stirred in her stomach. It wasn't just that the flat was clean. It had been stripped of practically all of Suzie's personal possessions. Stella's unexpressed fear took hold. Bored and frustrated at being marooned with a sprained ankle, her mum had decided to up sticks (literally) to Sydney and sublet her flat. She had left Stella behind.

Her thoughts racing, she didn't hear the front door and jumped when a voice exclaimed, 'There you are!'

Pulling off leather gloves and unwinding a Burberry check cashmere scarf bought duty-free at Heathrow, Suzie Darnell asked as if it were Stella who was late.

'I thought you'd gone...' Now that her mum was in front of her, holding a half-pint of milk, Stella's idea of emigration appeared ridiculous.

'What do you think?' Suzie flapped her scarf at the room and crowed, 'I'm a new woman!'

'It wasn't on the job sheet,' Stella muttered huskily.

'What job sheet?' Suzie was lurching and limping around the room, swooping and dipping as if doing some outlandish dance. Reliant now on one crutch, she flourished it. 'Relish the space that's been liberated, breathe the air, bathe in the light!' Suzie did a twirl where the armchair had been. Excited by the 'liberated space', Stanley cavorted joyously around Suzie. 'Come and see the rest! Not that there *is* anything to see, that's the point.'

Suzie took Stella to what had been – and still was if she had a reason to stay – Stella's bedroom. It was where her brother stayed when he visited. As Clean Slate's first office it had once housed files, a printer, shredder and computer. Now it was as bare as a nun's cell.

'Where are the photo albums and my dolls?' At any other time, Stella would have been pleased to see her dolls – never played with – had gone. 'And that little Sydney Opera House Dale gave you?' Stella went along to her mum's bedroom. There was nothing on the shelves. The model she had done of the family dog when she was six – a lump of clay with no likeness to any animal that Stella never understood why her mum kept – was missing.

'The cleaner was meant to do what Jack did.' In her confusion, Stella couldn't think of the woman's name. She returned to the living room and was strangely disorientated by the space. She sat disconsolately on the edge of the sofa. She had seen the flat go through a drastic change before. When Jack had first cleaned, he had persuaded Suzie to get rid of the towers of newspapers her mum had hoarded from when they moved there in 1973. Somehow he'd made it feel like the home she had shared with her parents. Jackie said Jack had the knack of transforming the starkest place into a home. Now her mum's flat was as bare and unfriendly as it had been on the day they moved there. Stella was reminded of Natasha Latimer's basement. Although a fan of straight lines and clean empty surfaces, she felt a stranger in a place she knew well. Stella dimly understood that her irrational fear that her mum had emigrated had come from the fact that it did look as if she no longer lived here. There was no trace of her.

'Where is everything?'

'Banished!' Her mother spun about on her good ankle. 'Look at me, light as a feather.' She windmilled her arms.

'She shouldn't have done this without permission.' Stephanie Benson, that was her name.

'She had *my* permission!' Suzie cast herself on to the sofa beside Stella.

'Stephanie Benson's remit doesn't cover carrying heavy furniture. If she had injured herself, she could sue for breach of contract. It wasn't fair to ask her.' Stella made herself breathe as Jackie would advise. The last time she had felt like this was when she found a body while she was cleaning. In fact she felt worse.

'Stephanie. Sweet thing although she's a bit doleful. Shifty too. Good cleaner, I grant you. But then all this freed space makes cleaning a doddle.' Suzie fiddled with a lock of hair, girlishly. 'Zigzagging increases tension. She's cleared a straight path. Not that it's why I hired her.' Suzie stretched out her bandaged ankle while her other foot rested on one of four dents in the pile where the legs of her other armchair had been. Stella spotted tracks from Stephanie Benson's vacuuming.

'It's not why you hired who?' Stella felt foreboding.

'Daphne Merry,' Suzie crowed happily.

'Who's Daphne Merry?' Oh God. Stella pictured her spreadsheet: *Daphne Merry (Declutterer) Dog (Name?)*. Merry lived at number 3 Thames Cottages and had brought Jack cake. It was Daphne Merry who had found out that Steven Lawson's daughter had seen him following Helen Honeysett to the river. Merry had brought back the Honeysetts' dog Baxter the night Helen Honeysett vanished.

Suzie beamed at Stella. 'She lives next door to your victim!'

'She's not my vic— Mum, you asked Daphne Merry to declutter?' Stella felt as if her worlds were colliding.

'It's not only Lucille May-Every-Time who can play detective. I don't "play" – I was married to one. I know how to get the canary singing. You gain the suspect's trust and once they're putty in your hands apply the palette knife.' She clapped her hands in the uncluttered air. 'I went undercover!'

Suzie had told Jack that she had been happiest in the early days of her marriage when Terry shared his cases with her. *Before he left her*. As it was her mum who left her dad, Stella had assumed this wasn't true.

'Daphne Merry isn't a suspect,' Stella retorted, although she and Jack had agreed to keep an open mind. Terry said everyone was a suspect unless they were dead at the time of the murder.

'Everyone's a suspect unless they're dead at the time of the murder,' Suzie announced. 'The subject came up naturally, or so Daphne thought!'

'How could the subject of a dead estate agent come up naturally when Merry was here to declutter?' They might hate each other, but Lucie May and her mum were similar: they scattered obstacles in their wake as they chased a goal.

'I said I'd seen her mentioned in one of those dreadfully penned articles by Citizen Kane on the Honeysett girl. I left it there and burbled about being fascinated that Merry entered people's homes and expunged their rubbish. She didn't take long to spill!' Suzie snatched up a cushion and hugged it to her chest.

'She called Honeysett "feckless". Lives and dies by the sword does our Daphne. No prisoners cluttering her jail. Adroit. She never suggested I throw something away, she guided me towards the decision. It means, should I wish to, I can't blame her.' She tapped the cushion rapidly. 'I liked her.' An express touch-typist, her mum often tapped out words as she talked. Jack said it was a sign of intelligence: Suzie needed stimulation or she got bored. The last bit Stella agreed with.

Regardless of Suzie's mood or dubious method, Stella had to admit Suzie had found a way to interrogate a suspect. To date Stella hadn't intentionally interviewed any of the residents of Thames Cottages. Stanley had led her to Sybil Lofthouse. Jack – and now Suzie – had befriended Daphne Merry and Stella had twice been ambushed by Adam Honeysett. Nevertheless, between her and Jack, they had met nearly everyone living in the street when Honeysett vanished. They had yet to find Neville Rowlands – dead or alive – and Megan Lawson and to interview Bette and Garry Lawson. Stella didn't count Natasha Latimer, being born the same year as a crime was a watertight alibi.

Meanwhile, her mum had only had the file for the time it had taken Stella to cook an omelette, eat it and clear up, but she'd gained a grasp on the case and grilled a suspect. Stella relented. 'Did you learn anything else from Daphne Merry?'

'She carries a sadness. In that way she's similar to Stephanie Whatsit. Their burdens dictate their demeanour,' her mum intoned like a fortune teller. 'It goes beyond Honeysett's disappearance, far back into the mists of time.'

'How do you know?' Suzie and Lucie May both let fanciful theories get in the way of fact.

'When I said I had a daughter – that's you – Merry nodded as if she had one, yet there was no mention in your file of family. In 1987 she was living alone. Where is this daughter, I thought?'

'Actually I can tell you—'

'She said it was cruel to leave a baby to cry. We never let you cry.' Her mum pursed her lips. 'Or I didn't, your dad wasn't there.

That's what made you cry.' She patted the cushion complacently. 'I teased it out of her.'

Stella resisted saying what Jackie had told her about Daphne Merry's daughter dying. It would spoil her mum's triumph.

'Daphne was coming back from a holiday in France with her husband and their seven-year-old girl. It was early in the morning, Charles Merry had been driving all night, he refused to let her take a turn at the wheel although she said she was a better driver than he was. She begged him, but he refused even to take a break; he was determined to get the early ferry. Which they did. Daphne and her little girl – she never told me her name and I was far too sensitive to pry – were asleep in the back. The next thing Daphne knew, she was hanging upside down by her seat belt on the A23 at some place called Pyecombe. Her husband was crushed by the steering column, he died of internal bleeding at the Royal Sussex County – where Terry was taken – and her little girl was thrown out of the car. She died instantly.' Suzie's hands lay still on the cushion. 'She looked asleep. It wasn't until the police arrived that Daphne realized she was dead.'

'Was he driving on the wrong side of the road?' Stella asked at last.

'Police think he fell asleep. They swerved off the road at seventy-five miles an hour and hit a tree.'

'What did she say about Helen Honeysett?'

'You know that Daphne found their dog on the towpath. She brought it to Adam Honeysett, but of course he was out with his mistress.'

'How do you know about the mistr—' But Stella didn't need to ask. Daphne Merry had indeed been putty in her mother's hands.

'... she put a note through his door saying she had the dog. It was called Baxter, would you believe! Daft name for a dog.'

'Didn't she think it odd when Adam Honeysett didn't come asking for the dog?' Stella didn't think Baxter was any dafter as a name than Stanley. His name hadn't been her choice.

'She said they were a young couple and often out. She would hear the dog barking when it was left alone in the house. She said she wasn't one to judge. I should coco! She bristled with disapproval. I gathered she hates carelessness. It's an obsession.'

'I suppose if you're a declutterer, you would hate carelessness,' Stella pondered.

'More likely the one led to the other. Like you and cleaning. After you had that flu when you were fourteen you became a Finickety Fanny with a duster.' Suzie fussed Stanley's ears. 'Then you started Clean Slate.'

'Sybil Lofthouse had a dog.' Stella felt an obscure need to demonstrate that she too had been interviewing suspects. 'The killer might not have had an accomplice who disposed of the body. Helen Honeysett would have trusted Merry and Lofthouse.'

Her mum shook her head. 'I read that Lofthouse was in bed when Honeysett vanished. She had to be up early.'

Stella tried to remember what Sybil Lofthouse had said. She would check the notes she had made after meeting her. Something about that meeting nagged her.

Suzie banged the cushion. 'According to your file, Lofthouse was fifty in 1987.'

'That's not old.' Stella would be fifty in about seven months. It was just another birthday.

'Fifty then was today's seventy. Seventy is the new forty-five.'

Stella hadn't heard this. Suzie would be seventy this year (*No fuss, no party!*) and was as defiant about ageing as Lucie May, whose age was a movable feast. Stella viewed her mum as twenty-seven, the age she had been when Stella's parents separated.

Stella said, 'Sybil Lofthouse kept calling Stanley Whisky.'

'It would have been her dog's name. Old people get confused.' Suzie implied that ageing was outside her own experience. 'You want me 'umble opinion, me learned lud, your killer is the plumber's wife!'

★

Stella got in the lift outside her mum's flat. She'd been disappointed that Suzie had changed her mind about going out. Having the flat decluttered seemed to have tired her out.

As the mechanism creaked and jangled its way downwards, Stella wondered again why Natasha Latimer had a JCB digger walled into a vault in her basement. Latimer was the second client who'd omitted information from a brief. The digger wasn't critical, but it was odd she'd not shown them. When the lift reached the lobby, Stella recalled a comment her mum had made when she came back with the milk. Stella took the lift back up to the top floor and opened the flat door. Stella felt her heart flip. Her mum was hunched on the sofa, clasping the cushion; she seemed to have shrunk. In the bright and airy room she looked lost.

'Mum.' Stanley sniffed his way along the skirting. Without the sofa, he had an uninterrupted path. 'You called Stephanie Benson shifty. What did you mean?' Of course the cleaner wouldn't be good enough.

'Terry died five years ago today.'

Stella stopped in the middle of the carpet. 'I didn't remember.' She did remember the moment when she was told. She had jotted the words the policeman said in the margins of a cleaning equipment catalogue as if they'd make more sense that way.

'... failed revive... dead on arrival...'

Outside the sun had gone in. The sky was grey, the glass flecked with darts of rain. As well that they hadn't gone to Richmond Park.

'I had a look at her application.'

Your father is dead.

'Sorry?' Stella stared at her mother.

'Stephanie Benson. I checked the details in the database.'

'That's confidential!' Stella groaned. 'Normally a client wouldn't see the database.'

'Pish posh. I input her details myself!' Suzie swatted the air with her crutch. 'Stephanie put that she'd spent twenty years in Sydney. I told her I loved Sydney, the Harbour Bridge, opera house, Abbey's bookshop and best of all Dale's restaurant. She said she loved them too.' Suzie bashed the cushion. 'Dale has never heard of her.'

'Australia's a big country, why should he know her?' Suzie's injured ankle was forcing her to spend too much time thinking. Perhaps a trip to see Dale was the answer.

'Their population's smaller than the UK. Dale's like you, he knows everyone!' Suzie Darnell seemed pleased by this idea. 'Whatever Stephanie was doing for twenty years, it wasn't at that address. She made it up. The question is, why?'

'Mum, you don't know that.' Stella was still fazed by the decluttered living room.

'She couldn't recall where she'd lived.'

'Maybe she didn't want to say. Our handbook discourages personal conversation with clients.'

'It encourages *polite* conversation. All she had to do was say where it was. No, she's never lived there.' There was no shifting her mum once her mind was made up.

'Jackie would have checked her references.' Stella hadn't forgotten she'd once discovered that two solid-sounding referees didn't exist; it wouldn't happen again. Jackie was training Beverly to chase up references. This made Stella nervous because Beverly trusted everyone. Had Benson's check been one of Beverly's? 'If she's cleaning how you like...' No matter how good Benson was or that Suzie actually liked her, no one worked for Clean Slate if they had lied in their application. *No one except Jack.* Clean Slate entered people's homes, they had to be trustworthy. Stella put from her mind that Jack, while not utterly trustworthy – it was he who'd provided the fictional references – was her best cleaner.

'She's hiding something.' The fortune-teller voice again.

'I'll clean until your ankle's better,' Stella decided.

'I want Stephanie!' her mum exclaimed.

'But I thought—'

'How will I find out her secret? Loose ends are a detective's nightmare. Your father learnt that the hard way.' Her fingers busied over the cushion.

'Mum, it's not ethical—' Was it really five years since her dad died?

Your father is dead. The words still baffled her.

'It's for her own good. It corrodes the soul to be inauthentic.' Suzie gave a peremptory sniff and her fingers fluttered to a stop on the cushion.

'Are you OK with what Daphne Merry's done?' Her mum had thrown out pictures of herself as a girl. Stella had an album Suzie had made for her and pictures her dad had taken of her up until the age of seven after which he'd seen less of her. But now there were no photographs of her grandparents or of Suzie.

'I can't take clutter with me.' Suzie stretched out her leg and contemplated her bandaged ankle. 'Like Daphne said, you and Dale won't want to take it with you either.' With the agility of a forty-five-year-old, Suzie Darnell sprang from the sofa. She zigzagged across the carpet to the kitchen.

She said in a small voice, 'Funny, with no clutter you don't know who you are.'

Chapter Thirty-Six

Sunday, 10 January 2016

HELEN SUSPECT BANKRUPT
By Lucie May

The prime suspect in the disappearance of Helen Honeysett (pictured left) was facing bankruptcy. Plumber Steven Lawson's (35) final job before drowning himself in the Thames and abandoning his wife and children was to fit a washing machine that subsequently leaked. Ankle-deep on her puddling lino housewife Shirley Falcon told us, 'Steve was charming. I'm sorry he's passed, but how am I meant to get the washing done?'

Customers told us of boilers failing to ignite and stone-cold radiators after Lawson had 'fixed' them. Examples of shoddy workmanship have 'flooded' our post bag. Contemplating the water, Mrs Falcon cried, 'If he's a cold-blooded killer, he'll never sort this out now.'

His business 'leaking' customers and with a family to support, Lawson was desperate. (Pictured below.) He relished the innocent attention of the pretty blonde estate agent (26), a glamour model before she sold houses. Gorgeous Helen, described by friends and family as loved by all who knew her, made Lawson feel special.

Every day, Rosemary Honeysett (inset pic) grieves for her lost daughter; with no body, she is deprived of a funeral while Lawson got a send-off at Mortlake Crematorium (left).

Detective Inspector Ian Harper told us, 'Helen's disappearance is being treated as a missing person's inquiry at this stage. This is a direct appeal: Helen, if you are watching, please do make contact with police to tell us you are OK.'

Lucie's piece was heavily biased towards the plumber as the culprit. Jack had noticed this with all her articles. Crude adjectives like 'pretty' and 'gorgeous' were par for Lucie's course, but the level of venom towards a man who hadn't been charged with murder and had since committed suicide was harsh even for Lucie. Constrained by legal implications, she had been content with heavy hints that Steven Lawson ('Lawson') was guilty.

Adept at working heart-strings Lucie had portrayed a flirtatious man as careless of his work and his family. Even his good looks played against him. Lucie often claimed to shine a laser beam on the truth. In fact she concocted the 'truth' first. She spared nothing and nobody in pursuit of a story. Lucie disliked her copy being 'ripped to shreds' by her 'septic tank of an editor'; she had needed a cool-headed editor for this story. His heart missing a beat, Jack considered that Lucie May was one person you didn't want as an enemy.

In the photograph accompanying Lucie's article, he could see that the comparison to Paul Young was justified. Steven was better looking even. In Honeysett's original file, Jack had seen a shot of a grim-faced Steven Lawson leaving Richmond Police Station where he had been questioned. The snap of him smiling was designed to underline a 'devil-may-care' attitude to life, and to death. A visual cue to direct the reader to his unassailable guilt. Perhaps he was guilty.

A smaller shot showed the hearse with Lawson's coffin under the arch outside the crematorium chapel. Jack had been inside the art deco building for more than one funeral – including Stella's father's. Three years earlier he had got trapped in the 'locked-down' grounds when Margaret Thatcher's coffin arrived, the hearse escorted by police outriders. Risking arrest, he'd had to hide behind a bush until her ashes were removed from the oven and the police had gone. He had left by the gate on the towpath, little guessing that he'd be as good as living there one day.

Jack flicked through the copy Stella had given him of Adam Honeysett's real file. His attention was caught by a headline; it was the article they'd seen on Latimer's computer: *The Secret Lover!*

Jack laid the article beside him on the sofa. Another one by Lucie. She had been busy on the case. Despite the gaping hole rent in Honeysett's bereaved-husband image, Lucie had reserved her judgement for 'Drake', whom she painted as lazy and indulged. In comparison to Steven Lawson, Lucie had been lenient on Honeysett. What had happened to Jane Drake after Honeysett had told the police about her? She'd have needed her luxury penthouse pied-à-terre to keep Lucie and the rest of the ravening press pack at bay. Jack hoped she'd passed her exams.

He became aware of squeaking. *The ghost?* Jack looked down the length of the basement. In the glass he saw his repeated reflection – phantom Jacks – and as he walked towards his mirrored self the panels slid aside. The sound came from beyond the end wall. Jack hesitated. Unfazed by creeping about someone's house without their knowing, or walking on a dark and lonely towpath, he felt unsettled by the JCB digger entombed beyond the wall. The squeaking had stopped.

He pushed on the brick. The heavy door swung inwards. He was hit by an icy draught. It had been cold last time, but not like this. He felt every hair on his body stand up; the tingling in his palms warning of danger was electric. He should leave the house, walk until he got a signal and call Stella. He climbed into the chamber.

Who am I and what have I done?

He stopped. Blood pounded like a mallet. The whispered words were in his head. Behind him the basement lights went out and he was plunged into blackness. He felt in his coat for his Maglite and realized he'd left it on the sofa with his phone. It was metres away, but way out of reach.

He found the light switch. He heard a slapping sound. It was the river hitting the sides of the bank. He smelled mud and gasped as if the viscous substance might suffocate him. He put a hand on the leather seat of the digger and snatched it back. It was warm. He waited until his heart had regained a semblance of a normal beat and touched it again, this time with the back of his hand. Definitely warm.

Jack had made dank cellars his home, knowing should a True Host find him, he would die. Yet in a house in which he was living legitimately, he was afraid. He tried to conjure up his mother's lilting voice:

Ride a cock-horse to Banbury Cross,
To buy little Johnny a galloping horse.

Emboldened, he climbed on to the digger. He grabbed a lever as if to manoeuvre the machine as, with his mother as passenger, he'd 'driven' the 27 bus up King Street clutching the seat in front and doing revving noises. He pulled on the lever. With a drawn-out squeak the giant claw rose, jagged teeth silhouetted in the bleak light. It was the sound he'd heard. A ghost didn't operate diggers. Who had been here?

The sound of the river and the smell of mud meant one thing. As he'd said to Stella, the chamber had an exit. He climbed off the digger and felt his way along the wall, coming to a narrow opening. There was nothing. The light didn't penetrate inside. One step more and the darkness was absolute. A whisper slid off the cold sweating bricks, '*Who am I and what have I done?*'

An exit was also a way in.

Chapter Thirty-Seven

'No drama. I didn't tell you because it's not relevant,' Natasha Latimer bellowed. Stella held the phone away from her ear. Beverly had brought her a mug of tea; she took a sip, but it had gone cold.

That morning Stella had visited Jack on her way to work.

'Latimer has an intruder,' he'd told her.

'What?' Stella quelled a thud of dread.

'Come and see this,' he whispered as if someone could hear.

He had taken her into the brick room with the JCB and led her along a low passageway. At the end was a grille. Holly and bramble branches poked through the bars.

'It leads on to the towpath. It's hidden by bushes; a casual passer-by would miss it. Although not an inquisitive dog.'

'You are kidding!' Stella rattled the grille. 'It's locked. Natasha Latimer must have a key. It doesn't look forced.'

Now Stella asked Latimer, 'Do you have a key to the grille at the end of the tunnel in your basement?'

'Somewhere.' Latimer was impatient. 'Don't bother cleaning there. No one need see it.'

Careful not to panic Latimer, Stella asked airily, 'How many people have keys?'

'Just me, of course.'

Stella remembered Jack's point. 'Could your builders still have a key?'

'My builders were honest.' But Stella detected doubt.

'Did you change all your locks when you bought the house?'

'No need, the Banham on the front door is impregnable and that grille is locked.' Without seeing her face, Stella sensed Latimer absorb her unspoken words.

No lock was impregnable if you had the key.

Tentatively, Stella said, 'I wonder if you should call the police.'

'Keep the place clean for sale. Do *not* call the police. They'll do nothing, but they will record it in their stats. It'll wipe thousands off the asking price. Please ask your man to sort a locksmith.' The line went dead.

Stella took her tea through to the office. 'Natasha Latimer told us that Neville Rowlands, who rented the house before her, is dead. But what if he isn't and he has a key? Or someone else...' Stella saw that Jackie was on the phone.

'Lots of people don't change the locks when they buy a new house.' Beverly looked up from her computer. 'They think it's OK cos they bought the place off of someone. But what if someone else has a key? Some boy I was at school with took the key for a flat where his mum used to feed the cat. The new people didn't know she had one. He nicked things regularly until he was caught red-handed with the TV!' Beverly rocked back on her chair then shot forward, 'As for the digger, Jackie got me to do research.'

'Research on what?' Stella couldn't help worrying when Jackie let Beverly use her initiative. Unfair, because one thing she did know was that Beverly learnt from her mistakes.

'I uncovered – yay, good pun! – there's hundreds of diggers in basements around London. At least a thousand, it says here!' Beverly read out: 'Once a basement is excavated, the digger is extracted with a crane. The street has to be cleared of cars and obstacles to get the crane in. The operation costs more than the price of the machine so basement construction companies have calculated that it is cheaper to leave the digger in situ.'

She took a breath. 'Shall I find out about the man?'

'What man?' Regardless of house price, Latimer should call the police.

'The old man you said rented before she dug a great hole under the house.' Beverly's pen was poised. 'Mind you, if he's dead, it can't matter that he's got a key.'

'Bev'll have it for you in no time.' Jackie was off the telephone.

But Stella wouldn't have staff work beyond their remit. 'It's not in your job description.'

'It could be!' Jackie arched her eyebrows at Stella.

Assuming disinterest, Beverly did a spin on her chair.

'It would have to be reflected in the salary.' Stella was stern.

'We can sort that. Stella, if this detective agency is going to get off the ground, you're going to need a new office and more staff.'

'In the meantime, dead or alive, the old man might have the key to the secret passage!' Beverly spun around the other way.

'OK,' Stella agreed cautiously. 'He's called Neville Rowlands. Cross-check with the electoral roll. The name can't be common.'

Jackie had said *'if this detective agency is going to get off the ground...'* Was Stella serious about it? What was putting her off? Vaguely, she supposed Terry would be laughing at her. But Terry was dead. And she didn't believe in ghosts.

'That was Angela Morrish on the phone.' Jackie interrupted Stella's thoughts.

'Who's she?' Stella forced herself to concentrate.

'The woman who owns that chain of solicitors we pitched for? The washroom contract? The one who let Stanley sit on her posh suit.' Jackie raised her eyebrows. 'I'm afraid we lost it guys.'

'No way!' Beverly jumped out of her chair. Stanley, sensing threat, flew from his bed and raced about the office barking. 'That was *so* in the bag! I gave her two cups of tea *and* we got biscuits.'

'She probably took one look at this place and decided we were smaller than we are.' Jackie pulled a face.

'We deep cleaned it before she got here!' Beverly had gone red, her eyes were blazing. 'Who got it?'

'Premark Environment. Their specialism is washrooms. They've got a brilliant track record,' Jackie said.

'Crap!' Beverly flumped down on her chair.

'I've heard of them. They're good.' Stella couldn't remember when they'd last lost a pitch for a major job. Angela Morrish had visited the same day as Natasha Latimer and Claudia brought the 'ghost job'. Stella had been out doing a domestic estimate. She should have stayed. No, Jackie and Beverly were good. She said, 'We stood no chance with Premark Environment in the frame. Maybe it was this office too.'

'If we had to lose to anyone it was to the best,' Jackie agreed. 'Angela said it was close. She's keeping us on file. I liked her, she sounded like she really meant it.'

Stella nodded vaguely, she was no longer listening. If someone had a key to Natasha Latimer's house, Jack shouldn't stay there another night on his own. She should have said so this morning. She was zipping up her jacket when her mobile phone rang. Mum Barons Court. Stella had lived in the flat until her twenties, but had never considered it either her 'home' or her mum's.

'I was bang on!' Suzie always shouted into mobiles, as if she or Stella was on a mountain top.

'About what?' Her mum was always bang on about something.

'Stephanie Benson. I got her address in Sydney out of her. I rang Dale and he says it doesn't exist.'

Stella looked at the clock; it was ten past two. 'Mum, it's the middle of the night in Sydney. Dale must have been asleep.'

'He's like you, he never sleeps.' Suzie was dismissive. 'Stephanie said she lived at the junction of Olola Avenue in Vaucluse. That's near to Dale. You have to have serious cash to have a house there…' Her mum gave a sigh of pride. 'Where she's supposed to have lived is a patch of grass with trees. Look it up on Street View. Dale says that unless Stephanie's a possum, she can't have lived there!'

Stella rubbed her temple. She had expected Suzie to have issues with anyone who took over from Jack, but not this.

'Stephanie claimed to be housekeeper at a house there. What was she doing, picking up leaves and mowing the grass?' Stella could hear Suzie tapping her cushion. 'Whoever she is, she's not Stephanie Benson!'

Stella faced off her mum's implacability. 'I don't see why not.'

'I've twice called out to her to come for coffee and she hasn't come.'

'Was she vacuuming? Maybe she didn't hear.'

'She heard the lift alarm when she was vacuuming and we know from that time I was stuck in it that *no one* hears it. Listen, darling girl, I've been around the block enough times with your papa to spot a false identity. She doesn't answer to "Stephanie". False name, false past. You're a detective: find out who she is. Follow her!'

Stella rubbed her face. 'Spying on staff is not company policy.' She nearly suggested Suzie ask Stephanie Benson, but she didn't want her mum quizzing staff about their private lives.

'Just like your dad,' Suzie groaned. 'Can't or *won't*?'

Jack would love it, but Stella drew the line at tracking people, especially a woman. This was partly why she was hesitant about the detective agency. A detective had to follow people. A cleaner did not. She lit upon a cast-iron objection. 'We don't need to follow her; we have her address.'

'It will be false. She's changed her name and lied on her reference. *Tail her!*'

'Mum, I—'

'And don't sack her, she's a damn good cleaner!'

Good or not, Clean Slate didn't employ dishonest operatives. Stella should ask Jackie to let Benson go. Again she thought of Jack; he was not the most honest person she knew.

As she drove along Shepherd's Bush Green, it occurred to Stella that her mum had never called her a detective before.

Chapter Thirty-Eight

Tuesday, 29 March 1988

The tide on the river was on the ebb, receding waters exposing the muddy foreshore scattered with debris.

On the Thames towpath a girl in school uniform traipsed along, dodging puddles, stopping and peering through foliage at the water's edge. The distant chime of bells carried on the breeze, four in all, and this appeared to galvanize her. She started running, splashing along the track, hampered by something in her duffel coat.

'What are you doing down here?'

The voice brought her up short. The firefly light of a cigarette bobbed as a woman emerged from under Chiswick Bridge. In a fur coat with padded shoulders and high-heeled boots, she negotiated the muddy path with confidence, the cigarette held away from her face.

'I came to see you.' Megan Lawson was crestfallen; had Aunty El forgotten their Secret Assignation?

'Megs! I said *on* the bridge in the light, not by the river where anything could happen. Your ma would have forty fits. As it is, I'm persona non-fuckwit. 'Scuse the French.'

'When we had Smudge, Dad and me came here all the time. There's no one to do anything now.' Megan was briefly taken aback by this fact that she had never before voiced.

'There's always someone to do something, sweetheart, your

dad wasn't the only badass.' Swinging into an American accent, her aunt drew fiercely on her cigarette, an eye screwed up against the smoke. 'There's plenty more where he came from.'

'You're here by yourself,' the girl countered.

'I can take care of myself. It's my job to walk in the footsteps of the good, the bad and the downright evil.' She gave a low laugh. 'How is it back at the old homestead, Megsy? They still giving you a hard time for doing the right thing? Any joy from your saintly brother?'

'Garry still says I killed his birds. Mum is trying to prove Dad is innocent.'

'My sister believed in Father Christmas.' Her Aunty sketched a circle in the air with her cigarette. 'Forget I said that, honey-bear!'

'Garry won't believe it was Helen Honeysett.' Megan spoke in a whisper.

'Wait a sec. Helen Honeysett killed Garry's birds? Are you kidding me?'

'No. I didn't mean that.' Megan had long ago got truth mixed up with hopes and dreams. Helen Honeysett was supposed to be nice. Everyone missed her because she was missing. Or was she missing because everyone missed her? The little girl tried to square this with a woman who had made her feel strange, but she couldn't remember why. And anyway she was wrong to think badly of her. She hurried on, 'Mum says there's no evidence linking my dad to Mrs Honeysett. Only me telling the police I saw him go after her. Mum says he didn't know Helen Honeysett was there and he went to "clear his head". She says Helen Honeysett might not have gone to the towpath, she could have gone somewhere else. She says it might not have been her I heard.' The girl heaved a breath as the words tumbled out.

'You don't believe that, Megs?' She eyed her niece through narrowed eyes and dragged on her cigarette. 'More likely your esteemed dad planned the quarrel with your mum as an excuse to go after Honeysett.' She always called her 'Honeysett'.

'I don't know.' Megan was confused. That anyone could plan to have an argument was inexplicable.

'It's not all about evidence and context. He was your dad, lovey, so it's hard for you and for Garry to accept he's done wrong. My father was a shit, so no surprise if he'd done this. Your dad charmed snakes out of their baskets with his baby looks. He charmed my sister. Me, I scare off the baddies.' Her aunt ground her cigarette out on the path with a pointy-booted toe and lit another. The flare of the match briefly revealed black eyeliner and red lipstick.

'I do *except* he's done wrong,' Megan assured her.

Her aunt snapped to business. 'Did you get it?'

'Yes.' The girl undid her blazer and produced a flimsy notebook. She held it as if reluctant to part with it. 'Mum would kill me if she knew I took it. It's her secret. She doesn't know I know.' She didn't say her theft of the notebook was the more terrible because of whom she was giving it to. Her mum said Aunty El was never to be trusted.

'Good girl!' Cigarette between her lips, her aunt reached for the book.

Megan hesitated. 'Maybe I should ask Mum first?'

'Bit late for cold feet. Listen Megs, *darling*, your ma is my little sister, I'll walk on hot coals for her, but about this she's buried her head in the sand. Once I prove that your dad did this thing, then, tough though it'll be, Bette and Garry can move on. And, more importantly, that poor family can bury their girl. No need to ask your mum.'

Tremulously, Megan regarded the exercise book clutched to her chest. 'Mum will kill me.'

'Whatever else she is, unlike Steven pretty-boy Lawson, my sister ain't no killer. It's like ripping off a plaster, do it *fast*.' She snatched the book from her niece. In the lamplight from the bridge above, she flapped it open and scanned the pages. 'Mmm. Perfect. Megan, you'll make a journalist one day.'

'I'm going to be a De-Clutterer.' Megan's spirits lifted at the prospect.

'Aim higher than that, kiddo! You sound like my sister. She could have been a doctor like the pater, but settled for being a friggin' nurse.' She tucked the notebook inside her voluminous fur coat. 'Gotta scram, have to file a story by midnight.' She went over to the steps to Chiswick Bridge. The little girl lingered on the dark towpath. Perhaps her aunt recalled some responsibility, because she stopped and said, 'Chop, chop, Megs. I'll pop you home.'

Aunt and niece didn't see a shadow under the arch of the bridge. Nor were they distracted by a dog lead swinging as from a disembodied hand. To and fro.

On the bridge, Auntie El unlocked a white 2CV parked on double yellow lines with one wheel on the kerb. She swooshed a penalty ticket out from under the windscreen wipers and stuffed it into her coat pocket. She told Megan, 'Darling girl, each of us has to fight our corner. I won't let your dad drag his family with him into his grave.'

'Mum might be cross when she sees you,' Megan mumbled apologetically. She had loved her aunt's visits. When Aunty El had breezed into the tiny cottage in a cloud of smoke, it meant noise and adventure. It was over a year since she had been. Megan wasn't allowed to say her name.

'She'd be apoplectic!' She gave a mirthless cackle. 'Luckily she won't know. I'll land my broomstick on the green and you jump off and whisk away home.' She tipped her niece's chin to the lamplight. 'Smidgen, cheer up, you've done the right thing.'

Chapter Thirty-Nine

Tuesday, 29 March 1988

'Have a nippet, darrl-ing,' she said in a grating drawl.

'Do you know, don't mind if I do?' A mouse squeak. 'Don't go mad with tonic, darling.'

'Down the hatch!' Megan raised her tooth mug to her reflection in her dad's shaving mirror still propped on the window sill in the bathroom and took a draught of tap water. 'Have a fag,' her voice grated.

'Don't mind if I do.' The voice started low for her Aunty El and soared to a cry as Megan realized this was her line. She puffed an imaginary cloud of smoke at polystyrene tiles on the bathroom ceiling.

It was three minutes past eight. Megan had said goodnight to her mum and was putting off going to bed. She was regretting giving Aunty El the notebook. Now that she was home, she no longer felt like the brave De-Clutterer assisting where she could. She would be in terrible trouble if her mum found out.

Garry was in the aviary. In the darkness, unseen by his mother and sister, he was crouched on the ground below the nest boxes staring at the stars. His dad had told him to use Orion as a starting point to identify other stars. The boy considered that the brightest star was his dad. He kept having stupid thoughts. Garry told no one he had seen his dad on the 27 bus, on Chiswick High Road, in men he passed in the street. Some sightings were literal.

The media kept alive the story of the baby-faced killer who had cut short a young woman's life and then drowned himself in the same river where he'd dumped the girl *loved by all who knew her*. He saw his dad in passengers' newspapers on the bus, in newsagent windows and on television. The boy had begun to avoid shops and, when he could, people. He'd stopped catching the bus and walked home along the towpath. The only way to get away from accusing eyes and his dad's happy face was with his birds.

Clasping his knees, oblivious to the cold, Garry, who jeered at his sister for believing in fairies, willed the stars to turn all that had happened into a dream from which he could wake.

Bette Lawson never noticed that a job which used to take her son fifteen minutes now lasted an hour. Every night, when the silently eaten meal and washing up was out of the way, her children slipped out of the room and out of her consciousness. She remained at the kitchen table, her gaze resting vaguely on Steven Lawson's chair opposite. On the table before her were newspaper cuttings. She would scour them, trying to find a key fact to show her husband innocent, to prove her sister wrong. She studied the words and pictures for something she had missed that – impossibly – could bring Steve back. She sorted the paper into piles and then rearranged them into new piles. Hours later, unaware her children were in bed – not asleep – she would shovel all the piles into a carrier bag and hang it behind the ironing board.

She went to the kitchen drawer and from a jumble of assorted objects – elastic bands, old key rings, washers – she took Steven's Estimate Book. He had a scribbled note of his last appointment. Fitting a washing machine was a simple job although he'd grumbled about installing it in a tight corner. When he heard it had leaked, flooded the kitchen and seeped through the ceiling below, he had gone to the towpath. Her sister said he'd gone to meet Helen Honeysett or why didn't he take the dog? Bette had forgotten what her argument for this had been. Why hadn't he taken Smudge?

After he died, another plumber reported that the pump in the machine had been damaged so the flood wasn't Steven's fault. No one reported that in the paper. Her sister had scoffed, '*Fractured pump causes washing machine leak.* Sensation!'

'Did you find anything?'

Bette hadn't heard Garry come in from the garden. 'No, love, but if I keep at it, I will. Dad was innocent of this business.' She never said Helen Honeysett's name. She never said why she was so sure that Steve hadn't done it.

'I'll kill the man who did it.' Garry dashed his shirt sleeve across his face.

'She mightn't be dead. We don't know what happened,' Bette remarked.

'I'll kill *her* if she comes back alive. She's ruined everything.'

'What good will that do? I want no more of that talk.' Bette shut the Estimate Book and laid it next to one of the piles of papers. 'Stick the kettle on, there's a pet, I'll have a coffee.'

Garry gestured at the papers. 'I'll help you.'

'The best way to help is by staying strong. It's what your dad would have wanted.' Bette sounded less confident. Her sister said Steven was a weak man who'd let his family down.

Garry made his mother a mug of instant coffee. He was leaving the kitchen when she asked, 'It's over a year, so a long time, but try to remember. You were in our bedroom with Megan when Dad went out that night. Are you sure you didn't see him?'

Garry Lawson didn't turn around. 'I said, didn't I? Megan's a liar.'

'Yes, love, but you could have forgotten,' Bette suggested carefully. 'Like I say, it's been a long time.'

'Not that long. I won't ever forget.' Garry smacked aside the bead curtain and went out. Bette wanted to hold him and stroke his hair to soothe him, like when he was a little boy. She and Garry were the only two in the world who believed in Steven's innocence. Not that Garry did believe it: he couldn't bear to think his dad was a murderer. That left only her.

Her coffee cooling, Bette tried to muster up Steven's face, but only saw Honeysett's photo from the Christmas party over a year ago. In the last few weeks of his life, Steven had been bad-tempered. He hadn't told her he wasn't getting the work. He'd laughed enough at the party, especially when Honeysett pointed her camera at him. After he was questioned, Lucie put the picture in her paper. Under a headline *The Face of a Monster*.

Upstairs, Bette saw light under her daughter's door. Megan was asleep on her back, her arms above her head like when she was a baby. The tooth mug was beside the bed. It was empty, but for a slice of lemon at the bottom.

Chapter Forty

The church clock struck four as Beverly answered the phone. 'Clean Slate for a Fresh Start, I'm Beverly, here to help with your query.'

'Bev, it's me.' Stella was parked on Kew Green. She had organized for a locksmith to come to Natasha Latimer's to change the locks. She was on her way to tell Jack. As she was crossing Hammersmith Broadway, Suzie had rung and asked if she'd found out Stephanie Benson's true identity yet. Stella couldn't admit she'd forgotten and had rashly agreed that she would. Now she was wrestling with how to get out of this without lying. 'Is Jackie there?'

'She's gone to meet Graham. They're going to IKEA, remember? Jackie said we might never see her again, she always gets lost there.'

Stella hadn't remembered. This was a reason not to go through with the plan. Then she imagined telling her mum and said, 'Bev, would you turn on my computer, please?'

'Your computer! Are you sure?' Stella was loath to let Beverly near her machine since she'd wiped out Suzie's database.

Everything was backed up; Stella decided to take Jackie's advice and trust Beverly. She grimaced. 'Yes. I'm sure.'

'I've turned it on,' Beverly hissed as if she had ignited a fuse. 'I'm leaving your room now.'

'No, stay at my desk. Go into the client database. You've done it before.' Stella put from her mind what had happened in the past as she heard Beverly tapping on the keyboard. She pictured Suzie's precious database reduced to a blank screen.

'Then what?' Beverly sounded uncharacteristically timid.

'Look up Stephanie Benson. She's an operative.'

'Ooh, yes, Stephanie's *lovely*.'

'How do you know she's lovely?'

'She passed my test!'

'What test is that?' Stella kept her voice level.

'At her interview Stephanie thanked me for giving her tea.' Beverly was confidential. 'If interviewees are polite to the lowly office minion, they must be nice. Doesn't mean they're great cleaners, but it's a start.' She gave a neighing laugh.

'You're not the office minion.'

'Some people think so,' Beverly replied simply. 'They don't thank me for the tea or look at me.'

It was the kind of criterion Jack would apply. Stella saw the sense in it. She wondered what test could tell her that clients bringing detective cases were guilty of the crime themselves. Adam Honeysett had lied about seeing livery on her van and about being with Jane Drake the night his wife disappeared. Were that a test, he would have failed. Did it make him a killer?

'Stella?'

'Sorry. What's Benson's last cleaning job today?'

There was tapping and then Beverly reeled off an address that was literally around the corner from Kew Green.

Stella moved the car to outside the newsagent's further along Kew Green. Although she was in a white van and no one – apart from Adam Honeysett – would know it was from Clean Slate, Stella's photo was on the company website and had been featured in media interviews: she couldn't risk Benson recognizing her.

An *Evening Standard* stand outside the newsagent's read

Bowie dies at 69. Not a music fan – although at school she and her friend Liz had liked Duran Duran – Stella had a soft spot for Bowie's 'Rebel Rebel'. She grabbed her phone, but the person she wanted to tell, her friend Tina, was also dead. Stella rarely let herself think about Tina. Then out of the blue something – a newspaper headline – hit her with the force of a sandbag. She couldn't meet Tina for coffee and chew over business issues with her. Stella got out of the van and took a paper from the stand. Bowie had died on 10 January. Returning to the van she noted it was the same date as Terry's death. Jack would definitely call it a sign.

She looked up from the paper in time to see a woman coming out of the house she was supposed to be watching. She couldn't be sure that the woman was Stephanie Benson. Her Clean Slate uniform must be hidden beneath a bulky parka coat. If she had asked, Beverly would have given her a description. Jackie said Beverly would make an excellent witness, she recalled the most trivial detail. Stella berated herself. Terry wouldn't have staked out a suspect – not that Benson was a suspect – without knowing what they looked like. Then Stella saw that not only was she carrying a Clean Slate equipment bag, but she was walking towards her. She shrank down in her seat and pressed her nose to the glass on the driver's side. Behind her she sensed Stanley become alert. She prayed he wouldn't bark when Benson passed.

Instead of barking, he was mewing. She understood it. Stanley had met Stephanie Benson when she came for her interview. Mewing meant he'd liked her. Stella's guilt at tracking her shot up several notches. She fumbled at the ignition and, head low over the wheel, pulled out as Benson reached her. At the top of the street, she flung the van through a six-point turn and returned. She scoured the pavement for Benson. *Nowhere.* Terry wouldn't have brought a dog to a stakeout. Nor would he have been distracted by dead rock stars and dead friends. He kept his mind on the job.

On the South Circular Stella got a break. Stephanie Benson,

bag on her shoulder, was ahead of her. In the stop-start rush-hour traffic, Stella made sluggish progress towards Chalker's Corner. She beat a rhythm on the steering wheel as Benson dodged the lights and walked briskly between the cemeteries. Seven cars crossed the line and the lights went to red. For a crazy moment Stella had the urge to fling out of the van and give chase on foot. At last she was at the top of the queue. She took stock. It was a simple equation of density of traffic and light-changes. She wouldn't catch up with Benson.

The stonemason's Chalker and Gamble that had given the junction its name had long gone, replaced by a vet's surgery. A man emerged from the building carrying a cat box. Behind him a woman led out a small dog on a lead not unlike Stanley. Stella's gaze drifted across the road and she caught Stephanie Benson turning into the cemetery gates. Stella puffed out her cheeks; she was crap at tailing a target.

The lights changed and Stella was off. In the cemetery she braked sharply beside what had been a greeting lodge with ornate carvings. It was boarded up and slathered with graffiti tags. She sat for a second looking at the serried ranks of headstones – no doubt clients of Chalker and Gamble – blurred by the approaching twilight. As she looked at the stones, many covered with lichen and London dirt, Stella hatched a plan.

She took a bucket and scrubber out of the back of the van and, Stanley at heel, wove between the plots keeping Benson in sight. She was fifty metres ahead by a line of yew trees. Stella tripped on a plastic vase of plastic flowers and stopped to right it. Rushing on, she suddenly jerked Stanley to a stop. Benson had either doubled back or Stella had unwittingly cut a corner because the operative was only metres away, standing by a grave. Stella crept as close as she dared before Stanley would give her away.

Stephanie Benson was ripping at weeds on a grave that was a tangle of brambles and tall grasses. No great reader of human behaviour, Stella nevertheless saw the woman was upset.

Stella put her plan into action. She chose a grave off the path with a clear view of Stephanie Benson. This grave was little better tended, but Stella wasn't a gardener. She knelt on the cushion of grass tussocks and squirted astringent on to the headstone. She set about scrubbing it. Appearing intent on her task, she kept watch on Benson.

Although she was 'undercover' Stella was gratified to see the difference she was making. The stone was coming up pale in the dwindling light, the lettering almost legible.

Within the limits of his lead Stanley rooted around, sniffing and snorting as he burrowed into the soil. He unearthed a bald tennis ball, the rubber perishing.

'Leave!' Stella hissed. She was struck with horror that he might dig up a body. She looked to see if Benson had heard. But she was still weeding, her movements mechanical as if she was in a trance.

Stella's phone buzzed. It was Suzie. In the comparative quiet, Stella's voice might carry. Her mum would be wanting an update. Stella texted *I'm undercover* and regretted it. Suzie would be fired up. Right on cue, her phone buzzed again. She stuffed the phone in her jacket. There was no one at the other grave.

Stella clambered to her feet. Benson was carting a bundle of weeds away between the yew trees. Stella gathered up her bucket, tossing in the bottle of gravestone cleaner and the brush, and, Stanley's lead wrapped around her hand, wended her way between the mounds. In the time she'd been working on the grave, the light had almost gone.

For all her hard work, Stephanie Benson had made little impact on the grave. Tall weeds grew at the foot of the plot. The epitaph was barely decipherable.

IN MEM   O STEVEN LAWSO , A OOD   SBAND AN   ATHER. R.I.P.

It was no great feat to work out what letters were missing. Had she buried her own father, Stella would have chosen a similar message. No birth or death dates. No sentiment or fuss. She gave a start. Steven Lawson was the name of the prime suspect in the Honeysett case. The man who drowned himself in the Thames. This must be a coincidence: the headstone looked a lot older than nearly thirty years. Jack said there were no coincidences.

Stella walked around the grave. Something was carved at the back, just above the line of the mown grass. Like the inscription, it was eroded almost smooth. Stella sat on her heels ignoring Stanley who, presuming a game, began to bash the ball he held between his furry jaws against her shoulder. Stella traced indentations with a finger as if reading Braille. An eight. A seven. Steven Lawson committed suicide in 1987. This had to be his grave.

It was dark. No sign of Stephanie Benson. Stella floundered towards a string of lights that must be the South Circular. Stanley coughed as his collar constricted his throat, an eerie sound. Stella was furious with herself; gallivanting in graveyards at night was Jack's thing. He'd let slip that he went on walks at night with Bella. Stella had hoped that the botanical illustrator might deter him from going out. Now Stella was doing it and without Jack. Idiotic to have listened to her mum. At last Stella saw her van, ghostly white against the wrought-iron gates.

Her relief was short-lived. The gates were shut. She read the noticeboard by the lodge. Closing time was nightfall. Beyond the gates, the traffic crawled by. The drivers, cocooned in their vehicles, stared ahead. No one would hear her shout.

'You're trespassing!' Stella spun round. Headstones and statues floated wraithlike in the semi-dark. Stanley emitted a guttural growl. A sign of danger.

A man in a hi-vis jacket held a shotgun. Stella backed against the gate. He had an insignia on his jacket. It was the logo for Richmond Borough Council. The gun was a garden rake. Only marginally reassuring. 'No cars are allowed in without permission.'

Jack would start speaking and trust to whatever came out. Stella liked to plan and speak the truth. 'I was tending a grave.'

Being a detective was leading her down ever more complicated paths of duplicity.

'In the dark?' the man snarled.

Stella was alone in a locked cemetery with a man with a rake. Contrary to policy in the Clean Slate handbook, Stella had told no one of her whereabouts. Her mum knew she was following Stephanie Benson, but not where that had taken her. Her dad had said that a perfect place to commit murder was in a cemetery.

'It wasn't dark when I started. The stone was dirty.' She rattled her cleaning bucket.

'Whose grave were you cleaning?'

'Steven Lawson's.'

'Why do you care about him?' The man was sharp.

'He's... he's my father.' Stella clenched the inside of her cheeks between her teeth. A cleaner never lies.

The man seemed to soften. 'Never seen you here. It's a right mess. A disgrace.'

Stella was taken aback; it had never occurred to her that he might notice who visited a grave or the state of it. Then it came to her. In West London the Helen Honeysett case would be notorious. A hundred years earlier Lawson couldn't have been buried in consecrated ground. It was likely that even in 1987 his interment had caused controversy.

Stella kicked herself for not making up a name; the man couldn't know everyone who was buried here. She was caught in her own trap.

Her phone buzzed again. Stella delved into her jacket and answered without checking who it was.

'Stella, how's it going?' her mum whispered hoarsely.

'I've cleaned it.' Stella spoke loudly into the mouthpiece. 'Like you wanted.'

'What did I want? Cleaned what?'

'The headstone looks brand new, Mum.' That much was true.

'What headstone? Listen, Stella, I've got something to tell you.'

The man was gesticulating at her. Stanley growled. 'I can't

give you special treatment, but seeing as you're his girl...' He was unlocking the gates.

'Thank you,' Stella said weakly.

On Kew Bridge she called her mum back.

'Since when did we offer headstone cleaning? Good idea, mind!'

'What were you calling about?' Right then, Stella wished that headstone cleaning was all she did.

'Stephanie is not Stephanie!' Suzie's voice boomed out of the speakers. 'Guess who she is. *Hah!* You won't get it!'

Stella pictured the woman squatting by the weed-choked grave, distraught in a futile endeavour to tend it. 'Megan Lawson.'

After a beat of silence. 'How do you know?' Suzie sounded deflated.

'How do *you* know? Tell me you didn't make up some story to get her talking.' She had just passed herself off as Steven Lawson's daughter.

'*Per*-leese! Terry sneaked around the houses but, like I told him, you get results by being straight. I taught you that.'

Suzie had got Stella to tail Stephanie Benson. It was always pointless to highlight her mother's changes of tack.

'I asked what her real name was and she told me.'

It was no coincidence that Megan Lawson was at her father's grave. Cause and effect. Cause: Suzie unmasked her true identity. Effect: Megan Lawson returned to her real past. From the state of Steven Lawson's grave, Stella guessed that his daughter – or any of his family – rarely went there.

Chapter Forty-One

Monday, 11 January 2016

'It can't be coincidence that Megan Lawson, the daughter of the man considered guilty of murdering Helen Honeysett, is working for Clean Slate.' Stella was perched up on the JCB.

'No, it can't. Did Suzie ask her why she applied for the job?' Jack stood at the mouth of the tunnel. A thin draught chilled the back of his neck. Stella had said she wanted to explore the hidden vault properly, but since she was drawn to gadgets and machinery – usually ones that cleaned – he suspected her keen to go on the digger.

'She said she needed a job. If there's another reason – and I think there is – she didn't admit it to Mum. She told her she'd changed her name to escape the press. Mum promised her we wouldn't sack her for lying. I guess we won't.'

'Hats off to Suzie.' With forensic curiosity and a cavalier willingness to cut to any chase, Suzie Darnell would have made a good detective. Perhaps that was part of what Terry had seen in her. 'We must talk to her.' His voice bounced off the brick passage. If someone was lingering on the towpath at the other end of the tunnel they would hear every word. He moved away.

'We'll go tonight in case since talking to Mum she's considering doing a bunk.' Stella was examining the controls on the digger.

'We should cancel the locksmith,' Jack said.

'Why? Latimer never changed the locks. Anyone could have a key.' Stella was regal on her gleaming yellow throne.

'Exactly. We need to catch them red-handed; that means not stopping them getting in. This is no ordinary burglar.'

'Why do you say that?'

'Whoever started this rumour about the ghost – I don't buy Daphne's theory that Latimer's psyche is haunting her – doesn't want her to sell the house. We know it's her sister who believes in the supernatural. This could be a vendetta. Who are her enemies?'

'My dad said start with that question. But most people don't have enemies, just those who don't much like them. I couldn't name mine.'

'That's because you don't have any. I bet Natasha Latimer's spoilt for choice. Only Sybil Lofthouse has had a good word to say about her. A likely candidate, dead or alive, is Neville Rowlands, who lived here with his mother and was kicked out.'

'Beverly's looking him up.'

'Beverly?'

'Jackie thinks we should establish this detective agency officially. She suggested Beverly as an assistant, she spots things. Are you OK with it?'

Jack liked being a team with Stella and was wary of others joining in. And of anything official. 'I guess.'

'I could call Martin. Off the record – Natasha Latimer needn't know. Get his take on whether someone has actually broken in. There's no sign of forced entry. It's an excuse to find out what the police are thinking on the Helen Honeysett case.'

'Cashman will close us down.' During the Kew Gardens case, Stella and Cashman – her father had been his mentor – had had an affair. The policeman had gone back to his wife. The break was amicable, but even before that there had been no love lost between Jack and Cashman. Jack would accept Beverly on their team but never Martin Cashman.

Stella had explained why the digger was there. Jack would love to have a big yellow digger in his house.

'Lucie's written loads on Helen Honeysett. She'll know about Rowlands.' His stomach fizzed. A sign that his motive wasn't pure. He'd brought Lucie May up out of pique because Stella had suggested Cashman. Tit for tat.

'That's a good idea.' Stella didn't play games. She was craning around the lever, peering into the giant claw. 'There's a bracelet in there.'

Jack leant in and, mindful of the jagged teeth on the rim of the bucket, fished out a cracked brown leather ring from the bottom. He tilted it to the light bulb. A tag hung from the buckle. 'Whisky. It's a dog collar.' He passed it up to Stella. 'It has the owner's number on it. 0208 948, that's the Kew exchange isn't it?'

'Whisky's the name Sybil Lofthouse called Stanley. Mum said it was probably her dog's name and she'd got confused. This might be hers. But why is it here?'

'I suppose when the basement was constructed, it got unearthed.' Jack couldn't recall seeing it there when they dis-covered the digger. 'Or it could belong to someone who lived here. There are those pet graves outside.'

'Does one have the name "Whisky"?' Stella asked.

'No, but it was dark so I could've missed it.'

'Why did you go there in the dark?' Stella asked.

Jack felt the vault reel. He'd had time to legitimately explore the garden, but hadn't done so. He hadn't been there since the night he broke into the garden. He had given himself away.

However, Stella went on: '... Beverly found a story of builders excavating a basement in Twickenham who found the skeleton of a baby that had been there for seventy years. Police traced the DNA via the nephew of a woman who'd lived alone in the house in the 1940s. A church-goer who gave piano lessons, she'd have been disgraced for being pregnant out of wedlock. She had killed the baby and buried it in the garden. They find weird stuff: there was a suitcase of valuables from a burglary twenty years before, Roman coins, several sets of dentures, letters.'

'A garden's a good burial place,' Jack said. 'After that, a dog collar's a bit tame.'

'Let's go and see Megan Lawson.' Stella pulled on a lever. With a squeak – the squeak that Jack had heard in the basement; the squeak that Latimer had complained of – the digger arm rose upwards.

Chapter Forty-Two

Wednesday, 8 January 1997

Megan scurried past the gaggle of reporters crowding around a policewoman with a man, mooching in a wax jacket, on the towpath. Hood up, a scarf wound around the bottom half of her face, hands crammed deep in the pockets of her duffel coat; no one noticed the nondescript woman. This was as well because had they recognized her they would have pursued her. A snap of Steven Lawson's seventeen-year-old daughter by the river where he drowned – Megan resembled the dead plumber – would have been a prize.

It was ten years since the estate agent had vanished and the police were holding an anniversary press conference. Adam Honeysett was making what would be dubbed in reports as an 'impassioned plea to camera' in the hope of jolting someone's memory or conscience. It was a cursory affair: everyone believed the detectives had their man. No one had gone missing by the river since Steven Lawson died.

Megan passed the house where Brian Judd lived. The man with the beard had an alibi for that January night. He'd been seen in his office at Hammersmith and Fulham Council. Everyone was doing something else when Helen Honeysett went missing. Everyone except her dad. Her dad had liked Helen Honeysett. *She had liked him.* Megan stepped into the tunnel under Kew Railway Bridge.

★

'This is my one.' Megan lifted a yellow budgerigar off the perch where it had been preening itself and held it up for Helen Honeysett's inspection. 'I hand-reared her. She's called Mindy.' She enunciated the words with aplomb.

Helen Honeysett made a bird-like motion with her head. 'You shouldn't have picked it up so fast. How would you like to be swept off your feet unexpectedly?'

'It doesn't mind,' Megan mumbled, reddening. Garry swept them off their feet all the time. Did budgies have feet? She thought it was claws. He was at Scouts and he didn't know she had invited Helen Honeysett to his aviary. He would be livid because, Megan knew, he was secretly planning to ask her to come because he'd accidentally told her. It wasn't her fault Helen Honeysett was here. 'I'm desperate to choose my budgies!' she'd said.

'Remind me of the price?' Helen Honeysett had insisted on coming right into the aviary.

'Two pounds for blue ones and two pounds fifty for the yellow budgies because they're worth more than blue,' Megan inflated the prices she'd told her at the Ewell-tide House-Warming Party.

'He's enterprising, your bro! He'll be rich one day.'

'He spends it on more seeds and things.' Megan scuffled her feet on the dirt floor. 'I made him promise not to sell Mindy.' She raised the bird to her lips and kissed it.

'I want her!' Helen Honeysett made a cooing sound.

Megan closed her fingers around the bird. 'There's others.'

Helen Honeysett posted the black thing she called a pager into one of the roosting boxes and thrust her hands out for the bird. 'I want a hold.'

If she had been Angie, Megan would have said no. But it was Helen Honeysett so in case she got more 'desperate' Megan passed over the little bird.

It wasn't going to plan. After school, Megan had gone through *the gate in the back fence to see Mrs Merry, but Mrs Merry had trodden on poo which belonged to Baxter, the Honeysetts' dog. She had sent Megan away with no De-Cluttering.*

'Can it speak?' Helen Honeysett kissed the bird. Megan tried not to mind.

'I don't think so,' she faltered. 'I fed her from a pipette when she was little or she would have died. My dad says I have a way with animals.'

'Your dad has a way with the ladies!' Helen Honeysett did a funny laugh. 'Where is he? I thought he'd be here.'

'He had an emergency. He gets more money for those ones.' Megan remembered a conversation the night before between her parents. 'Daddy wishes that people had more floods.'

'I bet he does,' Helen Honeysett hooted.

'He's left me by myself, but he said to go to Daphne. She's through the garden. But she's busy with clearing up and...' Megan remembered her exciting idea from earlier that afternoon during the nature lesson. 'Actually I'm saving up for a corn snake.'

'A snake will kill you.' Helen Honeysett blew on one of the budgerigars swinging on the perches and clinging to the miniature ladders. The bird began frantically preening itself.

Suffused with disappointment about Helen Honeysett's reaction to the corn snake, Megan tried to take Mindy back from her, but Helen Honeysett didn't see. 'I think they're hungry. Garry's late giving them their supper. He'll be back any minute.' This was a warning to make Helen Honeysett go. Garry would be cross with Megan, not with Helen Honeysett for being there.

'Gorgeous Garry is the little entrepreneur, isn't he!'

Megan had no idea what that was, but guessed it was to do with budgies. Garry wasn't 'little'. 'He'll be thirteen in May. That's a teenager.'

Helen Honeysett flicked at one of the perches, making it swing. The yellow budgerigar tipped off. It flapped wildly and then flew up and clung to a ladder. Helen Honeysett said, 'Let's feed them!'

'I'm not allo— It's Garry's turn.' Megan couldn't admit she

wasn't even supposed to be in the aviary. She didn't want Helen Honeysett to know she had brought her without permission. She remembered another thing she could tell her. 'My dad made this aviary. He's a plumber not a carpenter so he says it's "a bit of a lash-up".'

'A "lash-up"!' Helen Honeysett did another funny laugh. 'I wonder though, isn't it cruel to keep birds in cages? I might let this one fly free.'

'That's what I think too!' Megan agreed with a heartiness she didn't feel. In a small voice, she cautioned, 'Except not outside cos of cats.' And not Mindy.

'Cats can't fly!' Helen Honeysett blew on Mindy's feathers. Maybe it was all right to do that? Helen Honeysett must know about it, she knew everything.

'Adam's getting me a Victorian cage for my birthday, the sort they used to put linnets in. To go with my grandmama's chaise longue. I'm going for a nineteenth-century feel in the house. Do they need all this clobber? It's not aesthetic.'

'No they don't!' Megan assured her fervently. Plastic toys and tufts of feathers were scattered on the ground; the wire sides sagged. Poo was splattered on platforms nailed crookedly to the central pole that no longer looked to her like tree branches. Suffused with shame, Megan wished she'd cleaned and tidied before she came. But how was she to know she was coming? Garry would be angry just for that. Scrutinizing the cage with the eagle eye of a De-Clutterer Megan saw a terrible muddle.

Megan urged the yellow bird, still clinging to the ladder, back on to the perch where it resumed picking and nuzzling at its feathers. Helen Honeysett shouldn't have blown on it, but Megan didn't want to spoil things by saying this

'Got to run!' Helen Honeysett declared. 'Tell your dad I came. Tell him our ballcock is stuck. He'll understand!' She thrust Mindy at Megan and unlatched the door, letting it swing wide after her.

'Me too.' Megan grabbed the door and shut it. She realized

*that Helen Honeysett might mean a real run and not that she
was busy and felt foolish. In a rush she deposited Mindy in
her nest box and latched the aviary door. She caught up with
Helen Honeysett in the kitchen. Helen Honeysett flung aside
the bead curtain, setting it swinging in all directions. Following
her, Megan got tangled up in it. At the front door Megan heard
Helen Honeysett swear without noticing, 'Shit, I've left my pager
in your dad's lash-up!'*

'I'll get it.'

*'It'll only take a second.' Mrs Honeysett pushed through the
curtain again; strings of beads trailed over her shoulders. A
draught whistled through the house when the back door opened,
rustling dried flowers in a vase in the hall and making the bead
curtain sway as it gathered strength. The front door slammed
shut as she reappeared.*

*'Did you find it?' Her pager was another reason why Helen
Honeysett was quite different from everyone else.*

*'Yes. Can't be without that. My lovely boss'll have my guts!
Does Steve have a pager?' She seemed more interested in that
than about the corn snake.*

'Yes he does!' Megan gasped at her impromptu untruth.

*'Cool. I'll page him. I have his card.' At the gate Helen
Honeysett blew Megan a kiss.*

*Megan felt a rush of happiness. It made up for the fact she'd
forgotten to say she was Mrs Merry's Trusted De-Cluttering
Assistant. The visit was a success after all.*

Dusk was drawing in. The reporters and the police had gone
from the towpath. The tide had covered all but the top step at
Kew Stairs.

Megan had seen his coffin trundle into the furnace, yet ten
years on she still looked for her dad. Now she scanned the
towpath, yearning to see him strolling towards her out of
the shadows with Smudge loping along by his side. Instead she

saw Daphne Merry with her dog. She passed Megan without recognizing her. Daphne Merry didn't have a De-Cluttering Assistant any more. Her mother said that losing her seven-year-old daughter had driven her mad. Did losing someone you loved drive you mad?

Through a hole in the hedge, she saw a face. Megan rushed inside and straight up the stairs. Ignoring the 'Trespassers Keep Out' sign she barged into her brother's bedroom. 'Garry!' He wasn't there. The bed was a heap of sheets and blankets, covered with bird breeders' magazines and the Transformers he said he was too old for, but wouldn't let her play with. His school uniform was crumpled on the carpet. The room smelled of him. Garry would make the man stop staring. So would her dad if he wasn't in Hell. Because of her.

Her heart knocked against her chest. Megan went to her parents' bedroom and tried to see into the park, but the hedge was too high. Exhausted, she sat on their bed.

She was still there an hour later when Bette Lawson came home from her shift at the hospital.

'What are you doing in here?' she demanded not unkindly as she began to change out of her uniform.

'Sitting,' Megan replied blankly.

'I can see that.'

The man from number 1 was in the park again. Megan rehearsed the sentence, but couldn't say it. After her dad, she was scared to make trouble and Mr Rowlands was only sitting. Helen Honeysett had said he was a sweetie.

'Would you like a cup of tea?'

'Lovely, thanks, Megs.' Bette was bundling her uniform into the snake charmer's washing basket by her dressing table. She went to the wardrobe and pulled out a pair of jeans and a jumper. She lingered in front of the open wardrobe and then eventually said in a faraway tone, 'I need to get rid of these.'

Megan saw her dad's best suit that he wore at Aunty El's wedding. 'The shortest marriage in history,' he had laughed when her aunty divorced. Megan said, 'I'll help you.'

'You've done enough.' With a tight smile, Bette shut the wardrobe.

Filling the kettle, Megan didn't know if her mum had been nice or cross. Garry was always cross. Had he known Helen Honeysett visited his budgies before she went missing, he'd be crosser. Her mum came into the kitchen. She chucked her pager down on the table.

'Does... did Daddy have one of those?' Surprised by her own question, Megan stood with the fridge door open.

'Wish to God he had...' Bette Lawson poured hot water into her mug. 'I could have paged him...' She heaved a sigh. 'Wake up and pass me the milk, Megs!'

'Helen Honeysett had a pager.'

'Shame she forgot it when she went to the river.'

'She forgot it in the lash-up.' Megan pictured the bird poo in the aviary. Her time with Helen Honeysett and the budgies – over a year ago – had gained mythical signifance to the eight-year-old.

'What are you on about now, Megan?' Distracted, Bette took the milk bottle from her daughter.

'I wish I had a pager.' Megan had forgotten that Helen Honeysett's visit was a secret she must never tell.

'We're not forking out...' Bette trailed to silence. She returned the bottle to the fridge and went out to the living room.

Megan followed her. She twitched the curtain. It was too dark to see Mr Rowlands, but she knew he was there.

Megan was leaving home tomorrow. She was going to Sydney. Her childhood friend Keith had emigrated there when they were six. She didn't know where he lived, Australia was a vast place and she didn't expect to find him. But it was something to have a friend of a kind somewhere.

Megan pictured the word printed in blood red on the posters
ten years ago. *Missing*. No one would miss her.

Who am I and what have I done?

Chapter Forty-Three

Monday, 11 January 2016

The spots of rain spattering the windscreen were insufficient to lubricate the wipers and the rubber blades squeaked across on the glass. The sound was like the squeaking of the digger's claw. Jack shivered at the memory.

The clock on the van's dashboard said five past eight as they pulled in to a car park in Kent Road off the South Circular. A car was leaving. Jack caught the muffled chorus of 'Starman'. All the radio stations would be playing Bowie.

Megan Lawson lived in a shabby block of eighties-style flats with greying-white plastic trim around the rim of the flat roof. Each flat had a Juliet balcony and a picture window.

'Read me the number on that dog collar you found in the digger.' Stella pulled up the phone app on her handset.

The ringing came through the speakers. Jack counted nine rings then silence. Stella reached for the red button. He stopped her.

'Hello? Anyone there?' Nothing. He reached to the dashboard and turned up the volume. Someone was breathing into the mouthpiece. The quality of the silence changed to dead air. He said, 'Someone was there, then they cut the line.'

'Why do that?'

'Curiosity overcame a judicious intent I'd say, at a guess.'

'What?'

'Whoever answered knew they shouldn't pick up the phone, but they couldn't resist hearing who was calling.'

'If they had spoken we could have told them who we are.' Stella pressed redial.

'True.' Jack knew that urge to step from the shadows to see who was there.

Stella tried again and this time the phone rang on. No one picked up.

'Waste of time.' Stella took the phone off the dashboard cradle and got out of the van. 'Anyone could have left the collar in Latimer's basement. Probably the person's frightened of con men and kept quiet to avoid getting embroiled in some scam.'

'Maybe.' Jack wasn't convinced.

He joined Stella as she was pressing a button on a door panel. The top half was glazed wired glass giving a view of an insipidly lit lobby. Junk mail lay scattered across the concrete floor. Jack read *Miss S. Benson* on what looked like a bill.

Stella said, 'The line I suggest we take is we don't think her father is guilty or she'll clam up.'

'We don't think he is guilty, do we?' Jack said. 'We have open minds.'

'Yes, but if we say that she'll probably interpret it to mean we think he's guilty. Best to seem to come down on her side. Do you want to lead?'

Stella was suggesting a less-than-honest approach and Jack's unease at the change in her increased. 'You do it. I'll be the friendly sidekick there to reassure her that we're nice.'

Stella frowned. Jack guessed she was considering that might be a tall order.

Her phone buzzed. 'Hi, Mum.' He heard twittering through the handset. 'Are you OK?' Stella changed the phone to her other ear. 'Have you fallen? *Don't* move! I'm coming!' More twittering. 'Oh, is that all… Oh dear! But it might be too late.'

Jack wondered what was too late. What had Suzie done or not done? The possibilities were endless.

'Give me a date and I'll send round a van.' Stella rang off.

'What's happened?'

'You know Mum got Daphne Merry to declutter her flat? She regrets it. She says she doesn't know who she is and she's lost her bearings.' Stella chewed her lower lip. 'She wants her clutter back.'

Wanting clutter would make no sense to Stella. And she had a very clear idea of who, and where, she was.

'It makes sense to me. The flat looked like it had been raided. All Mum's treasured possessions had gone.'

Jack groaned inwardly. Stella had confounded him again. 'Won't Daphne have thrown everything away?'

'Seems she has a cooling-off period. Suzie rang her. She was upset by Merry's response.'

'Was she rude?' Jack imagined that Daphne Merry would be professional about failure. Feeling vaguely that he must defend her, he murmured, 'It was a nice Jamaican ginger cake.'

'She was probably fine. I think Mum was hoping they'd be friends.' Stella's expression could be horror at the idea of a new friend or sympathy for Suzie. 'Could you be there when it's collected? It'll be a reason to talk to her again.'

'It will.' Stella was thinking like a detective. Jack didn't say that he too hoped that Daphne Merry might be a friend.

Megan Lawson's sitting room was a testimony to decluttering. There were no pictures, no television or sound system. Even Stella's house, while intended to give nothing of herself away, reflected the Stella he knew. Or thought he knew. This room was a negation of self, anonymous and unlived-in. Megan Lawson had to fetch two chairs from elsewhere in her flat for them which suggested she seldom had guests. Jack wondered what it had cost her to let them in.

'At this stage we have absolutely no idea what happened to Helen Honeysett,' Stella assured Megan Lawson.

'My father killed her.'

'Pardon?' Stella dropped her Filofax on the floor.

'My dad couldn't live with the guilt. He killed himself. The Metropolitan Police have no proof, but they know it was him.'

Megan Lawson was slight, and, Jack calculated, about his own age, late thirties. However, lines around her eyes and long greying hair made her look older. She was not much over five feet and when she opened her front door he and Stella had towered over her. Her sparsely furnished sitting room was as chilly as Latimer's basement, but not, Jack guessed, due to soulless design, but because Lawson skimped on heating. Her fleece, worn jeans and scruffy trainers suggested she skimped on most things. She avoided eye contact and stared at a spot above Stella's head when she talked. At one point, Stella glanced up to see if there was something there. Megan Lawson had the disconcerting habit of humming under her breath when she wasn't talking. Jack was redundant; she wouldn't care if he and Stella were nice, she was barely aware of them.

He felt he had seen her before, but couldn't place her. He encountered many people, passengers on his trains. He would study the rows of blank faces of the people waiting on platforms in his search for a True Host. Megan Lawson had probably been a passenger.

'Your mother doesn't agree.' Stella was taking a combative tack.

'Do you always agree with your mother's view of your father?' Megan Lawson retorted. 'Mum's obsessed with proving my father innocent. She won't accept the obvious. He murdered a woman and disposed of her body. My aunt said Mum won't move on until she does.' She resumed her tuneless humming.

'You put on your application form you lived in Australia. It wasn't true,' Jack said.

'I said to Mrs Darnell: go on, *sack* me.' Megan Lawson shot him a hostile look. 'If your father was a murderer, wouldn't you want to be someone else?'

Jack could only agree with this.

'Jackie Makepeace told you we won't sack you.' Stella tapped a blank page of her Filofax with her pen.

'I did go to Australia,' Lawson said abruptly. 'I got my dad arrested. It might have been the right thing, but it's never felt right. I tried to kill myself. Twice. The first time I stepped under a train at Wynyard Station in Sydney. They took two hours to cut me out. All I have to show for it is this.' She pushed up her sleeve to reveal a livid scar from her wrist to her elbow. She fixed on the ceiling above Stella again. 'When I came back to London, I kept away from the river. One day I checked in to a hotel near Charing Cross Station and overdosed on paracetamol. I shovelled down enough to kill me. My liver's shot: I'm on the slow train there.'

Jack regarded the pale wispy woman. Megan Lawson wasn't an imposter, she was struggling to live her shattered life.

'Why do you believe Steven Lawson killed Helen Honeysett?' Stella asked gently.

'Dad was a killer.'

In the silence, Jack heard kids shouting outside. 'Get him. *Wanker!*'

Stella put down her pen. 'What do you mean?'

'He killed his family on the day he drowned. My brother breeds budgerigars and sulks in his room like the teenager he was in 1987. No need for suicide, he's dead already. Mum's a survivor, she works at the hospital and keeps the home going unaware that it's already gone. We meet at her canteen sometimes. She can't have me in the house or Garry will go mad. Madder. I'm sure she'd rather I'd died. Dad's suicide put us in grooves: we go round and round like wind-up toys. My aunty used to be proud of me for speaking out. Truth is we're all in Hell.' Megan Lawson stared at the ceiling, humming. 'My aunty's too busy to see me.'

'You live near the river now,' Jack said.

'It's where I belong,' Megan Lawson said.

'The police let your father go. Why do you think he's guilty?' Stella persisted.

'I was a kid, I knew Dad liked Honeysett, she made him laugh, but I didn't think anything of it. Mrs Merry made me see. Like Mum, she's a survivor.'

'Why is she a survivor?' Jack hadn't meant to ask but, scribbling in her Filofax, Stella gave no sign she minded his interjection.

'Her husband and daughter were killed in a car crash before she moved to Thames Cottages.' Megan Lawson hummed a snatch of tune. 'It's why she spent time with me. I made up for her daughter.'

'If your dad liked Helen Honeysett, why would he kill her?' Stella steered her back on track.

'Honeysett was a gorgeous girl about town and Dad was a plumber with an overdraft and two kids. Fun to flirt with on the towpath, but end of. He made a pass and she gave him the brush-off.' She resumed her humming.

'How do you know this?' Stella turned to a clean page.

Megan Lawson shrugged.

'Did he have a temper?' Stella wasn't giving up.

'My mum could lose it. He was the silent type, he'd just leave the house.'

'Did he hit you or your brother?'

'He never hurt us.'

Stella said nothing. She would be doing a 'detective silence'. Her dad had said, *'Let a void open and the interviewee will fall into it.'*

Jack heard the thud of the lobby door, then footsteps, slow and ponderous, on the stairs. They paused outside her flat. There was the jangle of keys and a door opened and closed.

'Dad bottled up his emotions, but Honeysett got to him,' Lawson said eventually.

'What would he gain by killing her?' Stella was having to rejig the angle of her questions because rather than defending him, as they'd expected, Steven Lawson's daughter was a fierce exponent of his guilt.

'A person can be murdered out of fury.' Megan addressed the ceiling: 'I'm sorry, but I can't help you. In fact, I don't want to help. I don't need a couple of would-be detectives raking up the past. I told the police I saw my father go after Helen Honeysett. My brother saw him too, but swears he didn't. Go and torture him.' She broke into a hum and then, 'Like my aunty says, innocent men don't walk into the river and drown themselves.'

'Actually they do.' Jack shifted on his chair. 'Living under a cloud of suspicion can be too much to bear.'

'He wasn't the only one living under a cloud. He's made us all guilty. You have no idea what it's like to step off a platform in front of a train!'

'Well, in fact...' Jack trailed off. Drivers dreaded getting a 'One Under'. Many went through their working lives without someone jumping into the path of their cab, others had it more than once. He'd had one and been a witness to another. Most drivers found it hard to get over. Jack still saw the expression of the man who had looked directly at him as he jumped. It was unfair to resent Megan Lawson for choosing that way to end her life, but he did.

Perhaps Stella guessed his feelings because she changed the subject. 'Who lived at number 1 Thames Cottages in 1987?'

'Neville something. Garry said he murdered Honeysett, but he had an alibi. He was creepy, used to watch the houses through the hedge.'

Jack sat up. Now they were getting somewhere. 'Did you tell the police?'

'Nothing to tell. Like I said, Rowlands – that was his name – had an alibi for that night: he was caring for his mother. Besides, I heard Helen Honeysett with Dad on the towpath.'

'You were there?' Stella leant forward. 'Did you tell the police?'

'What business is it of yours?' Megan Lawson countered.

'Did your family know that you left your house?' Jack asked. Stella had mentioned reading in Adam Honeysett's file that Megan had gone to the towpath. How had he known?

'No! My mum would have told the police. Garry knows. He just can't bear to face it.'

'Adam Honeysett knows.' Stella had remembered too.

If it were possible Megan went even paler. 'We went out for a drink a few months ago. I forgot I told him.'

'Why did you go out?' Stella pursued.

'Not on a date if that's where you're going.' Megan hummed and then interrupted herself. 'He was quizzing me about that night. Like you are.' More humming.

Jack knew it wasn't the first time a wife had helped cover up a murder for her husband. Was this why Garry Lawson couldn't leave? He wasn't being the husband his mother had lost, he was making sure she didn't reveal the truth about Steven Lawson.

'Did you see your father with Helen Honeysett?' Stella was filling her Filofax page with her neat script.

'I was hiding on the riverbank.' Her humming sounded like a variation on the theme for *The Good, the Bad and the Ugly*.

'What did you hear?' Stella kept her eyes on Megan Lawson, although the other woman never met her gaze.

'She said, "Oh, it's you!"'

'How close were you?' Stella was her father's daughter.

'No idea. About ten feet?'

'Why were you sure it was Helen Honeysett?' Jack asked. Stella's slight nod told him it would have been her next question.

'Who else could it have been?'

If Stella had been tempted to answer 'pretty much anyone' she resisted. 'What did you do next?'

'I climbed up the bank. I'd been stupid; the tide was rising. If I'd slipped I'd have fallen in. There was no one on the tow-path. I ran home. My mum was in the kitchen, she was crying, but she hid her face. She never knew I'd been out.'

'Mrs Merry found Helen's dog on her way back from Kew Bridge.' Stella made of show of looking back on her notes. 'Could it have been her that you overheard?'

'No.' More humming.

'Can I get this straight?' Stella was sketching a map of the towpath. 'Daphne Merry turned left from the cottages on to the towpath towards Kew Bridge and Helen Honeysett always went right and passed Mortlake Crematorium. So how come Merry found Honeysett's dog?'

'When Helen Honeysett was jogging, she never noticed him run off. Baxter tried to go home, but got confused and passed the steps to the cottages. Mrs Merry hated carelessness. "One day he'll drown," she said. Dad rescued Baxter once.' Despite her conviction that Steven Lawson had murdered their neighbour, Jack saw a fleeting look of pride at this memory. Again he saw the seven-year-old Megan Lawson had been.

'So Daphne Merry didn't have an alibi?' Stella was sharp.

'Of course she did, that creep saw her.'

'What creep?' Jack tried to hide his excitement. They were getting warmer.

'I just told you. Neville Rowlands was always following Daphne when she walked Woof.'

'Woof?' Jack echoed. 'Was that her dog's name?'

'Her little girl named him,' Megan explained.

The dog would have been all Daphne had left of her family. Jack remembered his meeting with Daphne on the towpath. 'Isn't Woof the name of her dog now?'

'I don't see her now.' Megan was curt.

'Why did Neville Rowlands follow Merry?' Stella was on point.

'He wasn't following her, he was walking his dog.' Megan looked irritated. 'Helen said he was a sweetie.'

'Why did she think he was a "sweetie"?' Personally, Jack was happy to move Neville Rowlands up to pole position on their suspect list.

'She said that about everyone. You couldn't trust her.'

Stella didn't disguise her surprise. 'Why not?'

'She let my brother's birds escape. Some died. Neville Rowlands found one in his garden and brought it back. I told

Helen Honeysett. She wouldn't confess what she'd done. She said that if Neville Rowlands moved out, the owner could do up the house and make a fortune. He'd lived there all his life. Like my parents he was a tenant. When Mum dies Garry will be homeless.' A shadow passed across her face. Garry Lawson had cut off his sister for suspecting their father of murder. Yet still Megan worried about his welfare. Must be a sibling thing. Jack liked her for it.

'How could Neville Rowlands have seen Daphne Merry on the towpath if he was at home looking after his mother?' Stella missed little.

'He took his dog for a pee. He said he saw Daphne coming back from Kew Bridge with Baxter and Woof. His mother confirmed he was away for five minutes.' Megan roused herself. 'Neville Rowlands wasn't a sweetie, he was a total creep, but don't go pinning this on him. Or anyone else. My dad did it and then killed himself.'

'Who else was on the towpath?' Stella was contemplating her map. 'In 1987 everyone in the street owned a dog.'

'How should I know? Since I heard my dad, it's irrelevant.' Jack noticed that Megan Lawson had a fine line in couching conjecture as unstinting fact.

'You didn't say you heard your dad.' Stella's tone was even.

'I heard her and he was with her.' Megan stood up. 'The one you should be talking to is my aunt. She's written articles on it. She'll write a book one day.'

'Your aunt is a reporter?' Stella remained sitting.

'An *investigative journalist*. Dad called her a "hack".' Megan carried on humming.

Megan Lawson was familiar, not because she'd been on his train or on a station platform, but because she had the same brown eyes and full mouth as someone he and Stella knew all too well. Someone who was going to write a book 'one day'. Someone who had a fine line in whisking up fact from hazy supposition.

'Who is your aunty?' Stella knew.

Megan Lawson stopped humming and fixed directly on Stella. 'She's called Lucille May.'

Chapter Forty-Four

Tuesday, 6 January 1987

The bedroom door burst open. Megan dropped her pencil on the carpet.

'You've done it now.' Garry's fists were balled. Despite this threatening pose, Megan only noticed that his cheeks were wet with tears.

'Garry! What's happened?' *Had Mum gone to the river?* She put out her hands to hug her brother.

Choked by sobs, Garry spluttered, 'You killed them. *Murderer!* You killed...' He dashed a sleeve across his face and swept the drawing pad and a jar of colouring pencils off the little desk. He retrieved the pad and began systematically to rip up each page, flinging scraps of paper in all directions.

'Stop! Please,' Megan protested feebly.

'What's going on in here? Garry, put that down now!' Bette Lawson stormed into the room and snatched what remained of the pad off her son. She dropped it on the uncluttered desk, giving the pad a pat as if that might restore it. 'What's the matter?'

'She's evil!' Garry's voice trembled with suppressed fury. 'She's killed my birds!'

'Do *not* talk about your sister like that. What do you mean she's killed your birds?' Bette Lawson went to the window, but it was dark so she couldn't see the aviary.

'She went in without my permission. She left the cage door open on purpose.'

Megan came to life. 'I did not!' She set about gathering up the bits of paper. Garry gave her a kick; it wasn't hard, but it knocked Megan off balance.

'Garry! Whatever Megan has done, we don't have violence in this house.' Bette Lawson paused, perhaps registering there was no 'we'.

'*She* is violent!' Garry scrubbed at his hair with both hands. 'She killed my birds.'

'I did not!' Helen Honeysett's visit was her secret. 'I made 'specially sure the door was fastened properly. I did your drill. Make sure no budgies are by the cage door, back out and put the latch on behind you. I did that. That's what I did.' She ran out of breath.

Bette Lawson would have liked to do what Steven did when things got difficult and take the dog for a walk. Let the kids fight it out. Let someone else sort out the mess. But as per Steven had left her to deal with it and gone off to do a job. Or so he said. Bette had picked up what remained of Megan's pad and was twisting it, bending the spiral spine.

'Are you sure you shut the cage when you left, Megan? Better to tell the truth.'

'I did. I am sure.' Megan saw Helen Honeysett's retreating figure, the beads slung around her shoulders. She had gone back for her pager thingy. Megan stared blankly at her mum... She couldn't tell her mum about Helen Honeysett visiting or her mum would realise who had left the cage open. Yet it was quite impossible that Helen Honeysett would do such a thing. The afternoon with Helen Honeysett felt suddenly wrong and strange.

'What's happened?' Bette Lawson turned her attention to her son.

'Three birds got out and the dog that belongs to the old lady at the end killed one.'

'Which bird was killed?' Megan asked tremulously. Her brother ignored her.

'Garry, if Megan says she didn't leave the cage open then she didn't.' Bette wearily took off her mac and folded and refolded it. Absently, she corrected her son, 'Miss Lofthouse isn't old.'

'The one you hand-reared. Its head is ripped off.' Garry was stony-faced.

Megan went white. 'Mindy's dead?'

'Garry!' Bette dropped the mac on Megan's bed and took him by the shoulders. 'Stop it!'

Megan said, 'Can I help bury Mindy?'

'Stay out of it.' Garry shook off his mother's hands and slammed into his bedroom.

In that moment, Bette Lawson saw the man that her son would become. A stolid and silent individual who would no longer love her.

Megan subsided on to her bed. In her seven-year-old way, she too saw that Garry was properly gone. 'I *was* telling the truth,' she said to no one in particular. 'I fastened it tight shut.'

Weeks later everything was different. Helen Honeysett was missing; Steven Lawson lay on a slab in the Richmond Morgue; his daughter Megan sat at her bedroom window staring out at the night. The lawn was patterned with moonlight and she could just see the aviary; the mesh, washed with silver light, was like cobwebs. The birds would be in their beds. Except for Mindy. Where was she? With her dad, she hoped.

Dubious about God, because if there was one it would be true that her dad was in Hell, Megan gazed towards the rose bush where Garry had buried his birds.

Mechanically, she whispered the Lord's Prayer:

'Our Father in heaven,
Hallowed be your name...'

Hours later, drifting into a fitful sleep, Megan saw a tiny feathered form lying on the floor of the aviary. She looked closer. Its head was missing.

Your kingdom come,
Your will be done,
On earth as in heaven...

Chapter Forty-Five

'Lord Peter Wimsey and Miss Marple!' Lucie May's voice crackled from a speaker beside the front door. 'Come to update me on what's occurring in the murky subterranean worlds of deep cleaning and late-night passion wagons?'

Jack and Stella waited.

'*Entrez!*' the Dalek voice gargled. Jack pushed on the front door; it held fast.

A static cackle. 'Harder, Jacko!'

Stella tried; still the door remained stubbornly shut.

'Lucie, could you please come and open it?' Jack addressed a badly concealed camera amid a clump of ivy above the door.

'*Harder!*'

'It's locked.' Talking to the ivy, Stella was unruffled. 'You need to wire the lock to open when you activate it. This is a mechanical lock, it works manually.'

Jack mouthed at Stella quizzically.

'She's installed a Wi-Fi doorbell. It rings on your phone and you can see who's there and talk to them. But not if—' The door flew wide and, waving her mobile phone, Lucie May was before them.

'Bloody thing.' She sashayed into her sitting room. Dressed in her late-night garb of a baggy shirt that was her 'hated ex-hubby's', a jumper slung over her shoulders and tight black

leggings, she was already curled in her corner of the sofa, legs
tucked under, nibbling on a carrot by the time they joined her.

'What's that smell?' Jack asked as a sharp tang assailed
him.

'Lemon oil. Wards off depression and mosquitoes.' Lucie
wagged her carrot at Stella. 'It's better than bleach for cleaning
showers and whatnot.'

'Are you depressed?' Jack was concerned. He had feared that
the noxious mix of driven ambition and constant disappointment would take its toll.

'Have I the time or luxury?' Lucie chomped up her carrot and
reached for another from a line of crudités laid in a row on the
coffee table before her. 'Nippets, both?' she warbled cheerily and,
springing up, flew across to her 'Nippet Station'. She unscrewed
a bottle of Gilbey's gin, doing a skipping motion that belied any
suggestion of depression.

'No thanks,' Stella said. 'Actually alcohol is a depressive.'
Lucie's shoulders stiffened. Jack knew Stella wasn't judging – she
was a stern judge only of herself – she was stating a fact. Wary of
each other, the two women were polite for pragmatic purposes.
If they were going to fall out, Jack wanted to be far away.

'Not in small doses.' Lucie filled her glass with a generous
helping of gin and a cursory splash of tonic. She tossed in an
ice cube and a sliver of lemon from a dish on the pull-down
flap in her cabinet and meandered back to the sofa. 'Sit down,
Thompson and Thomson!'

She brushed aside papers and chocolate wrappers scattered
on the sofa and signalled to Jack to join her. She appeared to
have forgotten Stella was there.

Stella removed more papers and a wizened carrot from an
armchair at a distance from the sofa and sat down.

Lucie took a slug of her 'nippet' and produced, from beside the
rank of carrots, a phial of lemon oil, sprinkling it indiscriminately.
Drops fell around Jack's polished brogues. He scooted his feet
back. He didn't care about many material possessions, but he

did care about his shoes. 'Feel your mood lighten and the cogs in your minds whirr,' Lucie trilled.

'We've met your niece.' If Stella intended to break Lucie May's light mood, she succeeded.

'What niece?' Lucie hugged her knees, the pose of a girl. She suddenly looked old, her hands bony and trembling.

'Megan Lawson. Although she goes by the name of Stephanie Benson.' Stella unzipped her jacket and settled back in the chair. 'She's your sister's daughter,' she reminded her. Jack could see Lucie didn't need reminding.

'Nothing wrong with changing your name, especially when it's tainted.' Lucie snatched up her glass and took a gulp, grimacing as if it was medicine. She drank some more. 'I told her to go to Clean Slate. She'll raise the bar on standards and turn your business around.' She gave Stella a gladiatorial glare over the rim of her glass. 'So, Miss Prissy-Poos, did you sack her for changing her name?'

If Stella was surprised by this news, she was the perfect poker player. 'Megan suggested we talk to you about Helen Honeysett. We've been asked to investigate her death.'

'By my niece?' Lemon oil notwithstanding, Lucie's mood had become as dark as an impending storm. Jack tried to catch Stella's eye; it was time to leave.

'By Honeysett's husband.' Stella eyed Lucie, unblinking. 'Megan said you'd shed light on the background.'

'Actually, Stella, we should be—' Jack tried to get up, but the squashy sofa had swallowed him and he couldn't get purchase.

In record time Lucie assembled another gin and tonic and had left the room. They heard her call from above, 'You want background? I'll give you fucking background.'

Jack had never been upstairs at Lucie May's. Although she had decorated the sitting room, the landing had not been touched since at least the 1960s. Wood chip wallpaper, orange above the dado, cream below. Neither colour, stained by nicotine, likely to be the original.

'Where's she gone?' Stella indicated three doors, all shut.

'Let's go,' Jack whispered. 'This was a mistake.' Recently he'd made a lot of mistakes. He'd left his home and his memories and Bella had left him. Now they were mired in Lucie's very private life. He backed down the stairs.

Stella tapped on the nearest door. 'Lucie?'

'Come.' The voice didn't sound like Lucie.

Jack had no choice but to go with Stella. Keeping close to her, when she stopped abruptly, he banged into her. He saw why.

The walls were papered with photographs of a woman, posing in a graduation gown and cap, leaning on railings with a river behind her and smiling into the lens. Some in black and white, others in lurid colour, on newsprint and glossy photographic paper. One wall was given over to a vast whiteboard ribboned with yellow and pink sticky notes and scribbled observations. Coloured arrows spoked out from a name circled in red and hatched in black as if behind prison bars, 'Steven Lawson'.

Jack had once stumbled upon a murderer's shrine. There too were images of a young woman, raising a glass of wine in a toast, eyes bright, perfect teeth pearly white. Here was another young woman bathed in summer sun, her hair glossy as a shampoo advert. Helen Honeysett laughed into the lens as if she might confidently evade her fate.

Jack had always supposed Lucie's 'Captain Kirk Bridge' was on her sofa within reach of a nippet. He'd picture her, fingers flying over the keyboard, churning out bread and butter stories for local newspapers, always chasing the Holy Grail of a scoop and the syndicated big time. But her true sanctum was her spare bedroom.

All around them, under headlines such as *Cold-Blooded Killer*, *The Quiet One*, *The Towpath Monster*, Steven Lawson's baby-faced features beamed out. Jack recognized the seven-year-old Megan Lawson with an older boy – her brother Garry – and Bette

Lawson at Mortlake Crematorium. In the girl's tight features, he saw the woman they had met earlier that evening. Garry Lawson clutched his mother's arm. Megan was a pace apart from them. From the set of his shoulders, Garry wasn't just supporting Bette Lawson, but ensuring Megan couldn't get near her.

'Sit down. Stop hovering like a pair of lily-livers!' Lucie barked.

As he shut the door, Jack went cold. A sheet of paper was stuck to the back of it with four drawing pins. 'Who am I and what have I done?' The writing was jagged, in thick red felt pen, and the letters, larger with each word, gave a different sense on the question typed in Courier font that had floated on Natasha Latimer's screensaver. Was Lucie the intruder? He tried to sound hearty: 'So, this is the nerve centre!'

Seated at a table heaped with newspapers and files, used mugs and foil takeaway containers, Lucie span around in her chair to face them. 'Welcome to the "Murder Room".'

'Lucie, we ought to lea—' Jack began.

'Steven Lawson lured Helen Honeysett to her death.' Lucie might have been reading a bedtime story. Jack felt a creeping chill down his back.

'You know he did?' Stella appeared unaware of Lucie's strange controlled state.

'He had motive, opportunity and means. Done deal.'

'What was his motive?' Hands behind her back, Stella strolled around the room examining the walls as if she were in an art gallery.

'He was terrified Helen Honeysett would tell his wife – my baby sister – he'd made a pass at her. He needed Bette's money, his business was down the pan – pun intended – and he needed the respectability of a family. Besides, Honeysett didn't want him. He was desperate. She had to go.' She spoke with the same certainty as Megan Lawson, although their theories about what had happened differed. Megan assumed her dad had wanted to be with Honeysett; Lucie was saying he'd killed her because she threatened his status quo.

'And the means?' Stella asked.

'A plumber has an armoury of murder weapons at his disposal.' Lucie grabbed a bag of crudités from a drawer in her desk and ripped it open with her teeth. Carrots spilled across her papers. She snatched one up and began sucking on it furiously.

When Lucie was chasing a story she was tenacious. She had provided them with leads and on more than one occasion was present at a crucial moment. But this mystery involved her own family and it seemed she couldn't be impartial. Jack knew she would dislike them talking to her niece; Lucie liked to hold all the cards. He was shaken. In the past he'd relied on her ebullient if dark humour, but tonight there were no jokes. Lucie May was a stranger. Time to go.

'Helen Honeysett's husband had a motive too.' Stella was steadfast.

'He had an alibi. His mistress vouched for him. Crap for the "heartbroken hubby" routine, but it got him off the hook. He couldn't be in two places at once. Everyone in that street had an alibi except Stevie baby.' Lucie crunched on a carrot. A piece dropped on to her shirt and she bashed it off with a violence that unnerved Jack.

'Adam Honeysett could have hired a contract killer,' Stella said.

'This isn't James Bond.' Lucie was chilly.

'Honeysett and Jane Drake could have done it together. They had joint motive.' Stella still had her back to Lucie. Jack was relieved she couldn't see Lucie's if-looks-could-horribly-kill expression.

'Jane Drake was seen buying cheap plonk from an off-licence at Kew Gardens station at the time Honeysett left the house. Another witness saw her returning to her flat minutes later. She had no chance to get to the towpath and do away with fair Helen. Face it, PC Clean-Up, they're in the clear.'

'The murderer might not have lived in Thames Cottages?' Stella was tenacious too. 'Anyone could have killed Helen Honeysett. A customer or a colleague at the estate agent's.

A perfect stranger.' She had obviously abandoned her method of working with limited suspects.

'Top marks, Inspector Clouseau! I never thought of that!' Lucie snarled. 'No one reported seeing strangers on the towpath. Only dog walkers go there at night. Whoever it was had an intimate knowledge of the girl's routine. *Means*: Lawson lived two doors down and walked his dog with Honeysett. *Motive*' – she thumped her fist on the desk – 'the chap was a sex maniac. *Method*: Lawson attacked her on the towpath, weighed her down with lead piping and chucked her in the Thames. She sank without trace. My brother-in-law ticks all the boxes.' Lucie's ferocity had gone up a notch. 'I told my sister to steer clear of him. She looked OK, she could have had anyone. Bette has no self-esteem, so she went for the first man who batted his eyes.' She seized another carrot. 'Ma and Pa had me, but they wanted a boy. Second go – and that was a miracle, they couldn't stand each other – was another friggin' girl. The poor kid had failed before she was out of nappies. Mr Ballcock comes to mend our boiler and wham bam! My blokes have been disasters, but at least I never fell in love. Pater wouldn't as much as speak to my "beaus", but with Bette he didn't care. I'd come home and find Pipe-Cutter slouching on the sofa scoffing my mother's nasty parrot-seed cake. Next thing, Bette's prancing down the aisle and having his babies. Seventeen she was when she had Garry. A bright future flushed down the toilet.' Lucie could be blunt, but Jack had never heard her so vicious. He hugged into his coat in an attempt to disappear.

'The evidence against Lawson is circumstantial.' Stella was positively serene.

'As your daddy said, *Ste-llah*, feel the truth there!' Lucie thumped her stomach so hard Jack winced. 'Mine tells me Lawson murdered Honeysett. Ask yourself, has another girl disappeared by the towpath? Have other dogs been found wandering there? No! Lawson topped himself and since then no one's copped it.'

'Dad also said, "Don't let a hunch blind you to the evidence." Whoever killed Helen Honeysett may have killed again, but they got even better at concealing the evidence. The victim may be someone who's not been reported missing.' Jack could have hugged Stella.

'Get real!' Lucie gave a wintry smile. 'Even Lawson's own daughter knows he did it. Doesn't that tell you something?'

'Megan was a little girl. She may have been wrong or she misunderstood what she saw. Her brother doesn't think his father was guilty.'

'Garry has the brain of a budgie. Thank God for Widow Merry, that old dame has her head screwed on, unlike the other weirdos in that street. She's known real shit in her life, her man took their seven-year-old kid on a ride to oblivion. She bothered with Megan before Mr U-Bend drowned himself and Bette went to la-la land. The Merrys lived in Hammersmith; that crash in Sussex was my first story.'

'What year was that?' Jack asked. Lucie frequently claimed news events as her 'first story': it was impossible to pin down her age. Daphne Merry had been thirty-eight in 1987.

'Nineteen eighty-five.' Lucie tossed the remainder of her carrot at an overflowing wastepaper basket and missed. Shrivelled bits of carrot, dried and curling, encircled the wired basket along with screwed-up paper and chewing-gum wrappers.

'You have to be prepared to abandon a theory, follow the evidence.' Stella was looking at a picture of Steven Lawson being mobbed by a nasty-looking crowd and reporters outside Richmond Police Station. 'Avoid reaching a conclusion too soon and passing up a vital clue.' She moved towards the door; any moment she would see the question stuck there. Jack was suddenly certain that they mustn't tell Lucie where they'd seen it before. 'Your sister's convinced Lawson didn't do it.'

'That shit-bird plumber cruised through life scot-free. He won't get away with murder.'

'Steven Lawson's dead,' Stella observed benignly. 'He hasn't got away with it.'

On the window sill was an ashtray heaped with butts.

Although the ceiling was nicotine yellow, there was no odour of stale smoke in the room. As far as Jack knew, Lucie had given up smoking a good while back so the ashtrays must have been there a while. She must have spent years in her 'Murder Room' sifting through amassed information in search of the magic bullet that would finish off her brother-in-law. Bitter loathing had corroded objectivity. The focus of her investigation wasn't to find who murdered the estate agent, but to prove it was Lawson. Ordinarily Lucie was an effective – if judgemental – reporter, but venom had consumed her. With sickened gloom, Jack pictured her dead body slumped over her desk, Lucie having died in the attempt.

'Your sister says here she knew Steven Lawson loved her. He was *a family man.*' Stella was reading an article under the headline *Wife of Cheating Plumber Haunts Towpath.*

'Didn't Terry teach you about hiding in plain sight?' Lucie was nasty. Jack was miserable; this wasn't the Lucie that, for all her ruthless ability to snake and ladder to the finish, was his friend. 'Stevie had the face of a landscape cutey, but the saw-teeth of wolf!'

'No one can help their teeth,' Jack remarked. 'You never suspected anyone else? What about Neville Rowlands?'

'He's harmless. Poor bloke was stuck with his witch of a mother, never had a life. At her beck and call day and night. Daphne Merry saw him on the towpath; he'd sneaked out for a breather. Before you run with that one too, Rowlands was coming from the opposite direction to Honeysett.'

Stella had reached the door. Jack willed her to look at him before she saw the sentence that had been on Natasha Latimer's screensaver.

'What is this?' Stella demanded.

'They're the last words in the plumber's diary before he drowned himself. Guilty as sin!'

'I don't see how they prove Lawson killed Helen Honeysett.'

Wonderhorse! Jack stopped himself doing a jig. *They were a team.*

'That doesn't sound like the profile of the man you've been describing,' Stella continued.

Jack had kept quiet. Stella's composed manner was the ideal foil for Lucie's high-octane state, but his curiosity took over. 'You have to be a tad reflective to keep a journal.'

'Not a *journal*, Jack-Puss!' Lucie jabbed her carrot at him. 'He was as reflective as a shit-spattered mirror. After the police let him go, Lawson wrote a minute-by-minute account of each hour of each day to show he wasn't out on the towpath stalking innocent girls and murdering them. *Pathetic!*'

'Sounds like he tried to protect himself,' Stella said. 'After Helen Honeysett vanished, Steven Lawson must have expected to be questioned every time there was an assault or reports of a suspicious-looking man in the vicinity of the river.'

'Stevie was stupid, but no fool. He bent the truth, like he did his pipes.' Lucie sent her chair spinning again, this time sticking out her legs like a child on a roundabout. Jack felt mild relief; this was more like the old Lucie.

Stella turned to her. 'How come you've seen his diary?'

'My niece gave it to me after his death.' Lucie had the grace to look shifty.

Stella said, 'I've seen no mention of it in the press.'

'It's not in the public interest,' Lucie proclaimed piously. Jack guessed she shouldn't have the diary and with a book somewhere in the pipeline, didn't want its existence known. A moment later Lucie confirmed this: 'When I write my book, his diary will show the lengths Stevie went to get away with murder.'

'Technically the diary must belong to your sister.' *Go Stella!*

'The diary belongs to anyone willing to speak the truth.' Lucie grimaced horribly. 'Get this, Marple and Morse, take the advice of a seasoned investigative journalist. Don't go hunting a phantom murderer; save Honeysett's cash.' She glared at Jack. 'Yes, I know who's feathering your nest. Adam Honeysett's wife's murderer is mouldering in Mortlake Cemetery. Tell him to go piss on Plumber Lawson's grave!'

Chapter Forty-Six

Monday, 11 January 2016

'Lucie May seems intent on proving Lawson did it,' Stella said. 'She wasn't herself. She never sees us to the door.'

'Maybe she was in shock. She's carried a family secret for nearly thirty years, it must have cost a lot to talk to us.' Jack knew about keeping secrets. They were in Latimer's basement, the dead space a respite after Lucie's Murder Room. Exhausted by the encounter, Jack was grateful when Stanley chose to snooze on his lap. Settled on the sofa, next to him, Stella booted up her laptop.

'It's hardly secret. It was a high-profile case and she wrote articles about it,' Stella pointed out.

'Lucie never admitted her connection to Lawson.' He fluffed Stanley's handlebar moustache. 'If my brother was suspected of murder, I'd keep out of it.'

'Even if you believed he'd done it?' Stella was rummaging in her rucksack.

Stella was a police officer's daughter, she wanted villains apprehended and crime prevented. She wouldn't make exception for her family. Or him. 'I'd say nothing.'

'That would be illegal.' Stella laid a school exercise book on the sofa between them.

'That's Lawson's diary!' Jack exclaimed. 'I didn't see Lucie give it to you.'

Stella opened the flimsy book. 'It wasn't Lucie's to give.'

'You took it without asking?' He pulled on Stanley's ears, kneading them through his fingers. 'Isn't that illegal?'

'No.' Stella was firm. 'And if I'd asked, she'd have refused.' She slid the diary towards him.

Jack tried to focus. Within two columns, crabbed printed letters flattened at the base suggested Lawson had used a ruler. Like Lucie had said, it wasn't a journal, but a list of activities and precise times.

Time	Activity
6.34 a.m.	Showered.
7.15 – 7.32 a.m.	With Bette, walked Smudge on Kew Green. Mrs Merry by pond with dog. She said 'Good morning'.
7.32 – 8.30 a.m.	Breakfast with B, G and M.
8.30 – 9.01 a.m.	Went with Bette and took M to school.
9.01 – 9.55 a.m.	Hammersmith Library on bus. Bette to Charing + Hosp. Requested book on plumbing. Read by librarian's desk.
9.55 – 10 a.m.	Went to toilet. Told librarian.
10 a.m. – 12 noon	More reading, asked librarian for another book.
12 – 12.45 p.m.	Bette came. We had sandwich.
12.45 – 2.34 p.m.	Asked for book on history of Hammersmith. New librarian. Impatient at me for asking q's.
2.34 – 2.36 p.m.	Asked new librarian where toilets were. Man there. I dropped change on floor. 'Throwing your money around.' Didn't know me. Just friendly.
2.36 – 5 p.m.	Read at front table. Librarian knew who I was. Didn't smile.
5 – 5.07 p.m. (7 min. walk)	Left library. Asked time outside. Bought RSPCA sticker off lady on Fulham Palace Rd. Grey bun and blue eyes. Crossed road in front of car. Man shouted. White mini, D323 LPC.
5.07 – 5.30 p.m.	Told hosp. receptionist waiting for wife. Think he knew me. Waited.
5.30 – 6.20 p.m.	Walked to Hamm Bdy with Bette, train home. Helped G with birds.

6.20 – 6.23 p.m.	Lucie at Thames Cotts: 'How do you live with yourself'. No answer as police instructed. Bette lost it and said. Still no other suspects.
6.23 – 6.28 p.m.	Asked M and G to walk Smudge with me. Garry won't if M there. M stayed with Bette.
6.28 – 7.36 p.m.	Towpath with G. Saw Mrs Merry coming back from Chis Bridge – usual route. G called her evil. Told him off. I said good evening. She didn't hear. Saw Nev R. He greeted me politely like he didn't know me. Sybil Lofthouse acted like hadn't seen me.
7.36 – 9 p.m.	Tea. TV News.
10 – 10.17 p.m.	Walked Smudge with Bette. Saw B Judd. He didn't speak, but did see us.
10.17 p.m.	Bed. Bette there.
11.03 p.m.	Light out. In bed all night.

The diary continued with little variation in activity for twenty-eight days. At the top of each page, fastened with a paper clip, was a newspaper schedule for that evening's TV, some programmes circled in red, Underground and bus tickets, receipts for sandwiches and charity stickers.

'Lawson provided proof for everything he did.' Jack felt for the dead man: desperation emanated from every entry. 'He's made sure he had witnesses, even when he went to the lavatory.' Stanley shook himself and, jumping down, padded off down the basement. The panel slid aside for him. He jumped into the sandbox and started digging. Clouds of sand flurried up behind him.

Stella said, 'Lucie May has a point. This could be proof of guilt as much as of innocence.'

'Lawson couldn't know when he'd need an alibi.' Jack was sombre. He called to Stanley and pat-patted his knee to encourage him back. The poodle had nestled within his hollow in the sand.

'He bought badges and stickers from charity sellers so that they might remember him.' Stella flipped back to the first page. 'Looks like he tried to kill himself by stepping out into traffic.'

Stella glanced over at Stanley. 'He won't come if you ask. Show you don't care.'

'I *do* care.'

'That's why he won't come.' The glass panel slid closed and Jack couldn't see Stanley.

'I'm not sure it was a suicide attempt, it was another way of being remembered,' he said.

Stella flipped through the exercise book. 'He doesn't walk out in front of a car any other day.'

'Risky if the driver didn't see. Lawson couldn't hide at home and avoid abuse from the likes of Lucie or the public. He couldn't be alone, he needed an alibi.' Jack scratched his stubbly chin. He had forgotten to shave that morning. Living in Latimer's basement, his own routine had been disrupted. 'These days CCTV would have been his friend.'

'Perhaps Lucie's right. His plumbing business had dried up, and if he'd got jobs, he couldn't be alone with anyone, especially women.' The glass swished aside. Stanley emerged from the playroom and this time went to Stella's lap. She lifted her laptop out of the way and he jumped up on to her. '"Nev R" must be Rowlands. He seems to have been nice to him. Lawson had hate mail and from this it looks like his neighbours thought him guilty.'

'That could suggest Rowlands was guilty.' Jack patted his lap surreptitiously, but Stanley gazed at him implacably. 'He could afford to be nice to Lawson if the poor guy had taken the rap for what Rowlands had done.'

Stella ran her finger down the entries, turning the pages slowly. 'He sees him more than once. If he was guilty, wouldn't it be more convincing to put the blame on the man suspected of the crime, like everyone else?' Stella balanced the laptop precariously above Stanley. 'Bev's not found Rowlands yet.'

Jack didn't dare think what Lucie would do when she found out Stella had taken the diary.

'"Who am I and what have I done?"' Stella read out Lawson's last words. Unlike the other entries, this final one was scrawled in large letters across the ruled lines. 'He left the library at four thirty, half an hour earlier than usual. Did he write this at the same time or when he got home? There's no mention of buying badges off charity workers or asking the time. He left half an hour early.'

'He planned to commit suicide, he didn't need an alibi,' Jack said. 'This entry is the twenty-seventh of February, on the day he died. A Friday.'

'Is that key?'

'Wednesday used to be the classic day for suicide. I suppose it's a bit like an island with a sea between the weekends. But Lawson might have lost all sense of the days. It was one long nightmare for him.' Jack sucked on the arm of his glasses.

'Latimer can't have seen Lawson's diary – how come this question was on her computer?' Stella brought up a colourful spreadsheet. Jack put on his glasses and read details of the Thames Cottage residents. She'd done a map of the area. 'Bette Lawson would have known about it, and Megan, since she stole the diary. Garry Lawson may have read it.' She became animated. 'He's only next door, he might be Latimer's intruder! He could have got hold of a key when the builders were here, let himself in, changed her screensaver and manoeuvred the digger. Latimer said he was "strange".'

'Natasha Latimer would consider anyone not motivated by wealth and property strange. Garry's father was dubbed a murderer and killed himself. Enough to make anyone strange,' Jack said. 'For whatever reason, he doesn't have a job, he's in his forties and he lives with his mother and breeds budgerigars – none of that a crime. But it could be that his father's parting question haunts him and it leads him to haunt others.' He had to meet Garry Lawson.

'Garry Lawson is *alive*.' Stella was firm. 'He can't haunt anyone.' She sat forward on the sofa. 'He could be the murderer!'

'He was twelve at the time.'

'Twelve-year-olds are capable of murder. If Garry Lawson suspected Helen Honeysett and his dad were involved, he had the motive to kill her. He told the police he didn't see his father on the towpath, but Megan Lawson is sure he lied.'

'If he did see them it means he had an alibi,' Jack reminded her.

'Megan sneaked out to the towpath. Perhaps Garry did too. Steven Lawson could have guessed what his son had done and that's why he killed himself.'

'It's possible.' Jack picked up the diary. It was the nature of tabloids to persecute, but he had set Lucie apart from the gutter press. Tonight they'd seen a hard-nosed reporter who made allowances for no one. Jack had made the mistake of believing she was on his side. Lucie May was on nobody's side, not even her sister's. She had been part of a pack that had hounded Steven Lawson to his death.

'Lawson didn't leave a suicide note. The diary is evidence – flimsy though it is – that he killed himself.'

'I wonder if Bette Lawson knows Megan passed it to her sister. She certainly doesn't know we have it.' Having recovered from initial shock, Jack was excited that Stella had taken the diary. Lawson's blow-by-blow account of his last days gave a heart-rending insight to the prime suspect.

'Maybe Lucie May hasn't published the diary to protect her sister.' Stella was good at seeing the best in people.

Jack found this unlikely. 'Protect her how?'

'The verdict on Lawson's death was "Accident or Misadventure". He left no suicide note. If the coroner had seen this, it would probably have been ruled suicide and Lawson's life insurance would have been void.' Stella opened a fresh worksheet. She titled it *Suspects*. 'We must return it to Bette Lawson.'

But Jack objected. 'It will stir up more ill will between the sisters. Let's keep out of it.'

'From how Lucie was talking, it can't get worse.' Stella set up columns and coloured cells. 'I'll ask Natasha Latimer about Lawson's question: it might be coincidence and there's no link.'

'If you do, she'll know I opened her computer,' Jack said.

Stella looked at him. 'You said it came up on the screen when you were dusting.'

'It did.' Although this was the truth, Jack felt himself flush. Guilt was tingeing the few honest bits of his life. As if he sensed his shame, Stanley got up and, languidly, transferred from Stella over to his lap. Jack nearly crowed with joy.

'We do agree with Lucie May that Helen Honeysett's killer knew her routine and it wasn't a random attack by a stranger. That gives us five suspects.' Deftly Stella created a grid on the screen, titled columns and typed *Sybil Lofthouse*. 'She lives at number five and is the only resident of Thames Cottages Natasha Latimer likes. She worked at the Stock Exchange.' Stella tapped the keyboard. 'She told me she went to bed early then. She lived on her own then too; we have only her word that's what she did. She had a dog and went to the towpath.'

'She was fifty at the time. It's unlikely she overpowered a fit young woman and then got rid of her body. From your description she doesn't look like she could overpower a mouse.'

'She could have pushed her in the river. I'm nearly fifty, I could do it,' Stella said stoutly. 'Lofthouse could have caught Honeysett by surprise.'

'What was her motive?' Jack shuddered at the possibility of Stella killing anyone. Or being killed. 'Has Lofthouse benefited from her death?'

Stella played Devil's advocate. 'It may not have been about money, maybe she wanted her gone. Sybil Lofthouse seems harmless and daffy, but it could be a front. She might have had a grudge against her.'

As a guest of True Hosts, Jack knew that desiring the absence of a hated person was motive enough. Those who would never commit murder dreamt that someone who had made them unhappy would die. 'Daphne Merry was on the towpath. She found Honeysett's dog Baxter by the crematorium.'

Nodding, Stella added this to the section for Merry. 'Why attract attention by returning the dog?'

'So we wouldn't think her guilty?' Now Jack was the Devil's advocate. The only person he suspected Daphne of wanting dead was the man who killed her daughter and he was already dead.

'This is by the by. Merry had an alibi. Suspect number three: Neville Rowlands who lived in this cottage. Adam told me at our first meeting that Rowlands saw Merry. Unwittingly he gave her an alibi. It wasn't mutual because she said she didn't see him. He did say she'd two dogs with her, her own – Woof – and the Honeysetts' dog. When he was interviewed Rowlands couldn't have known Merry had found Baxter unless he'd seen her. His alibi was his mother, who claimed he was outside for no more than five minutes. But mothers can lie.' This idea seemed to silence Stella.

'One of the pet graves is dated 1987. It's for Hercules. The same year as Helen Honeysett.'

'His dog dying could have upset Rowlands and made him jealous of others who had a dog. Some people get attached to their dogs.' Stella spoke as if she didn't have a dog she was attached to.

'Rowlands is a stronger suspect than Lawson,' Jack said. 'Surely Lucie – or the police – saw that? There's something we don't know.'

'There's a lot we don't know. We have to take it stain by stain.' Stella jotted *Hercules's grave* in Rowlands' note section. 'He's on a par with Adam at the moment.'

'Who's next?' Jack was enjoying himself.

'Bette Lawson. If she suspected her husband of having an affair with Honeysett, she had a powerful motive. When she returned from the towpath, Megan said her mother was in the kitchen trying not to let her see she was crying. What if Bette had just got there and her agitation was because she had committed murder? Helen Honeysett saying "Oh it's you!" implied she knew the person she met on the towpath. She knew Bette Lawson.'

'She knew all the suspects,' Jack reminded her. 'Did Bette have time to kill Honeysett and throw her in the river before Megan returned to the house?' He was dubious. 'Megan was hiding on the riverbank, she would have heard a splash.'

'She might have dragged Honeysett into bushes, returned later and disposed of the body, probably in the river,' Stella mused. 'Even at night it would have been hard to move a body. You'd need a car and that would draw attention. Lawson had a van, but they checked it for DNA and found none.'

'Lawson's a nurse. Didn't they have to do lifting and manual handling in those days? She was probably strong,' Jack said. 'With knowledge of anatomy she could kill efficiently too.'

Stella tapped 'Strong' and 'Time-lapse' in Bette's section. Perhaps because she didn't rate his last suggestion, she left out 'Anatomy'.

'Next is Honeysett and the woman he was having an affair with, Jane Drake.' Jack didn't disguise his dislike of the man. He did disguise that he wanted it to be Honeysett. 'They alibied each other so discount that. They gained by Honeysett's death and we only have his testimony that she vanished that night. Helen might have found out about his affair and wanted a divorce. He had much to lose. He could have murdered her when he got back from Jane Drake's in the morning and gone to his meeting in Northampton. When his wife was declared dead, he got the house and her life insurance.'

'She wasn't declared dead until 2007. And don't forget Adam asked us to solve the case. OK, so you think that was to divert us from discovering his guilt, but it could be that he isn't guilty. He'd have been better to lie low and not hire private detectives or whatever we are. I wonder if Adam is still in touch with Jane Drake?'

'If he dissuades us from finding her, I for one will be suspicious.' Honeysett had withheld vital information: he was playing them.

'Good idea. Lastly, there's the "Person or Persons Unknown", the one we don't know about.' Stella filled in the last row of the grid.

Sybil Lofthouse (No. 5)	50 in 1987. No alibi for evening. No obvious motive. Means & opportunity: yes.
Adam Honeysett (No. 4)	28 in 1987. Alibi Jane Drake. Motive: Jane D and ££. Means & opportunity: yes.
Jane Drake (flat on Kew Road)	19 in 1987. Motive: Adam H and ££. Means & opportunity: accomplice to Adam H.
Daphne Merry (No. 3)	38 in 1987. Alibi from Nev R. No obvious motive. Means & opportunity: yes. Brought back dog (cover?).
Bette Lawson (No. 2)	29 in 1987. Alibi from Megan and Garry Lawson. Motive, means & opportunity: yes. (Contract killer?) Strong. Time-lapse.
Garry Lawson (No. 2)	12 in 1987. Alibi from sister which denied. Motive, means and opportunity: yes.
Neville Rowlands (No. 1) Deceased? Address?	Age unknown. Alibi Mother /saw Daphne Merry. Motive, means & opportunity: unknown. Hercules's grave
Unknown person(s)	Motive, means & opportunity: ?

'It's late. I must go.' She shut her laptop and motioned to Stanley.

'I'll take Stanley to the towpath for a pee,' Stella announced outside Latimer's gate.

'I'll come too.' This time Jack wouldn't let her go alone.

Stella and Jack went up the steps to the towpath and set off towards Kew Railway Bridge.

'Heel, Stanley,' Stella commanded as the poodle strained forward. 'He wants to go to that house again. I wonder who lives there?'

'Brian Judd,' Jack said promptly. Then he heard himself.

'If he was there in 1987, they are suspect number six.' Stella hadn't asked him how he knew. Jack let himself breathe.

They had gone beyond the lamp-post at the Thames Cottages steps and the dark closed in around them. Below was the wash of the river.

Stella put on her phone app torch. The pale light created baffling shadows that jerked and jumped with each step.

They emerged from the canopy of trees. Above, the sodium-stained sky sent an insidious pall across the path. They were outside the dilapidated house.

Stanley pulled harder. Jack let him lead him forward.

Someone was watching them through the lattice of cobwebs behind the grimy panes. He was sure it was the same face as he'd seen last time. Before he could stop himself, Jack gasped, 'Who's that?'

'Who?' Stella asked, looking behind her to the towpath. She turned to the house. There were only cobwebs. 'It must be that Brian... What did you say his name was?'

'Judd.' Jack was caught in a dust-laden cobweb of his own.

Before he could stop her, Stella plunged across the grass and gave the iron claw on the door three thunderous knocks. It triggered a tirade of shrill barks from Stanley.

No one came.

Then it happened. The question that he was waiting for. Stella asked him, 'Actually, how do you know he's called Brian Judd?'

Jack could think of only one way to divert her. A split second before he let go of the lead he cried, 'Oh *no*, Stanley's escaped!'

Stanley shot away into the darkness around the side of the house. Stella chased after him. Jack followed. It came to him that Natasha Latimer had talked about Brian Judd at her cottage. He could have said that. He'd let Stanley go for no reason. If something happened to the little dog he'd never forgive himself.

There was no one there. Where had Stella gone? Dimly aware that he was sick with himself, Jack tore along the side of the building to the back. He stumbled and fell headlong. He was cushioned by damp grass, short and springy beneath him. He rolled over and staggered to his feet.

'Stella!' At the top of his voice. He didn't care if Brian Judd heard.

'He's here!' In thin moonlight, Stella, etched in silver, was a hologram. She was peering through what Jack knew was the kitchen window. 'He's here. Whoever's in there has Stanley. I can see him. I'm calling the police!'

'No, Stella—' Judd would tell them that Jack had broken into his house. He hadn't worn gloves; if SOCOs checked for prints his would be all over the bathroom window. Cashman would be beside himself.

'There's no sodding signal.' Stella was waving her phone in the air.

In the midst of this, it occurred to Jack that she rarely swore. 'I'll sort it.' He hated himself for being the pseudo superhero. He went to the lavatory window and thrust up the sash so hard it crashed against the top. He flung himself over the sill.

The door was locked. *There was no key.*

There was whimpering through the door panel. 'Stanley! I'm coming.' He flung his weight against the door. Hot pain shot up his shoulder and down his wrist. The door held. He rubbed his arm and launched himself again. It wasn't there. He hurtled through space, shadows and shapes spinning about him. More pain as he fell flat on his face. Something hot and damp slathered his cheeks. It was Stanley. The dog snuffled around him, pushing at his hair to get to him, licking him.

'The front door was open.' Stella stood over him. She was holding up the key to the lavatory. No sympathy, she was being practical.

Jack dusted himself down. He had landed well, nothing broken.

'This place needs a deep clean.' Stella clipped on Stanley's lead. In the weak light seeping through the glazed front door, Jack saw that there were even more leaves and flakes of bark than the last time he had come. Wind off the river would send them in. It suggested that Brian Judd did use the front door.

'Hello!' Stella called up the stairs.

Jack grabbed her arm. 'Sssh!'

'You saw someone up there. Brian Judd presumably. He might be too frightened to come down. Mr Judd, it's OK, we were just passing by. We mean you no harm.'

Silence. Jack felt creeping chill. He sensed a presence. It emanated from the walls, the shadows, the stairs that wended into darkness. Someone somewhere was standing very still. Their mind was blank, their gaze vague. Waiting.

'I was possibly mistaken. It was more likely to have been a reflection or... or...' Jack could hear himself. He didn't sound convincing.

'Best we check. Brian Judd could be lying injured or unconscious. Or worse.' Leading Stanley, Stella crunched over the leaves to the staircase. She seemed unafraid. If there was a problem she would address it.

'Stop!' Jack exclaimed in a near shout.

One hand on the banister, Stella froze. 'Why, what's the matter?' Jack detected a quaver in her voice. Stella barely trusted him at the best of times.

'If Judd is there and is injured or afraid, Stanley could make things worse. All of us could overwhelm him.' Jack pictured the face at the window. The expression hadn't been fear. 'I'll go. Stay here.'

'There's only two of us. Stanley's on a lead and he's good at detecting.' Stella didn't relish chivalry.

Stanley detecting Judd was just what Jack did not want. He would meet the True Host alone. He could hardly explain this to Stella.

'Maybe he's phobic about dogs. Some people are.'

Stella got this. In her cleaning work she encountered many phobias. Dust being the main one. She let him go.

On the landing, pallid light leached from open doors along a passage. Judd had ample warning of his approach.

'OK up there?' Stella was whispering. For some reason this made Jack feel properly scared. He dared not reply and give

Brian Judd his position. Judd knew anyway. Jack felt him close. One of the shadows was not a shadow.

He took a step along the passage. He felt as if his skin was alive; every part of him tingled. Another step. Two more. He could no longer cover his back. He fumbled for his Maglite. His fingers closed around the little torch and he slipped the keys attached to the ring between his fingers. Crude defence. No True Host would be prey to violence. He couldn't use the Maglite. He couldn't face what he would see. He would die.

Jack backed away down the corridor and ran downstairs. Despite the chill, he was in a flop sweat.

Stella wasn't in the hall. In a second Jack got it. The point about a True Host was that they second-guessed you. Then they third-guessed you. The choice might be binary, but you had to out-think them. Judd had known Jack would want to confront him alone. He had known that Jack would prevent Stella going up the stairs with him. It was a classic chess move. He had left Stella alone. *Not alone.*

'Stella!' Jack rushed into the little closet. The window was shut. He pulled on it, but this time it didn't open. Blinded with panic, he hadn't seen that the latch had been fastened. His fingers trembled as he unscrewed it.

'This needs a chemical scour. Almost not worth doing except it's an antique.' Stella was shining her torch into the filthy lavatory pan. 'You were quick.'

'Yes, he's not up there.' Deception had a habit of snowballing. The distance between them was vast: soon Stella would be out of sight.

'Let's check out Judd's alibi. We don't have motive, but he'd have had the means to dispose of her.'

'He must have one since he's not a suspect.'

'We must test every alibi. The killer hasn't been found in thirty years. It's likely he has been interviewed by the police and dismissed because he has an alibi. Or she, we shouldn't assume it's a man either.' Stella was holding the bathroom key. 'There's no one downstairs, I checked.' She fitted the key on the inside of the bathroom door. 'Come on, let's get out of here.' She was already at the front door.

Jack lingered in the lavatory. He would come back. Brian Judd was expecting him.

'That wasn't here then.' Stella's boots crunched on the shingled towpath.

'What wasn't, when?' Jack had walked city streets at night since he was a teenager without fear. He was hunting those whom most people took care to avoid. Tonight, on the desolate towpath, the river black and timeless on his right, he was very afraid indeed. Honeysett's killer wasn't dead. He had just got better at killing. Whom had he killed?

Who would be next?

'In the photos of police searching the undergrowth for Honeysett in 1987, the towpath was churned-up mud. If someone had attacked Helen Honeysett, she could have slipped and fallen.'

'It was winter. The mud might have been frozen solid,' Jack said.

'She could have slipped on ice.' Stella stopped to let Stanley lift his leg by a bush on the bank. They watched his teetering hops on three legs – for a delicately built animal he lacked balance and co-ordination.

'There were no footprints indicating a struggle. The police couldn't isolate footprints. They knew dog walkers – Lawson and his daughter, Lofthouse, Helen Honeysett, Daphne Merry and Neville Rowlands and Adam – had been there. But there were joggers and other dog walkers that never came forward.' She continued walking. 'This surface would leave no prints.'

'Adam Honeysett could have parked on that road by Kew Bridge that goes to the towpath. There's businesses under the arches – a gym open until late – but in 1987 it would have been deserted.' Jack thought he sounded like Lucie May, intent on proving a man guilty regardless. He was playing for time. He must find out about Brian Judd himself. Nothing that Stella discovered would tell the real truth. True Hosts were not identifiable by National Insurance numbers or the electoral roll. He must find him and follow him. Except, Jack was sure that Judd, moving on soundless soles somewhere close, had found him first. In the next second, this was confirmed,

'He's heard something.' Stella put her finger to her lips. Stanley was straining back the way they had come, his tail between his legs.

'He'll smell lots of smells here.' Spears of dim light drifted through branches. *Someone was there.* Jack felt the coil of fear unwind.

'He's not sniffing, he's listening.' Stella wasn't mollified. 'Oh, I see, he wants a poo.' She dug about in her jacket pocket for a poo-bag.

Jack suppressed the urge to snatch up Stanley, grab Stella's hand and head for the lamp-post by Thames Cottages. Stanley circled one way, then the other; he padded a metre back towards the dilapidated house and circled again.

Hurry up.

'Good evening.' A pleasant greeting.

'Evening,' Stella responded brightly. Her lack of fear should lessen his own, but instead it was quadrupled. Jack couldn't speak.

As the man briefly entered the circle of light, his head torch dazzled Jack and he noticed a dog lead slung around his neck. It was clipped over his chest – the dog walker's way – so it wouldn't slip off. The man moved off into the darkness.

Perhaps Stella was spooked by the encounter after all because she picked Stanley up and hastened on. At the lamp-post by Thames Cottages, she stopped again. The man was nowhere to be seen. He hadn't had time to go into one of the cottages or to reach the alley. He must have gone on to the Kew Stairs.

Jack walked up the green with Stella and watched until her van joined the South Circular. As he shut the door of Latimer's cottage and paused in what he hoped was an empty house, the presentiment of evil he'd felt earlier crystallized. Helen Honeysett had been murdered by a True Host.

Who am I and what have I done?

Who had known that these were Steven Lawson's last words?

In the dilapidated house, he'd been within touching distance of Brian Judd. Judd hadn't been a suspect; he had an alibi. Stella was right to discount all the alibis. True Hosts circumnavigated circumstantial evidence and, with sleight of hand, manipulated assumptions. Jack must stop Brian Judd killing again. And he must do it alone.

Chapter Forty-Seven

Stanley started barking almost as soon as they were on the South Circular. Short sharp barks. He was asking something. Stella stopped the van minutes from Thames Cottages. He must have eaten something illegal and wanted to do another poo. She walked with him along Townmead Road. They passed the gates to the recycling centre and arrived at the entrance to the housing estate she had pointed out to Jack from the towpath. While Stanley did his circling this way and that, Stella regarded a sign: 'No Unauthorized Entry. Contact Concierge to Visit Residents.' The concierge's kiosk was empty so who would know?

Perhaps it was that, although after midnight, Stella's mind was busy and walking was preferable to trying to sleep. Or perhaps it was that Stanley changed his mind about pooing there. Instead of returning to her van and driving to her house in Hammersmith, Stella let Stanley tug her past the kiosk and, without authorized entry, into the estate.

Even in daylight the curving streets and terraces of faux Georgian houses in pale sandstone, with no cars parked on the kerbs or people on the pavements, was unsettling. Although Stella appreciated pavements free of litter and splodges of chewing gum, at night it was uncanny. She trailed after Stanley as he pottered and sniffed along the 'pretend' street.

Jack had seemed different. Was there something the matter?

She couldn't give him more cleaning, he was at Natasha Latimer's full time and when he finished he'd return to Suzie's and to the London Underground. Maybe he was missing Bella. Stella had no remedy. She wasn't aware of missing anyone if she wasn't with them.

Although she couldn't see cameras, she felt she was being watched. With each step, she felt the silence and stillness press in on her.

Stanley dragged her up steps where lighted bollards revealed a winding path mosaicked with cobbles. He nosed between the tall red ornamental grasses that Stella remembered seeing on the towpath. It was like a maze. They arrived in a circular clearing from which other paths led. Balanced on a plinth in the centre was a large stone ball. She hoped it was firmly fixed as Stanley beetled to its base and began to poo on the cobbles. Looking away to give him privacy, Stella rummaged in her jacket for a poo-bag. She tried every pocket, but only found loose change and liver treats. She had used the last one on the towpath. When Stanley had finished, she chose one of the paths, searching for something to use instead. She wished the man she'd seen earlier would come back this way.

She arrived at the top of steps leading to the towpath and went down. Something caught her eye. A crisp packet. Perfect. As she reached for it, Stanley snouted forward and snapped it between his jaws. He glared at her with wary menace. No amount of agility or obedience classes had trained him out of snatching litter or discarded food and possessing it with heart-stopping ferocity. Stella waved a treat under his nose. Recognizing a bribe, he whipped his head away. No use pretending she didn't care. He knew too well that she did care. It was freezing, the towpath was dark and the silence oppressive. Was it like this for Helen Honeysett?

She would walk Stanley back to his poo, and on the way maybe he'd drop the bag.

She must have strayed off her original path because she found

herself back at the towpath. She waited a moment, hoping the
man she'd seen earlier would return. But perhaps he'd been
going home.

This time she saw that there was another path a couple of
metres along. She took that one and at last found herself by the
stone sphere. And the poo.

Stanley's tail dropped. He growled. Not the growl of a dog
who has captured a crisp bag or the sharp squawky bark of a
dog who wants a poo. But a warning bark that signalled danger.

Stella took in reality. She was alone, far from anyone who
might hear her call for help.

'Who are you?' A woman appeared from behind the stone.

'I might ask you that.' Too late Stella recalled Terry's advice
about humouring strangers in dark isolated places. He had never
advised being haughty.

The woman wore a quilted jacket and trousers, long hair tied
back, her face immaculately made up. 'I live here, I don't have to
explain myself.' The air of entitlement bristled. Perhaps haughty
was OK after all. The woman leant on the stone ball. If it rolled
off the plinth it would crush Stella.

Hazily she thought the woman was from Neighbourhood
Watch and had seen Stanley poo. Worse, she'd seen Stella walk
away from it. 'I was about to pick—'

'I know who you are.' The woman was pacing around the
ball, narrowly missing Stanley's poo. 'I've seen you with Adam.
Think you can keep him when no one else can?' In contrast to
her clothes and make-up the woman's trainers were thick with
mud, her laces frayed and trailing.

Stella tried to summon up Terry's list of warning signs for
physical violence. Body tension, tick. Pacing, tick. Increased
volume of speech, tick. Terry had taught Stella to fell a strong
man in seconds. The woman was thin and, although she was
wiry, Stella was sure she could overcome her. Her dad had
advised 'de-escalation of the situation' as a first step. Stella went
for the truth. 'I hardly, er, know Mr Honeysett.' It was true, but

she sounded like she was lying. She said emphatically, 'I am not having a relationship with him.'

'I saw you coming out of his house.' The woman spat venom. 'I've seen you by the river with him.'

'I'm working for him.' But in that instant Stella realized she and Jack were working for *Helen* Honeysett, a dead woman who couldn't speak for herself. Not for her husband.

'Assess threat and risk and then come up with a working strategy...'

Terry had said that part of the strategy was to ask yourself if your action would resolve the situation. Running away was an obvious action. 'I'm sure if you talked to Adam, he'd—'

The woman hissed, 'Don't placate me. I was stupid. I believed he'd leave her. I was prepared to do anything for him. Even perjury!' She broke off one of the ornamental grasses and flung it at Stella's feet like a discarded spear.

So much for 'de-escalation'. The woman was blocking the entrance to the nearest path, a warning sign of violence.

'You committed perjury?' Stella had seen a younger version of her in Adam Honeysett's augmented file. Lucie May called her 'the Mistress'. Jane Drake was the nineteen-year-old with the pied-à-terre whom Adam Honeysett had been with when Helen Honeysett vanished.

'I told the police I was with Adam when his wife disappeared. That made me fair game for the wolves. People from the tabloids shouting through my letterbox, chasing me with cameras.' She snapped off another grass and flailed it at Stella. 'One bitch called me a whore!'

Stella found Drake's systematic vandalism of the grasses as disturbing as her words. 'Your alibi made Adam Honeysett the prime suspect. He'd been unfaithful. It gave him a strong motive for killing Helen. How was that a favour?'

'It got him off the hook. If it wasn't for me, he'd be in prison.' Jane Drake held a grass in both hands out in front of her as if she were involved in some arcane ceremony. She whispered, 'The night that woman disappeared, Adam was supposed to come to my flat. He rang saying he had to work late. He always told *her* that when he was with me, so I knew he was lying.'

'He *was* with you.'

The grasses shifted, a dry rustling. Neither woman noticed. Nor did they notice there was no breeze.

'I lied.' Jane Drake sat on the edge of the plinth, the giant stone ball behind her.

'I don't understand.' It was too extraordinary that Jane Drake had accosted her in a deathly quiet estate in the middle of the night. Drake must have followed her.

'Adam asked me to give him an alibi. He said he was walking the streets, nerving himself up to tell that woman he was going to leave. He couldn't prove he hadn't killed her. He worked out that it was preferable to confess he had a lover – he called me that – to being done for her murder. Preferable for him – it destroyed me. Nineteen eighty-seven was the year the film *Fatal Attraction* came out. I was the bunny boiler who destroyed their marriage. Adam, the two-timing shit, got off scot-free.'

'Are you saying he killed his wife?' Jane Drake seemed to have forgotten that she'd assumed Stella was in a relationship with Adam Honeysett.

Drake gave an exaggerated shiver. 'I need a drink.' She moved to one of the paths out of the grass circle. 'Coming?'

'I ought to... OK, thanks.' Stella distantly noted that her good manners were again overriding personal safety. But this was too good a chance to miss. She followed Drake along the labyrinthine path. Glancing at Stanley, crisp bag still between his teeth, she stopped. 'Do you have a poo-bag?'

'I don't have a dog,' Jane Drake retorted.

The sentence jolted a far-flung thought. But it was gone before Stella could get it.

'Use this.' Drake was holding out a tissue to Stella.

Stella returned to the clearing. There was nothing beneath the stone ball. Stanley's poo had gone.

Chapter Forty-Eight

Tuesday, 12 January 2016

I know a busybody when I see one. What is a lady doing walking her dog so late? She let her dog do its business and left the mess for someone else to clear up. Unforgivable, you would say. It threw me; the dog is a spit of Whisky. Leave her to me.

I am grateful that you are not here to witness her misdeed. She will never do it again. I dealt with it this time, but I won't be so tolerant if it happens again. She is a meddlesome creature. We can't have her – or her man-friend – sticking their noses in where they're not wanted, can we? You and I are of a single mind. I know what you are thinking. I am with you every step of the way.

By the way, a small thing, but I saw you with that young man. I have to say that wasn't wise. A casual observer could get the wrong impression. I have forgiven you. It is because you hope for the best from the worst of mankind. You are sadly mistaken, as you will soon discover.

You felt me watching over you last night. Never forget that I am there. *Always.*

As I said, please leave me to deal with this.

Chapter Forty-Nine

Tuesday, 12 January 2016

'Adam Honeysett used me and dumped me!'

Jane Drake's 'pretend' mews house was in a terrace that, but for the lack of flower pots, bins or cars, wasn't unlike Thames Cottages. It was a different matter inside. Stella was stunned. Drake could do with a visit from Daphne Merry. Ornaments and knick-knacks dotted shelves jammed with books; sofas, armchairs and a fold-up table jostled cheek by jowl. Despite this, a surreptitious finger test told Stella that someone dusted and polished regularly.

'I'm a husk!' Jane Drake declared.

Drake was red-cheeked and healthy and, given it was one in the morning, bright-eyed. The person Stella might compare to a husk was Megan Lawson.

Stella took a mouthful of tea from what she'd supposed was a cereal bowl and observed that another thing that detecting and cleaning had in common was the consumption of tea. Stanley sprawled at her feet, the crisp packet crackling between his teeth.

When she arrived, Stella's shock had been reserved for the walls. They were papered with photographs. Printed on paper, curled and warped, most showed a figure walking away from the lens. The images reminded her of the covers of the crime novels her mum liked to read.

Now Stella's eye was drawn to a sequence of pictures of two people seen at a window. She nearly dropped the bowl of tea.

Date- and time-stamped, they were taken over a duration of two minutes. Tuesday 5 January, just after midnight. That was the night Adam had asked her to investigate his wife's disappearance. One of the people was Adam Honeysett. Stella went cold. *The other was herself.* Stanley had barked when she was there. He had detected a person. She should remember that he was never wrong. Jane Drake had been outside with her camera.

She looked again at the walking figures. One was of herself; in another she recognized Jack. The date stamp for both was the same night. Stella's was before she was accosted by Honeysett. Jack was while Stella was in his house. What was he doing there? Perhaps the time on the photo was wrong and it should have been for the night after. Except it was accurate for her pictures. Stella felt a wave of unease and moved on to the other pictures. There was one of Sybil Lofthouse. Why was she on the towpath at night if she didn't have a dog? To the left of the frame was an elderly man with a stoop. It was the dog walker who'd passed her and Jack earlier. He was approaching the camera, which meant that Drake must have hidden on the riverbank to photograph him. In all the pictures was a shadow that Stella realized with a jolt was Adam Honeysett. He was out of sight of herself, Jack, all the other people in the photographs. Apart from the one time she'd met him on the towpath, Stella for one had not known he was there.

'More tea?' Jane Drake asked as if Stella had come for a cosy chat rather than stumbled into a stalker's den.

'I should be goi—' This was the second 'gallery' she'd encountered within hours. Lucie May's Murder Room focused on another man. Both concerned the Honeysett case. As Steven Lawson's diary recorded the minutiae of his last days, so Drake had documented those connected to Adam Honeysett. *She was mad.*

'I'm not mad.' Jane Drake cut into Stella's thoughts.

'I never thought—' Stella hid her face with the bowl and drank, hazily taking in that the tea was the nicest she'd ever had.

'I loved him from the moment we met on the towpath. I was walking my parents' dog and he had his dog. We instantly clicked. He's older than me, nine years was a lifetime at nineteen, and I thought him a God.' She gave a cheerless guffaw. 'He said he would leave his wife.'

'Did you believe him?' Stella had cleaned for enough women having affairs with men who promised to leave their wives, but never did.

'I planned to have his children. Tarquin for a boy and Miranda if it was a girl.'

Tarquin sounded like a cleaning product to Stella. 'Why did he want to leave?'

'She didn't love him. She teased him; nothing he did was right. He said that I was the best thing that had happened to him.' She slurped her tea. 'He wanted rid of her, not to be with me, but to be free. How stupid was I! His crime was banal.'

'Hardly banal. A woman died,' Stella remarked quietly. Terry had taught her to keep the victim top of mind in any investigation. Helen Honeysett might have been one of the figures walking off into the darkness.

'She fancied herself a bloody agony aunt.' Jane Drake, her fingers wrapped around her bowl, regarded Stella fiercely. 'She made people's problems worse.'

'Did she have enemies?' Despite her experience of the complexity of murder, Stella tended to regard the victim as nothing but blameless.

'Hah, did she! She poked about in her neighbours' lives, she took their pictures, watched their every move.' She waved a hand at the walls. 'This is nothing. She fancied herself as Queen of the Street. She told that man' – Drake pointed at a stooped man with a brush moustache – 'he mustn't be trapped by his aged mother, he must find a wife. Adam said she assured that clutter-woman whose husband smashed up her family in a crash she wasn't too old to start again!' Drake unlaced her Dr Martens with a snapping flourish.

'Who is that man?'

'Neville Rowlands. He had an alibi.' Jane Drake looked annoyed to be interrupted.

'Yes, I know.' Rowlands might be trapped by his mother, but she'd saved him from being a murder suspect.

'... can you imagine! As if that poor woman could just swap out one daughter for another and it would be all right. And as for the plumber: they were having an affair. She used to tease Adam with how he could do it more often than he could.' She stopped. 'Adam told me he didn't have sex with her any more. He must have lied.'

'She had sex with Steven Lawson?' Stella felt disappointment. Despite her open mind she had hoped that Lawson would emerge unscathed from the case.

'So she said. She lied all the time so who knows. He believed her. She was on at that woman who worked at the Stock Exchange – she called her the Duchess – to give up investment secrets. Enemies? Helen of Troy was spoilt for choice!' She kicked off her boots and curled her feet under her. 'She was all over me like a rash.'

'You met Helen Honeysett?' Stella put the empty bowl on a nearby table. Stanley, sensing a plot to steal his crisp packet, gnashed his teeth.

'I had to suss out the opposition. I went to her work and asked her to find me a house. She treated me like a silly kid until I flashed my Coutts cheque book and talked of a cash buy. I said I was selling my flat too. She practically wet herself showering me with properties – water closets, en-suites, walk-in wardrobes, panoramic views – and insisted on driving me to see a house near Kew Station. You could see dollar signs springing out of her head as she totted up her commission.'

Jane Drake was on their suspect list in tandem with Adam Honeysett, but she could have killed Helen alone. Adam must have worked their assignations around Helen's movements. Drake would have known when to intercept her on the towpath.

She could have pushed her in the river. *'Oh, it's you!'* Since Drake had met Helen, she would have known her.

'… I pictured her telling Adam how a Jane Drake was buying the most expensive property on the books and she would exceed her target for that month. He would have died from terror that she'd guess who I was.'

'If he was going to leave her, why would he mind?'

'I see the contradiction now. He said she'd kill him if she found out about us. The next day that was academic, when she vanished!' Jane Drake beat a tattoo on her front teeth with a finger. 'Funny, that!'

'If you suspected he'd murdered her, why give him an alibi?' Stella tried to untangle the confusion of lies and high-octane jealousy. If the story of the false alibi was true, it made Adam Honeysett the key suspect. Perhaps it was as 'banal' a crime as Jane Drake said. Honeysett murdered his wife and had by accident of circumstances got away with it. 'If he wasn't with you, where was he?'

'He *said* he was on the towpath.' Jane Drake spat out the words.

Stella glanced down at Stanley. He was snoozing; the crisp packet lay on the floor beside a paw. 'How come no one saw him?' She edged downwards, preparing to whip up the bag before Stanley realized.

'He was with another woman.' Drake looked briefly forlorn, but then resumed her expression of tight fury. 'He's a *murderer*,' she fumed illogically.

Stella tried to assemble the jumbled jigsaw of conflicting facts. On the walls the diminishing figures seemed to multiply. 'If he murdered Helen that meant he was on the towpath as he said.'

'He said he was going to tell her he was leaving. He lied!'

'Perhaps he did tell her.' Stella felt her way through the fog of possibility. 'Perhaps they argued and in the heat of the moment he killed her.' Had Helen encountered her husband by the river, she might have exclaimed, 'Oh, it's you!'

Stella continued: 'Where were *you*?'

'What?' Drake jumped up and came towards Stella. She tensed. Drake bent down and retrieved the crisp packet. Stanley continued sleeping. So much for being a guard dog – of the crisp wrapping or of her. 'I was in my flat. Adam got there at four a.m. He cried and said we had to finish and he must give his marriage another go. Talked shite about being too old for me and letting me live my life. Of course I saw soon enough that this was a ploy to cover his arse. He'd bumped off the Queen of Sheba!'

'And yet you gave him an alibi?' Stella felt she was trapped in a maze in which she returned to the same point again and again no matter which route she took. Drake and Honeysett's initial false alibi had put the focus of the investigation on to Steven Lawson. If the false alibi was false too and Honeysett was on the towpath at the same time as Helen, it altered everything. He was a prime suspect.

'Why are you stalking him if you think he's a murderer?'

'I'm not stalking him!' Jane Drake smoothed out the crisp packet over and over. Stella wanted to point out that it wasn't hers, that it came from the ground. 'I know how it looks. But I'm not a nutter who can't let go.' She scrunched up the bag and then flattened it again. 'Actually I am a nutter who can't let go. That's what he's made me.'

'If Adam Honeysett did kill his wife, you might be in danger too.' Stella spoke slowly as the idea dawned. 'If he feared that you might tell the police he'd asked you to lie, he might want you dead too.'

'I'm sure he wants me dead.'

'Unless it wasn't Adam that killed Helen. If he wasn't with you all night you don't have an alibi.' Adam Honeysett had given her a pile of hastily assembled papers on his wife. He had clumsily kept back information Stella was bound to find out. Jane Drake had kept a meticulous record of various people's movements in the street. She knew when there was likely to be no one about. It was against every rule in Terry's book – she had no phone signal, no easy means of escape – but, scenting a lead, Stella said, 'You had a motive, the means and the opportunity to kill Helen Honeysett.'

Jane Drake got up. She tossed the crisp packet in an overflowing wastepaper bin. She was coldly matter of fact: 'I didn't kill her. But I sure as hell wanted her dead.'

Stella took a wrong turning out of Drake's flat and found herself on the towpath. It was five to five in the morning; it wouldn't get light until half seven. Considering she hadn't slept she was alert, her mind clear. Stanley peed against the low retaining wall of the riverbank. Waiting for him to finish, Stella gazed off towards the towpath and saw a bright light. It floated off the ground. It was a man wearing a head torch. Avoiding the beam, she looked downwards and caught a glimpse of a lead clipped across his chest. A dog walker. Possibly he was the man she'd seen when she was with Jack on the towpath. He was familiar. She let herself breathe.

'Morning,' Stella greeted him. It was the man with the stoop.

He passed her without replying.

Stella felt a chill descend. His silence filled her with a strange dread. She whipped around. The towpath was empty. The light had gone out.

She was metres from the old house that Stanley had broken in to. Her heart missed a beat. A man was in the porch. She shrank into the shadows of the riverbank. If she kept very still, he wouldn't see her.

Stanley mewed loudly. The man looked towards Stella's hiding place. She shut her eyes as if it would make her invisible. When she dared open them, the man was coming towards her.

Chapter Fifty

Dappled light, melancholy and insidious, washed over the tow-path. Unable to sleep, Jack was walking. His ostensible reason for the nocturnal journey had been to walk until he had a signal and call Bella. He'd had the idea of asking her to reconsider breaking up with him, but when he tried to list reasons why she should change her mind – she would ask him to justify his request – he couldn't think of one argument in his favour. His mind was full of the fact that a True Host lived minutes from where he was staying. A man who had likely murdered Helen Honeysett on the towpath where he was now.

He was passing the dilapidated house. Pocketing his phone, Jack slipped down the path at the side of the house.

The key was still on the inside of the bathroom door. He unlocked the door and crept out into the hall. The post had gone from the mat. Avoiding dead leaves, Jack crossed the floor and climbed the stairs. This time he was not afraid. Although ostensibly he had come out to call Bella, he knew that all along it was to this house that he had intended to come. This time he was alone. He was ready and prepared.

On the landing, the quiet was all-encompassing. Jack's nerves were alive to the presence of Brian Judd.

Come out, come out, wherever you are.

The doors to the front-facing rooms were closed. He moved

along the passage and trod on something; it let out a strangled squeak. Crouching, he felt something soft and fluffy. He found his Maglite and flicked it on. Pale and insipid as gaslight, the light revealed a toy hen with a padded orange crest that matched an orange beak. An incongruously cheerful creature to find in this cold, uncanny house. Jack turned off the light. He crammed the hen into his coat pocket and crept along the passage to the last room on the right.

Last time he had been sure that Judd was just centimetres from him. He had felt the tingle of energy that passes between two human beings. Now he felt nothing. Was he alone?

He opened the door and went in. He risked the light. A low-wattage lamp cast light on a room chock-full of paraphernalia. It took him some moments to understand that the frogs, bears, squirrels, a rabbit with an eye and an ear missing that lay scattered on a rag rug were dog toys. A divan was littered with rubber chews in the shape of rings and bones. From a hook on the wall hung a string bag bulging with tennis balls. Copies of *Dogs Monthly: Fun Canine Stories to Fill Your Heart with Joy!* – were on a table. The horse might already have bolted, but this time, Jack had taken the precaution of wearing gloves. The thick dust guaranteed fingerprints. One shelf was heaped with packets of nappy sacks that he knew did for poo-bags, packets of wet wipes and bottles of dog shampoo. Brian Judd shopped in bulk.

A tartan dog bed was in one corner, a dog cage in another. Fur caught in the pins of a wire brush was cream-coloured like a sheep. A large bag of biscuits sagged beside this. Chicken and rice, for small-breed dogs. It depicted a cute portrait of a white-haired dog with a slip of a pink tongue, maybe a terrier – Jack only knew about poodles. Judd's dog was small. This only faintly reassured him. If so minded dogs the size of Stanley could rip you apart.

True Hosts didn't keep pets; they avoided any intimate connection. Brian Judd had given over an entire room to his dog. It didn't add up, Jack thought.

He lifted the bag of biscuits down from the shelf. Fishing his reading glasses from his coat he put them on. In the poor light he read the sell-by date: *June 2012*.

He needn't worry about being attacked by a small dog, it no longer lived here. Or anywhere. The room, neglected and deserted, was less a shrine for a loved animal than a sign that the owner couldn't face the immensity of his loss.

Jack placed the bag on the shelf, facing as it had been; a True Host would notice the smallest alteration. His attention was caught by a letter on the table. The name on the letterhead was Natasha Latimer's. This was a connection between Latimer and Judd. Although he was wearing gloves, he didn't pick it up.

DEAR MR JUDD,

You have received numerous communications from my lawyers re my purchase of your property. To date you have not replied.

Unfortunately the building has been allowed to deteriorate. It is in need of extensive renovation or demolition will be the only option. Enclosed is an increased offer that should expedite the matter. It allows you to relocate somewhere more suitable for you.

I look forward to receiving your acceptance, ASAP.

Yours sincerely
NATASHA LATIMER
Enc.

In the peremptory tone and the expressed expectation of success Jack recognized the woman he had met only once. The date of the letter was December 2010. Since Latimer hadn't bought the house, the 'matter' had never been 'expedited'. Number 1 Thames Cottages must have been second choice. This house, set back from the river, offered more scope for alteration than the house she'd bought. Jack, too, would prefer to live here, although he wouldn't instal a basement. Jack found he was obscurely grateful to Judd for not giving in to Latimer and keeping the house as it was. This too was not in the character of a True Host. Yet an atmosphere of malevolence pervaded the rooms.

Whatever Judd was, he must dislike Latimer. A True Host never forgave. Natasha Latimer, ruled by hard cash and a hard heart, would be haunted by her nemesis.

Jack lifted the letter up by one corner and slipped out a yellowed newspaper clipping. It was dated March 12 2011. Just a few weeks after he'd met Stella.

PENSIONER DEFIES DEVELOPER

By Lucie May

A man whose family has owned an eighteenth-century house by the river at Kew for 150 years has turned down an offer of £1.5 million. 'Mr Judd has let the house fall to rack and ruin. It's crying out for skilled restoration. It's my dream home,' property developer Natasha Latimer told us. 'Judd could retire to a little property. Only a fool would refuse hard cash.'

A recluse, Brian Judd walks his dog on the towpath before dawn and late at night. Police have warned Latimer to stop approaching the elderly man or they will charge her under the Protection from Harassment Act 1997. Judd, who declined our invite for a chat, has lived in the substantial riverside property all his life. Charles Judd, a prosperous wine merchant, bought the house in 1858 for twenty-two guineas. In the 1930s his grandson sold the family business and drank the proceeds. His son, Brian Judd, retired from Hammersmith and Fulham Council's accounts department in 2005 and has rarely been seen since.

Latimer's intended renovations include digging out a deep basement. Unmarried with no children, Latimer told us she didn't plan to sell on the improved building at a vast profit, she wanted to join 'in with the local community'.

Brian Judd's home is close to the towpath where, in 1987, 26-year-old estate agent Helen Honeysett went missing. Judd, like all men living in the vicinity, was questioned by the police. He was working at the office late that night.

Looks like Ms Latimer will have to keep searching for that Dream Home!

It was the kind of story Lucie loathed. People wrangling over a house wouldn't make her Journalist of the Year. Jack supposed that Latimer had tried to harness the press to drum up support. No one manipulated Lucie, and a champion of the underdog, she'd have backed Brian Judd over Latimer.

Latimer didn't talk of houses or homes, but properties and projects. It was a shame, he thought, that Helen Honeysett wasn't actually haunting her. A top-selling estate agent, it was likely they'd have got on. The Thames Cottages 'property' had come with Neville Rowlands as a sitting tenant; presumably Latimer had offered him a sizeable sweetener to move on. Jack shone his torch around the room filled with chewed and manky toys, a dog bed, magazines advising on defleaing or what to do on Bonfire Night. He felt a wash of grief for the small dog that had capered and snoozed here. Rowlands' dogs were buried in the family pet cemetery in the back garden. How much 'hard cash' had persuaded him to leave them behind?

Judd's bedroom might be a monk's cell. It was furnished with a single bed above which hung a plastic lampshade operated by a cord. On a stool by the bed was another *Dogs Monthly*, December 2010. Was that when his dog had died? A white MDF wardrobe, the fittings loosening, leant crazily against the wall. Jack prised open a door and a musty odour drifted out. Stella could identify a composite of smells in seconds; he settled for the predominant one of damp cloth and old man. Three jackets, a black suit encased in dry-cleaning plastic and two pairs of shoes, one black and one brown, all scuffed, the leather dry and cracked. True Hosts were particular about appearance. Jack kept his own shoes lubricated and polished.

He gripped the door. The man he and Stella had met on the towpath the night when Stella had scared Jack with her twenty-second hearing test had been wearing scuffed black shoes. He lifted one black lace-up off the rail. The soles were scratched. No mud. But then it hadn't rained and the towpath was shingled. The man had been walking his dog. There was no dog here. All the same...

Jack felt a change in the air. The minutest alteration. True Hosts moved stealthily; Brian Judd would give no warning of his return. Jack went to the doorway and, crouching, peeped out into the passage. People watched for intruders at head height. But a True Host would know to look down.

Thin light played tricks with distance and dimension and Jack took time to orientate himself. His skin prickled with the nearness of another human being. A weighted silence pressed in upon him. He hid his face with his coat collar and moved quickly along the corridor. He reached the dog's room and hesitated. Was Brian Judd waiting for him there? Or was he on the landing, patiently biding his time? Two choices. Jack tried to out-think him. He'd expect Jack to try to leave. So he was on the landing. Or Judd would expect Jack to think that's what he'd think and so he was in the dog's room. Or he'd think Jack would guess that and so he was on the landing after all. But Jack had thought that too. Judd would confound him by being in one of the other rooms in the passage. His head bursting, Jack crept into the dog's room. Something moved by his feet. He froze. The stuffed hen had fallen out of his pocket.

A slant of moonlight silvered the floor. Jack's throat tickled with dust that hung in the cold air. True Hosts disliked dust.

Who am I and what have I done?

Brian Judd had typed Steven Lawson's last words on to

Natasha Latimer's computer. He had a reason to hold a grudge against her. But how did he know of the diary? Jack counted to ten and crept back to the door.

The passage was quiet. He pushed the thinking on. There was one approach that a True Host never took.

Jack gathered his coat to him and ran down the passage. He leapt down the stairs and trampled on the dead leaves in the hall. The obvious exit was out of the front door. He veered left and slammed into wood. The lavatory door was shut. He rattled the handle, knowing already he'd miscalculated. The True Host was with him all the way. The door gave and barrelling inside, Jack flung himself through the open sash and tore up the path to the footpath.

True Hosts never showed themselves. Brian Judd would not have expected Jack to break cover. He had out-thought him. Jack stood for a moment in the shadow of the porch. He willed Brian Judd to join him.

Why did Judd lock the bathroom door from the inside? Jack felt a stab of doubt. Could the person who locked the door have no more right to be in Judd's house than he did? Did he already have a guest?

He heard a call. A cat or a fox. Someone was waiting in the shadows by the riverbank. *Brian Judd.*

A flicker. Small breed, pale coat the colour of the fur caught in the spines of the hairbrush in the dog's room. The dog wasn't dead after all.

Chapter Fifty-One

Tuesday, 12 January 2016

At Chiswick Bridge I decide to walk on. I hate lying to you. I would dearly like to escort you back to your cottage, but you appreciate me giving you privacy. Soon I will be with you and we will never be parted.

Instead I follow you along the towing-path. Keeping watch and keeping out of sight. It's not a good time to be out. I don't want you encountering that young man, you are far too trusting. When we get back to the cottage, you pull your curtains. You shut me out. I don't like that.

Chapter Fifty-Two

Tuesday, 12 January 2016

'Oh, it's you!' Jack fussed Stanley's ears as the little poodle smothered him with efficient licks.

'What are you doing here?' Stella sounded furious.

'I was...' Jack couldn't tell the truth. He turned the tables. 'What are *you* doing here?'

'Stanley needed a... Oh, never mind, we have to pay a call on someone.' Stella was steaming off into the darkness. He caught up with her as the lamp-post came into sight.

'Hang on, Stell, look.' He plunged into thick bushes beside Latimer's cottage. 'This must be where that tunnel in the basement comes out.' Stanley, proficient at agility, nimbly jumped over brambles and snuffled inquisitively through the bars of a rusting iron grille.

Stella peered into the gloom of the passage beyond the bars. She looked down at the dog. 'He's seen something.' She squatted beside him and ran her fingers under the metal frame.

'Careful he doesn't get his head stuck,' Jack warned as Stanley nosed forward. Health and safety was Stella's thing but, filled with contrition at almost being caught trespassing, he was eager to make amends, however trivial. Or futile.

'Here we are.' Stella slotted a key into the lock and pulled on the grille. Impeded by the brambles, it opened a few centimetres. Her voice echoed in the dank passage. 'Either this is a spare or our intruder leaves the key here. I'd bet on the latter.'

He should tell her that he had a good idea who the intruder was.

'I think I saw that man again.' Stella stepped into the passage. 'The one we met on the towpath.'

'Stell, watch out! Judd might be in there.' *Idiot.* Jack smacked his forehead. Truth time. 'Actually, I have an idea who the intruder is.'

'Who?' Stella sounded far away. She'd switched on her torch app; ghostly light flickered on the brick.

He must get the key off her and lock the grille. It was never good to thwart a True Host. Jack cannoned down the tunnel and found her in the vaulted chamber sitting on the digger.

'Latimer made enemies before she moved here. She tried to buy that house on the towpath, but the owner, who's called Brian Judd, wouldn't sell.' He was out of breath although he hadn't been running.

'How do you know?' Stella operated the lever and raised the claw. Stanley barked uproariously, a strident sound that made Jack's ears ring. Worried that the dog would be crushed, Jack picked him up.

'Lucie May wrote an article.' He compounded his stab at the truth with a lie: 'It was in Honeysett's second file.'

'I didn't see it.' In the semi-darkness, Jack couldn't tell if Stella doubted him.

'Maybe I saw it somewhere else.' He sounded lame. He remembered what Stella had said earlier. 'Why did you say the case was wide open?'

'Like you said, everyone living on this terrace in 1987 could have murdered Helen Honeysett. Or it could have been team-work. She upset all of them.'

Stella told him she had met Jane Drake. While excited by the information she'd gathered, Jack felt frustration that, again, she'd met a suspect without him.

Stella jumped off the digger. 'Show me the back garden.'

'It's dark.' Jack didn't know why he'd said that.

'It was dark the first time you saw it.' Stella headed back down the tunnel.

Jack was hot with confusion. *How did Stella know?* In a flash he understood. Jane Drake. He ran after her. 'I'm sorry, I was impatient to see the house and—'

Stella unlocked the garden door with the grille key. 'One key fits two locks. It probably used to work the front door before the Banham.' Stanley tumbled out of Jack's grasp and whisked inside. They went after him. Stella locked the door. Jack hoped that, rather than keeping Brian Judd out, she hadn't shut him in with them.

She would know about his breaking in to Judd's house too. She knew him much better than he knew her. She knew him better than Bella. 'Stella I—'

Stella trained the torch on a headstone. 'Someone's been cleaning this.'

'Cleaning it?' If he told Stella about his visits to the dilapidated house, she would refuse to work with him. At least he'd have told the truth. Jack felt he was teetering on a cliff edge.

'Hercules died in 1987, but the headstone's lighter than that one over there for Max who died in 2012. Max's stone is better quality – granite is hard-wearing – than the lighter one for Hercules. Why should the older, poorer stone look newer? Answer, it's been cleaned.' She bent and sniffed the 1987 stone. 'Mrs Cooper's Concentrate.'

'How do you know?' Silly question. Stella could identify a cleaning astringent in one sniff.

'It gets rid of algae and moss as well as dirt.' She arched her back in a stretch. 'Could Rowlands be buried here? I suppose not, that's illegal.' She raked the beam over the headstones.

'Actually it's not. According to the Burial Laws Amendment Act 1980, if Rowlands had owned the house, he could be buried in his garden. A body is classed as "Clinical Waste" and provided you've registered the death—' He interrupted himself. 'The thing is, Stella, I went into...'

Stella had gone. He went round the hedge. She was craning over the little bridge at the green glass skylights. 'That's not right.'

'No, it's not. I'm really sorry. I should—'

'The lights only work if triggered by movement or body heat.' She pointed down.

'That's right.' He saw why when he'd first seen the glass he'd mistaken it for water. He imagined dropping a stone and making ripples on the glowing surface.

Stella's voice was a murmur. 'Jack, there's someone in the basement.'

Chapter Fifty-Three

Tuesday, 12 January 2016

Jack switched on the light in the hall. Stella couldn't hear anything below.

At the top of the stairs, a finger to his lips, he whispered, 'I'll go first.'

'Better I go, I've got Stanley.' As if illustrating this doubtful advantage, Stanley hopped on to the first step and forged on down, forcing Stella to push past Jack.

On the River Wall, a solitary light twinkled on the water. The basement lights came on. The glass panels slide aside. At the end of the sweep of ice-like floor, Stella saw that the door to the hidden chamber was open. They had just been in there. The door had been shut.

Jack strode past her, patches of blue light illuminating the floor where he stepped. He kicked open the brick door with a crash.

'Oh, it's you!' she heard him say.

'Where were you?' a voice demanded.

'In your pet cemetery.'

Illuminated in the dirty light, Natasha Latimer sat on the digger. Her sister Claudia was leaning against it, gazing up as if waiting for her go. Stella gathered her wits and signalled to Stanley to sit.

'Your ghost isn't a ghost, he's as alive as you or I,' Jack said. 'But I think you already know that, don't you?'

'Ghosts are real.' Without her bobble hat, Claudia seemed slighter, like a ghost herself in the dim light of the bulb.

Straining on his lead, Stanley began scuffling in the dirt. 'Leave!' Stella hissed. The poodle shook his head; something was flapping between his teeth. *A dead creature.* Stella tried to see, but he gave a gurgling growl. If Stanley was being a hunter, he wouldn't give up his prey. She shone her phone down. It was a scrap of rag. She let herself breathe. It wasn't as enticing as a crisp bag; he'd soon lose interest.

'I don't know what you are talking about.' Natasha Latimer batted her sister away. 'You've dragged me here in the middle of the night for what?'

'The night is the best time of the day,' Claudia said dreamily. 'We will meet our ghosts. That's why I said to come.'

'Oh, yes, it is the best time!' Jack agreed. He looked up at Latimer. 'In 1987 those renting had more rights than they do now. If the landlord had wanted to get rid of a sitting tenant, they'd have had to offer an incentive. How much did you offer Neville Rowlands to leave?'

'Enough.' Natasha Latimer smiled. Stella knew that was a bad sign. Why was Jack discussing tenants' rights?

'I said she should let him stay.' Claudia buffed the yellow paintwork with her blanket cloak. 'It wasn't good karma to make him go.'

'I agree,' Jack said. 'But Neville Rowlands has been coming back and you knew. You hoped we'd boot him out. You couldn't tell the police because the press would love the story of the young property developer who picks on elderly men.'

Latimer folded her arms across her chest. 'Rowlands is dead.'

'Dead to you,' Jack said. 'After you got him out, you didn't care what happened to him.'

'I didn't tell the police about Rowlands breaking in because I didn't bloody know!' Natasha Latimer turned to Stella. 'Are you going to let him talk to me like this? He's the bloody cleaner!'

Stella had never heard Jack so brutal and unforgiving. If he were a cleaner, she'd have to sack him. But he was a detective so she did nothing.

'What's the harm?' Claudia flapped her cloak. 'Nev visits his animals. We must have access to our dear departed. He's not a criminal, he's a sweetie!'

Latimer scowled down at her sister. 'No one is a sweetie.'

'It's only bricks and mortar, Nats. Love conquers all,' Claudia said apropos of nothing.

Natasha climbed off the digger and, speaking as if her sister didn't exist, said to Stella, 'Ask your operative to stay until the locks are changed and then leave.' She went through to the basement.

Light slanted into the chamber as the lamps in the basement lit up. Stella heard the panels swish open and shut. Then silence. Stanley had dropped the rag; she snatched it up and stuffed it in her pocket.

'Could one of you tell me how to drive this?' Claudia was perched on the digger, her cloak billowing.

'Let me show you,' Jack said.

'So Claudia gave Neville Rowlands a key,' Stella said.

Lights dotted the River Wall. Residents of Strand on the Green across the Thames were waking and starting the day. Natasha Latimer and her sister had gone. Stella and Jack sat on the lips sofa in the basement. They had drinks, tea for Stella, hot milk with honey for Jack.

'One thing I'd liked about Latimer was that she spared the pet graves. Yet it didn't fit with who she was. I knew she must have paid Rowlands to leave, but what sum was worth leaving his pets behind? Looks like he and Claudia shafted Latimer! Hoorah for Claudia.' Jack wondered if he'd see her again.

'It was still trespassing. It's against the law.' Stella got off the sofa and went over to the River Wall. The river appeared to subsume her. Jack had the dreadful notion she might drown and silently urged her to come away. When she spoke it even sounded as though she was under water. 'Was it Claudia who started the haunting rumour? And why Helen Honeysett specifically?'

'Claudia Latimer is in touch with spirits. She's a sensitive soul. She will feel Honeysett's ghost here.' Jack was inclined to go with Claudia on that, but he wouldn't push it. 'This entire area is imbued with Helen's disappearance. That's a haunting of sorts.'

'That doesn't explain who put the question on the screensaver or operated the digger.' Stella had palpably had it with spirits.

'Maybe Rowlands isn't the sweetie Claudia thinks he is. She sees the good in us all. Megan Lawson said Helen Honeysett called him a sweetie too, although I expect she called everyone that. Rowlands took Latimer's money and kept a key to her house. It must have been tempting to indulge in a touch of revenge for being booted out. Yes it's against the law, but I kind of get it.' Jack totally got it, but refrained from saying so.

'How would Rowlands know what Steven Lawson wrote in his diary?' River light played over her.

'Lucie complained that Neville Rowlands was the only resident of Thames Cottages who'd talk to her after Honeysett vanished. One guess how he found out.'

'Lucie told him? Surely she wouldn't give up her secret!'

'A few nippets and I'm betting she wouldn't be able to help herself.' Jack tried to formulate how to express his conviction that Brian Judd had murdered Helen Honeysett. They were wasting time on Rowlands. Stella's open mind had limits and tonight – or this morning – he'd challenged it with spirits, so True Hosts would close it with a clang. He ventured, 'What was Brian Judd's alibi?'

'He was at work.'

'Who said?' True Hosts made themselves visible if they wanted to give the impression that they were somewhere when they were not.

'A colleague, I think. We must double-check.' Stella came back to the sofa and, sitting down, pulled the Honeysett file from her rucksack. She was going to look for the article on Latimer's tussle with Judd. Jack shut his eyes. *Tell her where you saw it.* 'I can see Brian Judd would dislike Latimer, but why would he murder Helen Honeysett?' Stella pulled out a newspaper cutting and, frowning, said, 'I haven't seen this one before... Oh my God!'

Eyes on the River Wall as if it could swallow him up, Jack raked his fingers through his hair. When he tried to tell the truth something always got in the way.

'What?' Jack felt a wash of guilt. She knew. *No.* How could she know?

'The colleague was Graham Makepeace. Jackie's husband. I'll call him and ask for details. Let's hope he remembers.'

'Although Jackie hasn't mentioned it, I doubt he's forgotten that a colleague was a suspect in a murder case!' Jack steepled his fingers, feeling relief and then more guilt that he had something to hide from Stella. He was an idiot! He mustered himself. 'Stell, that article I read about Brian—'

Stella was excited. 'Adam told me all the neighbours came to their house-warming party at Christmas in 1986, days before Helen vanished. That would include Neville Rowlands.' She waved the photograph of Steven Lawson smiling. 'We've identified all the others in the picture. Except for that man.'

'That's Lawson.'

'No, there.' Stella was patient. 'It's blurred, but I think he's the man we met on the towpath. And who I saw just now on the way back from Jane Drake's. Look at the way he's standing, as if the ceiling's too low. The dog walker on the towpath had a stoop.'

Jack fished his glasses from his shirt pocket and crammed them on his face. He peered at the fuzzed figure of a grey-haired man soberly dressed in a black suit and tie standing behind Lawson. He jerked his hand, slopping milk on his coat. Stanley appeared from nowhere and began busily to eradicate the stain. Jack had seen the suit an hour earlier, encased in plastic in Brian Judd's musty-smelling wardrobe. 'He looks rather formal for a neighbours' party,' he commented inanely. The man wasn't Neville Rowlands, he was Brian Judd. He looked out of the photograph with the impassive stare of a True Host.

'I'll show this to Beverly,' Stella decided. 'It'll help if she can put a face to a name.'

Jack blurted, 'What if it's not Rowlands? We couldn't see the man properly, his head torch was blinding.' Again he considered that True Hosts were sartorially stringent; Judd's suit bagged at the pockets and his tie was crumpled.

'Adam will know.'

'It could be this Brian Judd fellow.' Jack hated himself for his craven duplicity.

'Would a recluse go to a party? Especially with neighbours?' Stella limited interaction with her own neighbours to hasty greetings. She'd never accept an invitation to a party. She angled the picture towards him. 'Who's he looking at?'

Jack shrugged. 'Helen Honeysett?'

'No, Judd or Rowlands – if it is him – isn't looking at the lens. Compare him to Lawson who is definitely smiling at Helen. That man's gaze is off to his right.'

Jack hadn't touched his drink. He was rather going off milk. He looked at the photograph. 'You're right, he's not looking at her.'

'He seems upset.'

'Not upset.' Jack shifted to face Stella. 'Say when I get it right.' He glared at Stella with a furrowed brow.

'You look furious.' Stella held his gaze; her own expression was one of concern. 'What's the matter?'

He let his brow relax a fraction. 'OK, how's that? Compare me to Judd.'

'You look the same!' Anxiously, Stanley bounded on to Jack's lap and began licking his face.

'There!' To avoid Stanley's tongue and to hold the expression, Jack was tight-lipped like a ventriloquist: 'Ask ee ah I veel?'

'How do you feel?' He loved Stella for falling in with him.

He pulled Stanley off. 'Burning in my stomach like hot coals. Outrage. No, not outrage.' He took the picture off Stella. Their fingers brushed. Hers were warm although the basement was as chilly as death. 'Jealousy. Gnawing jealousy that could drive a person mad. That's Judd's expression.'

'What would he be jealous of? If it is Judd.'

'Not "what", whom. If Judd isn't looking at Helen Honeysett, whom is he watching?' Jack spoke on a sigh. 'We'll never know.'

'We might!' Stella was examining the other photograph. A group, by a mantelpiece decked with tinsel, balancing paper plates of food and glasses of wine, were chatting with pretending-to-be-fascinated faces. A younger Bette Lawson was talking to a middle-aged woman in a silk shirt with a rose quartz pendant and silvery hair swept into a bun. Slightly apart, drooping in studied languor, a teenaged boy – probably Garry Lawson – was holding out a tumbler of orange to a small, childish hand off 'stage left', likely to be Megan's. 'Sybil Lofthouse hasn't changed.' Stella pointed at the pendant woman. 'I don't recognize that woman.' She gestured at a tall woman with soft brown hair and a beaky nose with Adam Honeysett, behind Sybil Lofthouse and Bette Lawson.

'That's Daphne!' Jack enthused. 'It was only about a year since her husband and daughter were killed. Amazing she's at a party.'

'Life has to go on. She still had to earn a living,' Stella said. 'So that's Mum's declutterer!' Stella held the picture up to the light. 'Merry was attractive.'

'Still is.' In the eighties, even in a Lady Diana-style ruffled blouse, Daphne had been striking. Yet closer scrutiny betrayed a sombre truth. Her face was a mask, her eyes glazed; she was hardly present. She had suffered what every mother fears: the death of a child. If anyone was haunted anywhere, it was Daphne Merry.

Jack felt annoyed: Daphne was listening politely to a twenty-something Adam Honeysett. Flamboyant in mascara, sparkly jacket with epaulettes, a scarf tied around his head, draping down one shoulder, Honeysett might be Simon Le Bon. Daphne was clasping her glass as, holding a bottle of champagne, Honeysett leant over her. *Prat*. It was nearly thirty years ago, but Jack longed to intervene and save her.

'This was taken seconds before the one of Lawson with the man in the suit behind him.' She tapped the time stamp in the corner. 'Helen took this picture, then swung around and took Lawson, and caught Judd-stroke-Rowlands – or whoever he is – unawares. Wait a sec...' She placed the pictures in parallel on her knee and grabbed her Filofax from her rucksack, tearing out the plastic rule from the diary section. She laid it between the photos, tracing the man's gaze towards the group picture. 'He's watching Daphne Merry.'

'Stella, you are the greatest of Wonderhorses!' Jack grabbed her hand and flapped it up and down. 'He saw Honeysett forcing drink on Merry and resented it.' Jack had felt the impotent resentment himself moments before.

'Resentment isn't jealousy,' Stella pointed out.

'No. It's not,' Jack agreed. He let go of Stella's hand.

'Watch me.' She pulled a hideous face at him. 'What's that?'

'Blood-curdling rage?'

'Jealousy,' she huffed.

'You never get jealous.' He heard the annoyance in his voice. Stella didn't mind about the things that most people – him included – suffered over. Her mum fussing over Dale, Lucie claiming Terry for herself, him being with Bella...

'Maybe the man in the suit liked her.' Stella would avoid the word 'love'. 'He looks fit to brain Adam with that bottle if he could.'

Jack pushed his glasses over the bridge of his nose. 'If Brian Judd or whoever was in love with Daphne he'd hate Adam Honeysett leering at her.'

'Judd was a recluse, how would he have the chance to fall in love with her?'

'Walking his dog on the towpath?'

'How do we know he had a dog?'

'When we went into his house I saw dog things,' Jack said too quickly. Stella looked over the top of the photograph at him. In that second, with the force of a gale, it hit him. *She knew he was lying.*

'That's why Stanley goes there,' Stella said. 'He can smell the dog. But it's not a motive for killing Helen. Mum said Merry still lives on her own. So whatever the man in the black suit felt for her, it wasn't – or isn't – mutual. And like I say, it doesn't explain why he'd kill Honeysett.'

'Perhaps Helen upset him. It doesn't take much to tip a True… someone over the edge,' Jack said.

'How did imitating Judd – or Rowlands – tell you he was jealous?' Stella asked.

'I noticed how it made me feel. I felt jealousy.'

'It doesn't help us prove Brian Judd broke in to this house. Nor does it get us nearer to knowing what happened to Helen.' Stella looked at the photograph of Steven Lawson smiling at the camera. 'It could be him.'

'Who could be who?'

'Judd or Rowlands. That man I said I passed again, who was walking his dog on the towpath again tonight – this morning. It was as I was coming back from Jane Drake's. I was going the wrong way.'

'Are you sure?' Jack clenched his fists. The True Host had got him in his sights. He was watching the person Jack was closest to. Stella.

Who am I and what have I done?

'Perfectly sure. My van's parked by the recycling place. I got lost on one of the paths in a maze-thing in the estate and ended up on the towpath.'

Everything ended on the towpath.

'I mean are you sure he was the same man that we met?' *Brown scuffed shoes.*

'I'm *not* sure. I couldn't see his face. He was wearing that torchy thing. I was dazzled. I said goodnight. He didn't reply.' She paused. 'It freaked me out. It can't have been the same man because the one we met was polite. He asked about Stanley being obedient. Another thing...' Stella flapped her hand in dismissal. 'Stupid.'

'What's stupid?' Dread coiled upwards.

'That was the thing that's been nagging at me since I was with Jane Drake. I asked if she had a poo-bag and she said she didn't have a dog!'

'So what?' Jack tried not to sound panicked. The man must be Judd.

'That night we met the man, do you remember seeing a dog?'

'No, but it was dark. It was probably rummaging in the bushes like Stanley does.' He had not seen a dog. A chill crept down his back. Stanley had gone into the playroom. Through the glass, Jack could see him nestled in the sandbox. 'Or he didn't have a dog. People can go for walks on their own. I do.'

'After midnight and at five in the morning?'

'Well, yes, that's when you met me—'

'He had a lead slung across his chest.' Stella stopped, then said, 'He had a bag with poo in it. I said it was stupid.'

Jack didn't trust himself to speak. Brian Judd was too many steps ahead. The man they had met together on the towpath last Wednesday had a lead across his chest. Where was his dog? Following her own train of thought Stella hadn't noticed his silence.

'... Helen's dog was found on the towpath by Daphne Merry. We should check if other dogs have been lost around here since January 1987. Lucie May would know, but after last night, I don't fancy asking. You'd have better luck.'

'I doubt it.' Jack cleared his throat. 'You could ask Martin Cashman.'

'No way!' Stella was keen to forget her fling with Cashman. It was mean to remind her. Trying to wind back, Jack made it worse: 'We do know of one dog found on the towpath.'

'Do we?' Stella never spotted meanness.

'Stanley. You and Thingy rescued him from falling into the river near Kew Bridge.' Jack was being mealy-mouthed. He knew Thingy was called David. The man hadn't been good enough for Stella. Jackie maintained that Jack didn't think any man was good enough for Stella.

'*David* reported finding Stanley to the police. No one claimed him,' Stella answered stiffly. She wouldn't want to think about David any more than Cashman.

Jack began polishing his glasses as if cleaning would undo his hurting her.

Stella was gazing at the photograph of Adam Honeysett with Daphne Merry. 'Adam looks like Simon Le Bon, don't you think?'

'Not really,' Jack huffed. Although moments earlier he had thought this himself. He sniped, 'Are you sure David Barlow reported Stanley missing?'

'Of course I'm sure.' Stella was staring at him. 'Is that you being the man in the black suit again?' She was geared up to guess the feelings behind his expression.

'No.' Jack wiped a hand down his face to erase his expression of gnawing jealousy.

Chapter Fifty-Four

Tuesday, 12 January 2016

Stella clipped the signed job sheet into her folder. It was five past nine. She'd started the shift late because a lorry had broken down on the Great West Road. Lawyers and clients were arriving at the Hammersmith Magistrates' Court.

Dark clouds scudded across a leaden sky. Stella's mood wasn't affected by weather, but being late made her tense. She zipped her jacket up to the collar; the fur lining protected her cheeks from the sharp gusts whipping across the car park. Her van was in her allocated space by a cluster of wheelie bins.

'Got you bang to rights have they, Detective Darnell?' The corncrake laugh, harsh and mirthless, carried on the wind. Lucie May sauntered over to Stella, the heels of her knee-high boots clicking on the asphalt. 'Been eradicating stains?' Her eyes gleamed coldly at Stella.

Stella decided things couldn't get worse. 'I want a favour.'

They had formed a fragile rapprochement the year before last when Lucie had helped with Stella and Jack's last case, but the visit to her Murder Room had undone all of that. In the chill of the winter morning they eyed each other as if preparing for a duel.

'Knew you'd come pecking. Being a detective ain't such a box of birds after all!' Lucie barked. 'The favours are all run out. I have to get into court.'

Stella cut to the chase. 'Jane Drake wasn't with Adam

Honeysett the night Helen Honeysett went missing. He was on the Thames towpath at the same time as his wife.'

Lucie was rootling in a bright red imitation-crocodile handbag with a fearsome gold clip, and gave no indication she had heard. She pulled out a packet of Marlboros, flicked up the lid and, dipping down, snapped up a cigarette between lipsticked lips.

Since giving up smoking, Lucie had tried e-cigarettes, sticks of root liquorice and settled for chopped carrot from Marks & Spencer, which she munched compulsively. Stella didn't comment on the return to real cigarettes; it wasn't her business. 'Helen Honeysett's husband, Adam Honeysett—'

'I know Adam Honeysett. Who says Jane Drake wasn't with him?'

'He begged her for an alibi so she claimed they were at her flat. She's convinced he was with another woman. He insisted he wasn't. I think he's telling the truth because otherwise why ask Jane Drake to speak for him? Drake told me that Helen Honeysett upset everyone in Thames Cottages. Any one of them could have killed her. Lawson is not the only suspect.'

'You're wonderfully naïve, darling! So the Grieving Widower had another tart that night. I upset people all the time, so far no one's taken a pop at me.' The cigarette bobbed in Lucie's mouth as she coldly enunciated the words. She held a lighter aloft as if waiting to set off a controlled explosion.

A lesser mortal would have quailed, but Stella was unflappable. Facts were facts. 'Jane Drake had a motive for killing Helen Honeysett: she's obsessed with Adam Honeysett. She lives along the towpath, she stalks him and anyone he talks to. She stalked me. She has the pictures all over her walls, it's weird, like a shri—' Stella remembered Lucie's wall and stopped. 'Adam Honeysett was having an affair with Drake. It would have suited them both if Helen Honeysett was dead. It might have suited everyone living in Thames Cottages that she was dead. In fact the person it least suited was Steven Lawson. His life fell apart after she disappeared.'

'Your dad thought it was Lawson.' Lucie May drew long and hard on her cigarette, eyes narrowed.

A car door slammed; high above the clouds an aeroplane rumbled; a horn beeped. At last Stella said, 'They had Megan Lawson's witness statement saying she saw her dad going after Helen to the towpath.' Stella could do icy too. 'Megan told them her dad liked Helen and the police stopped following other leads. She never told them she went to the towpath herself and overheard Honeysett saying "Oh it's you!" to someone she assumed was her father. She never actually saw him. Megan told you this, didn't she?'

'Listen to you playing bad cop! Terry would be tossing in his grave.' Lucie flicked the lighter at her cigarette; each time she got a flame the wind blew it out. 'Go back to detective school! Our jails are packed with idiots who murdered without meaning to or were too stupid to cover their tracks. My esteemed brother-in-law's in the second camp. If it weren't for Megan, we'd never have known he'd left the house – Bette would have kept it zipped. He'd have got away with it. My sister hasn't fessed up about his diary. She was happy to take his life insurance.' Lucie May got a light, cupping her hands over the flame; she sucked on the cigarette until her cheeks seemed to meet in the middle.

'Whoever killed Helen Honeysett did cover their tracks. Someone has successfully disposed of her body without a trace. They did it in a short space of time because there were several neighbours walking their dogs on the towpath that night. Drake saw Daphne Merry, Neville Rowlands and Sybil Lofthouse. Megan Lawson was there too.' Stella decided against saying that Rowlands had gained entry into Natasha Latimer's cottage. Lucie would snap up the story. It wasn't Stella's story to tell.

'Do some first-base detection, Stella. Honeysett trusted Lawson, she'd have followed him anywhere. Stevie spun her a tale and, being a sweet young thing, she fell for it. My sister confirmed he was out of the house for twenty minutes. How long does it take for a dog to lift its leg? What was he doing? Where did he take her?'

'Steven didn't take the dog. As I understand it from my research, Lawson told the police he had gone bankrupt and went to the towpath to pluck up the courage to tell his wife. Bette Lawson – your sister – confirmed he did tell her when he got back.'

'Research! Some of us get out on the streets. You think you can solve a case with a mop and a bucket from your armchair.' Lucie scoffed. 'Since when did you pay attention to the wife of a suspect? Didn't Terry tell you about the "lesser confession"?'

A gust blew Lucie May's smoke into Stella's eyes, making them sting. Some might have feigned understanding. Not Stella. 'What's that?'

'When you've done something terrible, it's bound to show in your behaviour or your expression. So the trick is to tell the truth. Confess to something bad, but not too bad. Convince your loved ones – or the police – that you're innocent of the greater crime. So Stevie comes back, cries like a big baby and tells my long-suffering sis he's all washed up. He leaves out the bit about strangling a gorgeous young blonde and dumping her in the Thames.' Lucie took a final drag on her cigarette and ground out the stub under the pointed toe of her boot. Getting out the packet she lit another Marlboro. She flung the box into her handbag and shut the catch with a punctuating click.

'Maybe that's because he didn't strangle her. This new information widens the net of suspects to at least six.' Now wasn't the time to remind Lucie that Terry had also said it was important to keep an open mind. Nor would she say that Bette and Garry Lawson were also on her spreadsheet. Or that her mum had said Terry hadn't thought Lawson guilty. It would be a red rag to Lucie's bull.

'A net of suspects? What is this, a butterfly hunt? Who are your suspects? A silly young girl – now a dried-up witch – who flip-flops between truth and lies to snare Adam Honeysett. Two old women who couldn't drown a mouse between them. My sister. Now there I grant you have a point. She could be done for joint enterprise or at least as accessory after the fact. You've got the Grieving Husband who – in his infinite wisdom – hired you and Jackanory to solve a mystery that's already solved. The poor sod is forking out for a cleaner and a train driver to bumble about in deerstalkers spotting bird seed.' She gestured at the sky with her cigarette. 'I tell you, Agent Soapsuds, every day I thank whoever's up there that, unlike the Honeysett girl, my little sister is unharmed. It could easily have been her that monster got. What was the favour?' She eyed Stella through a curl of smoke.

'Can you tell me who the man is in this photograph?' Stella slipped one of the two prints from the Honeysetts' Christmas party out of her jacket pocket.

'It's the plumber!' Lucie rolled her eyes with exasperation.

Stella was patient. 'The man behind Lawson.'

'Oh, him. That's Nev. He couldn't swat a fly. Leave him alone! You're scratching around in barrel scrapings! He's a lonely old man who got kicked out of his home by a febrile young snappery-whipper scenting a quick million. At least he got to bite back!' Lucie cackled.

'You know that Rowlands was going into Latimer's house?' Jackie said Lucie knew everything. Stella felt suddenly very tired.

'*Who am I and have I done?* I put that on her screensaver. Genius, don't you think! You and Jacko moved in and spoilt the fun.'

'That's illegal,' Stella managed.

'Top marks! Hey Stella Artois, it's dirty down here in the real world!' Lucie regarded her cigarette. 'If you go running to your pet policeman, I'll deny everything! And that Martin Cashback knows better than to clip my wings.'

'Rowlands was thirty-six in 1987. He walked his mother's dog on the towpath that night.' Stella recited the facts.

'When I first met him, poor Nev was distraught. His mama died two days after Honeysett disappeared. You're a washerwoman clutching at clothes pegs.' Lucie was full of regret. 'I had high hopes of you, Stella Darnell.' She opened her handbag but then, perhaps thinking better of smoking a third cigarette, shut it and shrugged the strap on to her shoulder. 'Priceless! The poor bloke loses his home to that gold-digger and you try to pin a murder on him! Stop paddling in the shallows, Mrs Mop.'

Stella remembered the article Jack said he'd found in Adam Honeysett's file. The article she had searched for without success. 'What about Brian Judd? He had an alibi, but—'

'The man was a recluse, he only went out to walk his dog.' Lucie May hesitated as if taking in the implication of what she'd said.

Stella heard her phone ring. With a gesture of apology she answered it. 'Stella Darnell.'

'Stella, is that you?' The question her mum always asked when she called her mobile.

'Hi, Mum.' Stella's eyes watered as a bluff of smoke enveloped her.

'Stella, it's Mum. Don't forget Stanley has school tonight.'

'School?' Stella pinched the bridge of her nose.

'Agility training. It's moved to Tuesday this week, remember? Stanley mustn't miss it, he's doing so well. He was starting to work away from me and pay close attention to hand signals. *Don't be late!*'

Stella had forgotten about Stanley's class. She dropped the phone into her pocket. 'Sorry, that was my…'

A coil of blue-grey smoke drifted skywards. The car park was empty.

Chapter Fifty-Five

Tuesday, 12 January 2016

'... now bend that knee, no, the other one, to a right angle. That's it.'

'The body needs to be on the side so if they throw up they don't choke,' Beverly said. Someone was hurt. Stella threw open the door and rushed into the office.

'Yes, do that now. Gently roll her—'

'I have to pull on the knee,' Beverly said.

Stella dropped her rucksack. Stanley flew across the office, jerking to a stop as he reached the end of his lead.

Jackie lay on the carpet by the photocopier. Beverly crouched beside her. She was easing Jackie on to her side. A woman in a polo shirt and jeans stood over them, hands on hips.

'Jackie!' Stella shouted. 'Call an ambulance!' She grabbed the phone off Beverly's desk and stabbed at the keys. The handset was snatched out of her hand.

'She's fine.' It was Bette Lawson.

'I've got Jackie in the recovery position. I learnt it on the first-aid course.' Beverly was chatty as she positioned Jackie's arm under her head. 'Make sure the bottom arm prevents her rolling right over on to the face and open her airway.' She snapped Jackie's head back and pushed up her chin.

'Ow!' Jackie protested.

'Do it gently.' Bette Lawson replaced the phone in the holder.

'Keep her like that. Stay down there with her until the paramedics arrive, in case she vomits or fits.'

Stanley was frantically licking Jackie's face. She struggled to her feet and lifted him into her arms. 'Stanley could revive the dead, couldn't you, poppet!'

'That's CPR. I was doing the recovery position. But I can do CPR. Shall I show—'

'Not now, thanks, Bev. Though we're all a lot safer now you're the first aider extraordinaire.' Shifting Stanley further on to her shoulder, Jackie turned to Bette Lawson. 'Thanks for your supervision. That tea'll be cold. I'll get you another one.'

'No, you're all right.' Bette Lawson reached for a Clean Slate branded mug on Jackie's desk and drank from it.

'Stella, Mrs Lawson would like to talk with you about the Honeysett case.' Jackie was giving Stella her I'm-here-if-it-all-goes-wrong smile.

'Come through.' Stella handed Stanley's lead to Beverly and went into her office.

'Adam told me you're investigating Helen's murder.' Bette Lawson placed a file box down on Stella's desk.

Bette wore a pair of tortoiseshell glasses. Stella knew that Lucie disguised her short sight with contact lenses. She laid a folded blue coat over the back of her chair. Stella noted that the energy Bette had displayed while helping Beverly had gone. Lawson had a weary demeanour, as if crossing the room was an effort.

'You'll have read lies about Steve, most of them told by my sister. After Steve died I talked to everyone in our street, to as many of his clients as would speak to me, to his suppliers and his mates from Sunday football. I wrote up an account of all my conversations. Steve's not here to talk for himself, but if you read that, you'll find out what sort of man he really was. My daughter told me you're friendly with Lucie. I'm depending on the fact that your dad was a police detective, so you'll have inherited standards of good policing. Beverly's just told me you're a very good cleaner.'

Stella gestured for Bette Lawson to sit down. The Honeysett papers were at home. A detective could encounter a suspect or a witness at any time. She felt unprepared.

'Have facts at your fingertips: crime doesn't work to a schedule.'

She and Jack had been dubious that Bette Lawson would talk to them, yet now she had sought Stella out. Stella pulled a Clean Slate pad across the desk and wrote today's date on the top page.

'Steve wasn't having an affair with Helen. He was a one-woman man. He used to say that when he met me it was love at first sight. I never doubted him. Sure, he liked Helen – she was a nice woman, always seemed bright and cheerful. It's my guess she knew Adam was seeing someone else, but she wasn't a pushover, eventually she'd have made him fess up.' Bette patted her grey bob; unlike her sister, she had submitted to her natural colour. 'Lucie made Steve out to be a monster, but you have a read of this and you'll see how his customers loved him. Most of his business was repeat or word of mouth. You run a company, so you know what that's worth. Would the papers print that? Lucie didn't want to know.'

'Why was he declared bankrupt?' Stella steeled herself; she had to ask hard questions.

'Does the name Sarah Lawson mean anything to you?' Stella shook her head. Bette Lawson leant over the desk. 'Course not. Lucie wasn't interested. I love my sister, but she's stubborn, like our dad. Sarah was Steve's younger sister; there were ten years between them. She was spoilt, used to being fussed over and adored. She started shoplifting when she was a kid. Never got caught. Once her dad found a transistor radio she'd nicked and Steve said it was his. He covered for her every time. He was loyal. I wished Lucie was like that, protective, caring, but she's out for herself, always has been.'

'Are you saying Sarah Lawson killed Helen Honeysett?'

'There you go, jumping to conclusions.' Bette looked briefly disappointed, but then appeared to rally. 'I'm *saying* that Sarah cleaned Steve out.'

'Cleaning out' had one major meaning for Stella; a second association was 'decluttering'. She must have looked confused because Bette said patiently, 'I mean she emptied Steve's business account.'

'How could his sister get access to it?' Stella wanted to believe Bette Lawson. She couldn't recall a sister. Sarah Lawson wasn't in her brother's diary. She was cross with herself; Terry would have known the name of a suspect's cat.

'Sarah had been "borrowing" from their mum's pensions, and she couldn't meet the rent. Unknown to me Steve baled them out and told his sister to come to him in future. She nicked his cheque book, forged his signature and withdrew everything. That night, when the washing machine leaked, after he got back from the river, Steve told me what Sarah had done.'

'If it wasn't his fault, why did he kill himself?' Stella thought wryly that this was a motive for Steven Lawson murdering the sister rather than Helen Honeysett.

'Steve had been brought up to look out for Sarah. In their mum's eyes she could do no wrong. Steve said it would break their hearts if he told the police. He swore me to secrecy. After he died, I told Lucie, but she said it was respecting his wishes not to print it. Really it was that she knew a man who was bankrupted supporting his sister didn't fit the monster image.'

Who am I and what have I done?

Stella couldn't mention the diary. Bette Lawson was relying on the existence of the diary being secret. She was in denial.

'You've seen his daily diary,' Bette said.

'I... er... Sorry?' Was it a question or a statement? The cogs in Stella's mind raced at top speed.

'Lucie's got it. Megan gave it to her. She loved her Aunty El. She sneaked it out of the house when she was little. I hadn't the heart to tell her off. She will have thought she was doing the right thing.'

'You know?' Bette must also know Stella had the diary. She had come to get it.

'She thinks I don't know. Lucie never credited me with nous, she had to be the clever one.'

'You never told Lucie? Or the police?' Stella tried to sound neutral.

'Megan's suffered enough and what could the police do? Charge Lucie with theft. That wouldn't help anyone. Besides she won't print it.'

'Why not?' Stella wasn't in control of this interview, such as it was.

'It would put her in a bad light. A reporter who gets her niece to steal from her sister. Lucie's stuck with it.' Bette spoke without acrimony. 'After he was arrested and released, Steve wrote down everything he did. Being released meant nothing. He became the guy burnt on the bonfire. People had to blame someone. He could never be alone; the police were ready to pin any crime going on to him. Anything he earned went to paying the debt. Not that he got much work after Helen disappeared. His customers heaped praise on him after he died, but no one booked him before. There was the niggle that he might be guilty, especially after Megan went to the police.' She fiddled with the staple remover, snapping it open and shut the way Natasha Latimer's sister Claudia had done. 'That last morning he was ever so upset. I should have seen it.' Red blotches appeared on her pale cheeks. 'He told the dog – he always talked to Smudge when he had something difficult to say – he said that it'd be better in prison than living like that. At least there he couldn't be done for anything he hadn't done. I waited for him at the hospital and he never came. I was climbing the walls – with no mobiles then I couldn't call him. I went home and he wasn't there. Smudge was, though, so I knew he hadn't gone to the towpath.' She stopped abruptly and pressed a fist to her lips.

'It sounds like he was desperate.'

'He had to be to do that to his kids, didn't he?' Bette snapped shut the staple remover. 'If he'd seen Helen, I know for a fact he'd have gone the other way. He was upset, he'd have avoided her like the plague.'

Stella switched tack. 'Lucie didn't like your husband. Why was that?'

'Lucie doesn't like many people. You're lucky she likes you.'

Stella didn't think about whether people liked or disliked her. After the visit to Lucie's Murder Room and their encounter in the court car park, she suspected Lucie *didn't* like her.

'She was five when I was born. Lucie resented me. She had to have the limelight. She'd sit by the fire drying her hair, long and blond it was then, brushing until it crackled with static. She spent hours on her make-up. Men adored her. I was her little helper. No wonder I'm a nurse. Steve hardly noticed Lucie. He could flirt for England, but never did with her. It was me he wanted. She was jealous.'

'But she hated him.'

'Have you got siblings?' Bette fixed Stella with the same basilisk glare as Lucie May had that morning, and Stella saw they were sisters.

'A brother. He didn't grow up with me; I hardly know him.' Stella had never told a stranger this before. It wasn't much of a divulgence, but she would never have told Lucie May.

'Brothers might be different. Unless one of you is gay, he won't be after your other half. Lucie had to have every man she met. Including *your* gorgeous bloke, no matter he's half her age! I put it down to my dad never praising her. Lucie said Steve wasn't good enough for me, but he was worth a hundred of her blokes. She hated Steve for passing her up. Don't get on the wrong side of my sister!'

Stella already was on the wrong side of Lucie. She was about to say Jack wasn't her 'bloke', but Bette Lawson went on, 'Mum boasted her daughter met the rich and famous. It was crap: Lucie made that up like she does everything. When Mum got the cancer, Lucie would drop in for five minutes and rush off for some deadline. I'd started nursing so Lucie left it to me. I got the sharp end of Mum's temper, nothing I did was right, but she'd put on a big smile when Lucie breezed in. I once asked Lucie to sit with Mum because I had a shift. She was livid, went ape, saying how she had a career and wasn't twiddling her thumbs waiting to marry and have babies. She came when I told her Mum was dying, but she was like the kids on long car journeys asking when we'd get there: she kept on at me about when was Mum going to die, because she had an important interview. Steve said what was more important than being at your mum's deathbed? Lucie stormed out. Moments later, Mum died. Lucie was too busy to register her death and arrived late for the funeral. When she performed her eulogy – and I mean performed – there wasn't a dry eye in the crem.'

Bette Lawson looked drawn and pale. The prospect of nursing her own mum, or being there when she died, dizzied Stella. A strained ankle was a challenge. She wouldn't judge Lucie May.

'Lucie poisoned Megan's mind against her dad. Megan wasn't a girl who easily made friends. She called our neighbour, Mrs Merry, her friend. Daphne Merry's little girl was killed in a car crash, and she had time for Megs. I felt for Daphne. Don't know what I'd do if that happened to either of my two.' Bette fiddled with her wedding ring, twisting it around on her finger. 'I don't blame her for taking Megs to the police, in her mind she didn't want another husband getting away with it.'

Stella nodded at the file. 'Have you shown your interviews to the police?'

'They gave me short shrift. As good as said: Stick to your work and we'll do ours. They think Steven killed Helen so the case is as good as closed. When Adam said he'd hired you, I thought he was having a laugh. A cleaner! But I read about you. A cleaner's like a nurse, we're not prejudiced, we take people as we find them.'

'Adam Honeysett had a lot to gain.' Stella watched her closely. Did Bette suspect that Honeysett had killed his wife, and by default, her husband.

'He was with that girl, Jane Drake. Poor kid got chucked in the deep end of a media scrum.'

'Do you know a Brian Judd?' Stella asked.

'That old man living in the ramshackle house on the river? Only to say hello to. Not that he replies. He's a sociopath. Come to think of it, I haven't seen him for years. It wasn't him. He was at his office at the council till late.'

'Who do you suspect?'

'She was a little madam. Yes' – she raised a palm – 'it's bad to speak ill of the dead, but Helen got up a lot of people's noses. She could have upset anyone.'

'Did she upset you?' Stella knew what she was implying.

'She was silly around Steve, but he was a grown-up and he had bigger fish to fry. Probably did his mood good her batting her eyelashes at him. Besides, she put him in mind of his sister.' Bette exhaled. 'For all her faults Sarah was a lovely girl. I haven't seen her since Steve's death. She's a Facebook friend. Lives the life of Riley in Bali if Facebook is anything to go by. She'll always bounce back.' Lawson spoke without rancour.

'Did you think they were having an affair?' Jack wouldn't like her asking a straight question, but Stella thought Bette was a straight-talking woman.

'Mostly no. Like I said, I knew Steve loved me.' She snapped the jaws of the staple remover shut. 'I have my moments, those low times we all get when my imagination gets going.' She shrugged.

'So it was harmless flirting?' Stella pushed. If Bette Lawson did think her husband and Helen Honeysett were involved, Stella was sure she wouldn't sit by and let it blow over. She'd put a stop to it.

'Yes it was. Although maybe not harmless since in the end it killed him.' Bette Lawson pushed the box file towards Stella. 'Steve was as good as murdered and the murderer was Helen Honeysett. But for her my Steve would be here. She ruined it for him, for all of us. Garry's the ghost of the little boy who was into everything, chock-full of plans. I'll never get my son back, but before I die I want to see Steve cleared. I want my kids to have some peace.'

'We'll find who did this.' Why had she said that? After Bette

Lawson had gone, it occurred to Stella that Helen Honeysett had upset Bette very much indeed. If you had nothing to lose, that might be a motive for murder.

Stella sat at her desk. She never made rash promises to cleaning clients and this case was the hardest one they'd had. No body, a clutch of suspects and all the time the possibility that the killer was a random stranger long gone from the towpath.

Stella was startled out of her train of thought by Beverly. She tripped merrily into the room. 'I've got something for you.'

'Have you found Neville Rowlands?'

'Yes!' Beverly looked briefly deflated that her thunder had been stolen.

Stella sat up straight. 'That's great, Bev.'

'I came up with a plan about what to say on the way there.'

'On the way where?'

'To see Neville Rowlands.'

'On your own?' Stella exclaimed, horrified.

'Yes of course.' Beverly tossed back her hair with affected nonchalance. 'When he answered I said "Oh no, I've lost my cat!" I was practically crying! He said he hadn't seen it. Which was true obviously and he said I should stick a notice on lamp-posts! He was nice about it.' Beverly flung back in her chair. 'But he didn't invite me in.'

'You've lost your cat?' Stella didn't think Beverly had a cat.

'I don't!' Beverly hugged herself. 'I went undercover!'

'Bev, you must be careful!' Stella jumped up and pulled her jacket off the coat stand. 'How did you know it was Rowlands?'

'I asked his name.' Beverly was looking at Stella strangely. 'Are you all right? You've gone a nasty colour. Get in the recovery position.'

'I'm fine.' Stella gripped the coat stand. 'Bev, listen to me. That man might be a murderer, you should *not* have gone to see him by yourself!'

'Murderer! Yeh right. He was like my granddad. A total sweetie!'

Beverly had said Neville Rowlands was renting a bedsit in Hammersmith. Stella had been disturbed to see his address was right round the corner from Aldensley Road where her ex, David, lived.

She parked the van in a free ticket bay, halfway along the road. Rowlands' was the only house in the street that had escaped the gentrification of wrought-iron railings, elaborate trelliswork, renovated tiles or the inevitable basement excavation. The next-door house was boxed behind hoardings advertising the Bargain Basement Company.

A sagging picket fence enclosed cracked hard standing that was scattered with sweet wrappers, takeaway cups and other rubbish. The centrepiece was a rusting motorbike draped in filthy tarpaulin. Yellowed ice had frozen in dips in the plastic, the tyre on a protruding wheel was flat, the rubber rotting. The house was as dilapidated as the one on the towpath, but lacked a Gothic feel. Cream pebbledash stucco was cracked and engrained with dirt. A sheet was draped across the downstairs window. The front door was a faded red with a peeling notice saying 'No Junk Mail'.

None of the bells said 'Rowlands'. Stella checked the address. Beverly had written 'motorbike' under the postcode. It was the right place.

There was a bell on the other side of the door. It had a light and looked newer than the others, but no name. If it was Neville Rowlands', he couldn't get many visitors. Perhaps he didn't want them. Stella rang it.

The elderly man who answered the door – Stella estimated him to be late sixties – was smart in an ironed shirt and black suit trousers. His shoes were scuffed. This didn't particularly surprise her. Stella had clients whose homes were pristine, but their lavatory needed cleaning. Rowlands' comb-over was oiled and he was freshly shaven. Apparently retired, he was kitted out as if for the office. Stella had said to Jack that murderers came in all guises. Beverly was spot on, Rowlands could be anyone's respectable granddad.

'Neville Rowlands?' she said.

'Yes.' Rowlands was in the shadow of a hallway that smelled identical to the entrance to Clean Slate.

'Stella Darnell. I'm a private detective. I believe you used to live at number 1 Thames Cottages?' On the way, Stella had decided on a direct approach. 'Could I talk to you about Helen Honeysett? I understand you were her neighbour in 1987. The year she vanished. Would it be possible to come in or would you like to choose a more convenient time?'

Rowlands regarded her with a penetrating gaze. His eyes were an intense brown that gave nothing away. 'I'm not sure how I can help you. I talked to the police and to the press. I don't know anything new.'

Stella knew the smoothly pleasant tone. It was the voice of the man on the towpath. It was the voice of the dog walker she'd met on the towpath with Jack. The man who had passed her without greeting after she'd been with Jane Drake. The man who had been walking with a dog lead, but no dog.

She'd been in too much of a hurry to bring Jack – *stupid*. They were a team and, besides, she'd just torn a strip off Beverly for coming on her own. Rowlands was capable of sneaking into Latimer's house and waging a campaign of revenge. At least Beverly and Jackie knew where she was. But Jack should be here; this was their case.

'I'd like to hear your perspective.' Stella moved away from the door, a counter-intuitive tactic that worked with Stanley when she wanted him to drop a ball. It worked now.

'You'd better come in.'

Stella followed Rowlands up a dingy staircase to the top of the house. He had a stoop. She felt her blood chill. *He was the towpath man.* There was no sound from any of the doors they passed. Was she alone with Rowlands?

The landing was lit by weak light trickling in from a grubby skylight.

'Do excuse my tiny living quarters. However, I can offer you tea.' Rowlands unlocked a door and ushered her into what was indeed a small room. It had a bleak outlook over rooftops that Stella, her sense of direction as acute as her sense of smell, guessed were the houses in Aldensley Road. Rowlands snatched something from a cupboard by a divan that must make up into his bed and shoved it underneath. He invited her to sit and asked if she'd like a drink.

Stella accepted tea because it would mean he had to leave the room. As soon as he'd gone downstairs, she leapt up and quelling guilt – as a cleaner she never looked at people's things – eased open an alcove cupboard. A scent wafted out. Her stomach swooped. Gillette Splash Cool Wave. The brand preferred by her father, and Martin Cashman. Was this one of Jack's signs? She must not let the man's choice of aftershave lull her into a false sense of trust. This was the man who had attempted to terrorize Natasha Latimer.

Inside was a rack of ironed shirts, arranged in colour order, from left to right, pastel blues, greens and stark white. Stella approved. Three ties hung over a rail on the back of the door, dark red, dark blue and black. No other shoes. Rowlands was a man of simple tastes. In two narrow drawers she found black socks, paired and balled up, and neatly folded underwear. Rowlands favoured Y-fronts. She made herself feel beneath the garments. She had no idea what she was looking for. She was used to removing the contents of drawers and cupboards when doing a thorough clean, but she never looked at the items she took out. This felt very wrong indeed.

In the other alcove on a shelf was a faded set of Everyman volumes. Fixed to the wall above was a coin-operated electric meter half shrouded by a strip of loose wallpaper that had lifted away from damp plaster. The radiator in front of a fireplace blocked with pegboard was cold. Whatever pay-off Latimer had given Rowlands, it wasn't enough to rent somewhere more comfortable. But anything in what was quaintly called Brackenbury Village would be pricey.

No dust. Stella caught the faintest whiff of beeswax polish and noted the brush marks on the carpet. Rowlands was house-proud. Daphne Merry would approve of the lack of clutter.

She felt a stab of doubt. What was she doing here? Even if he did admit to coming into Latimer's house, she wasn't going to press charges. They had nothing to link him to the night Helen Honeysett vanished beyond proximity and a weak alibi.

She took out her phone and keyed in Clean Slate's number. It seemed overkill, but she'd promised Jackie to call if needed.

Rowlands had hidden something under the divan. Aware that any moment he would come back, Stella got down on the floor and ran her fingers along the gap between the divan and the lino-covered floor. No dust. In a hurry, she pushed whatever it was further under. She used her phone to bat it out, but only propelled it away. Sweat pricked her brow. *It took three minutes to boil a kettle and make a cup of tea.*

She crammed her hand right under the divan and, ignoring a graze – from a splinter or a tack – got a purchase and managed to manoeuvre the object out. It was a small silver frame. Inside was a grainy black-and-white photograph. It was of a young woman, her features clouded by another figure. The print had been double-exposed. Stella examined it. It wasn't double-exposed: the picture had been shot through glass, a window perhaps, and the superimposed figure was the reflection of the photographer holding the camera. The woman hadn't known her picture was being taken. Something about her rang a bell.

Rowlands had hidden the picture from her. Already guilty for rooting in his clothes cupboard, she scooted the frame back where she'd found it. She sent it too far to the back. He would know she'd seen it. With a jolt, Stella knew that Rowlands expected her to search his room. *He had set her a trap and she had been caught.*

On a cupboard beside the divan was an old-fashioned travelling alarm clock and another framed black-and-white photograph. A young man in regimental dress of buckled tunic, cradling a bearskin, was arm in arm with a woman in a bridal gown clasping a posy of flowers. The couple looked timid, their smiles rictus.

'My parents,' Neville Rowlands said. 'My father died weeks after that was taken. Not in the war. He was run over by a tram on Chiswick High Road in 1951, the year I was born. My mother never got over it.' Handing Stella a mug of tea, he murmured, 'I hope I made it the right colour for you.'

Stella hadn't heard Rowlands come upstairs or open the door. Her heart thumping, she assured him the tea was perfect. She could see how he had moved around Latimer's house undetected.

Rowlands sat down at the other end of the divan, his legs crossed. He hadn't made himself tea. 'You want to know about Helen Honeysett.'

'I'm talking to everyone who lived at Thames Cottages in 1987,' Stella told him.

'As I said, I'm not sure how I can help.'

Stella put her mug on the little cupboard and got her Filofax from her rucksack. She had been going to ask how long he'd lived in the street, but opted instead for a Jack question: 'Did you like Helen Honeysett?'

Impassive, Rowlands flicked an invisible speck off the knee of his trousers. He was stalling.

'If I'm honest I didn't care for her. Too brash for my taste, but that was the way of the young in the eighties. Mrs Honeysett wasn't afraid to come right out with what she thought.'

'What did she think?'

'She told me, "Your mum's got you clamped in a vice. Get out, find a sexy young thing and have the time of your life!"' Glancing at the wedding picture, Rowlands blinked rapidly as if confessing to the woman with the posy.

'How did you take that?'

'She was right. But Mother needed me. Besides, I didn't want to leave the street.' Without expanding on this, Rowlands got up and went to the cupboard.

Stella's blood went cold. A scrap of pastel green cloth was poking out. She must have caught one of his shirts in the doors.

Apparently unconcerned, Rowlands released the fabric, smoothed the shirt and shut the door. He returned to the divan and, gazing out of the window at the white-grey sky, asked, 'Who wants you to investigate this case?'

'Adam Honeysett.' Stella saw no harm in telling him. 'He wants to move on. It will be thirty years next January.'

'It will indeed be. I still wonder why now.' Rowlands interlocked his fingers on his knee and appeared to cogitate. 'It is possible that the man who could help died weeks after Helen Honeysett disappeared.'

'You think Steven Lawson did it?' Stella was prepared for this. If Rowlands was the killer, he would want to keep the focus of guilt on the plumber.

'Once upon a time it was "No body, no murder", but that principle was abolished in English Law in 1954. Until then you couldn't be tried for murder without the corpse. As I remember it, the evidence against Lawson was circumstantial, no DNA or cross-contamination, nothing sufficiently compelling for him to go to trial. A sad business. The public were quick to apportion blame. To my mind we have too many armchair detectives.'

Whether Rowlands counted Stella as an armchair detective was unclear. His knowledge of criminal law and forensics suggested he'd done his fair share of sit-down detection. She wrote, 'No body, no murder.' Nowadays police had a choice of 'proofs of life': CCTV, mobile phone and broadband usage. In 1987 they'd have been reliant on whether Honeysett's bank account had been accessed or passport renewed. Witness sightings were unreliable. 'What do you remember about that night?'

'It was dominated by my mother's illness. She was in pain. I couldn't bear to leave her, but had to walk our dog. I told the police, I didn't see Helen Honeysett. I went out earlier than she did and towards Kew Bridge. She always jogged the other way. That girl brimmed with energy.' He gave no hint as to what he thought of this. 'Daphne found the Honeysetts' dog. That alerted the police to the fact that something was seriously wrong. Poor Daphne. She's a kindly lady.'

Daphne. He was on first-name terms. Adam Honeysett had said that Rowlands and Merry were not friends, indeed that no one in the street were friends. Maybe it was that no one was friends with Honeysett. 'Are you still in touch with Daphne Merry?' Stella was casual.

He darted a look at her. Anger, annoyance, Stella couldn't tell. His reply was ambiguous. 'I see her often.'

'What about Sybil Lofthouse...' Stella's question was lost amid a terrible grinding as if the walls were caving in. Instinctively she ducked and her Filofax fell to the floor. 'What was *that*!' she exclaimed when at last it stopped.

'I do apologize for not warning you. They're digging a basement next door. Incredibly, one gets used to it. And then I'm not here much of the time.'

Stella knew where he was much of the time. She was tempted to tell him that Latimer was getting the locks changed. Perhaps he knew.

'I wondered about Sybil Lofthouse.' She kicked her Filofax under the divan and bending over, retrieved it. The action would explain to Rowlands why his photo had been shunted so far back. *No, it wouldn't.* Coupled with the shirt in the cupboard door, it told him that she'd searched his room while he was making the tea. She clenched her jaw to stop her teeth chattering.

'Miss Lofthouse did something at the Stock Exchange. I read that in the papers; she would never talk about herself to me. She is an intensely private lady. We'd exchange pleasantries if we met on the towpath, always about our dogs. There was no love lost between her and the dead girl. At the Honeysetts' Christmas drinks party the girl had wheedled away at Miss Lofthouse to give her inside trading knowledge. She seemed to be joking, but Miss Lofthouse didn't like it one bit. Nor do I think that Helen Honeysett meant to be funny. Miss Lofthouse left the party. A day or so before the disappearance, I was with Miss Lofthouse by the river and that young madam came galloping up as she did. She started up again about Lofthouse keeping secrets. What else did she know? *Please tell!*' He did a high voice in imitation. 'Miss Lofthouse looked fit to kill. Pardon the expression. That girl didn't notice the effect she had on others. It started with the Christmas tree.'

Stella would not ask. She waited.

'She took pictures of all of us without us knowing. Her husband made an invitation card with all our faces stuck on the tree. No one liked that.'

'Did you mind?'

'Me? No, it was a bit of fun.' Rowlands smiled blandly. 'It all came from wanting to be liked. She went the wrong way about it and she paid for it. It takes years to join a community. My family moved here – there – during the Great War.' He clenched his hands together. 'Those Honeysetts thought they could waltz in and woo us all. Poor Daphne had been through enough.' Neville Rowlands had reddened; he sat forward on the divan, suddenly animated. Was Daphne Merry the reason Rowlands had been reluctant to leave home and the reason why he went back?

'What had she been through?' Stella asked innocently. She wanted his take on the car crash story.

'A moment of carelessness cost her everything. She abhors carelessness. She came to Thames Cottages to put her life together. When that Megan Lawson befriended her, it was like a second chance. It wouldn't bring back her little girl, but it was a salve of sorts. I encouraged that. Such a sweet little girl she was. But after Daphne called the police to talk to the girl, that family wouldn't let her see the girl any more. Damn near destroyed her.' He got up and adjusted his parents' picture frame. Noticing Stella's mug, he remarked icily, 'You haven't finished your tea.'

'It was lovely,' Stella assured him, although it was too strong.

He sat back again. Stella noted he was 'fidgety'. Jack was good on body language.

'Honeysett didn't mince her words. In front of the neighbours at the party, she urged Daphne to have another child, said it would heal the pain. Daphne took it graciously of course. I agreed with her, but you have to go about these things carefully. Daphne is fragile.'

'It does seem that Helen Honeysett upset several people.' Stella wasn't sure she would have liked Helen Honeysett. She told herself that didn't matter. Her job was to find out why Helen had been killed. Stick to facts. Stella did wonder if her mum's comment that a victim wasn't implicated in their death was right. Had Helen upset someone so much they had wanted her dead?

'Oh yes,' he agreed readily. He seemed oblivious to the possibility that he was one of them. 'Like I said to that reporter, the smallest thing can cause the nicest person to snap. And then there's no going back.'

Had he really not minded Honeysett's clumsy advice to abandon his mother? Stella wouldn't like Suzie to be likened to a vice. Did nothing provoke him?

'We've met before.' Stella touched the phone in her pocket ready to ring for help. *What had her dad said about not antagonizing a suspect in a small space?*

'I don't recall.' Rowlands was studying her with surprise. 'I am sorry…'

'You were walking your dog on the towpath.' His surprise looked genuine. Stella felt a ripple of doubt.

'I don't have a dog.' He looked around the little room as if to check.

'Is this yours?' Stella fished the dog collar from her pocket.

Neville Rowlands took it from her. 'Whisky. Where did you find this?'

'In Natasha Latimer's basement. I assumed it was yours.' She watched him closely. 'I thought you'd left it there.'

'My mother's terrier was called Hercules.' He was as smooth as silk. 'Sadly he passed in 1987. My last dog, a spaniel, went a few years ago.'

'I've seen your pet cemetery,' Stella said. *Max 2000–2012. Lost to us.*

Rowlands brightened. 'Are the graves still there? I presumed the woman who bought the house would have dug them up.'

'It must have been strange to move after all those years. Having to give back the key...' Stella looked at him. He looked back at her. She looked away first.

'It was.' Neville Rowlands' face was a mask. He stood up and, brushing down his trousers, said, 'I wonder if too much water has passed under the bridge since 1987? As I said to that Lucille May from the paper, Helen Honeysett has taken her secret to the grave.'

On the doorstep, Stella thanked Rowlands for his time and, driving away, considered that the impromptu interview had told her nothing. Would Jack have got him to admit that the collar belonged to his dog? Honeysett had been rude about his mother: it was hardly a motive for murder, but as Rowlands himself had said, people snap.

She'd hoped to come away from the meeting certain that Neville Rowlands had murdered Helen Honeysett. She was far from certain.

Was Lucie May right and it *was* Steven Lawson? After all, she had known him well and she had spent years since his death researching the case. She had been subjective, her mind tight shut, but that didn't stop her being right. Jack had once said a stopped clock was right twice a day.

Stella saw she was on Aldensley Road. Eyes steadfastly ahead, she drove on. The last person she wanted to see right now was David Barlow.

★

Stella opened Bette Lawson's box file. It contained stapled papers, each labelled with the interviewee's name. Used to writing up patients' notes, Bette Lawson had stopped short of noting blood pressure and temperature. On top was Neville Rowlands 'aged thirty-six, psoriasis on lower arms, mother recently deceased'. She wondered if he still had the condition.

Bette Lawson described him as gentle. As he'd told Stella, Rowlands had gone briefly to the towpath with his dog and then returned to nurse his sick mother. Perhaps the fact that he was a carer had warmed Bette to him, because her notes were kindly. 'Mr Rowlands is worn out with caring and bereavement, but was good enough to talk to me...' 'I'm sorry to say I saw Steven going in the same direction along the towpath as Helen Honeysett...' He had seen Daphne Merry walking her dog towards Kew Bridge, '... the opposite way to your husband and the dead girl'. Stella consulted her map of the towpath. Rowlands hadn't seen Megan and she hadn't seen him. He hadn't told her he'd seen Daphne Merry or Steven Lawson. This meant Rowlands must have gone back into his house before Megan came out since she hadn't mentioned seeing him. Or someone was lying.

The afternoon passed in a blur. Stella worked her way through Bette Lawson's file, pausing to tap notes into her spreadsheet. Beverly and Jackie brought her tea at intervals that Stella, deeply absorbed, vaguely supposed were minutes apart. They removed the mugs of cold tea without comment. When she emerged from her office they had gone, their screens blank, chairs tucked in. Stanley was curled up in his bed by the filing cabinets. He made to move when he saw her, but she stayed him with a hand. It was dark outside. Lights from the top deck of buses passed across the office wall.

She returned with a cheese sandwich from the mini-mart. She'd been disappointed not to see Dariusz Adomek; since expanding his business to two shops, Dariusz was often at the other branch. Her anglepoise trained on Lawson's papers, Stella continued reading.

As the clock on the wall reached five past six, Stella, scrutinizing additions to her spreadsheet, gave a start. She found Bette Lawson's notes for number 5 Thames Cottages. Sybil Lofthouse was fifty when Honeysett vanished. Working early shifts at the Stock Exchange, she told Bette Lawson, and the police, that she'd been in bed by eight. She hadn't gone to the towpath. Stella flipped to her Filofax for her own account of meeting Lofthouse. She was dumbfounded. When she had transcribed her notes on to the Excel file, she had missed something out.

By the time the big hand reached quarter past, Stella had set the office alarm and was running down the stairs to the street, Stanley leaping after her.

Jack was in the dead zone; it was no use texting. She must see him.

Stella had reached the street when she got a text from Suzie. *Don't forget agility. At 6.30. Mum. X.* She stopped beside the minimart's fruit and vegetable stand, lurid in the neon red of the Coca-Cola sign. It took her only a moment to make the choice.

Chapter Fifty-Six

Tuesday, 12 January 2016

> *'Hey, my kitten, my kitten,*
> *And hey, my kitten, my deary!*
> *Such a sweet pet as this*
> *There is not far or neary.'*

Jack heard his mother's voice singing to the dance – manic and joyful – that they did every day. Had she sung it to him? Had they danced? The jigging figures dwindled like gossamer.

The air in the garden was still and cold. In the light of his Maglite, the headstones were like rocks among the rough grass.

'Hercules 1981–1987'. 'Max 2000–2012 Lost to us'. It had been kind of Claudia to give Neville Rowlands a key. Were Stanley Jack's dog, he couldn't abandon Stanley's bones to strangers who cared nothing for his memory. He would find a way to visit.

Jane Drake told Stella that she'd seen Neville Rowlands and Daphne Merry on the towpath on the night Helen Honeysett vanished. Hercules had died in 1987. He must have been the dog Rowlands had taken for a last walk. There were no reports that suggested that Merry or Rowlands had seen Drake.

Jack caught a movement. He swung his torch round. There was a bird on Max's headstone. He made out blue plumage, bright in the torchlight. There were parakeets all over West London, descendants of escapees in the twentieth century, but parakeets were green. It was a budgerigar. 'Hello, you!' he greeted the bird as he stealthily moved towards it. It too was an escapee and he knew exactly where it had escaped from.

'Is this yours?'

A dull-eyed man regarded Jack through a gap in the half-opened door.

'He – or she – was in the pet ceme— in the garden next door.' Jack held out his cupped hands to the man and opened them a fraction. He felt a fluttering of feathers, the faintest warmth on his cold fingers.

'I keep the aviary locked.' The man made no move to take the bird off Jack.

'Are you Garry Lawson?'

'What if I am?'

'I'm staying next door. Doing the cleaning, looking after the place.' Jack tipped his head back and forth in a lame attempt to appear jaunty. Lawson gave no sign that he'd heard.

Jack was adept at moving through rooms, tunnels, under bridges, as intangible as a shadow. Deception served its purpose. Stella preferred a transparent approach. If she were here, he knew what she would say. He launched into his speech: 'I'm also working for Adam Honeysett. He wants me and my friend to find out what happened to his wife. We're talking to everyone who was living here in 1987. You'd have been about nine – do you remember that time?'

'I was twelve. Nearly thirteen.' Lawson made to close the door.

'Twelve. Your sister Megan was seven.' Hoping to soften Garry, Jack clicked his tongue at the budgerigar. The ploy only appeared to rile the man. Hurriedly Jack went on, 'You didn't see your dad go to the towpath. Megan says she followed him to the towpath.'

'My dad didn't murder her.' Lawson thumped the door jamb. The change in tempo made Jack jump.

'Very likely not,' he agreed. 'Murder shines a spotlight on other lives and reveals secrets unrelated to it. The evidence against your dad was entirely circumstantial. It's why he wasn't charged. If you'd seen him going to the towpath, that wouldn't mean he was necessarily meeting Helen Honeysett.' He raised his cupped hands. 'Shall we return your budgie to your aviary?'

'Budgerigar.' Lawson reached out. 'I'll do it.'

'I'd love to see it. I had a budgerigar once.' His mother had said Jack would be allowed one when he was old enough to care for it, so this was nearly true.

Garry Lawson frowned at the darkness of the park opposite. He was a thickset man, black hair combed back and thinning at the temples: Jack could tell he was Steven Lawson's son. Garry was in his early forties – a bit older than Steven Lawson when he died – but he lacked his dad's boyish charm. His expression was stolid; he was getting a second chin and had a slight paunch.

Garry took the bird off him and went to close the door. Jack bounded inside before he could stop him, a fixed beam on his face. 'Brilliant!' He rubbed his hands together as if now, after the boring old chat, a truly exciting task awaited. Appearing to admit defeat, Lawson pushed through a bead curtain hanging across a doorway. Untangling himself from the beads, Jack followed Garry into a kitchen. It seemed that Bette Lawson was out. Jack was mildly relieved: he had wanted to see Garry on his own.

Jack had expected the Lawsons' cottage to be languishing in a time warp. Their lives had stopped in 1987 and the décor would reflect this. It would be neglected, shabby and outdated. Yet the kitchen was sleek and streamlined. White cupboards, oiled wooden surfaces and grey floor tiles. Bette Lawson's family might be fractured – Steven was dead, his daughter lived in self-imposed exile and Garry was a zombie – but her home was spick and span.

In the light from a lantern on the house wall, Jack saw a

trim rectangular lawn with a path down one side. Frost had settled, giving the grass an uncanny whitish gleam. Jack sized up the situation. No exit. If Garry Lawson attacked him, Garry would win. He was shorter, but well built and, his life shattered by tragedy and hate, had nothing to lose. Stella would avoid antagonizing a dangerous man in a dark garden with no one nearby to help. No, she wouldn't. Twice in the last few days she had put herself in danger. Now it was his turn.

'What sort was your budgerigar?' Garry unfastened the door to a flimsy-looking structure that was lit inside by a bulb. Chicken wire ballooned out from a wooden frame, crudely reinforced with lengths of wood at angles like a child's frenzied crossing-out of a drawing. Plastic toys dangled from struts and were suspended from the mesh ceiling.

Jack hadn't realized there were 'sorts' of budgerigars. 'Yellow,' he said, looking at one of Garry's yellow birds.

'You can't hurt my dad now, but if you hurt my mother or my sister, I will kill you,' Garry said suddenly.

'I wouldn't dream of it.' Jack hadn't protected his mother, what right had he to tread on this man's thin ice? Lawson, like him, had lost a parent in a needless death: they were brothers of a kind. 'Garry, I think you saw your dad follow Helen Honeysett, but were scared to say so because, like your sister, you think he did it. You are protecting him. But what if he *didn't* murder her?'

'That Merry bitch was out with her dog. She said she saw my dad. It's her that made Megan hand him in to the police.'

'Daphne Merry only did what she thought was right,' he said gently. 'Have you thought it might not have been your dad? Neville Rowlands' mother was dying; she might have lied for her son. She had nothing to lose.' Someone, maybe the detective who had asked Jack lots of questions after his mother's death, said his mother had distracted her killer to enable Jack to escape. Jack had never corroborated this. Jack might have made it up.

'Mum wouldn't lie for me. Or Megan. She tells the truth.' Garry Lawson sounded tired, his fury spent.

'So she wouldn't say your dad was innocent if he wasn't.'

'My dad *was* innocent.' Garry scrubbed at the thinning hair on his scalp.

'What about Brian Judd?'

Garry shook his head. 'He's dead.'

'No he's not,' Jack nearly shouted.

'Have it your own way.' Garry released the budgerigar into the aviary and trudged back up the path to the house.

Outside on the front-door step, Jack tried again: 'Judd wasn't dead when Helen Honeysett went missing.'

'All I know is it wasn't my dad.' Garry shut the front door.

Jack's thoughts buzzed about in his head. He knew that Brian Judd wasn't dead. If a True Host vanished it meant they were planning something. Brother and sister shared the awful suspicion that their father was a killer. Jack felt a weight of sadness. Megan had told the police, but Garry had lied. Steven's children's fear of his guilt stopped them seeing he might be innocent. On that January night, a fatal confluence of circumstances had placed Steven Lawson in the wrong place at the wrong time.

The other estranged siblings in the family were Bette Lawson and Lucie May. Lucie, like her nephew, was shackled by fierce emotion. Unlike Garry, Lucie had staked everything on Steven Lawson. Meanwhile, whoever had killed Helen Honeysett was out there waiting to kill again.

Jack texted Stella. *We need to speak to Judd. Jx.* A message popped up. *You are offline.* Disinclined to wait for her, he climbed the steps to the towpath. In the river's swirling currents, he saw the capering figures of a little boy and his mother. He heard her singing,

> 'Here we go up, up, up,
> Here we go down, down, downy;
> Here we go backwards and forwards,
> And here we go round, round, roundy.'

Chapter Fifty-Seven

Tuesday, 12 January 2016

'Over!' Stella essayed an arc with a cube of boiled chicken. Her voice echoed in the draughty equine centre. Stanley ignored her. Suddenly he lit upon Kirsty the behaviourist who ran the agility class at the edge of the course. He circumnavigated the jump, galloped across the sand and leapt on to her lap. Kirsty commanded, 'Off!' He bounded down instantly and sat at her feet. 'Heel.' Kirsty escorted Stanley back to Stella and said, 'Try again. I'll go up into the stands where he won't spot me.'

Stella gave a tight smile. It wouldn't matter where Kirsty went or how many times Stella tried, Stanley wouldn't do what she asked. So much for Suzie saying he was good at 'working away' – Stanley wouldn't even work *with* her. So far that evening he'd done no agility.

'Stay,' she instructed Stanley. The chicken was greasy in her fingers. Again she sketched a wave to remind Stanley of the reward for leaping over the hurdle. There were three hurdles after this one, a tunnel – wired hoops encased in plastic – and lastly the seesaw. The small poodle, seeming even smaller in the vast sanded ring intended for prancing horses, regarded her with detachment.

'Over!' Stella heard her command, devoid of Suzie's authority. She was preoccupied. In the office, the sentence in her notes had struck her as crucial, but now she wasn't sure. She felt bad for seeing Rowlands without Jack and worse for coming away empty-handed. The question on the screensaver hadn't been Honeysett's killer, but Lucie May leading a campaign of petty revenge. She should have gone to Jack. Terry wouldn't have put their dog Hector before work. Stanley was washing his paw, nibbling at his pads with concentration. Stella rapped, '*Ov-er!*'

Stanley took off. He galloped away from the jump and away from Stella to the far side of the arena. He wove between poles arranged in two staggered lines with precise fluidity. He plunged into the tunnel. A ripple of laughter from dog owners waiting for their pets' turn carried across the chilly auditorium. Stanley trotted back and forth along the seesaw, keeping balance at the pivotal point. Up, along, down. Stella was mesmerized. Up, along, down. Jack's words niggled at her. *'Are you sure David Barlow reported Stanley missing?'*

'Had that been the correct course, Stanley would have got full points.' Kirsty was beside her. 'He's used to working with Suzie. In time he'll accept you.'

Stella led Stanley to her seat. David reported finding Stanley to the police, but no one had claimed him.

'Of course I'm sure.' Stella pulled out her phone and with swipes and jabs found a phone number. David Barlow was the first ex she hadn't 'erased' from her Contacts list after she left him.

Please could I see you? Stella Darnell. She put her name in case David had wiped her details or knew more than one Stella.

A text winged in by return: *Come now! Dxxx.* The kisses appalled Stella. Before she could change her mind, she made excuses and left the equine centre.

Chapter Fifty-Eight

Tuesday, 12 January 2016

'Hi, Daphne, I've brought back your tin.' On the towpath, Jack had been filled with a need to see the woman who had once been a mother, as he had once been a son. 'I do hope it's not too late to call.' Stupid thing to say; it was only seven.

'Jack! How kind, most people wouldn't bother! Woof, *sit*!' Holding her dog by his collar, Daphne waved Jack inside.

Unlike Latimer's cottage there was no hall, Jack stepped straight into her sitting room. He had expected that, as a declutterer, Daphne Merry's home would be as sparse as Latimer's basement. But he could hardly move for clutter. Boxes were stacked on the carpet – what he could see of the carpet – ornaments, figurines, vases, lamps, bowls crowded every surface.

'This is a client's clutter.' Daphne had sensed his dismay. 'It goes to the hospice shop tomorrow.' Whisking a heap of coats from a chair, she gestured for him to sit by the fire. 'Hot milk with honey?'

Jack felt a flood of happiness. 'How did you know?'

Daphne Merry smiled warmly. 'You drank that when I brought my cake.'

While she was in the kitchen, Jack surveyed the clutter. A wooden tea-light holder fashioned as a mouse, with leather ears and a curling thong for a tail, sat next to a blue fish jug with a gaping mouth. Stella had said that Suzie was upset because

Daphne had been frosty when she asked for her things back. She'd refused to invoice. 'There is no charge, I have not decluttered.' Daphne had insisted on hiring a van and returning everything. Whose belongings were these? Jack was unsurprised that Suzie had been put out; she liked to be liked even by those she didn't like (she claimed not to have cared for Daphne), but he felt for Daphne; by her response, he guessed she'd call that job a failure.

The mouse and the fish were bound for a new home among strangers. Jack's throat constricted and he willed their owner to ring Daphne and reclaim them. Suzie had said, 'Daphne Merry's taken my life!' He understood that too. Doubtless someone was missing the fish and the mouse. Jack was prey to experiencing others' feelings – they probably didn't care. He gazed into the blackness outside.

Someone was out there. He jumped up.

'What have you seen?' Daphne stood in the doorway holding two mugs.'

'Nothing.' He didn't want to frighten her. It was freezing; no one could be out there. He took his milk and sat down again. 'Who lived in Natasha Latimer's house before her?' He warmed his face in steam from the mug; suddenly he didn't fancy drinking it. Milk was for babies. It was a nice thought. He stretched out his legs, and came up against a nest of occasional tables.

'Why are you interested?' Daphne Merry seemed surprised.

'Cleaning a place is an intimate relationship, I learn every inch as I work. I wondered who else the house had known.' Involuntarily he cast a glance at the sitting room, no skirting board was visible behind boxes and sundry objects.

'I won't have a cleaner; they'd never do a proper job. I'm sure you're an exception, Jack.' Daphne had read his mind. She said neutrally, 'Neville Rowlands had to leave when the house was sold.'

'I've some post for him, but have no forwarding address.' Daphne knew he was lying. Jack gulped his milk, quelling sudden revulsion. It seemed he'd gone off milk. 'It must have been a wrench to leave, after such a long time.' Daphne had told Suzie that her family had died in a car crash: how had Suzie got her to confide? Suzie was a perfect detective's sidekick; no wonder Terry Darnell never got over her leaving. If someone was in the park they were invisible. A True Host. *Brian Judd.* Jack stared at his ghostly image staring back. Daphne's dog Woof, settled in a cramped space by the fire, seemed to sense nothing outside.

'Mr Rowlands and I exchange Christmas cards.' Daphne zigzagged between boxes and bags to a corner cupboard and returned with sheet of blue Basildon Bond notepaper.

'Did he write this?' Jack kept his breathing regular as he regarded the printed capitals. A True Host's hand.

'I imagine so.' Daphne Merry held the paper while Jack photographed the address with his phone.

'Were it me, I couldn't bear to stay in the area.' Jack froze. Suzie had said Daphne used to live in Hammersmith. She'd moved to Kew after her daughter died. Jack knew well what it was like to stir up very bad memories.

'Mr Rowlands was born in that cottage. The family dogs are buried in the garden. *Were* buried; I expect she dug them up for that basement.' If Daphne Merry disapproved of the graves or the basement, she betrayed nothing.

'They're still there. Hercules died in 1987. Perhaps you remember him.'

'I do. You've got the date wrong. I'm good on people's dogs, Hercules didn't die until the mid-nineties. Mr Rowlands didn't have another dog for some time after that. A spaniel that he named Max, he died in 2009.' Daphne Merry gazed at her spaniel, dozing contently on the rug. A wave of unutterable sadness passed across her face. 'Woof isn't long for this world.'

Jack had a photographic memory. He pictured the headstones:

MAX 2000–2012
LOST TO US

HERCULES 1981–1987
A FAITHFUL COMPANION
STILL MISSED

There was no reason why Daphne Merry should remember
the dates when Neville Rowlands' dogs had died. But if she was
right, then who was buried in those graves?

Chapter Fifty-Nine

Tuesday, 12 January 2016

All the way from Ealing to Hammersmith Stella invented excuses not to see David Barlow. Suzie needed her. Not that Stella relished admitting how badly she had done with Stanley at agility. She should update Jack; he didn't know she'd found Rowlands.

Jack would look for a sign. If the next set of traffic lights were red, she would go to him. The lights stayed stubbornly green until she had passed through them. All the way to Aldensley Road there wasn't a single stop light. If she couldn't park in the street, it was a sign to leave. There was a two-car space outside David's house. David was on his doorstep. There was no turning back.

Stella had forgotten that David Barlow had reminded her of David Bowie. With Bowie having died two days earlier and with ghosts on her mind, she found the resemblance uncanny. Except this David, in his early sixties, looked very much alive and if anything younger than when she'd last seen him. His still brown hair was immaculately trimmed, he wore tailored wool trousers, a plaid cotton-silk shirt buttoned to the neck with a tie. His Italian loafers, unlike Rowlands' scuffed shoes, were highly polished.

'You look lovely,' he breathed.

Hot and tired, her trousers streaked with sand from the equine arena, Stella didn't feel lovely. She had intended to be polite but, catching the irresistible tangy scent of David's aftershave, was thrown. 'I have to ask you a question.'

'Come in out of the cold.' David was already walking into his lounge.

Stella nearly shouted with dismay. Wispy cobwebs hung from cornices. The windows in the conservatory extension were opaque with salt. She wouldn't need to do her finger test to prove that the riser-recliner – a legacy of David's late wife – was veiled in a haze of dust. The carpet was stained. Lurking beneath the aftershave, Stella detected the greasy odour of grime. It would be easy to clean the room because, apart from the recliner, a television and a hard wooden chair, David's lounge and conservatory were empty.

David had cancelled the contract with Clean Slate when Stella broke up with him. Thus saving her from cancelling it. However, it seemed that David hadn't starting doing the cleaning himself. Stella would never try to worm her way into a man's life by cleaning his home. She liked to clean for its own sake, whether it be a blotch on the chemist's counter where she'd bought a freezer pack for Suzie's ankle or a plastic sushi tray dropped on a pavement. She liked to tackle mess and restore order. Jackie said it was why she was a good detective. Stella knew every inch of David's lounge. He had commissioned deep cleaning. She'd steam-cleaned his carpet, washed skirting boards and walls, polished his furniture and even vacuumed behind the bath panel. Everywhere were stains, dirt and spiders' webs. She stopped herself from fetching in her equipment bag from the van and setting to. Something else struck her. It wasn't her policy to ask personal questions, especially of an ex-partner, but she demanded hotly, 'Where are all your things?'

'I've decluttered!' David looked about him as if baffled by this. 'I've brought air and light into my life.'

The room was dingy and the air was stale. Stella didn't suggest he clean the windows and open the doors to achieve air and light because the phrase struck a chord. Where had she heard it? The day had been long, but too many things were eluding her.

David was talking. 'Tea? I have wine, but I remember you rarely drink.'

Irked by this – Stella was uncomfortable with him remembering anything about her – she was tempted to ask for wine, but she was driving and besides she wanted tea.

'Tea it is.' David left the room. Had Stella wanted to take the opportunity to open cupboards and examine objects while he was absent, as she had with Neville Rowlands, she couldn't have. There were none.

When David returned, she got to the point. 'Did you report finding Stanley by the river to the police?' The tea was milky just as she liked it. This too irked her.

'I told you I did.' He was clearly aggrieved at her doubt. 'They said he belonged to an old lady who'd died. Her relatives had reported he'd run away, but didn't want him back. The police said I could keep him.'

Stella had no memory that he had told her, but he must have. She knew where she had heard about light and air. 'What's the name of your declutterer?'

Perhaps expecting her to press him further, David looked surprised at the change of subject. 'Mrs Merry. Not that she was merry. When I said "call me David" she reacted like I'd made a pass!' He guffawed dryly. 'I've not seen inside your new house, but Mrs Merry would be hard pressed to find clutter there! Why do you ask?'

Stella was loath to tell him her mum had employed Daphne Merry. She regretted the visit; she should have texted. But she was stuck: the tea was hot and it would be rude to leave it. 'She's done a thorough job.'

'Hasn't she! I agreed to all her suggestions – she was like my wife, I was scared to upset her!' He smoothed his tie, perhaps concerned that mention of Mrs Barlow was a tactical error. He could have relaxed; Stella wasn't threatened by her partners' pasts. Mrs Barlow was dead and Stella was alive: it was illogical to be jealous. Anyway, she and David had broken up.

David Barlow swirled his wine in his glass. 'She wouldn't be upset. I suppose lack of empathy is a must for a declutterer.

She can't be bowing to every protest. There's things I miss. A mouse candleholder I'd only just bought. She assumed it was clutter and said it had to go. She told me at the start that she gets annoyed when clients object to throwing out things despite inviting her to get them to do just that. I was determined not to be one of those customers.' He was regretful. 'She said memories drag you down. I need light and air.'

'How did you hear about her?' Stella was astounded by the coincidence. Jack would say it was a sign.

'I saw an advert in the local paper. *Cut down on cleaning? Clear out clutter from your home!* Not that you want anyone cutting down on cleaning!' He eyed Stella over his glass. 'She decreed that recliner was clutter but when I pointed out it would leave me with only one chair, she relented.' He ran his forefinger around the rim of his glass. An insidious whine filled the room. 'It feels like a tomb.'

'You get a cooling-off period.' Stella realized she shouldn't know this, but he hadn't noticed the slip.

'I "cooled off" immediately, but didn't dare ring, I was sure she'd kill me!' David's finger went faster around the rim; the whine rose in pitch. Stella thought of Natasha Latimer's supposed ghost. If ghosts existed David would have a few.

'*Don't waste any encounter. Salient information comes in all guises.*' Stella's own 'ghost', Terry was whispering in her ear. Incredibly, David had met Daphne Merry. A suspect – if not top of the list – in the Honeysett case. Stella shouldn't pass up a chance to learn about her. Merry had been kind to Megan Lawson when Megan was little; that didn't fit with a 'cold fish'. She had brought Jack cake. Jack and Bette Lawson had reckoned Merry liked the little girl because her own daughter had died. David thought her scary and distant. Terry said 'How' questions drew the subject out. 'How was Daphne Merry like your wife?'

David stared, perhaps taken aback by Stella's asking about his wife or because the question was out of character. 'Mrs Merry said she hated carelessness. She dislikes dog walkers who don't pick up their dog's mess. People who put out their rubbish bags the night before for the foxes to rip open. She had a neighbour who did that. People who chuck litter out of cars or on the street. One dog walker dumps their poo-bags in her bin when it's out on the pavement for collection. She said the government should limit who owns dogs. I told her about Stanley.'

Stella had been with David when he rescued Stanley from falling in the river. Having established he didn't belong to anyone, David had kept him. When he'd had to go away for several months, he'd asked her to look after Stanley. On his return he relinquished ownership because Stanley had become attached to Stella. 'Did Mrs Merry say which neighbour leaves the dog poo in her bin?'

'No. I got the impression everyone did. She told me an old woman in her street saw a neighbour let his dog poo on the towpath and did nothing. That was another beef. She hates bystanders, people who let others take the rap. Not her words. She said they were as bad as a culprit. I agree.' David contemplated his empty wine glass. Stella didn't respond. They both knew that David Barlow had been a bystander in his time.

The only 'old woman' living at Thames Cottages apart from Merry herself was Sybil Lofthouse. She had made clear to Stella that she kept herself to herself. That would add up to being a 'bystander'. Stella wanted to get out her Filofax and jot down what Merry had told David. Whoever had killed Helen Honeysett had the strength to dispose of her body and dig a grave in the winter. It would take strength to heave her down the bank into the river. Again, Stella considered that she herself might have that strength – cleaning and dog-walking kept her fit – but Sybil Lofthouse was small and slight and had done a desk job. Adam Honeysett, Steven Lawson, Neville Rowlands, Brian Judd could have done it. Daphne Merry disposed of clutter: bric-a-brac not bodies. Bette Lawson had motive and strength and, until her husband died, she had got him to herself after Helen vanished. Did Steven Lawson know what Bette had done and it drove him to suicide? Did Lucie think her sister guilty too and out of loyalty blamed Steven Lawson?

'... be kind to walk him on familiar ground.'

'Sorry?' Stella hadn't heard a word.

'Mrs Merry said that since I'd found Stanley on the Kew towpath, I ought to take him there, it's his territory. She cared more about Stanley than my mother's teapot. It was worthless, but I can see Mum holding it, I can't *believe* it's gone.' He leant towards Stella as if to take her hand. Stella was horrified by a sudden wish that he would. Her mum insisted that marrying Terry had been her wrong turning. David represented a definite loss of direction for Stella. She wouldn't say Stanley had been to the towpath – David might ask to come. She gave a start. More than once, Stanley had rushed to the ramshackle house on the river. Terry taught her to follow hunches. 'Stanley's owner, where did she live?'

'A flat on the South Circular. Police wouldn't say where,' he answered promptly.

So much for hunches.

'This place needs a clean.' David fixed on her, eyebrows raised. 'A *deep* clean. I could walk Stanley on the towpath while you're here.'

Jack said Stella wasn't great at reading people – she trusted the untrustworthy – but she did recognize a chat-up line. David Barlow knew her well enough to use the bait of deep cleaning. She drank her tea to stop herself saying yes.

Chapter Sixty

Tuesday, 12 January 2016

Daphne let him in. I heard him use the paltry excuse of returning her cake tin. I know my Daphne, she is too nice to refuse. She puts herself out rather than be impolite. She offers so much, and gets nothing back. I will change that.

I heard her say 'Jack' when she opened the door. He calls her Daphne as if she was his friend. I've seen him on the towing-path sneaking about asking questions. He broke into the house and sneaked about; he knew I was there, but he was brazen. Now he's with Daphne. Drinking from her mug, as if he's right at home.

He is one of those self-styled saviours with a mission to cleanse the world of evil. They are dangerous because they don't operate by normal values. Charming and vulnerable, women want to look after them. Give them a home. Once ensconced they strike. This man is a creature of the night. I have to save Daphne from him.

Daphne smiled at me on the towing-path. A sign. Jack believes in signs: I've seen how he walks, avoiding cracks in pavements and so careful on the towing-path because he knows each step counts towards his fate. *Or someone else's.* Daphne's smile was like the sun. She appreciates all I have done. Mother would approve of Daphne. I will make her proud.

I will have to bring forward my plan. I removed that young woman and I'll remove you. *Jack.*

Through the window, I see Daphne smile. She gives him a letter. I move closer to see but Daphne pulls the curtains. She shuts me out. I have said before that no one should do that. *Jack.*

Jack, who are you and what have you done? I will shut you out.

Jack in the box.

Chapter Sixty-One

Stella planted herself in full view of the camera outside Natasha Latimer's cottage. If Jack was in the basement, he'd see her on what he called the River Wall. She rang the bell. When he didn't come, she rang it again. He must be with Bella. He was never there when she needed him.

Stanley growled, a curdling rumble. He strained on his lead towards the towpath steps. She looked. He was wrong; there was no one there.

'Sssh!' she told him. If Jack was with Bella, he should have a signal. She called Jack's mobile, remembering as she held the handset to her ear that it was a dead zone. To her surprise Stella heard Jack's voice on the other end. 'Jack, it's me—'

'This is Jack, who are *you*? Tell me after the beep.'

Stella paused, unsure how to articulate the barely formed hunch. She needed him to read her notes. She didn't leave a message. When she put her phone back into her pocket, her fingers brushed something.

It was the rag that Stanley had dug up when they were with Natasha Latimer and her sister in the basement. A scrap of towelling. Stella lifted it to the lamplight. It was a sweatband. She looked around for a bin. There'd be one in the park, but it would be trespassing to climb over the gate.

Another growl. Tail down, Stanley was still fixed on the steps.

He'd be wanting to go to the ramshackle house. 'Over!' Stella said, still in agility mode. She corrected her command: 'I mean *heel*.' Gratifyingly obedient, Stanley by her side, she walked along the narrow pavement. Passing Adam Honeysett's house she paused. She wanted Jack with her when she tackled Adam. They were meant to be a team. Plus she should make up to him for going solo on the Rowlands interview. But Jack was with Bella. He wasn't being a team.

So preoccupied was Stella that she forgot that Stanley was never wrong. As she walked up the path of number 4 Thames Cottages, if she had turned to her left she would have seen a shadow on the towpath steps and caught the glint of a dog-lead clasp.

This time Adam Honeysett took Stella through to the kitchen. He wore a faded denim shirt open to reveal a white tee shirt tucked into faded and ripped jeans. His stubble looked deliberate and his hair looked recently cut, short at the sides and messy and tousled on top. The tousle was held in place by product: Stella caught a whiff of L'Oréal gel. Adam Honeysett took care of his appearance.

He invited her to sit on a bright blue stool in the shape of an H and he chose a E-shaped stool that was the same yellow as the digger.

He didn't take the same care with the kitchen. Cardboard packaging – Stella recognized a shepherd's pie sleeve as the brand she liked – spilled across the floor to a cluster of at least thirty empty beer and wine bottles. She'd seen a similar mess in the homes of men whose wives had left them. Beards were grown, hair was unwashed and the recycling bin overflowed with empties. But Adam Honeysett's wife had left him in 1987, so this must be normal.

The table was a Lego-type construction of giant plastic bricks, raised circles acting as place settings. It gave her the odd sensation of being in doll's house. On a wall was a colour print of a food cupboard, the shelves chock-full of Marmite, honey, cereal, soup tins, spices and condiments. The contents weren't dissimilar to those in her own cupboard, not that she had need of spices.

Gingerly she sat on the stool. It was more comfortable than she'd expected. She cut to the chase. 'You don't have an alibi for the night your wife disappeared.'

'We've been through this.' His expression was thunderous. 'I was having an affair and yes, I feel shit about it, OK! But look, Helen was no angel. Death was her trump card. Now she's untouchable while I'm fair game.'

'You asked Jane Drake to lie and say you were with her. But that wasn't true.'

Honeysett leapt up. He kicked the E stool. It skittered across the floor, knocking down the bottles and coming to rest on the cardboard. Stella's nerves jangled; stupidly, she had not anticipated violence.

'Are you saying you were with her all night?' Jane Drake could be lying. Withdrawal of her alibi would be powerful revenge on Honeysett for not marrying her. But somehow, despite Drake's stalking her and her creepy shrine, Stella believed her.

'I walked around London. I had to clear my head. Jane's dad had found out about us; he was threatening to tell Helen if I didn't end it. He was livid I had my hands on his special little girl. You ask me, he wanted to have her himself. I tried to end it, but Jane went ape and I couldn't do it. Either way, it would wreck my marriage. I'd have nothing.' He bit back a sob. But, Stella noticed, his eyes were dry.

Jack walked the streets at night; if he were here he'd know what questions to ask. Something about atmosphere and feeling in touch with the past. She said, 'Where did you go?' She had told Lucie he was on the towpath believing that to be true.

'Nowhere. Everywhere. I wasn't following a route. I got a coffee in an all-night café at one point. No one could have noticed me or they'd have blown my alibi long before.' He righted the stool and sat on it.

Stella saw that the other stools were also letters. Another E, an L and an N. Belatedly she realized they spelled 'Helen'. Had Adam bought them after Helen disappeared to show the police and the press he missed her? Had they been a present for Helen because he was guilty about Drake? Or, and Stella thought of Latimer's Pow3r 1 number plate, Helen had bought the stools for herself. 'You've lied before. How do I know you're not still lying? You had motive and you had the means.'

'All I can say is I didn't murder Helen. I loved her and I want her back.' He splayed his hands out.

He was overdoing the emotion. 'Did you walk to the towpath?'

'I came back that way. I didn't see anyone, but then I wasn't looking. Don't you think I've racked my brains since? Was Helen lying unconscious on the bank and I walked right past her? Could I have saved her? If I'd been at home earlier she might not have gone out.' He leant on the Lego table and buried his face in his hands. 'I went home, crept in, so as not to wake her.' He sat back and smacked his forehead – careful, Stella noticed, to avoid his hair. 'If only I'd gone upstairs, I'd have seen she wasn't there. But even then I'd have thought she had gone jogging early. But all I was bothered about was making sure the fucking dog didn't hear me and wake her up.'

The semaphore might have been convincing had Stella not witnessed the same high-octane emotion when he'd described kissing his wife lightly on the lips before driving to Northampton.

'If you weren't with Jane Drake, she has no alibi. Could she have attacked your wife?'

'She was seen buying wine that evening,' Honeysett reminded her.

'She wasn't seen after that and now it seems you weren't with her.' Stella wanted to provoke a reaction. Jolt him out of his theatrics. She put out of her mind what Honeysett might do if he was cornered.

'Whatever Jane is, she is not a murderer.' He caught his reflection in the window and patted his hair. Suddenly he reached across the Lego table and grabbed her wrist. 'You have to believe me! Jane Drake is stalking me. I can't tell the police, because she'll tell them I lied. I'm at her mercy! You can stop this. Please find my wife!'

Chapter Sixty-Two

Tuesday, 12 January 2016

Jack checked his phone to see if Stella had called. He was disproportionally ecstatic to see that he had a signal. He would call her. He saw the time – ten to eight – Stella wouldn't thank him for interrupting Stanley's agility class. He pushed on the door and went in. With silent footsteps he climbed the stairs.

Jack gave a knocker on the paint-flaked door three sharp taps. He put his ear to the door, but only heard blood pounding in his head. The door opened and he sprang back.

'Oh, it's you!' Megan Lawson didn't look pleased to see him.

'Hello there, Megan!' Jack rubbed his hands with an enthusiasm that must look insane.

If she was surprised, Megan gave no sign. She said flatly, 'You can come in if you like.'

This time it struck Jack that Megan Lawson was like her apartment, clean and tidy; nothing in the room captured the eye or gladdened the heart. In contrast Daphne's sitting room, although packed with clutter, was warm and homely. Although, he reflected, the homely objects were not Daphne's own and therefore didn't accurately express her personality.

'Do you want a drink.' She made the question sound rhetorical.

'No thanks, I had hot milk at Daphne Merry's.'

It was as if Megan Lawson had been hit with an electrical charge. 'Why were you there?' she demanded.

'I was returning a cake tin.' It sounded ludicrous. 'She'd made me a cake.' Instantly he saw he had said absolutely the wrong thing.

'I never see her now.' Megan slumped in a chair. If it was possible she looked even more lethargic.

'She must work hard, uncluttering and what not.' Hazily trying to save Megan Lawson's feelings, Jack was gabbling. Beyond denuding Suzie Darnell's flat, he had no idea of Daphne's workload.

'She was my friend. I was going to be a declutterer.' Megan hugged her stomach as if in pain and started up her humming. 'Then my mum said I couldn't see her. I went anyway, but she sent me away. I might as well be dead.'

'No! You are alive.' Jack clawed at the air in a bid to reassure. However, he would feel the same. Daphne Merry had been drawn to Megan because it enabled her to be the mother of a little girl again. But when Megan grew up Daphne must have lost interest; she would have had no experience of mothering an older child. She hadn't seen her own daughter become a teenager. Megan would remind her of what she had missed out on. In a different way to Steven Lawson, Daphne had abandoned Megan. Jack could see that for Megan, as it had been for him when his mother died, a powerful blow had been dealt the day her father died. She was at once a seven-year-old girl, vibrant and curious, and a woman in her mid-thirties, tired of the life she had not had. Jack couldn't say that this was why he had come. He wanted to show Megan Lawson that she wasn't alone. Except she was alone. She lived by herself in a cold, shabby flat and he could do nothing for her.

'Has Mrs Merry got a dog still?' Megan stopped humming to ask the question and then continued.

'Yes. A spaniel, I think. I'm not good on dogs. Apart from poodles.'

'Mrs Merry was lovely with animals. She let me walk with Woof after our Labrador called Smudge went away.' Megan sat up straight as if someone had told her to.

'Woof! That's the name of her dog now,' Jack exclaimed.

'All her dogs are called Woof.' Megan started humming again.

'How confusing.' Jack felt a chill. He'd gone to clean for a woman who called all her cleaners 'Tracy' because she couldn't 'get those foreign names'. The client cancelled the contract when he invited her to call him Tracy.

'Daphne's little girl named the first spaniel. I suppose it kept the name alive.'

'I expect you're right.' As he had before, Jack warmed to Megan. He'd been right to come. If not for her, then for himself.

'Daphne found Helen Honeysett's dog Baxter on the towpath by Mortlake Crematorium and handed him in to the police.' Megan brightened as she remembered this.

'Adam Honeysett said they didn't take Helen's disappearance seriously until the dog was found,' Jack agreed.

'Mr Honeysett was with his... mistress. Daphne looked after Baxter.' Megan sat back, humming. 'Dad rescued Baxter from drowning once.' She screwed her hair behind her neck and twisted it tight. 'Dad didn't rescue Helen that night.'

'Is that why you think he was guilty?'

'If he'd brought back Helen's dog, the police would have suspected him so he left him by the river.' The light that had come into her eyes when talking about Daphne Merry went. 'In the end, because of me, he was suspected anyway.'

'A guilty man might have brought the dog back to throw off suspicion.'

Megan shrugged as if the topic tired her and said abruptly, 'It's Dad's birthday today. Mum and Garry went to his grave. I went yesterday to avoid meeting them.'

'You couldn't go with them?' Jack didn't say that he knew she'd been because Stella had followed her and got locked in.

'No! If Garry knew I'd been near Dad's grave he'd have gone mad. I think Mum is scared he'll do what Dad did. I won't risk him doing that.'

That. She wouldn't say 'suicide'. 'Did you tell your mum you go and tend his plot?' Jack shut his eyes. She had said nothing about tending the grave. Stella had told him that. She also said the grave looked *un*tended.

Megan didn't appear to have spotted his error; she broke off humming to answer. 'Mum thanked me. I said I didn't want thanks, he was my dad. I could see she wanted to say it was too late to care for Dad and did I think weeding would make up for what happened.'

'I'd imagine if your mum was the sort of person who'd think that, then she'd have said it.' Bette looked frail, but he suspected she was tougher than Lucie. She would take no prisoners.

'I still love Dad, whatever he did,' Megan Lawson asserted as if he'd contradicted her.

Jack asked the question. If he was honest – and he would try to be honest – this was why he was here. 'When you were little, did you know a man called Brian Judd?'

'I know who he was. Mum said never to tease him because he was frightened of children. That seemed mad, how could you be frightened of children when you'd been one? Now I understand. If you've been a child you know how frightening they can be. Judd was harmless. It was Mr Rowlands I didn't like. He went on the towpath even after his dog died. I thought he chased me once and I ran into the crematorium grounds. But the footsteps were Garry. He rescued me.'

Garry Lawson had threatened to kill Jack if he hurt his sister. Megan expressed worry that Garry would kill himself. Jack noted that, despite their estrangement, brother and sister still loved each other.

'He's dead now.'

'Dead?' Garry Lawson had said the same.

'I saw him lying on the towpath. I thought he was asleep. But he wasn't breathing.'

'When was this?' Jack sat up.

'The Olympics were on. So 2012. Everyone was watching TV; no one was on the towpath. I walked to Kew Stairs and laid flowers for my dad and when I came back he'd gone.'

'Did you hear what happened to him?' Jack felt creeping unease. *True Hosts played dead.*

'I didn't ask. No one mentioned anything was wrong. You saying I should have checked on him?'

'No, I mean...' It was what he was saying. 'Have you seen him since that day?'

'No, but then I don't go to the towpath much.' She flicked a look at her watch. Jack got the hint.

Despite having a signal, Jack had no messages or missed calls. On a whim, he texted Bella. *The ghosts are gone, can I see you?* He had walked twenty paces when his phone beeped.

No. The thing he'd liked about Bella was she didn't mince words. He wished she'd minced them now though. Another beep. Bella had changed her mind.

Jack read Stella's message twice before, his heart thumping, he called her.

'This is Stella Darnell, sorry I can't come to the phone, leave me a...'

'Stella!' His shout resounded in the empty street. He started dialling then saw he had no signal. He returned to Megan Lawson's flats, where he'd had phone reception, and held his phone up in the air. *Shit!*

Jack broke into a run, swerving down a lane beside the National Archives to the river, his coat flapping like giant wings.

Chapter Sixty-Three

Stella was inclined to go back to her house after seeing Adam Honeysett and write up the notes of their talk. The only reservation she had was that he'd brought them the case in the first place and she couldn't see how, if he'd murdered his wife, that benefited him, since they were bound to suspect him. But after her last meeting with him, she ratcheted him higher up the suspect list.

She knocked on the door of number 5 Thames Cottages. She had expected to be turned away but, to her astonishment, Sybil Lofthouse invited her inside and offered her a mug of tea. Stella had had more than enough tea over what was proving a long day so refused.

Jack would have hated Lofthouse's front room, she told herself. He liked warm cosy rooms full of clutter. The walls were grey, the furniture unyielding as if to discourage visitors from lingering. She'd obviously caught Lofthouse on a good day. The elderly woman was knitting, an occupation that struck Stella as at odds with recording mergers and acquisitions. Stella could see no sign of 'the Ancient Mutt' mentioned by Natasha Latimer. Perhaps it was dead.

'We'd had the Big Bang in October of 1986. There were hiccups around that, computers crashing, some lost their jobs. I was nothing to do with it, not my remit, but we were all affected.' Sybil Lofthouse concentrated on her stitches.

'Do you remember Helen Honeysett going missing?' Stella tried to keep her voice steady.

'Of course!' The needles clacked rhythmically. 'I don't see what it has to do with me. Nor you, come to that.' Smiling benignly; her needles barely paused.

'When we met outside your house, after you so kindly stopped Stanley running away, you said you left at five in the morning in a taxi.' Stella wouldn't be put off by the knitting – the woman was eagle-eyed – she ran a finger down her notes and stopped mid-way. 'You said, quote, "No trains at that time. There was no one on the towpath then except joggers and dog walkers."' Stella looked up. A wave of shock ran through her. Sybil Lofthouse was no longer the kindly old woman placidly clacking her knitting needles. Her eyes were cold steel.

'Did I, dear?' She loosened a thread of wool from the ball on her lap.

'How could you know who was on the towpath if you weren't there?' Stella's tongue stuck to the roof of her mouth.

'I walked my dog there. There were no paid dog walkers in those days.' Sybil Lofthouse smiled comfortably, but the humour didn't extend to her eyes.

'What about evenings?' Stella mustn't lose the thread. 'Did you walk your dog then?'

'I did. How extraordinary that you wrote down what I said to you. Is that strictly legal, dear?'

'I'm a cleaner, but I'm also a detective. I've been hired to find out who murdered Helen Honeysett. As long as I don't publish your quote without your permission, it *is* legal. I need to understand, did you go to the towpath the evening that Helen Honeysett was last seen alive? That was Wednesday the seventh of January?'

'The police asked me that.' The needles increased speed. Clack-clack-clack.

'You told them you were at work. But I'm thinking if you were on an early shift you'd have been home by eight that night.

That's the time when Megan Lawson saw Helen Honeysett going to the towpath.'

Sybil Lofthouse laid down her knitting. 'Do you know what it's like to be caught up in a major incident that has nothing whatsoever to do with you? I was expected to tell a policeman the intricacies of my life because a silly girl got herself murdered. I was valued at the Stock Exchange for being trustworthy and discreet. I was brought up not to broadcast my feelings, not like people do now, splashing their emotions all over the computer before they've barely felt them. I don't talk about my life and I don't talk about other people's lives. I don't ask personal questions and I don't answer personal questions. In my job I held secrets that could have brought down banks and ruined companies. People in my line of work can't be witnesses. I keep myself to myself.'

'No one is precluded from being a witness if they were there.' Was she Daphne Merry's bystander? Stella glanced down at her notes, 'Miss Lofthouse is the type to keep herself to herself.' Out loud she read, 'He was creeping past the crematorium, like he does, stalking that poor Mrs Merry.'

Click-clack. That man should mind his own business. He's no loss to this street. Click-clack.

Terry had been at ease asking personal questions; he struck up small talk with strangers. Stella would rather bring up the shine on a chest of drawers than probe into the activities of a woman in her seventies who was, by her own admission, intensely private. She forced herself to go on. 'This is about a murder. If you saw something it was your duty to tell the police.'

'My duty is to avoid a sordid domestic tangle and a court case. That woman was a menace.' The needles clacked on.

'You were seen on the towpath that evening.' This wasn't true. Stella held her breath and watched the woman knitting. Dimly she considered that you could do a lot of damage with a knitting needle.

'I expect I was.' Sybil Lofthouse unwound more wool. 'This

nonsense won't bring anyone back. Instead of focusing on the fat fee you'll get for stirring up pain, consider the lives you will shatter.' She began knitting faster.

Stella had absorbed the interrogatory gambits of her detective father and could ride out silence until the other party filled the void. She rested her eyes on the knitted wool, vaguely pondering what garment Sybil Lofthouse was making. The older woman's lips worked busily as she recited, 'Knit two, purl two, knit two, purl two.' Stella waited.

Stanley hadn't been schooled in the tactics of the Criminal Investigation Department. He stretched, yawned – a prolonged wail like a child in distress – and with a peremptory sniff, pattered to the door.

'... purl two. Whisky needs to pee.' Sybil Lofthouse didn't look up from her knitting. She snapped, 'Whisky. Sit down!'

'Why do you call him Whisky?' Stella enquired airily. She could apply tension every bit as skilfully as Miss Lofthouse was plying her wool.

'Isn't that his name?'

'He's called Stanley.' A year ago, when she was ambivalent about being in charge of a dog, Stella wouldn't have minded what someone called him; now she felt irritation that Lofthouse kept getting his name wrong. Stella recalled Jack's theory: 'Did you have a dog called Whisky? Perhaps you're mixing Stanley up with him.'

'Whisky! A banal appellation for anything but a drink. My dog was called Timothy Trot.' Sybil Lofthouse began a new row. 'Purl two, knit two, purl two...'

'*Follow whatever clues are laid before you.*' Terry could be talking to her via an earpiece. 'Who owned Whisky?'

'That fellow called Judd with the beard like an eminent Victorian. Litter bug! Poor Mrs Merry was forever picking up after him. A stickler for taking care, she would have flourished at the Stock Exchange. No flies on her. She sorted him out.'

'How did she sort him out?' Stella was channelling Terry.

Stanley was attracted to the house on the towpath because he'd picked up the scent of a dog.

The needles stabbed the wool. 'Carelessness costs lives.'

'Where did Judd live?' *Ask a question that the subject is happy to answer. Lull them with the dullest facts.*

'*Does* live, not that I've seen him for a good while. The house looks like a bomb's hit it. It's on the river near here. Natasha Latimer tried her damnedest to take it off his hands, but he wouldn't budge. Stubborn old codger. He could have moved somewhere warm with central heating. He'll go out of there in a box. Natasha made do with the cottage your man friend is supposedly cleaning. Neville Rowlands, the tenant, was none too happy about going.' Sybil Lofthouse wound wool around a finger and pursed her lips as if she had said too much.

'Was it Timothy Trot you walked that night?' Stella hadn't heard of a dog having a surname.

'Timothy was a wonderful character, worth ten of any dog,' she remarked gratuitously. 'Of course it was Mr Trot, who else? We saw that wretched man by the river stairs. He obviously didn't want company. I didn't let him see me – at the Stock Exchange, you have to read signals.'

'"Wretched man?" Do you mean Steven Lawson?' Unconsciously Stella was tapping her pen on the Filofax page in time to the needles.

'I called him Mr Lawson. We observed formality in those days.' Sybil Lofthouse talked to the knitting. 'Terrible thing to take one's own life. One sometimes came across it at work, those boys on the floor lived at such a pace. If it went wrong, they chucked in the towel, poor fools.'

'Did you see Helen Honeysett when you were out?'

'She always went the other way towards Chiswick.'

The same phrase as Neville Rowlands had used. '*She always...*' 'Did she go in that direction that Wednesday night?'

'Yes.'

'How do you know if you didn't see her?' Stella hadn't noticed that Stanley was back lying at her feet.

'If you are doing your job properly, you'll know she got as far as Chiswick Bridge. Daphne Merry found the dog by the Mortlake Crematorium. Daphne couldn't bear that it was untrained. It would lag behind Helen Honeysett and wander off. It wasn't neutered, you see. Chased for miles on the sniff of a bitch.'

'Steven Lawson could have thrown Helen Honeysett into the water by the pier before you arrived.' Again, Stella thought that a fifty-year-old could push a young woman into the river if that young woman was caught unawares. *'Oh, it's you!'*

Lofthouse snapped, 'The police never said she went into the river.'

'They never said she didn't either.' Stella watched the busy needles. Click-clack. Facts took on order. 'Can you tell me your own routine?'

'I don't know why I should, but if it stays confidential...' Sybil Lofthouse put down her knitting. 'I walked Timothy T. at seven-forty, after *The Archers*, washing up and setting out things for my early start. In bed by nine. I passed Mr Lawson sitting on the bottom step of Kew Stairs at eight-oh-five precisely on my way to Kew Bridge. He was crying. Terrible to see a man cry. These days they are always sobbing, but then it was most unusual. I grabbed Mr Trot and we stood still. If you do that, people don't see you – in the dark I was invisible. But he didn't leave so we moved on. He was still there on my return. Timothy and I slipped by and were home by a quarter past.'

'Are you sure it was Ste— Mr Lawson? Did you have a torch? Or did he?' Stella knew how dark it was on the towpath.

'The sky in London is never dark. I would take a torch now as I'm unsteady on my feet. It's why I don't have a dog: they're too easy to trip over and need so much walking—'

'No ancient mutt?' Stella interrupted. 'Kew Stairs is the opposite direction to the way that Helen jogged. If you'd told the police Steven was nowhere near her he wouldn't have been suspected of her murder. You were his alibi!'

'I would have been inundated by questions from reporters and the police. I couldn't have that.' Sybil Lofthouse yanked a needle out of the knitting and unravelled several rows. 'Pleasant though it has been to chat, it is time for you and Whisky to leave. I retire early.' She held the needle like a stiletto.

On the doorstep, Stella asked, 'Where on the towpath did you say you saw Neville Rowlands that night?'

'I think that you know very well that I didn't say, my dear. He was creeping past the Kew Stairs, sneaking like he does, stalking that poor Mrs Merry.' Sybil Lofthouse closed the front door.

Shapes resolved into trees, stones and the outline of Kew Stairs; the granite glistened. The river had ebbed. Stanley's apricot coat was a pale blotch at her feet. She gripped his lead. It was here that Steven Lawson had walked to his death. If he were on the steps now, she'd be able to see him, but where she stood, in the shadows of overhanging branches on the towpath, Lawson wouldn't see her.

Again and again Stella returned to the fact, sickening and certain. Sybil Lofthouse could have exonerated Steven Lawson. Her evidence was circumstantial, but so were the facts that had as good as incriminated him. Lofthouse said she had seen Steven at Kew Stairs at 8.15 p.m. Megan and Bette told the police that her dad had stormed out of the house at eight. Megan had seen Helen going to the towpath just before her dad. Daphne Merry had reported passing Helen jogging towards Mortlake. Lofthouse and Rowlands had said it was the way Helen always went. As Stella had said to Sybil Lofthouse, the crematorium was in the opposite direction to Kew Stairs. Helen's dog Baxter had been found by Daphne Merry near the crematorium so it was assumed that Helen had run that far. But the dog often ran off so where it was found might have no connection to where Helen had gone.

Lucy had confirmed that it was a tight time frame for Steven to catch up with Helen and kill her. Sybil Lofthouse had seen Steven sitting on the steps at a quarter past eight, which gave Helen at least fifteen minutes' head start on him. Lawson could have pushed her in the river on her return, but her run took half an hour each way so she couldn't have returned to Thames Cottages until around nine. Bette had said Lawson was back at twenty past eight. She could have been lying to protect him. But Megan also told the police that she'd seen him return at eight twenty. Given that she believed her father guilty, Stella counted Megan as a reliable witness.

Steven Lawson had to face that his sister had bankrupted him. Enough to make a grown man cry, but was he sobbing because he had killed Helen Honeysett? Stella doubted it. A man cool enough to have killed a woman and somehow dispose of her body wouldn't sit where anyone could see him – and he had been seen – and cry. That didn't add up.

She shone her torch app down the riverbank. The tide was on the turn. Soon the steps would be below the waterline. If Steven had been sitting on the bottom step – and Stella didn't doubt the accuracy of Lofthouse's report – then the tide had been out that night. If he had pushed Helen off the bank, she would have tumbled down the slope on to the foreshore. She might have been injured in the fall, but couldn't have drowned. Whoever murdered Helen Honeysett had either lured her somewhere else, or killed her on the towpath and disposed of her body. With the timings provided by Lofthouse Steven Lawson didn't have time to do either. That fact was insurmountable. Lofthouse had also seen Daphne Merry and Neville Rowlands although they hadn't seen each other or her. Stella rubbed her forehead. She needed a spreadsheet.

The person that Megan had heard on the footpath that night must have been Lofthouse. Megan and Lofthouse had both hidden. Neither could corroborate the other's story. Stella knew from her nights round at Jackie's that *The Archers* finished at 7.15 p.m. Washing up and preparing for the morning couldn't take more than twenty minutes. She'd have been out on the towpath by seven thirty-five at the earliest. She said she went out at twenty to eight and saw Steven Lawson just after eight. *'Eight-oh-five precisely.'* Had she lied? If so why? Stella knew the answer. If Lofthouse had been there longer, or arrived later, she might have seen more. Better to lie than be a witness to murder. She kept herself to herself. Lofthouse might not know who had murdered Helen Honeysett, but she knew who had not. She knew that Steven Lawson was innocent. But what if she also knew who killed her?

If Steven had seen Sybil Lofthouse, he would have asked her to shore up his story. Stella was there with Daphne Merry: a bystander was little better than a murderer. Lofthouse had effectively killed Steven Lawson.

Sybil Lofthouse, Adam Honeysett and Megan Lawson had all seen Neville Rowlands and Daphne Merry on the towpath. Sybil Lofthouse's words echoed in her head. *'He was creeping past the crematorium, like he does, stalking that poor Mrs Merry.'* Something didn't make sense. Then as if a fog rolled in, the glimmer of thought was gone. Stella took off her rucksack and dug out her Filofax. She leafed to her notes from their interview with Megan Lawson. Megan had said Daphne Merry found the Honeysetts' dog near Kew Bridge. *Not Mortlake Crematorium.* A seven-year-old, upset about her dad, who shouldn't have been out in the first place, was more likely to get a detail wrong than a woman in her thirties who abhorred carelessness and would, as Lofthouse had said, flourish at the Stock Exchange. She stuffed her Filofax back in her rucksack and set off along the towpath.

Adam Honeysett claimed to have walked all night – crossing London – battling with how to end his affair with Jane Drake. Merry couldn't have seen Adam or, a stickler for the truth, she would have told the police that his alibi – that he was with Drake – was false. Of all their suspects, Adam Honeysett remained the one with the strongest motive for murdering Helen Honeysett.

He had got the house and eventually, when his wife was declared dead, her death-in-service benefit and life insurance.

Deep in thought, Stella didn't notice the Thames Cottages lamp-post. She trudged on into the darkness, passing Latimer's long garden wall and the concealed entrance to her secret passage, and continued along the shingled path, desolate and bleak although it was barely eight o'clock in the evening, her footsteps hollow in the suspended silence. Below her the river was filling, water chasing into gullies, washing over bottles and cans, shifting and dislodging them. By now familiar with the riverside path, Stella gave no heed to the extraneous sounds, some explainable. Some not.

She was only jolted from her deliberations when Stanley brought her to a stop. They were outside Brian Judd's house.

Whisky. Stanley sensed Brian Judd's dog. The windows were dark. Sybil Lofthouse hadn't seen Judd or his dog for some time. But without Timothy Trot, she'd no reason to walk on the towpath after dark, when the article by Lucie that Jack had seen had said that Brian Judd came out. Lofthouse had told her that she'd taken Judd's mis-delivered post round to him but, unwilling to get involved, she'd have been unlikely to have knocked on his door to check on him. A recluse, Judd might not have answered. People baffled Stella. She knew someone could lie dead in their home for years and not be missed. But in Judd's house she hadn't smelled the tell-tale stench of decay; there were no fat bluebottles dotting the walls and windows. And Stanley would have rooted out a body. Judd hadn't been there, but someone had picked up his post. They'd not swept up the leaves or cleaned, but Stella had seen that scenario before.

She let Stanley lead her over the grass to the house. He scrabbled at the door with his furious cycling motion. She was disbelieving as the door drifted open with a spine-chilling creak. Stella was no bystander. With Stanley at her side, she stepped inside.

Chapter Sixty-Four

Tuesday, 12 January 2016

I feel like a small boy on the first day of school. Worse, because on that day Mother took me. Mother is in my heart, willing me on. I've rehearsed the words. Not that I need to. I know them off by heart. You will appreciate my meticulous care. It is what you love about me. *Love.* I dare to use that word. You love me. The time has come for us. I am ready and waiting.

The moon is full. I'm not a romantic, I won't bother you with the crude theatre of flowers and chocolates, but tonight all the signs are here. My beloved Thames flows like the blood in my veins. I can be poetic, but I won't be. You are a no-nonsense lady. I will tell you all I have done for you. The river that has watched over me all my life is my witness. I am your True De-Cluttering Assistant. I clear up for you. I keep you free.

The dog knows me. The cleaners could spoil everything. I will not let them.

Chapter Sixty-Five

Tuesday, 12 January 2016

The chill penetrated Stella's jacket and chilled her bones. The air was musty. A decayed body wouldn't smell once the flesh had rotted. She dismissed the notion. There was a smell, faint and overlaying the damp. Not a corpse. Stella's bloodhound nose identified it as Nivea shaving gel for sensitive skin. Sybil Lofthouse had described Brian Judd as having a beard like a Victorian. Stella hadn't known what she was talking about, but guessed that it didn't involve shaving.

'Hello?' Alerted by her call, Stanley growled.

The scent of aftershave was fresh. Gillette. The aftershave her dad and Martin Cashman had worn. And Neville Rowlands.

Stella crossed the hall; the floorboards groaned beneath her tread. 'Mr Judd?' She crunched over the dried leaves and tapped on a door by the staircase. Without waiting, she went in. She found the light switch and a glass lampshade in the centre of the ceiling dully illuminated the room. 'Anyone here?' Her voice was flat in the deadened air.

Stella's practised estimating eye took in the room. The only piece of furniture that looked like it was made later than 1950 was a boxy Hitachi television with a bunny's ears aerial on top and a telephone that lay on a small hexagonal inlaid wood table. A light on the phone was blinking with a message. Someone had called Brian Judd, but either he had decided not to answer or he wasn't in. Or he couldn't answer.

'Mr Judd?' Stella called up the stairs. Silence.

On the landing, her torch app picked out four doors, all open. In the first was a vast free-standing bath, lime stains tracking down the enamel from gigantic brass taps. The wooden toilet seat was up; beside it a basket-weave laundry basket doubled as a stool. No aftershave. No razor. Who wore aftershave? Stanley was straining on his lead.

'Heel,' she muttered absently. She let him nose on into the next room. He yanked her towards a tartan dog's basket that was at the bottom of a narrow bed so high Judd risked breaking his collar bone if he fell out. Had this happened? She checked either side of the bed; no one was sprawled unconscious on the floor. The bed – made with blankets and sheets – didn't look recently slept in. Stella bent to the candlewick counterpane and gave an exploratory sniff. The musky odour of a man who rarely washed. She knew it from deep cleaning houses of the deceased in preparation for sale. A phantom smell, Jack called it.

Stanley grabbed at the bed and clenching it in his jaws, gave it a shake. Stella knew it was his preamble to nesting. On an instinct she let go of his lead and took a few steps away, her back to the door. He leapt into the bed and, circling one way and then the other, flumped down as if perfectly at home. He shot her a dark look, daring her to challenge him.

'Whisky,' Stella said softly. Stanley shot up, ears pert, head cocked. 'Whisky!' He bounded out of the bed over to her. He trotted around her and arriving at the front, sat down. Distantly Stella registered Stanley had executed a perfect English Finish.

She didn't need Kirsty the behaviourist to tell her that Stanley was behaving as if he was perfectly at home in this dirty ramshackle house, because he *was* at home. It wasn't that he had smelled another dog. This was where he had lived.

Clumsily, Stella clipped on Stanley's lead. By now she wasn't expecting to find Brian Judd alive. She checked the other rooms on the landing but, as Jack had said when he had come before, there was no one there. One room was given over entirely to stuff to do with dogs. There was no sign of a dog, no smell, no hairs. Returning to the landing, she felt vaguely bad for doubting that Jack had looked. Yet she knew why she doubted him. He had known his way about the house too well. He had been there before.

Downstairs a cold draught made her shiver. The downstairs toilet door – the way Jack had come in – was open. Inside, the sash window had been raised.

Stella pushed the door against the wall. No one was hiding behind it. A creak. She spun round. Thin whisperings of light in the hall seem to shift. Stella shivered. A disparate collection of assorted circumstance and supposition fell into place. Rooted in rationality, Stella wasn't the fearful type. She felt fear now; stealthy and treacherous, it threatened to paralyse her. Stanley began to mew.

She fumbled in her pocket for her phone. Something fell out. It was the sweatband Stanley had unearthed in Latimer's basement. She went cold. Joggers wore sweatbands. She tried to summon up pictures of the police reconstruction of Helen Honeysett's last run. Was the policewoman wearing a sweatband? Jack had the photographic memory. All she saw was a blur of shadows and lights. It was freezing. January. Night-time. Surely Helen wouldn't have needed a sweatband?

She opened her phone to Contacts and, bungling it the first time, swiped through to Martin Cashman. Their affair didn't make him an ex: he was her dad's young colleague, so Stella had kept his number. She dictated her text, a trick learnt from her mate Tina who had dictated everything except her survival from cancer. Stella's voice shook and hearing it her fear escalated. She was staccato: 'Martin Full Stop Me Comma Stella Full Stop Did anyone report a dog missing on the Kew towpath in 2012 Question Mark'. About to send Stella saw she had no signal. She jabbed at the button, but the message remained red. *Your message has not been sent. Retry?*

The leaves and twigs littering the floor stirred in a breeze. Stella forced herself to think. *Stain by stain.* She had got phone reception near Jane Drake's, but the estate was ten minutes away along the towpath in the opposite direction to Jack. Jack was with Bella; she couldn't see him.

Someone had got into the house through the bathroom window and left by the front door or the other way round... She let herself breathe. There was no one here. Yet although the house was cluttered and dirty, it didn't look burgled. There wasn't much to nick; the burglar hadn't even bothered with the telly or the phone. *The telephone.*

Stella led Stanley back into Judd's lounge. As she snatched the handset off the cradle she was so certain that the line would be dead that she was momentarily puzzled by the buzzing. Whatever had happened to Brian Judd, his telephone still worked. It was an old plastic dial phone with the number in the centre and the emergency number of the police. Was there ever a time when people didn't know that? She froze. Although it was Jack that was good with numbers, Stella did remember those she had called. 0208 948... She had called this number before. It was the number on the dog collar that Jack had found in the digger. Had Brian Judd had been in Natasha Latimer's house after all? Yet Claudia had told them that the intruder was Neville Rowlands. With a shaky hand, she dialled Cashman's number.

He answered on the first ring. 'Hey, Stell, you all right, love?' Jackie said he called her 'love' because he loved her.

Robotically she repeated what she'd tried to text, talking as if dictating. '... towpath in 2012 Question Mark.'

'Eh? You sure you're OK?' He sounded worried.

'Yes.' If she said more, he'd know she was far from all right.

'Hold on, I'll check.' She'd steeled herself for a knock-back. He shouldn't be doing a private search and she shouldn't have asked him to. Jackie said Martin would walk a million miles for Terry Darnell's daughter. This wasn't true.

Cashman was still at the station. Dimly Stella recalled that the reason his wife had left him in the first place was because his work hours were silly. She'd said he was obsessed with the job.

'You there, Stell?' Martin was back.

'Yes.' There was rustling in the hall. The dead leaves, she told herself.

'Lost iPhones and iPods, you name it. Scarves, sunglasses, a copy of the London *A–Z* – why the fuck hand that in? No dogs found. Or cats.'

Stanley barked, sharp and shrill. He was looking towards the lounge door. Stella reminded herself he was alert to the most trivial sounds. It meant nothing. 'Are you sure no one reported finding a dog on the towpath in 2012?'

'Not a one. Sounds like it's not the answer you wanted!'

David had lied to her. *Whisky.* Fragments were coming together. She gripped the receiver with both hands.

She knew what was coming next. 'Stell, is this a cold case? Why do you want to know?' He'd be considering warning her off. *It's a matter for the police.*

'No, just wondered.' This much was true. Thanking him and non-committal about his offer of a 'quick drink sometime', Stella rang off.

The rustling had stopped. If the leaves were being blown by a draught why would the sound stop? Someone must have closed the toilet window. Stella felt her insides cave in. She'd been really bloody stupid. Martin was police: he would know about the sweatband. Joggers get hot whatever the weather. She should have told him everything. Stella pressed redial.

The line was dead.

Chapter Sixty-Six

Tuesday, 12 January 2016

'*Bonsoir*, Garry darling. It's your Aunty Luce-the-Goose!' Cigarette smoke coiled blue-orange in the lamplight. 'How are the little birdies? Tweet-tweet!' Lucie May croaked nervously.

The man, in a hooded fleece and jeans, gaped bleary-eyed at the woman in a film-star fur coat. Then he snapped to. 'Piss off!'

Lucie mashed the half-smoked cigarette on the path with her boot. 'Your mum in?'

'She doesn't want to see you.' Garry jutted an unshaven chin.

Lucie rocked on her heels. 'Bette's my sister.'

'She's my *mum*. Go away. And it's after ten o clock.' Garry Lawson tried to close the door, but his aunt jammed her boot into the gap. If Lucie had been wearing her beloved glittering Jimmy Choo Nude Shadow Pointy Toe pumps with stilettoes the force would have broken a metatarsal, but her Dr Marten boots – reserved for door-stepping – were ample protection.

'What happens after ten, you turn into Prince Charming?' She kept her boot in place. 'I have to see her, it's important.' Lucie was tired of being nice. Garry Lawson was taller and broader but, listless and dismayed, was no match for her fierce intent. 'Bette!' Lucie called. She thrust herself at the door with the velocity of a ground-launched cruise missile.

Garry stepped back, pitching her into the hall. His mouth

twitched as if with shame at the trick and he muttered diffidently, 'Mum's out.'

'At this time? Where is she, Garry?' Lucie was properly cross. *Shite merchant.*

'Dunno.'

'Listen, Birdman, you're going to tell me, or so help me, I'll open your cage and release all your fine feathered friends as a feast for our feline friends,' Lucie hissed with heat-seeking alliteration.

'She went to the towpath,' Garry Lawson muttered. 'She's putting flowers on the steps where...'

'You let her go to the towpath at this time of night by herself?'

'She wanted to go on her own.' He was sullen.

'And you do what Mummy wants!' Despite the years of enmity, Lucie had expected her nephew to be as susceptible to her charm as most men were. But Garry was like a sulky teenage boy and she had no clue how to work one of those. She decided to be placatory: 'Damn right, kiddo, wish I'd listened to my mum. And Bette come to that.' She treated him to a smile that did full justice to her expensive dental work. 'Shut the door – don't let in the nasty cold air! Don't want you getting a chill.' Turning on her heel, fur coat billowing, Lucie sauntered down the path, trilling the tune for 'Feed the Birds'.

'She never wants to see you again and nor do I!' Emboldened by the distance, Garry marshalled his courage.

'Never say never, Gazza-pops!' With the agility of a caffeine-fuelled gazelle, Lucie took the steps to the towpath in two bounds.

Lucie May had wanted the advantage of surprise when she met her sister but, baffled by the dark and the shifting shadows, she had to use her torch.

She had often come to the towpath in the last thirty years, hunting for proof of her brother-in-law's guilt. But apart from the reconstruction after Honeysett's disappearance, it had been in daylight. She had planned to sort stuff out with Bette in her cosy sitting room, hopefully – when things were patched up – with a gin and tonic. She had not reckoned on stumbling about in the dark at the shrine to the Drowned Hubby. But for Garry lurking in his lair, she'd go back and wait for Bette there. Lucie styled herself an intrepid reporter, but within reason.

Since meeting Stella Darnell in the court car park, Lucie had been mulling over what Stella had told her. Adam Honeysett had not been doing press-ups with his mistress as he'd claimed. Grudgingly, she had acclimatized herself to the crazy idea that Steven Lawson was innocent.

At different times and in very different situations, Terry and Stella Darnell had urged Lucie May to keep an open mind. Lucie argued that the engine of a good story was driven by emotion. It was the raw shit that made people buy papers. It was love, death and betrayal that kept the world turning.

Earlier that evening, Lucie had mixed herself a nippet and, with no immediate deadlines, retired to her Murder Room. She reread each paper, every article and all her notes. She pored over photographs and her hand-drawn maps of the towpath and the cottages. Her material was arranged chronologically and cross-referenced. Her access to Terry Darnell and other police contacts had netted witness and character statements, timelines of Thames Cottages residents, dog walkers, cyclists; all those nearby when the estate agent went missing. Lastly she had opened Steven Lawson's diary. She had discovered the diary missing as soon as Jack and Stella had gone. She'd assumed it was Jack; Stella Darnell was too much of a law-lady to steal. Lucie had more than one copy of all her material. Plenty more where that came from, she'd muttered to herself as she assembled a particularly potent nippet.

For the last years, Lucie had spent her scraps of spare time twisting and bending conjecture to fit her story. Steven Lawson had brutally murdered Helen Honeysett. This morning outside the court, the cleaning detective had zoomed her vacuum cleaner through a lifetime's work.

Beside Lucie on her desk was a little clay model of a dog, ears pinned back as if in a high wind. It had been Bette's when they were kids. Lucie had nicked it. She stared at the dog and the dog stared back.

One way to recall something or find a solution to a tricky problem is to walk away from it. Lucie rarely did this. If she forgot a fact or couldn't work out how to obtain information, she made it up. As she reread Steven Lawson's diary, her finger traced each line. She stopped and looked up at the dog – at some stage it had lost the tip of its tail – and everything fell into place.

Lucie rushed out of the Murder Room, then ran back and snatched up the clay dog. On King Street, she found a black cab decanting passengers and leapt in through the other door before the driver could turn the 'For Hire' light off. Fifteen minutes later she was arguing with Garry Lawson on his doorstep. Despite the rift between the sisters, it hadn't occurred to Lucie that Bette wouldn't see her. As she picked her way along the towpath, she felt creeping doubt.

'Bette!' Her torch lit up a figure on the towpath. Pulling the clay dog from her pocket – a gift would sugar the pill – she stumbled forward.

'Oh, it's you!' She didn't hide her exasperation. 'I can't talk now. Have you seen Bette? My sister.' He was of those bit-part players who wants a starring role.

'She's gone.' He was reassuring.

'What do you mean "gone"?'

'Are you all right, my dear? You seem flustered.'

Lucie shook her head impatiently. 'I must find my sister.' A glimmer of culpability in her brother-in-law's death dawned. Her fingers tightened on the clay dog. 'I've got to make it up with her.'

'I'm still your "man at the scene"!' In the watery moonlight she couldn't see his expression. 'That Miss Latimer is moving out.

Our little plan worked! I was hoping to see you. I had a visit from a private detective. I was careful not to give anything away.'

'Good one, Nev.' Lucie clutched the top of her fur coat together. 'Not now though. I need to see my sister.'

'Has something happened?'

'No. Yes. Tell me a thing. When that girl Honeysett vanished, a witness on the towpath reported hearing a woman say "Oh, it's you!"'

'Megan said Honeysett was talking to a man.'

'Steven Lawson,' Neville Rowlands said comfortably. Then, as if reciting a poem in class, said, 'Who am I and what have I done?'

'What was that? Why did you say that?'

'You told me. It was Lawson's confession. Our little secret!'

'And let's keep it that way!' Lucie snapped. 'Megan never actually *saw* Lawson.' She scoured the dark, dismal footpath. *Where the hell was Bette?* 'Megan jumped to that conclusion because she saw her dad leave the house after Helen Honeysett.'

'Best not detain yourself, my dear, there's nothing you can do now.' Rowlands sounded peevish.

'I must do something. Where's your dog?' She cast about her. Nothing moved on the dark towpath.

Rowlands said nothing. Slowly he took the dog lead from around his neck. The clasp flashed silver in the moonlight.

'The police were wrong. *I was wrong.*' Lucie fretted. 'I've reread Lawson's diary and something he wrote... I know who Honeysett was talking to— *Arrghuphmm...*'

Lucie May felt searing-hot pain and then she was aware of nothing more. Unconscious, she fell down the river stairs on to the snatch of beach below. Her body lay sprawled beside a bunch of flowers, the message already soaked by the incoming tide.

'Happy Birthday, Steve. Still fighting for you. Your loving Betsy x.'

Chapter Sixty-Seven

Stanley lived in Brian Judd's house by the river. BJ not report missing because dead?

Jack had heard the buzz of Stella's incoming text as he reached the lamp-post by Thames Cottages. He had a signal! He fumbled for speed dial, before the temporary reception dropped.

'I'm sorry, I can't come to the—' He spun around on the spot, his hands to his mouth. There was one other person. Jack rang her number.

He was startled by music, tinny like a transistor radio, some metres away. Gingerly, watching signal strength bars, he edged along the bleak towpath towards the sound.

It came from the river. Max Bygraves was singing 'Happy Days are Here Again'. Jack felt a whisper of dread.

Max Bygraves cut off mid-flow and the ringing in Jack's ear switched to voicemail. 'Keep trying. If I'm not picking up I'm on a scoop!' Lucie May cackled.

Pale moonlight etched a bundle of fur, half submerged, by Kew Stairs. A drowned dog. A light glowed. *A mobile phone.* Water lapped around it and as Jack watched, the light was extinguished. He was thrust aside. A man blundered down the river stairs, skidding on slime and falling on his knees by the fur thing.

'*Mum, no!*'

Jack swung his Maglite beam down. It wasn't a dog. A woman lay face down on broken bricks and stones, her legs washed by the rising river. It was not a trick of the light on the River Wall. Short blond hair, sodden fur coat, polished Dr Martens. It was real.

'Garry, it's not your mum.' Jack's tongue was thick. 'It's Lucie!'

'Call an ambulance!' Bette Lawson was beside her sister. 'I can't feel a pulse.'

Chapter Sixty-Eight

Tuesday, 12 January 2016

'I love you, Daphne. I have always loved you. You were the girl my mother meant for me. A cut above, she always said. She told me she could leave this world content because I have you.'

I stroke your hair and, unused to my touch, you tense. It is a shock when what you have wanted for so long comes true.

'My dear girl, you are safe. I have kept you safe.

'Sit back, make yourself comfortable. I will tell you who I am and what I have done. I did it all for you.'

Daphne is listening. Her eyes never leave mine.

'You remember how that Honeysett girl upset you...'

Chapter Sixty-Nine

Tuesday, 12 January 2016

'One day they'll get themselves in real trouble. Honestly, Gray, I worry more about those two than I do about Mark and Nick.'

'Stella and Jack have already got themselves into trouble.' Graham, Jackie's husband of thirty years, was scrutinizing an instruction sheet. 'Stella can look after herself. I'd say Jack's the worry. You said he wanders the streets in the middle of the night. If he doesn't get attacked, he could be picked up by the police for acting suspiciously. Perhaps you should have a word? He'd listen to you.'

'Jack listens to no one on that subject.' Jackie took a hammer from a concertina tool box on the sofa amid boxes of books and ornaments. 'He once stopped the walking for Stella, but she felt bad for setting what amounted to a curfew and "released him".' Laid out on the carpet were the components of an IKEA 'oak-veneer' bookcase. Jackie knelt beside a length of wood and with clean strokes, hammered a dowel into a hole.

Graham frowned. 'There's a screw missing.'

'No! Jack's just quirky. He's sensitive – he feels *everything*. It makes him caring and empathetic, but means he suffers over the smallest thing. He's done well to get over his mum.' Tweaking the dowel, Jackie confirmed it held fast. Graham handed her another one. 'Not that he has got over it. He sees death everywhere.' She whacked in the dowel with one hammer stroke.

'I don't know what I'd do if something happened to them. I love Jack and Stella like they're ours.'

'They are ours.' Graham got up from the carpet and, grimacing, arched his back. 'I meant there's a screw missing from this pack.'

'I wonder if this time they've bitten off too much.' Jackie positioned another plank of wood. 'Helen Honeysett was murdered in 1987. People's memories can be inaccurate at the time, but now must be very hazy. They've never found that poor young woman's body – if she *was* murdered. Only a clairvoyant with the forensic patience of a saint could solve it.'

'A cleaner and a train driver, a crack detective team, who knew!' Graham lifted up a shelf board and regarded it with resignation.

'And all the time the murderer might still be out there.' Jackie cradled the hammer head, frowning.

'The plumber's dead and the police aren't looking for anyone else.' Graham pressed his thumbs into the small of his back and groaned. 'It's nearly midnight, let's call it a night and finish this tomorrow.' A surveyor for Hammersmith and Fulham Council, Graham Makepeace had considerable attention for detail, but it had been a long day and he had no patience with the incomprehensible instructions.

Jackie ignored him and with a free swing hammered in another dowel. Had she missed she would have dented the oak veneer. But as Graham was fond of saying Jackie hit the nail – literal or metaphorical – on the head every time.

'My money would have been on that Brian Judd in accounts.' He yawned. 'Talk about a screw missing: he used to scurry about the corridors like the White Rabbit. He always wore black even in summer. Saying that, he was a whizz with budgets, he once found me an extra—'

'I forgot he worked at your place!' Jackie gave the dowel a last tap.

'More than that. I was his alibi,' Graham said with faint pride.

'Oh course! You saw him in his office at the time Helen Honeysett was jogging on the towpath. You saved him! Living in that house on the river by himself, he was an obvious suspect.' Jackie scrabbled under the sofa and retrieved the missing screw.

'Barry says he did the IKEA shelves in his office on his own without using these. But my brother thinks he's Superman.' Graham shook his head at the instructions sheet.

'Don't knock him. Your brother *is* Superman. Barry's saved Clean Slate thousands in car and office insurance,' Jackie said. Graham's older brother was an insurance broker.

'I didn't see Brian Judd in his office. The light was on, his case was on the desk and his cardigan on the chair, so he was obviously there. Fancy a cuppa?'

'You told the police that you saw him.' Jackie held the hammer in her right hand, the screw in her left.

'I as good as did see him.' Graham Makepeace was studying the instructions.

'Graham, you're kidding me! "As good as" isn't seeing! Did you actually see Brian Judd there?'

'Well, no, but—'

Graham was interrupted by the peal of the doorbell. 'Who's calling at this time?' A shadow passed across Jackie's face. Late callers meant bad news. She had been saying she dreaded something bad happening to their sons or to Stella and Jack. Not superstitious, it occurred to her she had provoked the very thing she feared.

Graham went out to the hall. Heart thumping, holding the hammer, Jackie followed him. Her foreboding increased when she saw who was on the doorstep.

'Stella and Jack are in trouble.' Brandishing a decorated walking stick, Suzie Darnell narrowly missed Graham as she carved the air. 'Come now!'

'How do you know?' Jackie grabbed her coat.

'Mother's intuition.' Suzie thumped her chest. 'Stella's not answering her phone.'

'There's no signal down by the river...' Jackie stopped. She never doubted mother's intuition. 'Gray, ring the police.' She ushered Suzie down the path.

Jackie fired the remote key at the car and called out, 'And tell them Brian Judd no longer has an alibi for Helen Honeysett's murder!'

Chapter Seventy

Wednesday, 13 January 2016

Jack raced along the towpath towards Thames Cottages, all the while willing signal bars to appear on his phone. He didn't let himself think that there had never been a signal there before, so why should there be now? There had to be. He pictured Lucie's body, her fur coat soaked by the rising river. Already it was too late. *No!*

He ran up the path of number 1 and, as he reached the front door, a bar flickered on to the screen.

'Ambulance. Police. The Thames towpath by Kew Stairs. Now!' he shouted.

'Are you with the injured—'

The screen went black. His battery had died. He heard barking, faint, almost as if it was in his head. A week ago he'd heard a dog when he was outside Thames Cottages. He'd thought it sounded like Stanley. This time he knew it *was* Stanley. It was his distress signal.

Stella!

Jack scratched his key in the lock and flung the door wide. Pin-pricks of light on the staircase danced as he ran down to the basement. The River Wall swirled with the cold black water that was closing over Lucie.

All the glass panels were open. There was a rectangle of light at the end. *Stella was in the brick vault.*

'Do come in.' A genial host. Bathed in dingy light spilling from the bulb, the man was ethereal. Black suit, hair oiled and combed over his balding scalp. It was the man from Helen Honeysett's Christmas party photograph. Brian Judd. *The True Host.*

Jack's heart contracted. Daphne Merry was sitting on the digger. Jack had the wild idea that she was posing, then he saw the nylon cord binding her hands to the lever. Trussed up on the big yellow machine, Daphne Merry looked frail and confused. He went towards her.

'Jack, don't!' Stella was in the shadows by the passage, Stanley at her feet. He knew the expression in her eyes as if he could read her mind. *Don't try anything or he will kill us all.*

'Untie her.' Jack had to help Daphne.

'Leave her!' Judd's voice was metallic.

'Daphne wouldn't hurt you, Mr Judd.' Jack found he was fighting back tears. 'It's OK, Daphne. You're safe. I'll keep you safe.'

'Oh dear. I think there's been some mistake, young man. *Jack.* I may call you that. I feel we are old friends. Mr Judd is out there. Neville Rowlands, pleased to meet you. How nice you could join us.' His cold expression didn't match the warmth of his words.

'What?' Impressions tumbled around him. A black suit in a dry-cleaning bag. The atmosphere of evil in the house by the river. Brian Judd had a black suit.

'Jack, I should have told you. Lucie told me that the man in the photo with Steven Lawson wasn't Brian Judd. This is Neville Rowlands.'

Before he could answer Stella, Jack saw the knife. Stupidly he noticed that it was one of Natasha Latimer's Sabatiers. Rowlands was holding it to Daphne Merry's throat. Jack moved forward.

'Don't touch her!' Stella's voice was absorbed into the bricks.

'Daphne hasn't done anything,' he protested.

'She has.' Stella was deathly calm. Whose side was she on? Stanley's lips were pulled back in a snarl. He growled up at Daphne as if she was his mortal enemy.

'Daphne Merry murdered Helen Honeysett,' Stella said quietly.

'What?' Jack couldn't make sense of her words.

'She strangled her on the towpath. Helen never said hello when she jogged past her. And let her dog poo on the towpath. On top of everything else it was the last straw. She snapped,' Stella said.

'Your lady-love is ahead of you, chappie!' Rowlands gave a snuffling laugh.

'Then in 2012 she killed Brian Judd when he was walking his dog by the river. David and I rescued the dog. David named him Stanley.' Stella spoke mechanically. 'Brian Judd had called him Whisky.'

'They deserved it. They were lackadaisical, uncaring. Judd dropped litter, he put his rubbish out early and the cats and foxes ripped the bags open. That Honeysett girl didn't understand what Daphne had been through. She thought you could start again at the drop of a hat. I ensured Daphne didn't pay for her actions.' Rowlands was gazing up at Daphne Merry on the digger. 'I decluttered for you.'

'What did he do?' Stella was keeping Rowlands talking.

Jack moved closer to him, but Stella's expression warned him off again.

'If he had let that spoilt rich girl buy his run-down house on the river, I'd still be here. My greedy landlords sold my home to her instead. I enjoyed consigning Brian Judd to the cold earth.' Rowlands clinked the blade against the digger.

'Max died in 2012,' Stella said. 'You buried Judd in his grave?' Neville Rowlands was right. Jack felt his heart sink, Stella had got there before him. 'You buried Helen and Brian Judd in your pet cemetery.'

'That ground is sacred; they don't deserve to be there, but I had to keep Daphne safe.' Rowlands was chatty as if going over the pros and cons of a knotty problem. 'When Honeysett came back along the path, she didn't thank Daphne for clearing up her dog's mess. "Oh it's you!" She didn't even stop to talk. I was watching, I saw it all. Who did that bitch think she was? Daphne had to kill her.'

'I didn't kill anyone.' The voice didn't fit the fragile woman tied to the JCB. Jack's blood went cold. Her eyes were blank. Merry said, 'Max died in 2014 and your other dog called Hercules didn't die until the nineties. You lied.'

'Yes, dear. I did lie. I did it for you.' Rowlands was congenial. 'How lucky that I was nearby when you killed that girl. Your DNA would have been all over her. Without a body, our venerable constabulary were stumped. But then you went and took Honeysett's dog back. You had no care for yourself. That was stupid.'

'I didn't kill anyone.' Daphne repeated the phrase. Seated upon the gleaming yellow digger she was an automaton. 'There was no body. There was nothing. I looked over at the seat and it was empty. She wasn't in the car. Gerald was still asleep, as if he didn't have a care in the world. My baby wasn't in the car. She was the most beautiful girl in the world. Not a scratch on her.'

Daphne spoke as if in a trance, unaware that there was anyone else there. She was unaware of Rowlands or of anyone. She was back at the accident on the A23, as if reliving it. Jack knew that for her, that day was when life had stopped.

'It was clever getting the little girl to implicate her father. He *was* guilty. Living on the never-never, thinking he was a cut above. You and I kept our secret for nearly thirty years. It was a precious pact.'

This seemed to bring Daphne Merry to life. She twisted on the seat. 'I made no pact with you, you unmitigated fool. You are a petty little creature trailing after me like some foolish mongrel. Helen Honeysett was careless and frivolous. Like Gerald. *Untie me now!*' Daphne Merry jerked her bound hands, forcing one of the levers up. The bucket lifted up with a hideous squeal and then crashed down. Jack felt the building vibrate. He heard creaks. Yet the digger wasn't moving.

'I dragged that girl along the towpath into my garden. I spent the entire night digging her grave – the ground was like concrete.

Mother kept calling for me. If the police had come, they would have seen the freshly turned soil. But they suspected the husband and it was his garden they dug up. They knew you and I are law-abiding citizens upholding standards against a permissive tide.' Neville Rowlands brandished the knife.

The police would be on the towpath. They would be looking for the man who'd made the 999 call. Even with his mobile phone off, they could track his GPS. A woman had been attacked: they would be doing house-to-house calls. It was only a matter of time, Jack assured himself.

There was a thud. The vault door had shut. The single low-wattage bulb hanging from the ceiling made ghosts of them all.

'I removed your clutter. It was as if those murders never happened.' White-faced, Rowlands seemed to have shrunk. 'You owe me your life.'

'You are a fantasist. A menace who walks the towpath without a dog. I took pity on you for pretending your dog was alive. I know what it is to lose a loved one. But you are pathetic!'

Daphne Merry truly believed that she had not killed Helen Honeysett or Brian Judd. She had walked away. She had twisted truth to suit herself. Neville Rowlands had cleared up her mess.

More creaks. And groaning. Stanley made a sound Jack had never heard before. A strange call, high and long. Sifts of dust trickled from the walls. Suddenly Jack understood the creaking. He yelled to Stella, '*Get out!*' Dust filled his windpipe. He lunged at her.

There was an ear-splitting roar. Caterpillar tracks trundled towards Jack; the giant claw blotted out the light. Neville Rowlands stepped into its path, the Sabatier blade thrust at the figure tied to the seat of the JCB. Jack glimpsed the kindly woman who had brought him home-made Jamaican ginger cake.

He tried to wrench Rowlands out of the way of the digger, but snatched at dusty air. The two men tumbled in front of the machine. The walls of the vault shook. Jack was aware only of Stanley licking his face.

Chapter Seventy-One

Wednesday, 13 January 2016

An ambulance was outside the Greyhound Pub on Kew Green, blue lights strobing. Jackie pulled in a few metres behind it.

'Stella!' Suzie flung herself out of the car with the nimble agility of Stanley's handler. Jackie caught up with Suzie outside Thames Cottages. A huddle of people were coming from the towpath end.

Jackie saw the paramedics. 'Suzie, get out of the way!' *Please let it not be Stella or Jack.*

'That's my daughter you've got there!' Suzie bellowed as if apprehending kidnappers.

The paramedic at the head of the stretcher was terse. 'Madam, I need you to stand back.'

'Her name's Stella Darnell, she was born on the twelfth of August 1966 in Hammersmith Hospital, she has no allergies—'

'Suzie...' Jackie took her arm.

'No it is not!' Bette Lawson's voice cracked. 'This is Lucille Florence May. My... my sister.' She was clutching the hand of an inert shape under a blanket on the stretcher.

'Lucie!' Suzie was immediately concerned. 'Oh my God! What happened?'

'Suzie.' Jackie was firm. 'Let's find Stella and Jack.'

Despite her distress, Bette Lawson must have heard. She said, 'A tall man rang for the ambulance. He never came back.'

'He never came back!' Suzie shouted. 'There's someone out there attacking my little girl and you never thought to—'

'*Suzie!*' Jackie grabbed Suzie Darnell by the shoulders. This was a risk; their relationship was fragile. 'She might be at the cottage.' With a sick sensation, Jackie registered that number 1 Thames Cottages was unlit. Why had she listened to Suzie Darnell? What the hell was 'mother's intuition'? When Nick broke his leg on stage in *Mamma Mia*, she'd had no idea until he phoned from hospital the next day.

Suzie was leaning on the doorbell, her ear to the door. She thumped the wood. The door held fast.

'Why did you think Stella was here?'

'Where else would she be!' Suzie retorted. 'She has killed them.'

Jackie felt a shock of fear. 'Who has?'

'Daphne decluttering fucking Merry. That woman ripped out my soul. She destroys lives.'

'She made Jack a cake!' Jackie heard how bonkers that sounded. From somewhere within she heard a squeaking and creaks. She looked about her, but the narrow pavement was empty. 'Did you hear that?'

Suzie aimed a kick at the door, scuffing the wood.

There were footsteps on the towpath. Jackie braced herself. A shadow slanted down the steps.

'Mum, what are you doing here? Jackie?' Stella paused in the cone of light from the lamp-post. She was panting as if she'd been running. 'Call the police!'

'Stella! You're all right!' Jackie saw that Stella was not all right. Her face was white as a sheet and she was trembling as if she was freezing cold. Jackie delved into her bag and fished out a foil thermal blanket. She shook it out and draped it around Stella's shoulders.

'This is a dead zone.' Stella started off along the pavement. 'I'll ask Adam to use his phone.'

'I've got a signal.' Suzie was waving her handset as if flagging down a speeding train.

'Dial 999. *Now!*' Stella came back.

Suzie spoke into her handset. 'Hello, there. Police please.' She seemed to have regained her composure.

Stella seized the phone from her. 'And an ambulance. Hurry or Jack will die!'

The creaking Jackie had heard was louder. It was like the approach of a juggernaut. She wheeled around. 'Where is that coming from?'

'The bloody house is caving in!' Suzie shouted.

Stella was running up the steps to the river, the blanket flying out behind her like Batman's cape. '*Jack!*'

Jackie would later have only a patchy memory of that night. She had flashbacks of plumes of dust and grit. Of slabs of brick wall crashing down and of the constant smashing of glass. Stella had fought with them to go into a tunnel that was concealed deep in thick bushes and was all that remained of Natasha Latimer's cottage. As she and Suzie struggled to keep hold of Stella, Jackie had had only one thought. They must not let go of her or she would die. Later she would tell Graham she wondered if she'd imagined that Stella cried, '*Jack's inside, I must get to him, I love him!*'

Chapter Seventy-Two

Wednesday, 13 January 2016

Stella pictured the vault. In the dusty circle of light Daphne Merry, a ghastly exhibit in a museum of horrors, was strapped to the bright yellow excavator. Stella had let Jack push her on into the tunnel thinking – *stupid* – he was right behind her. That wasn't Jack. He'd never leave anyone in trouble. He'd saved her from Neville Rowlands and tried to save Daphne Merry. He had risked his life for a murderer. The booms were as thunderous as cannon fire. Stella launched herself at the tunnel entrance. Strong hands held her. She yelled, but thick dust choked her. Jack would not hear her.

The upper floors collapsed down into the basement. Stella heard Terry's bedtime-story voice: *'If you're captured, play dead. Only try to escape if you're certain of success or things are desperate.'*

Things were desperate. She went limp and dropped her head. When the grip on her arms loosened she made a dash for it. But where *it* should be was a pile of rubble.

She was recaptured and this time held fast.

A figure drifted out of the fog. Ghostly white, it floated along the towpath. Stella's legs gave way.

'Jack!' She shut her eyes. Her mind was playing the meanest of tricks.

'It's OK, Stell.'

*

She dared to look. The 'ghost' was smothered with brick dust and plaster. She rushed to Jack. He caught her. She felt wet against her cheek. He was crying. Hazily she thought she'd never seen him cry.

'It's OK, Jack. It's all right. It's OK, Jack. It's...' A mantra.

'Stell, it's not OK...' He was shaking. 'I couldn't... *Stanley*...'

Stella held Jack's head between her hands and he sobbed.

Chapter Seventy-Three

Saturday, 16 January 2016

CRAZED PENSIONER KILLED
HELEN HONEYSETT
By Alan Porter

A mystery nearly thirty years old has been solved. Daphne Merry masqueraded as a declutterer, entered people's houses and stole their ornaments and treasured keepsakes. We all get irritated if our neighbours drop litter, accidentally open our post or leave dog's mess on the pavement. But for the regular church-goer these were terrible crimes. In 1986 Gerald Merry fell asleep at the wheel and drove the family car off the road, killing himself and their seven-year-old daughter. His widow couldn't punish him for careless driving; instead she wreaked carnage on the innocent.

One winter's night in 1987 Merry was walking her dog along the Thames towpath. She greeted her neighbour, 27-year-old Helen Honeysett. The promising young estate agent, wired to her Sony Walkman, jogging with her dog, didn't hear. Merry considered herself snubbed. When Helen returned along the lonely riverside track, the declutterer strangled her in cold blood and took her dog.

In 2012 another neighbour, retired finance officer at Hammersmith and Fulham Council Brian Judd, paid the ultimate price for failing to pick up his dog's waste. Judd's poodle was found by a courting

416

couple. Whisky was unclaimed. Judd was an elderly recluse who walked his dog after dark: no one missed him.

In the early hours of Wednesday morning Merry met her nemesis. Neville Rowlands (65) an ex-tenant of Thames Cottages, the little terrace known locally as 'Death's Pavement', lured her into the newly dug basement of property developer Natasha Latimer. Obsessed by Merry, Rowlands had stalked her for decades. He witnessed both her murders and removed the bodies. With no body, police had no clues to the killer or, in Judd's case, no evidence of a murder.

Certain his lust was mutual Rowlands told the murderess he'd 'decluttered' for her. She laughed in his face and, in frenzied dismay, he tied her to a JCB digger and tried to stab her with a kitchen knife. Fate intervened. The foundations of Latimer's deep basement crumbled and the evil couple were crushed to death under a ton of rubble.

Police forensics officers excavated a pet cemetery in the property's back garden and unearthed gruesome remains. Helen and Brian Judd were buried in the graves marked with dogs' headstones, Hercules and Max. Merry claimed to have no memory of the murders. Experts confirm it's possible for a person to erase a trauma from their mind as if it never happened. But Daphne Merry did retain one memory. As she stole their precious knick-knacks, she told clients how she'd found her child's lifeless body by the side of the A23.

The case was solved by Stella Darnell, cleaner turned detective. In a statement, she said she hoped the families of Helen Honeysett and Brian Judd would find closure.

Jack laid down that week's edition of the *Chronicle* and resumed cleaning out the grate in what had been his mother's den. He heard creaking and paused, the shovel of ash in his hand. Since the collapse of Latimer's cottage, he was alive to the slightest sound in his own house. He reminded himself that although the house in St Peter's Square was old, the foundations were firm. He tipped the ash into a bin bag and gave the grate a final sweep.

Alan Porter was no stranger to sensational prose or inaccuracy. He liked to think that Lucie wouldn't have written so unsympathetically about Daphne Merry. Daphne had been a genuine declutterer, he wanted to protest. He wanted to argue that, poisoned by tragedy, she'd struggled to bring light and air to others' lives. Nor had she stolen the 'clutter'. Stella confirmed Daphne used to give unwanted things to the hospice shop. The headline was probably the work of the editor for whom Lucie reserved her most pernicious insults, but Jack had to admit it could have been Lucie's. No, she would not have spared Daphne.

Jack was engulfed by a wash of sadness. Lucie was another of Merry's victims. Her rapier mind poisoned by the case, she'd lost objectivity and deeply wounded her sister and her family. Daphne had destroyed not just those she killed, but those caught in the backwash.

Jack regarded the pan of ashes. He too was guilty. A True Host had been right there and, wooed by Jamaican ginger cake and soothing tones, he'd failed to recognize her. Daphne Merry hadn't erased the trauma of murder from her mind: she had not been traumatized. She had murdered and moved on.

Earlier that day, Jack had returned to the river. It was early evening and already dark. The lamp-post at the top of the steps to the towpath was lit. He had walked along to the dilapidated house where Brian Judd had lived with his dog Whisky. After a few minutes, Jack walked back along the path to the streetlamp. There was no one on the narrow pavement beside the cottages. The park was dark and silent. He knocked on the door of the end cottage.

Sybil Lofthouse opened the door immediately. She showed no surprise. It was as if she had been expecting the tall man in the dark coat, half hidden in shadow. 'You'd better come in.' She shut the door after him.

★

Jack was jolted into the present. He was due at Stella's to debrief. He slotted the newspaper into the case file and carried it downstairs.

In the hall the polished newel post gleamed in thin light seeping through the fanlight. There was no shadow on the newly painted wall – white, nothing controversial, people's tastes varied. Jack held his breath.

> *One, two,*
> *Buckle my shoe;*
> *Three, four,*
> *Open the door...*

The voice in his head was his own. He put the file on the marble-topped table. There was a grey outline where the mirror had hung. His mother always checked her reflection when leaving or arriving home. That July morning, before they walked to the river, she had examined the cut on her forehead. She never came home.

> *Five, six,*
> *Pick up sticks;*
> *Seven, eight,*
> *Lay them straight...*

Stella and Jack had eaten two bowlfuls of Stella's lamb stew. Since looking after Suzie, Stella had started doing some cooking. Her brother Dale had emailed her the recipe.

'Hot milk with honey?' Stella held up a carton of milk.

'Could I have a cup of tea?' he asked.

'Sure.' Stella betrayed no surprise. She popped a tea bag into the London Transport mug she reserved for him and added hot water.

On the table beside the case file was a copy of the report they'd given Adam Honeysett on their investigation into his wife's murder. The report had been true teamwork. Jack wrote the first draft. Stella trimmed his screeds of description (... *on dark winter mornings, the towpath is deserted. Lights on the north bank of the Thames accentuate the darkness...*); she extracted facts and bullet-pointed them under headings. Beverly did the formatting and Jackie the proofreading. Beverly bound the document with the fearsome wire-binder machine at which she was expert. Jackie had calculated Honeysett's invoice because left to Stella – and Jack – the job would have been pro bono.

'I still reckon you solved the case.' Sitting sideways at the table, Jack stretched out his long legs towards the fridge. 'I was sure Brian Judd was the True... the murderer. I thought he was the man in the Honeysetts' party photo because he wore a suit.'

'Why did that make you think it was him?' Stella joined him at the table.

'Brian Judd had a black suit in his wardrobe.' He took a mouthful of tea; it was too hot to swallow. His eyes watered. 'I went into the house by myself. Before you and I went there.'

'I know,' Stella said quietly. 'Graham said that Judd always wore black at work. He's sick with himself for giving him an alibi. I said anyone could have done it. When I see Jackie's bag in the office, I assume she's around. Not that she'd murder anyone.'

'I went into Judd's house without asking him.' Jack tried again. Stella wasn't getting the point. He had broken the law.

'Brian Judd was dead. He didn't know you were there. If you want to kill someone a good trick is to leave your coat and bag where people expect you to be.' Stella sipped her tea and recalled his earlier comment. 'Sybil Lofthouse gave me a clue it was Daphne Merry at our first meeting, only I didn't get the significance of her remark. She said she'd seen Merry on the towpath with Helen Honeysett's dog. How had she? Lofthouse said she went out *before* Helen and was by Kew Stairs. Daphne Merry claimed to have found Helen's dog by Mortlake Crematorium. I believe her. She never lied. She left Helen and Judd's bodies on the towpath where they could have been found. I think Sybil Lofthouse saw

Steven on the Kew Stairs and then saw Daphne Merry murder Helen Honeysett.'

'Wouldn't Neville Rowlands have seen her?' Jack suddenly knew that Stella's hunch was right.

'Rowlands was watching Merry. But Merry could have seen Lofthouse,' Stella said. 'Although if she had she'd have killed her to stop her telling the police.'

'She wasn't bothered about being caught. Daphne Merry was the perfect murderer. She had absolutely no sense of other. She killed and she moved on. Absurd though it sounds she might still have despised Lofthouse for being a bystander. She knew Lofthouse had watched her kill Helen and done nothing.'

'We'll never get Lofthouse to confess,' Stella said.

'She'll carry that secret to the grave,' Jack agreed. 'Whenever she dies,' he added.

'At the least if Merry knew Lofthouse had seen Steven Lawson on the steps by the river she knew she was a bystander. Everyone was watching everyone, but nobody saw anything.'

'Merry had luck on her side. Megan mistook Merry's voice saying "Oh, it's you!" for Helen and assumed she was talking to her dad. If she'd known it was Merry, she would have told the police and alerted them to another suspect. Thank God Suzie had that intuition about you being in trouble,' Jack said.

'Hardly intuition. Mum thinks I'm in trouble if I don't answer her texts or call right away. And it was too late. By then I was in Latimer's house trapped by Rowlands. You rescued me. You saved my life.'

Jack pulled a face. 'Anytime!'

Stella flicked through the pages of their report. 'It's extra-ordinary Daphne Merry didn't try to hide the body. Either of them. If Rowlands hadn't buried Helen Honeysett for her it's likely she'd have been caught.'

'I doubt she'd have cared. The crowning event in Daphne's life was the death of her little girl. She lacked empathy. It made her a good declutterer. She didn't get attached to things or, apart from her daughter, people.' She hadn't brought him a cake to be nice. She was nobody's mother. She'd wanted to see inside Latimer's house, to check for clutter. He said, 'Rowlands mistook her lying to the police as their tacit understanding he'd "decluttered" for her. He kept Judd's house going, opened the post, paid bills and, after Latimer got him out, he stayed in there. He needed a reason to come to the towpath. He couldn't keep a dog in his bedsit, so took Whisky's lead and poo-bags.' Jack couldn't say that this was why he'd sensed evil in the house. Evil had gone now.

'I assumed he had a dog because the lead strung across his chest made him looked like a dog walker.' Stella gave a sigh. 'Rowlands must have got a shock when he saw Stanley and realized he was Brian Judd's dog.'

'Stanley witnessed a murder,' Jack breathed.

They turned to look at the little poodle. He lay in his bed, all four paws in the air. He had known trauma. Would Stanley forget that he had been trapped in the ruins of Natasha Latimer's basement for over twenty-four hours? They'd thought he was dead. Stanley had been found under the digger bucket; it had protected him from falling masonry and provided an air pocket. Suzie had given Stella a cutting from the *Sun* headlined *JCB Saves Poodle*.

'Merry said she wanted clients to have light and air. Maybe she cared a bit,' Stella mused as she watched her dog.

'She wanted light and air for herself. If Suzie had been in the room with Daphne when she asked for her stuff back she could have been her third victim. I know that flash of fury when someone cuts you up driving or pushes in to a queue. I've imagined killing someone who lets their dog poo and doesn't pick it up. Daphne did it.' Stella would never want to kill someone and certainly not for a petty reason.

'Me too.' Stella was still looking at Stanley. 'David was too scared to ask for his things back. He said she'd kill him.'

Jack had a lot more to find out about Stella.

'This case has been all about dogs,' Stella said eventually.

'Merry wouldn't have killed Helen if Baxter hadn't pooed on the path and she hadn't left it there. Dad used to say a detective must "get to know" the murdered person. Mum said that was blaming the victim. He said the victim was ground zero. Someone who lived and loved, like you and me. It wasn't just about getting them justice; he worked to restore the person they had been when they were alive so they didn't become known only for how they had died. What we've learnt about Helen Honeysett is that she was tactless and thoughtless and careless.'

'Fair enough. We all have flaws. She was also lovable, incorrigible and full of energy. She wanted people to be happy. If she'd been alive today I'm betting she would have found Natasha Latimer the perfect house without upsetting anyone.'

'The families can have closure.' Stella echoed the words of the press release that Jackie had insisted she put out. 'We always suspected Helen was dead within hours of going out to the towpath.'

Like Helen Honeysett, Stella could say it how it was. 'He'll have to find another way to make peace with her for his affair,' Jack said. 'An affair isn't a heinous crime, it took on enormity because she was murdered. She would have had an affair with Steven Lawson if he'd been up for it. Her death lent his infidelities an unmerited darkness.' He got up and filled the kettle. 'I still say you solved this case. You worked out it was Merry.'

'If you'd been with me when I first bumped into Sybil Lofthouse, you'd have spotted the comment about her seeing Merry by Mortlake Crematorium and worked out she could have alibied Lawson. I wrote it down but didn't grasp the significance. She had *seen* Merry. And if I'd taken you with me to interview Neville Rowlands you would have recognized the photo of Daphne Merry under his divan. And seen that he was the man in the black suit. I forgot to show you the sweatband Stanley found in Latimer's basement. If I had you'd have known straight away that it belonged to Helen Honeysett: you would have recalled the pictures from the reconstruction.'

'If I had recognized it, you'd have insisted we show it to Martin Cashman. He'd have taken the case over.'

'Would that have mattered as long as the case was solved?'

'Who says he would have solved it? You did fine, Stell. Just fine.'

Stella and Jack had disagreed about how to express the discovery of the killer in their report. Stella had cut Jack's bit about her deducing Daphne Merry murdered Helen Honeysett and rewrote it to include them both.

'It's the truth,' he had argued.

'"There is truth and truth."' Stella quoted words that Jack had once said to her back to him. 'We're a team. I still don't get why Rowlands left the dog collar in the digger.'

'It was Whisky's collar. Perhaps it was a sign to us that Brian Judd was in his grave.'

'He probably dropped it by mistake.' Stella couldn't do with everything being a sign.

'Neville Rowlands' only mistake was believing Daphne Merry loved him. Otherwise he was meticulous in everything he did.'

'Fancy loving someone so much you literally let them get away with murder.' Stella decanted the rest of the stew into a plastic freezer bag and sealed it. She washed the pan. 'So much for Claudia and her haunting theory. Most of the time the squeaking wasn't even Rowlands controlling the digger arm. It was the house straining on the compromised foundations. Graham said the signs would have been apparent long before it collapsed.'

'Claudia wasn't wrong. Helen Honeysett was buried in the garden at number one. She was haunting it. Now at least she can be at peace.'

'Wait a minute.' Stella snapped off her marigolds. She opened the box containing all their notes and the papers on the Honeysett file. She pulled out the photocopy of the diary and ran her finger down the first page. 'There!' Stella slid the copy over the table to Jack.

'"Saw Nev R. He greeted me like I didn't know him." What does that mean?' Again Stella was ahead of him.

'Do you know who I am and what I have done?' Stella snagged the marigolds into a plastic holder on the side of the sink. 'The line wasn't Steven Lawson's. He was *quoting*. What if that's what Rowlands said to him on the towpath? Rowlands couldn't tell Lawson the truth or Daphne Merry would be arrested for murder, but maybe couldn't live with Lawson taking the rap for something he hadn't done. He gave him a sign.'

'A sign!' Jack was jubilant, Stella was seeing signs. 'Steven didn't get the significance of Rowlands' question. Rowlands' love for Daphne destroyed him. He was consumed with evil. Like Suzie, he'd lost track of who he was. *Who am I and what have I done?*'

'Why didn't Steven Lawson just write, "It's Neville Rowlands"?' Stella passed Jack the tea bags. 'That's what I'd do.'

'You've never been suicidal or lived under a cloud of suspicion for murder. Lawson felt bankrupted in all ways. He walked into the freezing river, not as a cry for help, but to die. This question was all he could manage. He left it for others to decipher. He left it for *us!*' Jack added milk to their mugs of tea. 'And it wasn't Neville Rowlands. Maybe Lawson was a fair-minded man unwilling to point the finger without proof.'

'Bette has achieved her ambition to clear Steven's name.' Stella bundled the tea towel into the pan and rubbed it dry.

'At a terrible cost,' Jack whispered.

He returned to the table with the tea. They drank in silence. The bells of St Peter's Church struck eleven o'clock.

Chapter Seventy-Four

Monday, 18 January 2016

The hearse pulled under the arch outside the crematorium chapel. The pall-bearers came forward. One, a woman in a modish hat with a fantail, unfolded a black-draped gurney and trundled it to the rear of the vehicle. Jack and Stella stood close together as the bearers transferred the coffin – dark oak with silver handles – on to it and, stepping away, bowed to the coffin. This triggered a storm of camera shutters and flashes from press photographers corralled behind a barrier.

Instinctively Jack moved into the shadow of the arch. Stella kept close to him. Like him, she wouldn't want her picture taken. If Lucie had had anything to do with it, Stella would have been all over the front page. Or maybe Lucie would have respected Stella's wish for anonymity. She, like Stella, had never failed to surprise him.

When he heard that the funeral would be at Mortlake, Jack doubted Stella would attend. She'd been reluctant to go to Terry Darnell's funeral – he was cremated at Mortlake – although last year she did make it to the funeral of her friend Tina. Jack's mother had been buried. He had no clear memory of the ceremony, but he'd visited her grave and sat in the empty country church imagining he could hear her singing.

Nine, ten,
A big, fat hen;
Eleven, twelve,
Dig and delve...

The service passed in a blur. During the second verse of the hymn 'Before the Ending of the Day', Jack got a tickle in his nose and sneezed, drowning out the words:

'*... from nightly fears and fantasies;*
tread underfoot our ghostly foe,
that no pollution we may know...'

Stella handed him a tissue. She wasn't even misty-eyed. Some might have mistaken her cool demeanour for lack of feeling; Jack knew better. Stella handled painful emotions with cleaning jobs. The tissue reminded him that he'd met Bella at a funeral; she too had given him a tissue, assuming he was mourning the deceased. He told her later he'd been crying for his mother. Meeting Bella at a sad occasion was a bad sign – perhaps it had doomed their relationship? He had met Stella during a murder case. Was their relationship doomed too?

A loud sniff from along the pew. Stella drew out another tissue from her 'handy' pack and passed it to Bette Lawson. Mouthing silent thanks, Bette passed it on and, taking it, Lucie May blew her nose with a trumpeting snort. She grimaced at her niece Megan, seated on her other side. Her nephew Garry maintained a stolid disregard, a frown furrowing his brow. Lucie had started weeping as soon as the coffin was placed on the catafalque and hadn't stopped throughout the service. Jack understood. Lucie had planted herself amid her family, but the reconciliation was shaky. She had much to cry about.

As if Lucie blowing her nose were the 'last post', Helen Honeysett's coffin jerked through the curtain-framed aperture to the crematorium oven. The chapel filled with the plodding chords of 'Every Breath You Take'. The sinister song struck Jack as an unsuitable send-off for a woman who had been murdered. He supposed Adam Honeysett had chosen it.

Helen's body had been exhumed from the grave in which she had lain, under the guise of 'Hercules', since 1987. Brian Judd had been discovered beside Max. The police had dug up the other graves and a bone expert confirmed the skeletons interred were canine. Judd had been given what undertakers dubbed a 'Direct Disposal'. No cars, no flowers, no mourners. What the recluse would have wanted, Jack guessed.

He glanced at Stella to see what she was making of Sting's haunting anthem and was stunned to see a tear rolling down her cheek. Perhaps Stella would always surprise him. Perhaps he would never know her.

'Nippet o'clock, darlings!' Leaning on her sister's arm, Lucie May waved her intricately decorated walking stick topped with a gold snake's head – superior to Suzie's stick – like a rallying flag. She huddled from the cold in a bright green wool coat, a replacement for what Jackie called her 'fur monstrosity', which had been ruined by the Thames.

Bette Lawson put her hand on Lucie's arm. 'Come back to ours.'

'Is that OK?' Lucie May looked at Garry Lawson.

'It will be,' Bette mouthed.

'It's one hell of a tall ladder to climb to the top of your tree, Gaz.' Lucie gave her nephew a timorous smile. Jack felt for her brave bluster.

'I'm not bothered.' Garry pawed at the ground, head down. He had forgiven Megan, but would he be able to forgive his aunt?

'There's only one person to blame for this and that's Daphne Merry.' Bette Lawson nodded at the crematorium where Adam Honeysett was surrounded by journalists. So they'd got to him in the end, Jack observed. Honeysett had got what he wanted. They had found his wife. How would he live now?

Lucie had also seen Honeysett. She became animated. Jack saw her curb herself, perhaps recalling she was at Helen Honeysett's funeral to support her family, not as a roving reporter.

'Shame about that old lady,' Lucie said chattily. 'Police think she lost her footing.'

'What old lady?' Stella asked.

'Sybil Lofthouse. She drowned in the Thames. They think she slipped. They fished her out by Hammersmith Bridge. That sod of an editor's given the story to Frog of the Pond, Porter. I said I'd do it, but he said it's too close to home after what I've been through. I said, I don't live in the effing Thames, it's not my home and getting mugged is par for the whatsit! I'm over it!'

'Lofthouse is dead?' Stella exclaimed. 'How could she slip? She had no reason to go there, she didn't have a dog.'

'If she did slip.' Lucie tapped her stick on the ground in satisfied punctuation.

'I guess that's that then.' Stella looked at Jack. He held her gaze, keeping his face expressionless.

Eventually Stella said to him, 'We have to get going. We're collecting Stanley from my mum's and taking him for a walk.'

This was the first Jack had heard about the plan. But as Stella said it, he saw that taking the little dog for a walk with Stella was exactly what he wanted to do.

Epilogue

It was a perfect spring afternoon. Fluffy clouds hung in a turquoise sky. Thames Cottages were picturesque, roses trailing around doors, the laburnum outside the Lawsons' in flower. The park was washed in evening sunlight that coloured daffodils, violas and tulips in the beds vivid reds, purples and yellows.

Jack and Stella sat on Steven Lawson's bench. Stanley lay between them, head on paws, his lazy gaze fixed on a blackbird hopping along the branch of an oak tree by the entrance. The 'No Dogs' rule had been circumnavigated by Jack carrying Stanley. He'd maintained it didn't count if Stanley's paws didn't touch the ground.

'He's still in the park.' Stella, nervous of by-laws, had argued.

'The only person likely to object is Daphne Merry and she's dead.' Jack lapsed into silence.

Stella reread the plaque on the bench.

STEVEN LAWSON, A SPECIAL HUSBAND AND DAD
1952–1987

It might be an idea to get a bench for Terry. She frowned. A bench would mean he was dead. Which of course he was... She blinked and looked over the hedge.

It was now possible to see all the cottages from the bench.

When it came out that Neville Rowlands had cut a hole in the privet to watch Daphne Merry's house, residents and local parents petitioned for the height of the hedge to be lowered.

Stanley was interested in the blackbird, now hopping about on the grass near them.

Jack began rolling a cigarette. He didn't smoke; Jackie said he found the procedure soothing. But if he didn't smoke them, why was there room for more cigarettes in the case? Stella thought. A smoker couldn't rid themselves of the smell of smoke. Jack smelled of soap and clean fabric.

'Bella must be pleased. You know, now you're back in your house and can have visitors.' Stella had decided she should get to know Bella since Jack liked her. She slipped Stanley a liver treat to divert his attention from the blackbird.

Jack crossed his ankles, his face hidden behind a flop of hair. 'It's over with Bella.' He wheeled a bunch of tobacco along the Rizla paper.

The blackbird swooped off the branch to a flower bed a few metres away. Stanley was still watching it. Stella said, 'I'm sorry.'

'Don't be.' Jack recrossed his legs at the ankles. He too was watching the blackbird. 'She said she has to do the next bit on her own.'

What next bit? Stella changed the subject: 'I was thinking of changing Stanley's name back to Whisky. He does answer to it.'

'He answers to "Chicken" and "Biscuit". Maybe leave it as it is? He knows Stanley is his name. My name's Jonathan. Only my mum called me that and only when she was being strict.' Jack sat up straight. Startled by the movement, the blackbird flew back to the oak tree. He enquired airily, 'Did you take Thingummy-Thing's stuff back to him yesterday?'

'Yes.' Jack still couldn't say David's name, real or not. Stella shifted on the bench and Stanley, assuming they were off, stood up, stretched and shook himself. Most of the contents of Daphne Merry's lounge had belonged to David Barlow.

After Martin Cashman had told Stella that no one had

reported Stanley missing, shocked by David's lie, she'd erased his contact from her phone. She had found his number on her mum's customer database and rung to ask if he wanted his possessions back.

'Yes! I've lost all sense of myself. It's like a death.'

When Stella had arrived at Aldensley Road, David reiterated his request that she deep clean. This time Stella had no hesitation in refusing. He'd called out as she was getting into her van, 'Stella, there's something I must tell you.'

She had been about to say she didn't want to hear, but David was speaking: 'I never told the police we found Stanley. I wanted to keep him. He would be our dog. Yours and mine. I lied to you.'

'I know you did.' Stella drove away.

Stella gave Stanley another liver treat although the blackbird had gone.

Jack licked along the Rizla; sealing it, he laid the cigarette in his case. 'Let's go!' He snapped the case shut.

Stanley gave a gleeful bark and leapt off the bench. Stella caught him before he landed on the grass and swung him on to her shoulder. 'Go where?' She latched the park gate after them.

'This way.'

A typical Jack answer, but with Jack, as with Lucie May, it was better not to probe.

A three-metre-high hoarding on the corner of Thames Cottages hid the crater that had been Natasha Latimer's cottage. Stella knew the dog cemetery was a mass of churned-up soil, the headstones stacked against the wall. Repeated along each panel of the hoarding was an image of the proposed house. A legend read, *A quaint three-bedroom Victorian-style cottage in keeping with adjacent properties.* An inset diagram showed three downstairs rooms, two bedrooms on the second floor and an attic bedroom. There was no basement.

'If Natasha Latimer had been content to live in the house as it was, she might have been happy,' Jack remarked. 'Greed drove her to want more and she's ended up with nothing.'

Stella snorted. 'No one in this street is happy, with or without a basement.' She faced reality head on. Apart from the Lawsons, for their own private reasons, everyone in Thames Cottages had played a part in Helen Honeysett's death.

The basement company had gone bust so couldn't pay Latimer compensation for what Graham dubbed as 'grossly incompetent' building work. She owed over a million pounds in demolition and legal costs. Claudia said it was only money. She'd inveigled her sister to join her at a drumming festival in Wales. 'I promised Nats she can have her own yurt.'

At the lamp-post by the top of the towpath steps, Stella decided she'd invite Jack for his tea. She was a dab hand at omelettes now. Stanley tugged on his lead and broke free. He shot along the towpath. She groaned, 'I don't believe it! I should have known he'd do that.'

'He'll be fine.' Jack seemed unperturbed. 'We know where he's going.'

'There are people living there!' She hadn't been to the towpath since January. The house was no longer dilapidated. The stucco had been replaced and painted a warm cream that glowed in the warm evening sun. She could see figures in the downstairs rooms. The cobwebs and dirt had gone. A tea towel hanging beside the porch rather spoilt the effect. Stanley was sitting on the doormat, lead trailing, waiting to go inside.

'Come on, Stanley. This isn't where you live now.' Stella felt a pang. Stanley must miss Brian Judd and his home by the river. She waved a liver treat. He didn't notice. The front door was flung open.

'Oh! It's you,' Stella exclaimed. 'What are you doing here?'

'Waiting for you!' Jackie clapped her hands. A crowd spilled out of the brightly lit hall on to the path – the dried leaves on the floor had gone. Stella saw her mum; Lucie May was perched on a shooting stick beside Bette Lawson. Garry and Megan were behind them. Graham Makepeace picked up Stanley. Beverly swooped forward with a cake ablaze with candles. She lifted it and a sudden breeze blew out all the flames.

'Dale gave me his secret fruit-cake recipe!' Suzie crowed.

'You're all trespassing.' Stella was appalled. 'Who owns this house?

'I do!' With a flourish Jack whipped the tea towel from off the wall. 'I took your advice, Stell, I sold my parents' house in St Peter's Square. I've left my ghosts behind!'

Stella read out the words on a grey slate plaque: '"Stanley's House".'

'Now Stanley can come here whenever he likes.' Jack took Stella's hand and led her inside. 'You both can.'

Acknowledgements

The inspiration for this novel came from Alfred, our poodle. A fluffy, sometimes irascible writing companion, he's part model for Stanley. My working day is structured around dog walks and many Mondays end with his agility class.

A big thank you to top canine behaviourist and trainer Michelle Garvey of Essentially Paws for her work with Alfred. His family – and Stanley – are all the better for it...

My thanks go to the best of dog walkers; as we pace through the shadows in various groups, before dawn and over fields in all weathers, our discussions range far, from the state of the world to *The Archers* and *Bake Off*, and we swap nuggets of dog wisdom. So, here's to: Ian Anderson, Teresa Andow, Clare Biggs, John Gower, Nikki Gower, Gillian Hamer, Alayne Hayward-Tapp, Simon Hayward-Tapp, Margaret Healy, Tom Healy, John Hughes, Lucy Hughes, Miranda Kemp, Jillian Oborne, Martha Oborne, Isabel Oborne, Tina Ross, Danny Minnikin, Dee Minnikin, Catriona Murphy, Lucy Smart and Joann Weedon. None of whom bears resemblance to any characters in this novel, living or... murdered.

Thanks to Sandra Baker for telling me about being an editor at the Stock Exchange. Any mistakes are mine.

To Domenica de Rosa who, apart from being a good mate, gave me a mini-excavator – thank you!

Much gratitude to Dr Kath O'Hara for taking the trouble to provide me with detail of particular medical symptoms. Any medical errors are my own.

My thanks go to Philip Morrish and Angela Kaye, Master and Mistress of the Worshipful Company of Environmental Cleaners for introducing me to a new echelon in the cleaning world. Philip's was the winning bid in an auction in aid of St Peter and St James Hospice for his company and Angela to be named in the novel. They're responsible for Clean Slate losing a major contract...

I am lucky enough to work with Madeleine O'Shea and Laura Palmer, the finest of editors, thank you to them and to all at Head of Zeus, including Richenda Todd for her penetrating copy-editing eye.

As ever, I've had wise, considered guidance and feedback from Philippa Brewster at Georgina Capel Associates Ltd. My warm thanks go to all at the agency for their support, in particular Georgina Capel and Rachel Conway.

I continue to be grateful to Stephen Cassidy, retired Detective Chief Superintendent with the Metropolitan Police, and to Frank Pacifico, Test Train Operator for the London Underground, for their helpful suggestions and generosity.

Any inaccuracies around police detection or driving on the London Underground are mine.

I'm been lucky to be buoyed up by friends and family: Tasmin Barnett, Simon Barnett, Juliet Eve, Hilary Fairclough, Marcus Goodwin, Kay Heather, Nigel Heather, Lisa Holloway, Katherine Nelson, William Nelson, Alysoun Tomkins and Hannah Tomkins.

Lastly, but firstly, love and thanks go to my partner, Melanie Lockett, for everything.